THE NAKED TRUTH

Two Truths and a Lie
Book 1

ANA KIRK SHAW

For my kids.

I beg you, never read this. But if curiosity wins, here's your warning: some of it is embellished, a lot of it is true, and all of it is far too much information about me and your father.

Skip Chapters 2, 9, 10, 17, 20, 22, 23, 2—

You know what? Forget it. Close the book.
Just trust me when I say I wrote it so we could afford your childcare.
And probably your future therapy now, too.

You're welcome.

Mahal kita,
Mama

PROLOGUE

THE BUMBLING BOY WHO ONCE BEAT ME TO THE TOP has become a towering mass of a man who is, once again, very much in my way.

Unless I can make him useful for ending my twin sister's engagement party.

"What, Annie Li?" Nico growls, eyes narrowed. Those eyes are glazed and unfocused, listing sideways with the rest of him—but they still hold the same amount of malice as the last time I saw him. They also reflect the orange glow of the lit cigarette dangling from his lips.

Bingo. Party ender, acquired.

I reach for Nico's mouth and try to think of how cancerous it looks and not how pretty it's gotten, almost petulant, *pouty*—and then I'm distracted by the bulging bicep the size of a melon, which is extraordinarily inconvenient because I need to save my twin from this nightmare. Now.

I snatch the cigarette from between his lips. "Smoking is gross," I tell him as condescendingly as possible, as if I hadn't quit like, nine months ago.

"You're gross."

"I thought I got sexy," I purr, referring to his drunken slip from just moments earlier.

"You're so sexy it's gross."

I'm surprised to note that his Brooklyn accent, once the heaviest of anyone I've ever met, is far less pronounced than it used to be. I'd call him the dumb guido—his thick accent bringing things like *cannolis* and *baked ziti* and I don't know, *some gambling game involving dice* to mind, instead of *valedictorian of one of the best high schools in the United States.*

Thick eyebrows punctuate panicked eyes as I lift my arm. "Annie," Nico warns me with an outstretched hand, but he's too slow.

I give myself exactly one more look at my sister—defeated in the corner of the rooftop, standing next to her foul, leering fiancé—and decide subtlety is a lost cause.

I chuck my unwilling accomplice's cigarette at an artificial plant by the bar. My college degree wasn't entirely useless, I suppose, as it hits with the alarming accuracy becoming of a two-time beer pong tournament champion.

Nico's mouth drops open. "Are you fuckin' kidding me?" he chokes out. *There's* his accent.

Nothing happens for a beat.

Then—

Whoosh.

The thing erupts into flames.

I do the most sensible thing: scream.

"What the fu—"

I lunge past him and grab the nearest fire alarm and pull. A screeching siren blasts through the rooftop.

Half a second later, the overhead sprinklers go off—not above us, of course, but over the bar side of the rooftop. The covered side. The part with the flaming ficus and my twin's slumped shoulders and her fiancé's scummy face and the champagne tower and the dessert table... and the entire engagement party.

Amidst all the shrieking and scattering, I look back and lock eyes with Nicholas "Nico" Giannuzzi—childhood neighbor, high school nemesis, and source of all teenage anxiety.

Nico laughs once, a noise of horrified disbelief. "You look good, Annie Li, but you're still fuckin' insane."

ONE

Annie

One Year Later

Flirting with a porn star is definitely against the rules.

Different sets of rules. Sister Annie's rules. Hawk Publishing House's client relationship rules. Moral, ethical, spiritual, religious rules.

But because I can't help myself, I type: *Wow. How's your dick?*

This is also a question of genuine concern, however, and it follows right on the heels of watching this deliciously naked man groan, "Fuck," on my screen while clutching said appendage. "You would think I'd learn after the first few times. I should start wearing protection," he had said.

I chuckled and pulled out my phone to email him immediately, something I've been doing with regularity for the past several months.

As I wait for his reply, his sexy scholar voice continues over my laptop speakers. "But anyway, the reason I keep burning my dick is that oil splatters when moisture comes into contact

5

with it when it's hot. The water pretty much immediately vaporizes into steam, which expands quickly, which pushes the oil out of the pan." He lifts up on his tiptoes to stick his impressive length under a stream of presumably cold water running from the sink. "And onto my dick," he finishes in a deep baritone.

Goddamn.

His turning towards the sink allows me the perfect opportunity to objectify the hell out of him. Sorry, he's a client. I meant admire. Admire the hell out of him. Out of his ass, that is. Although 'ass' has never seemed like the proper terminology.

Badonk, perhaps?

Because the creator of *NakedReactions* is big. Beefy. Bulky? No, that's not right either.

Thicc. With two c's.

He's big all over, but not in a meathead, gym rat way. Obviously strong, but most of his muscle is covered with a thick, nay *thicc*, layer of padding. More bear over lion. More dad-bod than pro-athlete.

I wipe at the drool collecting at the side of my mouth.

He's hot as hell, and we don't even need to see his face to make that determination. His camera is always angled in such a way that his head is cut off. *For privacy reasons*, he told me. But he could still have the face of a melted candle and still be considered hot, because his body, combined with the deep intentionality of his voice and his clear intellect, is a solid recipe for success, as evidenced by his hundreds of thousands of followers on his subscription-based platform.

We love a smart beefcake of a man who cooks. In the nude. While explaining, in thorough detail, the science behind his cooking processes. Hundreds of thousands of people will even pay ten dollars a month to watch him do so.

Hawk Publishing House will pay him a hefty seven-figures

to make a cookbook out of his videos. And they will pay me, a desperate-for-cash failed poet under their employ, a (barely livable) wage to ghostwrite it.

My phone dings.

> *From: chef@nakedreactions.com*
> *To: ali@hawkpublishing.com*
> *He's out of commission for a while. I'm going to the doctor in a bit. I feel really sorry for him.*

I smile, and amidst the sizzling noise of potato sticks frying in hot oil and the creator's languid, professorial voice saying something about *pectin* and *starch granules* and *enzymes* and *pectin methyl*-something, my fingers start flying and I'm hitting send.

> *From: ali@hawkpublishing.com*
> *To: chef@nakedreactions.com*
> *Seems like a standard occupational hazard for you. But who could ever feel sorry for what you're packing?*

An imaginary nun reprimands me from my shoulder. *Annie*, Sister Annie snaps.

Fuck you, Sister Annie, this doesn't count! Flirting with a porn star—sorry, adult content creator (his preferred terminology)—may toe the line, but it certainly doesn't cross it. It might bend it, though, but at least I'm not getting bent over. By anyone other than myself.

Sex with myself doesn't count, I proclaim to Sister Annie from Rock Bottom, also known as my parents' basement. *And I'm totally sober. And you're gone in a month, anyway.*

I jam my fingers into my eyelids.

Sister Annie. This sanctimonious bitch. Guardian nun of my now-two-year-long self-imposed vow of abstinence: no sex, no drugs, no alcohol. A hard reset after a decade of reckless abandon, of nights blurred by strobe lights and fake friendships and sloppy fights, of rooftop misadventures and waking up in strangers' beds with nothing but a headache. She got the job two years ago, when my twin sister May kicked me out of our shared apartment and forced me to move back home. Here. Where I've stayed safely. Bored, but safe.

Until last year.

After I rose like a drunken phoenix (an insane yet sexy one —the two truest things that dumb fuck Nico has probably ever said about me) from the literal flames of May's engagement party, I made a promise. No more problems. No more chaos or relapses or ruining more things for May. I gave Sister Annie one more year. Her last day is on the day of May's wedding.

If it's something outside of my bed or this house, then it's off the table. Sister Annie has one job: to make sure that this time, I don't screw everything up.

From: chef@nakedreactions.com
  To: ali@hawkpublishing.com
  You're making me blush, Ali

However, flirting with an adult content creator is a bit of harmless fun, especially under the shroud of secrecy we're operating under. Immediately after my boss Patricia gave me this project, as soon as I contacted him, right off the bat, he demanded to communicate via email only. No real names. No texts or phone calls, no video chat. I could watch his videos to get his "general vibe," but that's all.

To him, I'm Ali, which is just my email address—short for Anne Li—so I've never bothered correcting him. Ali, the ghostwriter from who-knows-where. He didn't give me a name, so I call him by his email, too.

But it's tough to get a handle on someone's voice while they parade naked through a kitchen. Aside from the faceless hunk of meat, something about it seems impersonal. His voice is sexy but seems unnatural and practiced. Fake. I get that it's for privacy's sake, but... if I wanted to do a good job on this cookbook, I needed his real voice. So, in old Annie form, I started flirting him out of his shell. *So, fuck you, Sister Annie—it's for work.*

My phone rings, indicating a group video chat.

"Hey, everyone," I answer with a smile.

"That's one way to get his dick wet," Fernanda shouts, her eyes magnified by the thick lenses of her glasses, not one strand of hair out of place from her hairspray helmet.

"Jesus," Izzy says, "I'm walking down Broadway right now, Fernanda. You can't yell that shit."

"Don't tell me you're one of those people who blasts their music in public," Betty snarks. All I see is the underside of her wrinkled chin on my screen.

"A cry for help," Fernanda shouts once more, "some real main character behavior!"

"I forgot my headphones at home," Izzy mutters, topknot bobbing at the top of her screen.

"Your parents not give you enough attention growing up—"

"Did we want to discuss this episode or use this as a forum to air our grievances regarding sidewalk etiquette?" I chime in, heart filled with warmth for my best friend Izzy Flores and my two newest and realest friends.

After a few months of Sister Annie, I got bored in the basement. I figured the Brooklyn Public Library branch in my neighborhood was about as G-rated and safe as it got, so I started volunteering for a family literacy program, helping kids fall in love with books. I love kids anyway—they're chaotic little goblins like me. And Fernanda and Betty. I watched the two of them perform *Grumpy Monkey* for a group of five-year-olds, both of them wearing clothes that were blazingly loud and/or blindingly sparkly, trading off animal voices like a well-rehearsed comedy duo. I loved them immediately.

Still, I hung back. Sister Annie had me convinced that getting too close would somehow ruin their lives. But Fernanda and Betty vehemently disagreed. They barged their way into friendship like they'd done it before—maybe they saw something in me and decided I could use a little love. Maybe they just didn't scare easily. Whatever it was, they found me in a quiet place and gave me something louder: community. And not of the five a.m. afterparty in Bushwick sort.

Izzy loved them instantly, too. Which mattered—because after over a decade of being the "honorary triplet" to me and May, her stamp of approval wasn't optional.

"Izzy's the one watching pornography in public right now." Fernanda says the word "pornography" as loudly as possible.

"Jesus, can everyone please lay off? I have a privacy screen on my phone for work."

"This episode's pretty good," Betty interrupts casually, as if we are watching a normal sitcom with a laugh track and not a group of women ages thirty to seventy-five watching a naked giant explaining the science behind cooking the perfect French fry.

"I feel sorry for his dick," Izzy mutters.

"I could never feel sorry for what he's packing. Seems like a standard occupational hazard for him, anyway," adds Fernanda.

"*That's what I said!*" I yell.

Fernanda and Betty do not like to cook. Fernanda and Betty are, however, thirsty for all the men who cook on various cooking shows. After listening to their particularly long, pining soliloquy of "that mean daddy, Gordon Ramsay," I mentioned *NakedReactions* to them, and within the hour, they had each subscribed to his channel. We try to have a cute little watch party for all of his episodes.

"Aww," Fernanda coos eventually. "Look at him. He's all red in the places the oil splashed on him. It got on his weird tattoo."

I turn back to my phone.

From: ali@hawkpublishing.com
To: chef@nakedreactions.com
Sorry, did I say dick? That was supposed to say duck. How's your duck?

Chef has one distinguishing feature that could potentially help identify his body in case of kidnapping or murder by a super fan (not me, of course... I probably couldn't lift his arm, much less his entire corpse). It's an interesting tattoo on his left pec—a pink hallucinatory duck head with a surprised look on its face. The duck's bill is open in an 'o' shape. It dons a tiny chef hat and inexplicably has eyebrows, both of which are raised high. Right now, the duck is also kind of splotchy and red.

From: chef@nakedreactions.com
To: ali@hawkpublishing.com
Overcooked

I smile, and then my fingers go flying.

From: ali@hawkpublishing.com
To: chef@nakedreactions.com
Might need a taste test to confirm

I tune back into our group chat, where they're currently debating how much this naked chef can deadlift "with an ass like that."

"Me on one side of the bar and Fernanda on the other," Betty is saying.

"I think he could manage me in the middle, too," Izzy adds on, "because that is one strong-looking ass."

"You could bounce a damn coin off it."

"—whole piggy bank."

"Chip a tooth, probably."

The thirsty commentary eventually ends, and after everyone hangs up, I pull up my email again.

From: ali@hawkpublishing.com

To: chef@nakedreactions.com

Don't answer that. I've surpassed my flirting quota for the day. But here's today's Two Truths and a Lie.

1. I'm deathly afraid of flying.

2. I haven't drunk alcohol, done drugs, or had sex in almost a year.

3. I love my job.

At the beginning of our working relationship, I'd just been watching his videos and typing up standard recipes with some basic descriptions. He didn't like it. He wanted it to feel like more of a meaningful, personal story, he'd said, not so much just a collection of recipes. May and I used to play Two Truths and a Lie as kids to practice our twin telepathy, so I started playing it with Chef after flirting him out of his shell so we could get to know one another better, so I could get a better sense of his voice. For some reason, we just started putting the lies at the end. They've gotten pretty personal, and now, even worse than flirting with an adult content creator over email?

I may or may not have a crush on one.

I've gotten bits and pieces of his voice, his attitude, his humor, and what I've found underneath it all is warmth and kindness. Empathy.

I like him.

I finish taking notes on what Chef's saying about the French fries, but it's not at all what I want to write about. I'm dying to write poems about the man himself.

His thick hands twist and pluck, pinch and scoop, a rhythm of motion in the cramped space of his tiny kitchen. Massive thighs shift, moving him up and down the narrow aisle. The kitchen is sleek—modern and polished, the kind you find in any city apartment where square footage is sacrificed for skyline views. I don't recognize any of the buildings out the window. He could be anywhere. Chicago, maybe. Boston, Miami. Even Tokyo.

But here, in this sliver of space, his presence is overwhelming.

a quiet choreography—
each step
a negotiation,
a conversation
between body and space.
a warm cloud
pressing against the walls,
his body
swallowing half of it whole,
his energy
saturates the rest.

He's finished cooking. He lifts a fry to try one, and I hear an audible crunch. Damn. My salivating continues. He finally plates his French fries and shows them to the camera. They look incredible. His dick peeks out from under the plate, and honestly, like everything he cooks... there's just something about his dick that makes me want to put it in my mouth.

I shut my laptop and bang my head on the headboard behind me. I should not be watching this man's por—adult content in my parents' basement. I should not be flirting with the adult content creator. Even if it is for work. *Because* it's for work.

But I hope his dick is okay.

Nico

SHE EYES MY DICK SUSPICIOUSLY.

I cringe.

"How?" she asks.

"How what?"

"How did you manage to get second-degree burns on your penis?" the urgent care doctor wants to know.

"Uhh..." I panic. "...work." *Fuck.*

She peers at me through her glasses. "And what is it that you do?"

Fuck. "Postdoc." It's the truth, but not the relevant one.

"In what?"

"In chemistry."

She squints.

"Does it matter?" I half-shout.

"Yes, it actually does." She looks at my dick again. "Is it a chemical burn?"

"No. Hot oil."

She blinks, probably extremely confused and thoroughly unimpressed. She sighs and moves closer to inspect it. "It's infected," she finally announces.

"I fucki—I know," I tell her, teeth clenched. Even if she's not touching me, her proximity seems to cause me more pain. "That's why I'm here. I'm in freakin' agony, and I saw some pus."

She hums. "Are you allergic to anything?"

"Nope."

"Okay. I'm going to prescribe some antibiotics and some antibiotic cream. Take the pills three times a day and use the cream twice a day. Clean the wound first before putting the cream on. You can wrap it up, too." She chuckles at her little joke. "With some gauze and tape."

"What do I do about the pain?" I demand to know.

She shrugs. "Over-the-counter pain medication. Acetaminophen or ibuprofen."

I blow out a breath. "That's what I've been taking, and it's not doing much of anything."

The doctor studies me. She's either thinking about 'the general weakness of men' (as my sister so frequently refers to), or she's trying to judge if I'm some sort of junkie. "On a scale from one to ten, how bad is the pain without ibuprofen or acetaminophen?"

I shove all toxic masculinity aside and admit, "Eight." I am the proud fuckin' spokesman for the 'general weakness of men.'

She hums. "I don't feel comfortable prescribing you something stronger here. If the pain becomes unmanageable, I'd recommend the emergency room." The finality in her tone tells me there is no room for negotiation.

"Yes, ma'am." It's a wonder I don't scream it.

She wraps me up without any jokes, types some crap up on the computer, then stands. "You're all set. I'd lecture you on lab safety, but seems like you've already learned your lesson," she laughs on her way out of the room.

I've learned my lesson dozens of times, but unfortunately,

outside of ensuring I dry whatever I fry as much as possible, there's nothing I can do about it, and I've never been more acutely aware of that as I think about all the damn choices that have led me to where I am right now.

I, Nicholas Giannuzzi, the valedictorian of one of the best high schools in the country, am a fuckin' porn star. And it's all because of the choices I made. With my undergrad chemistry degree, I could've gone straight into big Pharma or something way more lucrative, but instead, I chose to do the doctorate because food chemistry genuinely interested me, because I had no fuckin' regard for my future or what came after I fulfilled this fun little thing I wanted to learn about. Then Ma got sick, and I wanted to move home to take care of her instead of going to any of the best food science PhD programs in the country, and suddenly I found myself living in squalor in a shithole in Ridgewood while at NYU.

I was out with May and some other friends and got to talking with a buddy of hers who turned out to be an actual porn star at this ethical, women-owned porn company called *Harlot*. They got a mission statement and everything. He mentioned they were expanding into creator content and said I could be a good fit for one of their subscription-based platforms. After a year of sinking desperation, I tried it out... and I made a bunch of money almost immediately. And then, what started as a side hustle somehow became my main gig. Which worked, because we were racking up hospital bills left and right.

It's been lucrative as hell. And I sure as hell ain't stopping anytime soon. As much as it fuckin' kills me. As much as I want to shrivel up and die every time I record a new video. I won't stop, especially not with this hefty cookbook deal, especially not while I'm in this postdoc, making even less than I did back then, and with Ma's bills behind us after the advance I got for this book? Fuck.

Listen. Sex work is real work, all right? I'm friends with lots of creators who I deeply respect, who own their hundreds of thousands, *millions* of dollars a year. But I don't own it. I do the opposite of own it. I'm embarrassed. I'd never tell anyone. Could never show my face. Can't even talk to Ali, the anonymously sassy, horny woman ghost-writing my book. But with this *Naked Reactions* gig, I make more in one month than I would be making in one year.

I'm out of commission for the next week, though. No one wants to see a red and blistered dick dangling around food. I'll have to dig around for some unused content I can post. Photos, maybe.

I head to the drugstore across the street, wondering what Ali is up to today, what videos she's watched. At least she thinks I'm hot. Is it possible to get hard from a work email (yeah)? Is it possible to have a crush on someone if you've never seen her face (yeah)? Don't matter though, 'cause she's never gonna see mine.

Still, every time her name hits my inbox, my brain lights way the fuck up, like she's rearranging the atoms in my head. She's kind and for some crazy reason thinks I'm cool. She's funny and sharp and smarter than me in ways that make me want to keep up. I tell myself it's harmless 'cause it's words on a screen. Just playful banter with someone I'll never meet. But the truth is, I've started writing back just to make her laugh. Even worse, to get to know her even more. I retype my answers three times. I even check my spelling.

I like her.

I'm wincing when I walk out of the drugstore. Right there, in the middle of the sidewalk on Broadway, I rip open the bags and bottles and pop an antibiotic along with three acetaminophen dry. I dig around in my pockets next. I know I have... yes. An edible. One of the candy ones. Ten hefty milligrams of tetrahydrocannabinol. Some people have pocket lint. I have pocket edibles. I pop that too. Then I waddle down into the subway station and hop on the train to Ma's, thinking of Ali the entire time.

———

The edible kicks in by the time we're crossing the Brooklyn Bridge, and I'm feelin' like a million bucks. I know it's kicked in because I started rapping *No Sleep 'til Brooklyn* in my head. Also, because I'm giving a standing fuckin' ovation to the acrobatic kids dancing and flipping all over the train car, even when one of them comes close to kicking me in the head. *Wow, what talent*, I think, while bobbing my head to their house music, instead of *if you fuckin' touch me, I will end you*. I throw a twenty in one of their snapbacks.

I'm whistling as I walk out of my stop, taking in the beauty of Bensonhurst, the neighborhood of my youth. I'm only somewhat kidding; it's pretty drab, but there's a certain kinda charm in the old-school butchers and pizzerias with the Italy flags out front mixed with all the seafood markets and bakeries with the signs written in Chinese.

I'm walking down the main thoroughfare, about to take the left onto my mom's block, when I run into May Li.

"May Li," I bellow. "*May Li!*" I've always called the Li sisters by their full names. Just feels right. Like a celebrity. Keanu Reeves. Dwayne "The Rock" Johnson. May Li. Annie "My Worst Fuckin' Nightmare" Li.

She smiles, going in for the hug. "Hi," she says. "Please don't mess up my hair."

I know it's May, even if she and Annie are identical twins. We all went to elementary school together way back when. We went to different middle schools, but we eventually went to high school together, too.

I learned to tell them apart around first grade. Everything

about May was always perfect. She had perfect posture, sitting ramrod straight even at six-years-old, feet flat on the floor at her desk, with perfectly combed hair with those plastic clips set at even heights on both sides of her head. Never had any scuffs on her little shoes. She was calm, kinda stiff, but always really nice.

Annie Li has always been a fuckin' demon child. I think she went to sleep with her hair wet or something, because it was always all crazy and sticking out all over the place, a radius around the point where her head was on the pillow. She always had skinned knees. Her desk was behind mine in Mrs. Silvio's class, and she could never stop moving her feet and kicking my chair. She was loud, bossy, and smart as fuck, the worst possible combination of traits in a child. If we ever played some sort of team sport in gym class, she was the type of kid who wouldn't physically do anything but would yell directions at everyone else. She was scary as all hell, and my ten-year-old masochist ass was into it for a hot fuckin' second until she called me an "illiterate sausage" for the sixteenth time. Or maybe it was after the fifth time she didn't pick me for her team in gym class because I "ran like a spilled pudding cup."

She was better, I guess, sarcastic but friendlier in high school, but for some inexplicable reason she flipped a switch and went full demon banshee our senior year.

Even last year at the engagement party, after thirteen years of Annie-free bliss, I still knew exactly which Li sister was standing in front of me, way before she opened her mouth to insult me. She was just... a *lot*. Everything about her was immediately overwhelming. She'd grown up to be so devastatingly beautiful it knocked the air outta me, and it was *a fuckin' lot*. The tattoos down her arms and legs were a lot. The slinky dress that hid no part of her insane body was *too much*, and then her eyes—sharp and gorgeous, cutting straight through me as she told me I'd aged like spoiled milk, every word rolling off those pillowy lips? It was *way too fuckin' much*.

She was so much that I had to pound vodka sodas just to take the edge off—to dull the intensity of our constant, violent, verbal sparring that picked up right where it left off thirteen years ago. It backfired, of course. Now she still thinks I'm a trashy, illiterate sausage who can't hold his liquor... and also thinks she's sexy.

I hate that she's right. Because yeah, the accent I've spent years trying to get rid of and the whole (checks notes) *porn thing* make me kinda trashy. I can read scientific journals and articles all day every day, but I can't make it past the first page of any sort of fiction book (unless it's by Tolkien, and even then, I was fourteen and it took me *months*), so maybe I am half-illiterate. I also really like sausage. In fact, I'm on my way to eat it right now like a walkin' freakin' stereotype. And anyone with eyes can see that thirty-year-old Annie Li is sexy as hell. In fact, anyone *without* eyes would be able to feel it, too, if they squeezed that curve in her waist.

After all these years, it's still incredibly frustrating to be reminded that Annie Li is always right.

I shake my head, redirecting my attention towards the nicer, better twin. "How's it hangin', beautiful? Visiting your parents?" *And the spawn of Satan?* I squeeze May and lift her off her feet, avoiding my penis and her hair.

She brushes my invisible cooties off her shirt after I put her down. "Yes, I need some things for the wedding," she says.

I realize I'm grinning like a lunatic when May manages to look down her nose at me while being a foot shorter. "Are you tired or are you high?" she asks me.

"Yes," I offer.

"Hmm." She doesn't judge because she's the much nicer twin. "How are you getting to the wedding, by the way? Just flying in for the weekend?"

Tom has some douchey qualities, and that includes an appreciation of glamour and glitz and a flaunting of wealth that can be a little cringey. Including having his rich as hell, very kind fiancé pay to have a wedding in South Beach. Because he went to the University of Miami. Ten years ago. I'm not complaining, though.

"I'm making a road trip out of it, actually. A whole bunch of restaurants down the eastern seaboard have been reaching out to our lab, asking for someone to come visit and check out their kitchens and menus and stuff. I'm leaving next Thursday, and it'll take all week. Staying in a bunch of rental properties. I'll be in South Beach the night before your welcome dinner."

My only search criteria for those rentals was 'fuckin' epic kitchen' so that I'd be able to film some real good content for *NakedReactions*. The nicer and bigger the kitchen, though, the nicer and bigger the house, so I'm renting out some pretty sick properties. Two of them even have a pool and a separate pool house. Maybe I'll throw a party for restaurant kitchen staff. I'm psyched, actually. It'll be a real productive week.

"Sounds fun."

"May Li."

"What?"

"You and I haven't hung out in mad long, and I'm going to your wedding in a few weeks. We haven't worked together for a bit." Over the last few years I've given May some insider info on city restaurants, and as an analyst she'd recommend them as "profitable investments" to her firm. "What gives?"

She shrugs. "My schedule doesn't leave a lot of room for 'hanging out.' I'm in the middle of an important recommendation." She thinks for a moment. "What are you doing tomorrow?"

"What's tomorrow?"

"Monday. Federal holiday. I have a rare day off."

"Ah. Well, nothing." Rubbing cream on my infected dick.

"Want to come to the beach with me and Tom? Rockaways?"

I think about it. The ocean could be good for my dick. The osmotic pressure would help reduce the swelling. I know that the high salt concentration lends itself to antibacterial properties. And there are a bunch of minerals in the ocean that also have anti-inflammatory properties. Although this may only work for surface wounds. Maybe not infections like mine?

I realize I've been thinking all of this out loud when May Li very kindly says, "I probably wouldn't go into the ocean with an infected penis."

I laugh because May Li can be hilarious. "'Tis but a scratch, May Li. Cooking accident." I make a decision. Why not? "Okay, I'll come and stay out of the ocean. Text me where on the beach."

We give each other one last hug. May makes sure to leave space between her and my dick, and I continue my way down to my mom's.

———

"You're high as a fuckin' kite," is the first thing Ma says to me, smacking me on the side of the head.

I bring her in for a hug, her fluffy hair tickling my face, glasses mashing into my chest. "I missed you, too."

"You got any more?" my sister, Valentina, asks from behind her.

I dig around in my pockets, pushing crumbs of unknown origin and some change around. I find two, pick some lint off of them, and hold them out.

My mother and my sister each take one, knock them together, and pop them in their mouths.

"You're late," Ma tells me, walking back into the kitchen. I throw my bag on the ratty couch and take a deep inhale at the sharp tang of garlic and tomato and oregano and the warm yeastiness of bread and pasta and immediately feel my soul heal. Valentina and I grew up helping Ma with Sunday dinner, the whole to-do of it, and it's what got me involved in my doctorate concentration. The *NakedReactions* channel, too, I guess.

"I ran into May Li," I tell her, kissing Valentina on the head and moving to the plates to start setting the table. None of the plates match, so I make sure to pick my favorite ones—the heaviest and the thickest and the weirdest shaped. "Remember her? The twin?"

"Is she the normal one or the crazy one?" Valentina asks, sitting down to shave parm.

I cringe. "The normal one, I guess. I'm going to her wedding in a few weeks."

"I always liked the crazy one," Ma says. "I remember when youse guys were out on the block playin' Manhunt and she kicked Bobby Pinto in the nuts 'cause he pushed your sister onto the pavement."

This checks out.

Valentina cackles. "Oh yeah, I remember that. She took me home after, too."

This also checks out, because Annie Li may be batshit, but she was always fiercely protective of people she liked or who couldn't defend themselves. Including quiet, perfect May Li. And my sister, I guess. Not me, even if I never stood a chance in hell of defending myself against anyone. Including Annie Li.

"I heard she went *real* crazy, though," Valentina adds on. My neck prickles at this, considering I *did* watch her rip a cigarette from my mouth, light a plant on fire, pull the fire alarm, and flood an entire fancy-ass party. Which was a travesty, really, because the cookies on the dessert table were from one of the best bakeries in the city, and I had been planning on pocketing some to bring home.

"What do you mean?"

"I was out with some people from Stuy a few years after you guys graduated from college, and we ran into her at some warehouse party at like three in the morning."

"Valentina, what the hell?" my mom demands to know. She stands with her hands on her hips, the apron my dad gave her twenty years ago bulging around the words *I AM THE SECRET INGREDIENT.* "Three in the morning?"

Valentina rolls her eyes. "She didn't look good. I mean, I definitely didn't look good either, because it was three in the morning, but she looked high as hell, and not in the good way. In the scary, empty way. Like in the 'took too much about three hours ago' way. And she was hanging off some scrawny dude with a face tattoo."

"Jesus Christ."

"My friends weren't surprised, said that was just what she was up to nowadays."

"That's what she's been up to? Fucked up at three in the morning at some illegal underground party in Bushwick, sucking some molly dealer's—"

Ma throws a dish towel in my face, the one with the picture of the oven that says, *When in doubt, pull it out.* "Nico," she warns.

Valentina shrugs again.

What the fuck? Annie Li, salutatorian of Stuyvesant High School? I roll this around in my mouth like it's a taste I'm unfamiliar with. This doesn't check out, and it makes me feel kinda sad. I wouldn't wish something like that on my worst enemy, and she *was* my worst enemy.

"Poor baby," Ma says. "Hope she's okay. Nico, can you grab a serving spoon?"

I go to open the drawer, but it gets jammed halfway

because of the sheer amount of shit in it. I jiggle it until it opens and grab a spoon.

"Have you seen her for any wedding stuff?" Valentina asks.

"Yeah. Once last year at the engagement party." I dip my finger in the gravy. Perfect. "She looked fine." *Fine as hell. So hot she caused a fire, in fact.*

"She's the one you had that valedictorian beef with, right?"

I shrug like that "beef" wasn't the single most stressful and dramatic year of my life. "Yeah."

"What'd you do to her again?"

"I didn't do shit. She was the one who made my senior year a living hell for some unknown fuckin' reason—"

"Okay, enough gossip about the poor girl," Ma says. "Come sit down."

Valentina and I battle for the other good chair, the one that isn't Ma's. No one wants the wobbly chair. Valentina is victorious. I sit down at the other one and immediately tilt to one side.

"Let's say grace."

We all take each other's hands. "Rub a dub dub, thanks for the grub. Yay, god," we recite.

We're fake Catholics.

"Love ya, Joe." My mom blows a kiss towards the ceiling.

"Love ya, Dad," Valentina and I chime in.

We dive right in.

"Nico," Ma says in between bites. "Where's Tara been?"

My fork stops on its way to my mouth. "We broke up months ago, Ma."

She clicks her tongue and stabs her fork in my direction. "What the hell, Nico? She was great."

Tara *was* great. *I* was not. I could never be honest with her about *NakedReactions*, which was totally unfair to her, so I broke it off. "Just didn't work out," I tell my mom.

"I wanna see you be happy," she tells me.

Ditto, I want to say. So I'll keep doing this thing until you're good.

———

On my way back to the subway, I pull out my phone.

From: chef@nakedreactions.com

To: ali@hawkpublishing.com

How dare you deprive humanity of the full force that is Ali? Bad girl. Why'd you need to do that?

Are we getting into past relationships and inner wounds now? Wow, the big stuff. Look at us go.

1. My dick is infected.

2. None of my relationships have ever lasted longer than a few months.

3. I love my job.

THREE

Annie

———

I AGREE TO MEET MAY AND HER FIANCÉ TOM AT THE beach because I'm Very Supportive, but seeing them together right now puts me in a fresh panic that I still don't have a way to get to their wedding.

Right, because Tom decided to get married in *South Beach*, of all places, and to May, whatever Tom says, goes. Despite her twin sister's *severely serious fear of flying*.

It's partially my fault. I'll take some accountability. She asked me time and time again if it was okay, and because I'm behaving and not causing her anymore wedding-related drama, I said it was fine, that I'd figure something out and not to worry her pretty, perfect little head, because I am now the unproblematic Sister Annie and the most helpful Maid of Honor there's ever been.

Now, the wedding is in two weeks, and I still don't know how I'm getting there. I don't have my driver's license, never needed one as a born and bred city girl. A train ticket is approximately a million dollars, at this point. I set an alarm on my phone to just bite the bullet when I get home because I don't have another choice.

"So, are you guys all set for the wedding? Do you need me to do any last minute things, Plum?" I ask now, totally overcompensating for my ineptitude as a maid of honor and reaching for her childhood nickname like it's a lifeline.

"No, our wedding planner has been amazing, and I think her team's got everything covered."

Because she's perfect May with the perfect wedding. "Great," I tell her. "I'm excited to get ready with you. It'll be like when we used to do each other's makeup in the basement."

"Except you always made me look like Ursula, and I'm going for a more natural look."

"Hey, Ursula is a queen bitch. You should be honored to look like her."

A man walks by dragging a cooler through the sand and yelling, "*NUT*-crack-*ERS*!" in that way those guys do. I would kill for one of those right now, New York City's unofficial summer drink. Fruit juice, Kool-aid, and four or five or six different types of the cheapest liquor blended into a tasty slushy treat. A guaranteed good time. At Pride a few years ago, I found myself in the middle of a party, in a complete stranger's kitchen in the West Village at four in the morning. How many nutcrackers did that take? I'm not sure. I lost count (and consciousness) after the third.

"You got your dress, right?

"Yup. It's all set, and I got a travel steamer for it, too."

"When do you leave again?"

Fresh panic. "Uh, the Thursday?"

She frowns. "The day of the welcome dinner?"

"Uh, no. Wednesday."

She stares at me. "You don't have a way to get there yet?"

Shit. "I do. Well, I don't," I amend, after seeing her face. "But look, Plum." I show her my phone. "I set an alarm to buy a train ticket tonight!"

"How much are those tickets now?"

"Don't worry about it, Plum."

May hums, smelling bullshit from a foot away despite the overuse of her beloved nickname. "Please just make sure you're there in time for the welcome dinner," she murmurs.

It stings. Not because she's asking, but because she has to ask. Because she still thinks there's a nonzero chance I'll flake or screw it up. The only thing she said to me after the engagement party disaster was a tight, "Please don't do anything like that again." And now here we are, and she's not wrong.

"Of course I'll be there for the welcome dinner, May," I say, trying to sound steadier than I feel. "My twin sister is getting married." *To an asshole.* "I'm going to be with you every step of the way," I add, and I do mean that with every fiber of my being.

"Hey," Tom suddenly bites, and my heart drops into the pit of my stomach. *Did I say that asshole part out loud?*

"Uh—"

"Hey," someone says from behind me, and my heart keeps sinking and sinking and sinking and continues its way down my intestines until it feels like I need to shit it out.

I look up to my right, and for the second time in my life, I'm in Nico Giannuzzi's shadow. But literally, this time.

May and Tom jump up to give him a hug while I find myself glued to the sand. I start cycling through excuses to leave in my head. Am I sick? I could be sick. I hear the flu is really making its rounds. It spreads easily through... the heat. Of the summer. Very contagious in the summer, when everyone is outside in the open air.

"Annie," Nico deigns to acknowledge me, sitting below him at his feet, and this with my name in his mouth activates all my fight instincts. Just fight, no flight—like he claws the nasty out of me and all I want to do is be combative and tear his fucking face apart.

This is Sister Annie's time to shine. *You will use every ounce of your strength to stay seated right there on your towel and not climb on his gorilla shoulders and tear his eyes from their orbital bones or strangle him using only your thighs,* she says.

"Hi," I grit out.

May smirks, clearly still entertaining her decades-long running theory that I'm harboring a crush on this overgrown ape.

I give her a tight smile in return.

Thankfully, Nico can probably smell my rage pheromones, some primal warning carried through the breeze, so he lays his towel out as far away from me as possible, on the other side of Tom and May.

Now, the only time I've seen this asshole in fourteen years was on a dark rooftop, so I'm suddenly grateful for my sunglasses, a perfect shield for spying and getting a real look at him.

It's a shame really, because he looks unfairly good, almost aggressively handsome. He's always been big, maybe he played football or something, but he's filled out and then compacted and solidified into strong, firm planes, making me think of how easily he could throw me—apologies, a football—around. His hair is still the same thick mess, his face scruffy in a haphazard, lazy way that only accentuates the sharp cut of his jaw. His clothes look expensive and fit him well. His sunglasses (which have the audacity to be Tom Ford) scream *effortless ease,* as does the nearly sheer white linen shirt draped over his broad frame, sleeves rolled just enough to tease at strong fore-arms. I can't wait for him to take it off.

Annie, Sister Annie reprimands.

Enough out of you. I'm temporarily celibate, not dead.

"Anyone hungry or thirsty?" a still-clothed Nico asks the group.

"What do you have?" Tom asks.

Nico pulls out a big brown paper bag with grease stains on the bottom. "Fries. Homemade. Just made 'em myself."

My lip curls. "Old, cold, soggy fries. The ideal beach snack."

May pinches my leg.

"Don't have any then," he says in my direction. "Your loss."

Tom takes a handful. I hear a crunch. Whatever.

"Nutcrackers?" Nico goes on to ask.

"What flavors did you get?" Tom asks.

"He only had piña colada and..." he looks between the two separate bottles, "...blue."

"Hit me with the blue."

Am I salivating? I distract myself by considering the ineffable enigma of the flavor 'blue.' "What *is* the flavor blue?" I ask everyone because I'm being nice and behaving.

Tom shrugs. "It's just... blue," he says, like the inarticulate dipshit he is.

May loves this game—another one we've played since we were kids. "Is it raspberry?"

"Not quite... But it's definitely tart and sweet," I add on.

"A little citrusy."

"Fruity."

"It's more of a concept than a flavor, I think," Nico adds.

"Yes," May laughs. "It's a feeling."

"Like melted popsicles and childhood nostalgia," says Nico, shocking me with an insight and a depth well below kiddie pool.

"Like disappointment in a bowling alley."

"Like skinned knees and fireflies."

"Blackout descents into jungle-juice oblivion," I mutter.

May squeezes my hand. "Nico's a chemist," she offers. "Why do you think the flavor blue turns your tongue blue?"

she asks him, deftly diverting the course of the conversation, because she is the best sister in the universe.

Chef should've gone over this in his Chemistry of Candy episode.

Nico looks contemplative. He mutters something that sounds like "synthetic organic compound" or maybe "pathetic botanic ground," but who knows, because he's an illiterate gorilla. He eventually shrugs, because of course he doesn't know. Because he's an illiterate gorilla chemist, apparently.

Tom glugs half the bottle. I brace myself for the Red Flag Hulk. I hope he gets a brain freeze.

"You guys excited for the wedding?" Nico asks.

I take this opportunity to lay back and disassociate on my towel, overwhelmed by everything happening right now. The dense ape, the soon-to-be drunk dipshit, my Kryptonite summer drink, the impending three thousand dollar train ticket.

"I'm going to walk up to the bathroom," I hear May say after some time. "Be right back."

My right eye twitches. I recenter myself.

"Sunscreen?" Tom asks.

"I'll take some," I say, so very kindly, because really, I'm not going to deny myself the opportunity to watch my worst enemy's tortured face while I rub cream over my legs and tits.

Tom tosses the bottle over.

"Pete, my ex, always said the best form of tattoo care was sunscreen." And most of my hands and arms and legs are covered in them, so I'm constantly reapplying.

"Pete," Tom snarks in his weasel voice, "was he the prison tattoo artist or the junkie coke dealer or both?"

And there it is. There is an immediate activation of the fight response, especially because he never tries this shit in front of May, and I suddenly have a newfound understanding of why people are moved to extreme acts of violence.

Nico even glances over at Tom, the picture-perfect image of *concern*, thick eyebrows furrowed, full mouth pursed.

"Fuck you, Tom," I mutter under my breath. I say it quietly and don't scream it because I am behaving and being nice even if Tom's a *dick* and I'm embarrassed as hell that perfect, apparently rich and successful Nico just heard all of that.

And you know what? Pete *was* a coke dealer, but he is also a world-famous tattoo artist, and these are actually all really beautiful tattoos that people would pay thousands of dollars for, and I got them all for free, but Tom doesn't deserve to know that.

Pete is also in prison now, but no one here deserves to know that, either.

"Aw, don't be embarrassed, sis," Tom starts.

"I'm not your sis," I mutter a little louder.

"Everyone has trashy tattoos," Tom continues, as if I haven't spoken.

"They're really nice tattoos, actually, fucker," I answer, at the decibel right below 'shouting,' because he is *trying me now*.

"I have a Marge Simpson on my ass—" Tom tries.

"You're comparing my work to a *Marge Simpson ass tattoo*?!"

"Even Nico has a bad tattoo," he says.

"Tom—" Nico interrupts, and this isn't okay because the last person I need standing up for me is perfect, handsome *Nico*, of all people, and now I'm in fight mode.

"Tell me all about your *bad tattoo*, then, Nico," I sneer. *It's on, let's go.*

"No," he says, and the tips of his ears are turning red, which only activates me more because now it's his turn to get embarrassed.

"It's hilarious," Tom says, as if no one is talking except for him, which is his default.

"It's not—" Nico attempts a little louder.

Then we are all shouting.

"Does it say 'Gym, Tan, Laundry' across your ass?" I scoff.

"Oh, *real original*, Annie," Nico snarls.

"'Property of Snooki'?"

"Keep 'em comin', honey." Nico's whole body is turned towards me now, stiff and tight with anger.

"Robert DeNiro, then," I shoot back.

"Tony Soprano, actually," Nico jeers.

"Actually," Tom offers, "Nico's tattoo is a—"

"Fuck," Nico cuts in. "That stick's been stuck up your ass for fourteen consecutive years, Annie."

"You wish your dick was stuck up this ass," I purr.

"Honey," he laughs easily, "If I got my dick up your ass, you'd be wishin' for it for the rest of your life."

I am *appalled*. Who the hell is this guy and what the hell has he done with the kid who bawled like a baby when I took his holographic Charizard Pokemon card? I stand up and start moving, to do... something, *anything*—

"Where you goin', sweetheart?" Nico drawls.

I stop short and look around. "I'm sorry, is this some sort of active construction site? Are you going to tell me to smile?"

"But you'd be much prettier if you smiled."

"You'd be much prettier if you kept your scammy fucking mouth shu—

"What's going on?" May calls out from behind us.

FOUR

Annie

____

WE ALL SHUT OUR MOUTHS AS SHE FLOATS BACK
to us.

"Nothing," I say sweetly, quickly sitting back down. "Still
discussing the flavor 'blue.' Nico just told us it's the only icee
flavor his cousin Vinny serves out of the cooler at the end of
his driveway."

Nico grumbles under his breath, but thankfully decides to
keep his pretty lips sealed.

May looks at him.

I hold my breath and hope I've successfully deflected.

Her eyes light up, and I exhale in relief.

"Annie," she says excitedly.

I blink. "Yes?"

"Nico's driving down to the wedding. He's doing a whole
road trip the week before."

Nico's head whips up.

There is a sudden roaring in my ears. "Oh?"

"You should go with him!"

Entire civilizations rise and fall in the silence that follows.
Empires are forged, coups are staged, alliances crumble. A

medieval bard pens a tragic ballad about the pain currently tightening my spine. Somewhere, a tiny peasant child throws a tomato at a guillotine.

Until Tom breaks it with a laugh.

"I don't think—" I start.

"No, May—" Nico tries.

She ignores him. Both of us. "It'll be great!" she insists. "You two will get to hang out before the wedding," she says with a smirk towards me, "and you don't have a way to get there yet, Annie," May says. Fuck. "Nico already has a car and lodging—"

"I'm not sharing a hotel room with—"

"He has rentals. I assume they have more than one bedroom." May looks to Nico for confirmation.

"That's not gonna work, May," Nico attempts carefully, the tips of his ears even redder than before.

"You can help pay for gas, Annie. It'll be less than the three thousand you would spend on a train ticket."

"Honestly, I'd rather spend three million dollars than be trapped in a car with Joe Pesci for a week," I mutter. My heart is pounding in my ears. I'm slowly devolving into panic.

Nico hears me. "Fuck off with that shit, Annie, and get off my dick about my accent," he says, frustration evident despite his attempts to wrangle said accent into submission. "Honestly, there's no way I'm taking *or* paying for this miserable fuckin' hurricane of serious issues who causes fuckin' problems for everyone around her—"

"Hey," May cuts in, a hair more forcefully.

I, on the other hand, am forced into a shocked silence. Of all the things that have come out of Nico's mouth thus far, this is the only thing that manages to creep through my defenses and slice directly into my chest. I feel my ribcage collapsing around the wound. *Flight* is now activated.

"Don't talk about my sister that way," May warns. She says

this quietly and calmly, but there is an undercurrent of a rarely seen danger and intensity.

Nico manages to look contrite. He scrubs his face with both hands, then drops them. "I gotta go to the bathroom," he mumbles, then gets up and storms away.

I swallow the lump in my throat. Shove it down with all the other bad feelings that came up with it.

May isn't looking at Nico; she's looking at me. "I'm sorry," May whispers. "I thought I was being helpful, and that—"

"What a terrible idea, May," Tom cuts in.

May recoils slightly, then shrinks even more.

"*Excuse* you?" I growl. Did my teeth just get sharper? I run my tongue along the canines.

"—With her?" he continues. "We're going to be reading our vows while she leaps into the seats and pummels Nico with a bouquet—"

"Not if I stuff it down your throat first," I spit at him.

"—then sets the entire hotel on fire."

"With you in it, hopefully," I shoot back.

"—that's a ridiculously stupid plan, May—"

I turn back to May, hoping—

I freeze.

The look on her face hits me like a gut punch. That tight, apologetic twist of her mouth, the nervous knot in her brow, the way she tries to make herself smaller. That's the *exact* look from her engagement party, the look I've spent my whole life trying to protect her from. Not sadness, exactly. Not even fear. Just... that she's not doing the right thing. That she might be wrong, or not enough. That she might hurt someone.

She doesn't deserve to carry that. And for as long as I live, she will *never* carry that.

"May, you're right," I grind out.

So I do it again—I shoulder it before she can feel the weight.

"It's the perfect solution to the problem." My voice comes out cool and smooth. A little smile, practiced and polite, wraps around the words like ribbon around broken glass.

Tom's lip curls.

"Annie—" May starts.

My jaw clenches, eyes flicking between May's face and Nico's retreating back.

"Fuck you, Tom. May is *always* right," I grit.

"No—"

I stand up. "Wait," I call out. God*fucking*damnit.

I start moving, ignoring May's protests.

"Nico," I huff out, panting at the effort it takes to run over a few feet of sand. Damn, how do volleyball players do it? "Nico," I try one more time, louder, and he takes me by surprise when he whirls around.

"No, Annie Li," he tells me, pushing his stupid sunglasses up into his hair, which is frankly extremely overwhelming, because the now two times in fourteen years I've seen Nico's eyes have been in the dark or behind sunglasses, and here, now, in the bright of the sun? They are *intense*. A clear, rich brown, steady and bright throughout, with only a darker rim tracing the outer edge. No flecks of gold or hazel, not a lighter brown in the middle, nothing. The same pure brown all over. Warm and sure. A pool of melted chocolate. Ready to sweep me away to an unfortunate end. Like one of those kids in *Willy Wonka*.

"Please, Nico," I manage.

"Annie, I just fuckin' got here and feel an overwhelming urge to get away from you. And you know how fuckin' long it takes the A train to get down here?! I'd rather sit on that train for four hours than spend thirty minutes on the beach with you, on this gorgeous freakin' day," he rages. "Not to mention, in the two times we've seen each other in *fourteen years*, we've set a *bar on fire* and scared away all the seagulls on the beach with our screaming. How the hell could we ever manage three thousand miles inside the three cubic meters of a car?"

"Well, technically, the fire was your fault—I mean, it was *your* cigarette, and I *told* you that smoking was disgusting, and seagulls are totally just beach rats, anyway—"

"Goodbye," he says, turning on his heel and walking away.

I gnash my teeth together. Is this even worth it? This cannot, by any means, be worth it. I look back towards May, who's curled into a tight ball and looking down at the sand while Tom rages, gesticulating wildly.

Damnit. "Nico!" I run after him and grab his arm (which has the audacity to be harder than it looks) and swing him back around. I have to tear the next few words from my throat. "I'm sorry. I'm really sorry. Maybe we can spend the trip learning not to kill each other at their wedding?" I offer weakly.

"The wedding won't matter, Annie, because we'll kill each other before we even get there!"

"Not if we're learning not to kill each other!"

He opens his mouth to say something else, but I cut him off.

"I'll be good. I promise. Please, Nico. Please."

His eyes flick to me on the second "please." He chews on his lip, then sighs, looking past me towards the ocean.

"What are you thinking? Tell me," I demand.

Nico cuts his eyes back to me. "I'm calculating a physics problem."

"Huh?"

"Velocity."

I rack my brain for high school level physics. "Velocity equals distance over time?"

He nods, only somewhat impressed.

"Velocity for..."

"The velocity I'd have when I launch myself into the ocean."

"Ha."

"Distance from here to the ocean?" he continues. "Maybe ninety meters."

I smirk despite myself. "Time?"

"Dunno," he shrugs. "ASAP."

That gets him a smile—a real one, and I receive a look of surprise in response.

Nico shakes his head, blinking. "I really do have to work," he says. His eyes dart all over my face in confusion. "The road trip is for work."

"Doing what, exactly? I promise I won't distract you from your urns and crucibles and elixirs."

He frowns. "Are you... referring to alchemy?"

I wave my hand. "You won't even realize I'm there, I promise. Just leave me at whatever rental you have while you go stir your vat of mercury."

His mouth twitches.

Gotcha. I go in for the kill. Take a step closer. Push my shoulders back, flip my hair over my shoulder.

His eyes shoot down.

Annie, Sister Annie warns.

Ugh. Fine.

"I need to do this for May," I tell him. "I'm sorry I've been a jerk. I'll rein it in. This wedding means everything to her. I fucked up her engagement party. I'm doing this for her. Please."

Nico blows out a slow breath, pushing the hair back from his face. It doesn't listen to him and flops back down in a way that has me looking around for movie cameras. "How are you still ruining my life?"

Bullseye. I grin. "Ditto, Nico. It's like we're soulmates or something."

"If by soulmates you mean we're meant to eat each other's souls."

I agree. "Soulmates in hell."

The open air of the beach consolidates into a small dome around us. We search each other's eyes, and I'm acutely aware of my pulse beating in my neck. I glance back at May and swallow.

"Please, Nico."

He bites the inside of his cheek and looks up at the sky as if someone there will help him. "If we die in a fiery accident, I'll kill you," he finally says.

"Done."

He sucks his teeth. Shakes his head. "I'll pick you up on Thursday."

From: ali@hawkpublishing.com

To: chef@nakedreactions.com

I had to rein her in. Ali went a little feral, and humanity had enough of her. But seriously, how dare you deprive humanity of years of regular access to what you're packing?

I think we've reached that point in any normal, functioning relationship (not that either of us would know, clearly) where we get to the good stuff. So yeah. Yes, Chef. Give it to me. Fuck me up.

Here's mine.

1. I think you should be proud of your job, because it's cool and hot as fuck.

2. So hot, in fact, that I [Redacted for Work Email] to every one of your videos.

3. I've had several fulfilling and non-toxic relationships with amicable and respectful break-ups.

FIVE

Nico

"JUST DON'T, ANNIE." I SCRUB MY FACE.

She just stares, an inscrutable look on her face.

"Just hold it in," I tell her. Minute one of this road trip and I'm already descending straight into the first circle of hell. "Don't—"

"*Really?!*" she bursts out.

I sigh.

"You know, most times it really isn't my intention to ridicule you, but..." she gestures at the car. "You just make it so *easy.*"

"I didn't—"

"—you're *truly* just a walking stereotype—"

"—choose this car—"

"Like, *really?*"

"—only car left—"

"Not only is it a Mustang, but it's *yellow?!*"

"—didn't have a choice—"

"—and a *convertible?!*"

I sigh again. "Get in the fuckin' car, Annie." I really didn't have a choice. It's not like I asked the car rental place to give

45

me the tackiest car they had. Maybe I should've kept the top up, though, but it's a nice day out and I may as well embrace it all.

Annie doesn't get in the car. "The gas mileage is probably terrible on these things," she says instead.

"You don't have to pay for gas," I offer, because I'm sick and tired of talking about it. "Just get in the car."

"And really? An American car for a two thousand mile road trip? You couldn't go Japanese?"

"I told you I didn't have a fuckin' choice, Annie—this is all they had at the rental place." Maybe this is all some sort of cruel, sick joke from the universe for saying fake grace and cheering on a god I only nominally believe in.

"We're totally going to break down before we even get to D.C. in this American piece of shit. *Always* go Asian," she says with a saucy wink.

I spent my entire freshman year at Duke wrangling the Bensonhurst out of my voice and learning how to speak in a neutral accent that isn't aggressively loud or full of swear words. I'd say it's mostly gone, except for when I'm drunk or angry. I showed up at her parents' house intending to fully tamp down the accent for this trip so Annie would have less fodder for ridicule. However, here I am, supremely pissed after thirty seconds with Annie Li, and the Bensonhurst smashes back into my voice like the Kool-Aid Man. This becomes evident with my next statement.

"Get in the *goddamn fuckin'* car, Annie Li," I bellow.

"Jeez," she answers, completely unbothered, walking around and popping the trunk and throwing various pieces of luggage in. "Someone overdid it on the steroids this morning."

I grip the steering wheel. It seems like a safe place for my hands. They wouldn't be able to wring her pretty little neck there. We haven't even made it a centimeter out of Benson-hurst, and I already want a cigarette despite having quit a year ago. And no, I did not quit the second after Annie Li told me it was gross. Most certainly not because of that.

"What's all this camera equipment?" she asks, slamming the trunk shut. The buzzing starts in my ears. I feel the flush climbing up my neck. "Filming an episode of *Jackass*? Holding your dick above a Bunsen burner or whatever they have you do in your lab?"

I wince, because she's not too far off.

I must have pissed the universe off real good, by the way, for this. I *need* to record at least one video for *Naked Reactions* on this trip. My subscribers pay for it, and they missed out last week because of my infected dick. I think I can time it so that I film at one of the properties with the separate pool house, send Annie to stay there while I record, but fuck. The risk? Total Annihilation by Annie Li? Total Annie-hilation? If she finds out I post videos of my dick for money? It's a huge fuckin' risk. I'd rather throw myself out of a moving car. Which I guess will be easy to do, if Annie Li does find out. I clear my throat.

"I told them I'd make them a wedding video," I answer, praying she doesn't push it, but I forget about it as soon as she opens the door of the passenger seat because I am suddenly inundated with two things: books and *skin*.

Annie dumps what seems like twenty books onto the floor of the passenger seat before her long legs climb in. She's wearing what's gotta be the shortest shorts known to mankind. And a crop top. Skin on her legs, skin on her arms, skin on her stomach. Tattoos on all the skin. Despite them being prison tattoos or whatever Tom said, they're really well done. And hot as sin. And even if it's less skin than she showed on the beach, the fact that it's a foot away from me, in the confines of this car? I wrench my eyes ahead.

"Which parts do you want to film?" she asks.

I almost answer, *For our sex tape? Well, all of it,* when I realize she's talking about the wedding.

I clear my throat again.

"Are you sick?"

"Sick and tired of your shit, maybe," I tell her.

"Clever boy."

I look out the window and see her parents standing at the top of their driveway, waving. Annie returns one half-heartedly.

"Don't worry," I yell towards them, "I'll keep her safe and get her down there in one piece."

They smile and wave even harder.

"See you two in a week!" I say. "Travel safely! Congratulations!"

Annie yells something in Cantonese, and I pull away from the curb.

"At least your parents like me. They think I'm charming as fuck," I tell her.

"That's because they neither speak nor understand English."

Huh. "Well, maybe I give off charming vibes. They can just feel it."

"Your vibes feel like a hernia," she says seriously.

"Have you had a hernia? Do you know what it feels like?"

She thinks. "Well, at first it's a mild irritation, like... a nagging pressure that you try to brush off," she starts.

I heave out a breath.

"But then, out of nowhere, he shoves his way in—"

"Oh, it's a 'he' now?"

"—sharp, insistent, and completely unwilling to be ignored. Every movement reminds you of his existence. A stabbing, pulling sensation that flares up when you least expect it—"

"May I remind you that you forced me into this—"

"If you try shifting or adjusting or bargaining with the pain," she continues, "it doesn't matter. He's there. A relentless, throbbing, burning discomfort that makes even the simplest tasks unbearable. And just when you think he might ease up, he digs in deeper, a cruel reminder that he's here to stay—"

"Again, this is on you—"

"—and you'll probably need professional help to get rid of him."

I mull that over. "Is there an assassination implication there?"

She shrugs. "Surgical removal."

I sigh. Four sighs in five minutes can't be good for my lungs.

"So what are you filming?"

I have a mild panic attack before remembering the wedding. "I guess I'll film the... ceremony and vows and like, the first dance or whatever." I have no intention of doing so, but those are the film-able parts of a wedding, right?

She scoffs. "You really wanna get Tom on camera thanking May for funding his chino and boat shoes collection?"

I glance over. "You're real mean, you know that?"

Her long hair starts flying all over the place once we really get moving, and she ties it back. More skin. Skin on the elegant line of her neck. I'm gonna need some of those blinders they put on horses, or else we're going to get into an accident before we even get on the highway.

Annie rolls her eyes. Or at least it feels like she does. I'm not looking because I have pretend horse blinders on. "Only to dicks."

"Like me and Tom?"

"You said it, not me."

"Whatever. I can admit he's kind of a douche. But he's harmless. We've been friends since we were all kids."

She shrugs. "Birds of a feather."

"What the hell does that mean?"

"Cut from the same cloth?"

"Huh?"

"Like calls to like," she tries.

"That makes even less sense."

"Take it up with the romantasy girlies."

I give up.

"Are you sure you can read?" She doesn't drop it.

"I can write, too."

"Your name? Impressive."

"A one hundred and seventy-eight page dissertation on the science of umami."

A subtle wince. "A dissertation?"

"Yeah, Annie Li. It's Dr. Nico to you. And I'm doing my postdoc now," I say with not a small amount of pride.

Annie takes a while to digest this, and I can almost hear the neurons firing and her jaw cracking under the effort. Finally she asks, "Umami? Like MSG?"

I'm not surprised this is what she brought up, but this is what most people associate with umami, the fifth basic taste after sweet and sour and salty and spicy. "That's an example of umami, yeah. Other popular ones are parmesan, anchovies, and some dried mushrooms." My interest in all this started when I was shaving parm in Ma's kitchen, when I realized I couldn't identify what parm actually *tasted* like. It was a little salty, yeah, but something more, something funkier than that.

"What's the science of umami entail?" she demands to know, because she demands everything. Time, attention, answers. The last thread of my sanity.

"Investigating chemical interactions between..." I put myself in *NakedReactions* mode, thinking of how to explain complex chemical concepts to lay people. "Between umami flavor compounds. Glutamates being one of them. MSG stands for monosodium glutamate. Also investigating things like fermentation, aging, and slow-cooking to naturally intensify flavor."

"Like kimchi?"

I nod. "Exactly. Kimchi. Soy sauce. Miso. Fish sauce. They're all loaded with umami."

She pauses, chewing on that—mentally, not literally. Then, "You know, it's wild how white people demonized MSG for decades while shoving parmesan into their mouths like it was nothing."

I glance at her, and there's something sharp in her gaze. Almost like a dare.

"Yeah," I say slowly. "Whole campaigns built on junk science and yellow peril, racist, xenophobic bullshit. Made 'Chinese Restaurant Syndrome' a punchline while Western chefs were bathing in glutamates from truffle paste and dry-aged steaks."

"Right," she says. "And now it's in every bougie *Bon Appétit* video."

"Every fancy New American tasting menu."

"Every white dude who thinks fish sauce is edgy."

We look at each other.

She hums, and I feel like I've passed some sort of test. "So you do food science stuff."

"Yep." In more ways than one.

She hums again.

"Have I done the impossible?" I ask her. "Impressed the permanently unimpressed Annie Li?"

"With five minutes of Googling? Nah."

"Six or seven years of research and experiments, but sure."
And one very successful adult content page.

"So can you explain the flavor 'blue'?"

I got real obsessed with figuring out the answer to this after the beach this past weekend. I try to keep myself in *Nake-*

dReactions mode. "It's blue because of the artificial food dye. It's called Blue Number One. That's the stuff that stays on your tongue," I tell her, trying to keep the eagerness out of my voice, lest Annie massacre me about being a nerd. "The flavor is created through a combination of artificial flavoring chemicals that contribute to a fruity profile. Pineapple, banana, and cherry are in there," I tell her. "Along with childhood nostalgia," I add.

"Among other things," she murmurs.

We're silent for a few beats.

"Lightning trapped in a summer night," she says after a while.

I smile, because this is the part of Annie Li I didn't actively dislike in high school. "Pretty."

She grunts. It's almost comical.

Pretty soon I see the city getting smaller and smaller in my rearview, and thus begins the desolate wasteland of I-95.

"So what's the great Annie Li up to now? Pulitzer Prize winner? University professor? Both?"

She cuts her eyes to me. Her shoulders tighten. Her chin goes up in something that looks like defiance. "I'm a writer."

"That's what you wanted to do in high school, right?"

Annie shrugs.

"Explains the books, too," I say, nodding towards the small hill of them over her feet.

She relaxes, but only by a hair. "Yep."

"You were always walking around with a library's worth of books." I chuckle thinking of little Annie and the giant backpack she toted around. "In your arms or your backpack. You definitely threw some at my head a few times."

Annie sniffs. "I would never desecrate a book in such a manner." Her shoulders move away from her ears a little more.

"You're also bossy as hell, so Annie Li making people read her writing makes sense. Forcing it into their hands, daring them to feel something. Probably yelling about metaphors until they cry." I pause. "I don't know what kind of stuff you write, but you definitely give off chaotic free verse energy."

I think I get a small smile from this one. For some reason, like it did on the beach, it makes me feel like I climbed to the top of Mount Olympus and met Zeus, who handed me a leather-bound book whose table of contents listed I. The Cure for Cancer and II. World Peace Action Items.

"What are you writing right now?" I ask.

However, with this question, Annie closes up again, like steel reinforcements slamming down on her windows like in the movies. She picks up one of the books at her feet.

"Do you have a book?" she asks, and with that, she decides my question is irrelevant and that train of our conversation is finished, and I can't decide if all this whiplash is making me irritated or hard. Or both. Both, probably.

"What do you mean?"

"You could probably write a cool book about your research."

I glance over at her, the back of my neck prickling. "Not... Well, my dissertation was technically bound into a hardcover book."

She shakes her head. "No one wants to read that. Maybe something non-chemists could digest. Like, a cookbook would be cool."

"A cookbook... would be cool," I repeat lamely.

"Okay," she says with finality, out of freakin' nowhere. "I'm going to read now. Focus on driving, please. Eyes on the road."

I don't even bother responding, the whiplash feeling intensifying, now feeling like I've been punted off Mount Olympus but still pretty impressed we managed to share space without resorting to violence. But I guess quiet is better than arguing.

SIX

Nico

WE DON'T SAY ANOTHER WORD UNTIL WE START seeing the signs for Philly.

"Wanna eat?" I ask her.

She starts. She seems to drift for a moment, as if she's trapped in the pages of her book-world, before slowly lifting her gaze. Disoriented, as if she just remembered she was in a car with her worst enemy. I can only see her out of the corner of my eye, but I'm sure she looks particularly gorgeous right now. "Yeah," she says. "I can eat."

"I know a good place."

"I love chicken parm."

"I don't only eat chicken parm, Annie." I did have it for dinner last night, but she definitely does not need to know that.

"Are you saying that if I cut you open, you wouldn't bleed marinara sauce?"

I sigh (should I get a nebulizer?), and thankfully she's silent until I pull the car into the small parking lot.

Annie looks around. "Okay, cheesesteaks I get, because

we're in Philly, but we're not going to go to one of the famous places?"

I turn the car off. "This place is ten times better."

She eyes the storefront suspiciously. "You sure?"

"Positive."

I climb out and start making my way to the other side of the car to open Annie's door, force of habit really, because Ma would slap me upside the head if I didn't, but then I stop short when I realize that Annie Li would fuckin' hate it and would never stop raggin' me about it if I opened that door for her.

She stares at me with an eyebrow lifted in a dare and opens her own door.

I, at the very least, hold the door to the shop open for her on the way in.

It's a small place, a little more renovated than the last time I was here, but it's crowded as all hell, way more crowded than the last time I was here. I make my way to the counter, to the woman running the register. "Hey. Is—" but I don't need to finish.

"*Nicoooo!*" Gino yells as he walks out of the kitchen. "Nico! Cheryl, check out this kid. Come here, you gorgeous, brilliant boy, you." He steps out from behind the counter and wraps me in his arms. Now, I consider myself a pretty big guy, got some meat on me because of the nature of my job and all, but Gino makes me feel like a delicate ballerina.

"Gino, my man," I say into his chest.

Gino wraps my head in an arm, a half approximation of a headlock, presenting me to the middle-aged woman behind the counter. "Cheryl, you know who this is?"

"Nah, Gino," she answers.

"This guy here deserves the Nobel Prize or some shit. Smartest kid I ever met. Saved this business, made it what it is today," he says, gesturing to the crowds of people in the shop.

"Nice to meet you, Cheryl," I nod my head.

She sucks her teeth, as if acknowledging me has cost her something.

I suppress a smile.

Gino turns to Annie, who is standing there looking a little bewildered.

"And who's this stunning bambina, Nico? This your girl? She's too pretty for you."

She snaps out of it. Her face breaks into a huge smile, a wide grin that knocks me speechless for the second time because I'm so used to her scowling or glaring at me like she wants to flay the skin from my flesh. I ignore the stab of awe in my chest, but I stare at her. I mean, I gotta. She's a gorgeous pain in my ass.

"You're right, I am too pretty for him," she tells Gino, striding up to him to shake his hand. "I'm Annie. I'm his nothing. My sister is marrying his friend, and we're driving down to the wedding together. Nice to meet you."

"Gino. Nice to meet you, and congratulations to your sister."

"Thanks. I don't think it's worth celebrating though, since Nico's friend is a massive—"

"Annie," I warn.

Gino turns to me and slaps me upside the head. "Not so smart after all, kid, if pretty Annie is your 'nothing.'"

"She hates me," I say, at the same time Annie says, "I'm not his type."

Gino looks between us. "What's his type, then?"

"Someone who isn't a miserable fuckin' hurricane of serious issues who causes fuckin' problems for everyone around her," she says out of fuckin' left field, with a smile that's so fake it looks like it's slapped on and scotch taped. What the hell is that? What...

It suddenly hits me like a battering ram, and I realize with a start that those are *my* words. My words from when I was pissed on the beach.

I stare at her some more. At the current forced nonchalance of her posture and smile. And if I'm reading her right… Is that… No. It can't be. She's *hurt*. Prickly, thorny Annie Li, with skin so thick that even the weight of the world would barely make a dent, who at eight-years-old kicked a boy twice her size in the nuts because he pushed my little sister, is *hurt* by a comment I made. "Annie—"

"Or maybe like a cheerleader or something," she interrupts, "and certainly not this," she gestures up and down her body, seemingly at the tattoos that cover every inch. "Didn't you play football in high school or something?"

Huh? "If by football, you mean *Dungeons and Dragons*," I reply slowly.

She frowns at me. "I seem to remember you being a dumb sports jock at Stuy."

"Annie, I was valedictorian. You know this, so fuckin' enough about that. But I was also the captain of the Science Olympiad team and the Mathletes team. Not to mention president of the chess club and sci-fi club."

Annie stares at me, incredulous and slightly horrified. "You didn't play sports?"

"I think I played ping-pong for a minute?" I scratch the back of my head. "But back to that other thing—"

"Well," Gino says, clapping his hands together once and cutting me off, "looks like you guys got some issues that need workin' out, so why don't you two go sit down and I'll get you something to eat." He shoves me towards an empty table, with Annie following not far behind.

We sit. I take her in while she looks me directly in the eyes with another dare in hers. She doesn't back down, doesn't flinch, doesn't avert her gaze. But still, it's there. I can see it. A flicker of pain, of hurt, of self-doubt. Something soft. And just like that, I have to apologize to Annie "My Worst Fuckin' Nightmare" Li.

At least, I try to.

"Don't," she says quietly, cutting me off. She finally looks away. "I don't want it."

Gino takes that moment to plop down two cheesesteaks. "Davey just made these. Fresh off the grill. Bon appétit."

We mutter our thanks, Annie blasting Gino with that megawatt smile. The real one.

"So how did you help Gino do all of this?" she quickly asks after he walks away, erecting another wall with breakneck speed.

I don't answer. "Annie. Come on, honey."

The fire in her eyes reignites. "I'm not your honey."

I blow out a breath. "Fine." I'm not going to win. "I taught him about a particular chemical reaction."

She takes a huge bite of her sandwich. "Holy shit," she says around a mouthful of steak. "This is incredible."

I nod, because it is. "The reaction happens when proteins and sugars react at high temperatures and create hundreds of tasty as fuck flavor compounds. I used the tenets of that to give him a bunch of tips for improving his sandwich."

"Like what?"

I chew and swallow a bite. Damn, this really is incredible. "You gotta remember that browning is good. So I told him to use thin-sliced ribeye 'cause its marbling allows for faster rendering of fat, which enhances browning. To heat his griddle real hot. Also to cook in small batches for a proper sear. Too much meat on the grill will make steam, and that'll stop the reaction and browning from happening."

"And you just strolled in here like Robin Hood and told him that?"

I shrug. "Kinda. I dated someone who lived nearby for a

hot second. I came in here all the time when I came down to visit. We got to talkin'."

"Nice of you."

I eye her. "Despite this ridiculous image you have of me, I'm a nice fuckin' person, Annie."

"That courtesy seems to extend to everyone else but me," she says cooly.

"Christ, Annie, I wanna apologize for what I said on the beach, but you won't let me."

"Because that's not all of it, not even a fraction of what you need to be apologizing for, so I don't want it, Nico," she growls.

I stare at her. "What the hell are you talking about?"

"Drop it," she says dangerously. "I told you I don't want it."

"You're giving me fuckin' whiplash," I tell her, running my hands through my hair. It's already a disaster from the top down of our car. "This is too much."

"Then *leave it*." She slams her hands down on the table. I half expect quills to shoot out of her skin like a cartoon porcupine. For the first time, I catch a clear glimpse of the tattoos she has across her knuckles. Her right hand spells out PLUM. On her left, the four suits of a deck are etched across each finger—spade on her index, heart on her middle, diamond on her ring, and club on her pinky.

"Fine," I say.

Because she's right. I do need to fuckin' leave it. My life is already freakin' ridiculous as it is. This porn star does not need to add Sexy Enemy Apologist to his CV.

———

Our car doesn't start up again while parked at a rest stop in the

Middle of Nowhere, Maryland, and Annie vibrates next to me with barely restrained glee.

"Just don't, Annie."

"Oh, but I must."

"Just hold it in."

"I don't think I can."

"Try harder."

"*Told you*," she squeaks out.

I am unable to hold it in. "For the last fuckin' time, Annie, I didn't have a fuckin' choice about this fuckin' car so just fuckin' *enough*, okay?"

She tries to smother a grin and fails.

I pull out my phone and dial the rental company.

"I'm gonna go get some candy," Annie says, hopping out of the car and leaving me in peace.

A few minutes later, I finally hang up and will my blood pressure to go down.

"Earliest we can get to you is 8:30 a.m.," the rep chirped, like I won the car rental lottery. "But we've arranged accommodations for you about ten miles down the road. There's a hotel we partner with. You'll just need to get yourselves there."

I hung up the phone before I lost it on the poor customer service rep or threw my phone out the window.

I settle in to wait for Annie, already opening my email to find comfort in Ali's words. I immediately bathe in the stab of pride at Ali's first line, that what I'm doing is really cool. And then I get hard. Again. *We must refrain from sending our coworker a dick pic*, I chant in my head. I start typing.

From: chef@nakedreactions.com

To: ali@hawkpublishing.com

Why, thank you, Ali. It's rare that I get that sort of feedback. Regarding the job, I mean. I get all sorts of weird and inappropriate feedback about the goods, though (now that I think about it, for some strange reason, that doesn't include you).

Also, I don't like when you talk about yourself like that. Tell me more, but this time, don't be so mean to yourself. Tell me more about how Ali shines.

I'll start.

1. You have such a way with words.

2. A way with words that gets me [Redacted for Work Email].

3. I don't wonder what you look like every time I [Redacted for Work Email].

As I hit send on what I suppose some may classify as the written, not quite safe for work version of a dick pic, I hear a commotion outside the car. I peer out the window, over to my left... and my blood pressure spikes hard enough to shrivel my erection and cause legitimate medical concern. But underneath the alarm is something entirely unexpected: a visceral, primal surge of *mine, must protect.*

I decide to unpack this at a later time and jump out of the car and run over to where Annie, all roughly five feet and change of her, is standing toe-to-toe with a furious man about my size. Except he's built like he's been suckling pure HGH since birth.

"Annie, honey," I cut in, "step back."

Both she and the dude snap their heads toward me.

Her lip starts to curl back when the guy grunts, "She yours? Tell her to go get me a new—"

"Fuck you, you motherfucking roided-up jar of expired whey protein," Annie snarls, entirely ignoring my request and taking a step forward like she's not half this dude's mass. The violence of it stops me in my tracks. "You knocked into this poor woman and tripped over your own over-inflated ego—then you wanna cry about your soda? Get a fucking grip."

It's then that I notice the elderly Asian couple behind her —both half *Annie's* size, the woman clutching an all-white mobility cane, both of them visibly shaken.

I silently move to their side, at Annie's back.

Annie jabs a finger in the dude's face. "Go bench press some accountability, dick. You want a new drink? Why don't you wring one out of your nasty-ass, creatine-soaked compression shirt?"

The guy blinks, stunned, like the rage circuit in his brain shorted out from the sheer force of being verbally bodied by someone half his size. "What the f—"

The three of us behind Annie collectively relax, because the situation now reads *handled*. I wonder, briefly, if I should de-escalate or hold Annie's metaphorical earrings.

"Oh, now you're speechless?" Annie barks, arms out. "You've been snorting and grunting like a juiced-up buffalo and stomping your little hooves—," I glance down and his feet *are* comically small, "—and suddenly you can't form a sentence? Why don't you run back to your Mustang convertible—" I scrub my face at this, "—and drive back to whatever shithole gym you came from. Sweat out some of that toxic masculinity."

The dude shakes his head. "Crazy-ass bit—" he starts, and I go blind.

I take a step forward. "Careful." I surprise myself with the tone my voice has taken, all *metal* and *danger* and *murder*, while I am normally more of an *extra marshmallows, please* and *do-you-wanna-hear-my-ranking-of-all-the-Spider-Verses* kinda guy.

He glances between the two of us.

"You may have more muscle," I inform him, then point to Annie, "but she will set your Mustang convertible on fire."

He shakes his head again and storms off, muttering under his breath.

I look over at Annie as if to check her for injuries, but she's already moved towards the elderly couple, speaking to them in warm, soothing Cantonese. The man clutches Annie's arm with both hands. There is a lot of what I believe is "thank you."

Annie makes eye contact with me and gestures me over. "Let's walk them to their car," she says, and I've never moved faster to take someone's orders. The woman takes my arm with a frail hand, and we guide them across the lot.

After they drive away, Annie looks at me. I still feel juiced up with adrenaline and ready to, like, wrestle a hippopotamus or flip a tractor tire or scream into an abyss, or something.

Annie just nods, beautiful and serene. "Now I want a soda."

SEVEN

Annie

It's late by the time we get to the place. Nico gets us a big cab (I manage to squeeze in two *'cabs are here'* jabs) for all our luggage to take us to the... comically small murder shack that currently claims to be a motel.

"Is this some sort of sick joke?" I ask merrily.

He scrubs his hair sheepishly, but it's already a disaster thanks to our four hour long convertible ride. Mine is a bird's nest of tangles despite having it pulled back all day. "The rental place booked it for us," he says unhelpfully.

"Why? Because when we die here, they won't have to send us a new car?"

"Annie, please." Nico looks exhausted.

Nico, *Doctor* Nico, with the smarts and the whole 'helping old Italian men and their restaurants' thing, with the mad scientist hair that is tousled so handsomely it looks purposeful, who has my back in a fight with an actual meathead. With the warm brown eyes that turn *concerned* instead of *angry* when he's trying to do something stupid like 'figure me out.' Like I'm a science problem that needs analyzing and solving.

That was a mistake I let slip at Gino's. He wasn't supposed

to see that. That what he said on the beach affected me in a way that was both sharp and aching, that it left an imprint so clear and deep that I was able to memorize it and repeat it verbatim.

That isn't going to happen again.

I will also never again let that little part of me melt when he calls me 'honey.' When it comes out of his perfect mouth, I will not turn into an oozing puddle of goo. Or of honey, I guess.

Another tiny piece of me was almost disappointed when he didn't open my car door for me, because he knew (rightfully so) that I would tear him to shreds about it. But I think I secretly would've liked it. I'm never going to think that again.

Because he's already tired of me, and I need to make it to Miami.

I keep my mouth shut.

He doesn't look at me and jumps out of the van. "Thanks so much, man," he tells the cab driver with genuine warmth, because it seems that Nico really is that nice to everyone but me. Although he does unload all my luggage from the back, which is nice I suppose, but what's even nicer is watching his biceps flex to do it.

"Leave them," he tells me about my luggage. "I'll come back for them. Stay here and I'll go check us in."

"If you insist," I sniff. I'll give him this, because I didn't let him have my car door.

Nico walks back out with a room key and moves two doors down from where I'm standing. After a thirty-second battle with a key in the rusty lock, the door finally creaks open menacingly on its ancient, bloody hinges, signaling to the audience that whatever is in there is a Bad Idea.

I'm proven correct when Nico plants his hands on his hips and looks towards the sky. "For fuck's sake."

I inch towards him and peer around the door frame,

bracing myself for the man in a clown mask we've just awoken from a nap.

It's... a room. Technically. Everything is brown. Not chic leather brown. Not even trendy taupe. This is "fecal distress" brown. Shit-brown. The-color-of-shit brown.

One of the beds has a massive wet spot in the middle of it. We look up. The ceiling is leaking shit-brown water onto the shit-brown blanket.

"No, thanks," I say amenably. "I'd rather sleep in the pile of used needles in the corner of the parking lot."

Nico shivers. "I think I've just contracted Hep B."

We both creep backwards.

"I'll get us another room."

"What if we just got a cab to literally *anywhere else*—"

Nico blows out an impatient breath. "Tried that already. They won't give us a new car if we do that," he sighs, like he's just so burdened by logistics and not, say, the fact that the motel is leaking disease.

"Call me crazy," I say, "but I'd rather lose the rental car than my skin."

He drags his big hands down his face and groans. "Let's see what other rooms they have. We'll reassess if it's just as..."

"Fatal?" I offer. "Decaying? Haunted? Noxious?"

He trudges back towards the main office without a response.

I try not to scream when something rustles in the woods behind the murder shack, because statistically it's probably a raccoon and not a man named Earl who collects toes.

Nico eventually comes back out with a horrified look on his face.

"The only room left is the one they use for performing animal sacrifices," I supply for him.

"Worse," he mutters. "The only room left has only one bed."

The room itself isn't so bad. It's almost cozy, in a ratty, mouse-lair way. It doesn't smell damp or like Giardia or the blood of virgins.

Even so, we both still stare at the one bed as if it's soaked with the blood of virgins. Virgins with Giardia.

"Well," I announce, "Pile of needles, it is."

Nico looks like he is about to cry.

"I can sleep in the car?" I attempt to help.

"No one's sleeping in the car." He tears at his hair. "Is this really not gonna be okay with you? I can get us a new rental car and forfeit this one if it's not."

"How much is that gonna be?"

He shrugs. "For several days, booking on the day we need it... probably thousands of dollars."

I stare at handsome, successful Dr. Nico, who picked me up from *my parent's basement where I live*, devastating in the dim light of the shit-brown room. "You'd pay that?"

"If you're uncomfortable, then yeah."

Oh boy. "I..." My body immediately goes into fight mode. Sister Annie tries to wrangle Annie of the past into submission, because she is currently salivating and chomping at the bit at the opportunity to use this rich man for nice, free things. She is fortunate in her triumph. What the hell is wrong with me? "No. I can handle it. It's a big bed, and it's just a few hours."

All the tension leaves Nico's body, and I realize just how wound up he was over this. It almost makes me feel bad. No, it does make me feel bad. Because it's a reminder of just how unbearable I can be. Exhausting. Because that's what I am, or was to people. Just... effort, making everyone clench their teeth and flinch in advance, like I'm a slap they're waiting for.

"Even fewer hours than you think," he adds on, oblivious.

"I gotta get to DC to meet with this chef at his restaurant. You wanna come with? By the time we get back, it'll only be eight hours that we gotta be trapped in this room."

I blink at him. "It's ten at night."

"Yeah, but we haven't eaten yet. And it's a two-star Michelin menu. For free. Besides, they close at eleven, and I don't know if you know this, but kitchens after closing are usually a fuckin' party."

Oh *boy*! Old Annie shrieks with delight. Use this hot, rich man to throw down at a party that very likely involves a heavy amount of stimulants? Sign me the hell up. But alas, Sister Annie wins this round again and knocks her out. *Stay here.*

Nico remains ignorant of my internal struggle.

"I'm good," I mumble.

He frowns. "What are you going to eat, then?"

"I have the rest of that cheesesteak from Gino's."

"You'd rather eat an old, cold, soggy sandwich than have a highly regarded menu of extremely high quality, expensive food? For *free*?" he asks incredulously.

Not to mention free drinks, because I am, in fact, very familiar with a city restaurant after closing. I have to physically peel myself from the offer. Heart heavy, I drag my suitcases further into the rat lair.

Nico takes a few steps away, and I suddenly have a lump the size of a baseball clogging my throat. I know he's just giving me room to maneuver, but the motion makes my stomach clench, because again, this is what people have always done, what I've always been—sharp edges and emotional wreckage and a hurricane of serious issues that people learn to avoid or tiptoe around. "Enjoy, Dr. Nico, but don't get too fucked up."

"Why would I get fucked up? I have to chauffeur your ass bright and early tomorrow morning."

Oh right, because most people have an intrinsic pause

button. "Later," I call out, just as I enter the bathroom. "And thanks for driving," I tack on, because I am nice and behaving.

I shut the door, and I slump down on the other side of it.

I look around and decide to sit on the pink porcelain toilet instead of the floor.

Now, trapped in a busted motel rat palace—surrounded by shit-brown grout, cracked porcelain, and the kind of ominous dripping that usually precedes a murder in an abandoned meat locker—I decide this might actually be it. Rock Bottom. The End of the Line. The Big Sad. I've lived, I've laughed, I've made aggressively poor life choices. And now I'm here, in a mildew-scented purgatory that screams, "Your therapist was right."

I cover my face with my hands and take deep pulls of air that rattle through the space between my fingers. Then I pull out my phone and open up my email, compelled, after all of this, to find some sort of comfort in Chef's words.

I huff a dry laugh at what he's written. How Ali *shines*? By shines, does he mean spontaneously combusts and takes out a small village?

The door to the room slams shut, and instead of screaming *Take me with you*, I type instead.

From: ali@hawkpublishing.com
To: chef@nakedreactions.com

I'm a miserable hurricane of serious issues. But there's a reason for it, I think. It built and built and built through childhood into high school. Pressure and expectations from everywhere and everyone. Be the best. At everything. I didn't live in high school—I optimized. Studied like it was an Olympic sport. Worked. Played two instruments. Volunteered. Wrote. Perfected. Then I got fucked over. And then I wasn't the best, despite dedicating my entire existence to it. Then in

the city, on my own for the first time in my life? Free? I deto-
nated. Exploded into a million reckless pieces.

I leave the shit-brown bathroom to grab my toothbrush, brush my teeth and splash water on my face in an approximation of a night-time skincare routine, plod out, and get under the shit-brown covers. I hate it here.

I reread the deranged email draft on my phone. Then, I place my finger on the backspace key and hold it down.

I'm miserable.

And then I add:

1. I don't shine. I'm mean and miserable.

2. I'm trying my best not to, but I make really reckless, impulsive decisions just to feel something. Like Not That Safe for Work Sexting (S-emailing? Sexemailing?) with my hot porn star coworker.

3. No one has ever given up on me.

Then I scoot all the way to the edge of the bed and fall asleep.

EIGHT

Annie

I KNEW THAT IN SHARING A BED WITH SOMEONE, there was bound to be some accidental elbow brushing or perhaps a rogue kick.

I expected it, even.

What I did not expect, however, was to wake up draped over my worst enemy's hard body like a cold, clingy sleep koala trying to get warm.

But apparently, my worst enemy is a human mattress. A wet mattress like the one in our original room, because there is a spot on his shirt that indicates I've been drooling here a while.

Did I mention the human mattress inexplicably has faulty hardware, because there is a wayward pole currently nestled in right where it absolutely should not be?

Wow, this mattress feels good. Solid. Supportive. Extra firm. I grind down just a little bit, just to confirm the firmness for sleep science and also because I haven't had a human mattress with faulty hardware in *over two years*, and my eyes roll to the back of my head. Eleven out of ten, no notes. Or perhaps nine out of nine, now that I think about it.

Nico's big hands fly to my hips. "Again," he mutters, sleep in his voice.

I go rigid, because this likely constitutes sexual harassment. I remain frozen, praying he stays asleep so I can peel myself off the hot, firm, faulty mattress.

But because this is the worst day of my life, Nico displays all the telltale signs of waking. His body freezes under mine. His hands fly off my hips and smack flat onto the actual mattress. He clears his throat, which rumbles through his chest like a seismic event.

The sounds of our breathing rip through the silence.

To my abject horror, his hands start to move again.

One shifts up to tangle itself in my hair. The other inches towards my ass... and squeezes when it gets there.

Holy mother of—

"My worst fuckin' nightmare *and* my wettest fuckin' dream," he murmurs, his lips brushing against my ear.

My body lights up.

He thrusts up once, a tiny, almost imperceptible and unconscious movement, and we both let out unnatural, strangled sorts of sounds.

"Oh, wow," I squeak. That's some big, faulty hardware.

"Impressed yet?" he rasps.

"No," I say, with a small swivel of my hips, just to make sure.

"Lie."

I tilt my head up to look at him and immediately regret it. His hair's a mess and his jaw is shadowed with stubble, his gorgeous, infuriating mouth and the tips of his cheeks flushed a deep crimson. We search for something, anything, in each other's eyes before his flick down to my mouth. It's all too much.

I reach back and throw the shit-brown covers over the two

of us, enshrouding us in darkness, because if I can't see, then maybe this isn't actually happening.

"Talk to me, Annie." His voice is gravel and surrounds me in heat.

"I'd rather not."

He thrusts up once more, and our moans mingle together. I bury my face in his chest.

"What do you want me to do with this?" he grits out, now making small, incremental rocking motions that feel like heaven and hell wrapped into one big, non-faulty package.

"With what?" I grumble, now hating him for literally being the whole package. Smart, hot, rich, well-endowed Nico Giannuzzi. "The tiny sausage you have in your pocket?" I say, now meeting his thrusts with grinding of my own.

"Maybe I should feed you that sausage," he groans, taking his big hands and running them up and down my sides but over my shirt, along my waist, squeezing and kneading and learning as I all but purr in satisfaction at the feel of it. "Stuff it down your throat and make you gag on it."

An embarrassing sound, one that could technically be classified as a whimper, leaves my mouth at how much I *need* that. "It'd go down easy," I lie to him, "like a single strand of spaghetti." We're fully rocking together now, mimicking fucking without any actual penetration, his dick hitting just the right spot over and over again. I moan. A line of sweat drips down my back at the heat currently being generated under the covers.

"Want to test that out?" he asks, while inching his hand back down my ass to where I need it most. Oh god.

"Do you really have Hep B?" I blurt out.

His hand stops. "No. I'm clean. You?" he finally says.

"Same," I whisper.

"Am I fuckin' you right now?"

I swallow, rubbing along his length. "I'd never fuck an illiterate gorilla," I tell him, even while reaching down to my own underwear and pulling it to the side. One layer of clothing now separates us, and it belongs to him. It soaks quickly while I cover it in an embarrassingly wet glide back and forth. "Oh god," I whisper, rocking even harder.

"Perfect," he grunts, voice strangled now, "'Cause I'd never stick my dick in crazy," he tells me, as he maneuvers somewhere beneath me, and I feel a slide of fabric pulling down until I feel hot, smooth, solid steel right between my bare lips.

Our combined moans fill the blanket space.

"Fuck, Annie," he mutters, a frustrated whisper.

Something tugs at my head.

"Goddamn—"

It's not Nico pulling at my hair. No. It's the sudden ring of alarm bells.

"*You*—"

Not in the room. In my brain. Sirens begin screeching in my brain at the tone of his voice.

Shit.

Shit.

Because it's the obvious tension and exasperation in his voice that cuts through my horny, mattress-testing haze and reminds me who the fuck this is and how he feels about me and what the fuck and *what in the actual fuck am I doing?!*

I peel myself off and throw myself on the bed next to him while I try, with all my might, not to scream.

That doesn't count as sex, though, does it? Right?!

Sister Annie narrows her eyes at me.

Shit. *Shit*.

With *Nico*?!

SHIT!

We stare at the blanket still over our heads together, sweating and panting in a horrible, pre-coital silence.

Nico eventually blows out a big breath, one I know has a

lot of air, because I am now well acquainted with the sheer size of his chest and its subsequent lung capacity potential. "You are truly Hellspawn placed on this earth to torture me," he says.

"That's me," I say to the blanket. "Lucifer Li."

He turns his head in my general direction. "That's literally what your contact is on my phone."

"Funny," I grunt, "you're just Satan in mine."

"Funny," he responds, "because you mutter 'hail, Satan' in your sleep."

I don't answer that.

"That was a huge mistake," I say after a while.

His big body tenses next to mine. When he speaks, there's an unnameable emotion that's threaded through his voice. "Fine," he says, and something lodges itself in my throat.

We lay in quiet agony, sweating and listening to the murder drips coming from the bathroom.

"What's our next stop?" I ask casually, as if I didn't just grind myself against the bare length of my worst enemy's dick.

He clears his throat. "Richmond, Virginia. One of the fine dining spots down there." He pauses. "You should come with me this time."

I shrug noncommittally. "Maybe." No.

"Why not?"

The back of my neck prickles with residual panic and irritation. "I don't owe you an explanation."

"It's just food. Really good food, actually. Some of the best, according to a random tire company. Also the most expensive."

It's not just food. It's *Annie could ruin everyone's lives including her own, didn't I just prove that to you?* I find myself going on the offensive. "Is that what this all is? Wanna show off how fancy Dr. Nico is now? Rub it all in my face?"

There is a prolonged beat before he slowly sits up,

bringing the blanket with him. I'm blasted with fresh air cooling my feverish, sweaty skin, sunlight and reality illuminating my shame. "Huh?" he asks.

I look up at Nico and regret it again, because a messy, sweaty, aroused, *hard* Nico has to be the most devastatingly sexy things I've ever seen. There's a wet spot on his shorts above his obvious erection, *my* wet spot. *What the hell is wrong with me?* I have to keep going, a runaway train. "Not gonna work, dude." I sit up, too, relishing in the familiar waves of agitation now coming from my left. "Can take the kid out of Bensonhurst, but can't take the Bensonhurst outta the kid."

"You grew up two blocks away from me!"

"Yes, but I don't sound like a dollar-slice dimwit."

"I'm articulate as *fuck*."

My mouth twitches.

"What the hell is wrong with you?" he demands to know.

"Would you like an itemized list or a brief summary?"

"Gimme a summary."

I chew the inside of my mouth until I taste blood. Then I look him dead in the eye and say, "I'm a hurricane of serious issues." The words slip out before I can stop them.

Nico's whole body tenses. Then—boom.

"Fuckin' hell, Annie." His voice explodes through the room. "I'm sorry, okay? I'm so fuckin' sorry I said that, but I am trying to be polite and apologetic and helpful and you keep twisting it into somethin' ugly!"

He shoots up from the bed, pacing, running a hand through his hair like he's seconds from losing it. "I don't know what you want from me! I'm trying here. I'm really, really trying. And we almost just *fucked*," he snarls, with a twist in his face that pulls at my heart, pointing at the bed, at where we almost did, "and you immediately regret it, tell me it was a mistake, when *I* was the one who woke up to *you* grinding on my dick, and then you *immediately* insult me?! Why the hell do you always wanna pick a fight for no fuckin' reason at all?"

"There's always a reason," I mutter.

"Please," he snaps. "Enlighten me."

I stare at him, my chest rising and falling and hands clenched into fists. I could tell him. I could rip open every wound, every fear, tell him exactly why I can't let him be nice to me.

Instead, I say nothing.

He watches me for a long second, then exhales hard, full of something like frustration, like disappointment.

"We're leaving in thirty," he mutters. "Get your shit together by then."

I don't know if he means my luggage or my entire fucking life. Probably both.

He storms into the bathroom, and I'm left alone with the dull roar of adrenaline in my veins. But this kind of high doesn't feel good at all.

———

I blame the crying on a lot of things.

The book I'm reading is devastatingly sad—definitely not a light beach (or road trip) read. Especially not in a cramped replacement sedan with shitty A/C and nowhere to hide. I can't stop thinking about my email to Chef. At the sudden reappearance of the kid who started the downward spiral of my life. I can't stop thinking about my lack of impulse control, ashamed that I couldn't even make it one full year of Sister Annie *again*, rubbed on my worst enemy after *one day* of being around him because I was bored and horny and depressed. I'm also probably still coming down from this raging asshole yelling at me afterwards. And now I'm trapped in a four-door emotional pressure cooker with the asshole—the guy who ruined everything.

And I'm only here as a fucked up way of saving May. *And she still thinks I'm going to blow up her wedding, and she's right.*

And you know what else? I hate Sister Annie. What the hell has she actually done for me this year?

Because I'm *fucking miserable.*

I look out the window and surreptitiously try to wipe my eyes.

But it's Fuckin' Dr. Nico.

"Hey," he says quietly. He puts his large bear paw on my knee. "You good, honey?" I close my eyes and enjoy the gooeyness of my insides and the weight of his hand for one second before lifting his hand and dropping it on his lap.

"I'm not your honey," I warn.

He sighs. "I'm sorry about earlier, Annie." He sounds genuine, but too fucking bad.

"I'm not crying because of you, Nico," I snap. "I did enough of that in high school."

"Why are you crying then?"

I sniff and shift my body as far away from him as possible. "This book," I decide to say.

"Oh."

"It's beautiful."

"So it's a good cry?"

"It's certainly not a 'Nico Giannuzzi ruined my chances of getting into Harvard cry,'" I can't help but snarl. "That was more of a 'bawling my eyes out, sobbing so hard I threw up' cry."

To his credit, he blows out a slow breath, really trying to keep his shit together. "Should we just go ahead and address the elephant in the car then?"

"Which one?" I'm not touching high school. "How I'm

your *worst fuckin' nightmare and your wettest fuckin' dream,"* I taunt, "or how the townie humped a bunch of professors to get a doctorate?"

He looks at the road in front of us for what feels like several minutes.

I shift in my seat, picking at the ratty leather, the uncomfortable charge in the air prickling my skin.

"Why are you like this?" he finally asks quietly.

It is somehow the verbal equivalent of a slap in the face. Fighting Annie is shocked into silence. My lungs seize. I don't answer. *Why are you like this, Annie? Get your shit together, Annie. Do better, Annie. Be the best, Annie.*

"Jesus, Annie. You've gotta know it's truly exhausting," he says. "They may seem like funny little insults to you, but..." he shakes his head. "You chip and pick and chip away bit by bit until I finally feel like a giant gaping fuckin' wound."

Stop causing problems for everyone, Annie. I look out the window, clenching my fists so hard my nails dig into my palms. *Selfish, self-centered Annie. Worthless, stupid girl.*

"Did you know that after you harassed me for, oh I don't know, my *entire childhood* about what an idiot I sounded like, I spent an entire year trying to get rid of my accent?"

You're really good at insulting people, Annie.

"You know that I would try to avoid walking through the hallways senior year so I could avoid you belittling me for one reason or another?"

Tone down the nastiness, Annie.

"Well, that's a giant, gaping fuckin' wound," he tells me.

"You fucked me over," I finally whisper. It just comes out of my mouth.

"*I* fucked *you* over? Did I not just tell you that you made my entire senior year a living hell on earth?"

He has no idea.

"We're only on the second day of this road trip," he

continues, "and I already wanna give up. I just wanna stick you on a train and do the rest of this myself." He sounds defeated instead of angry, and somehow that cuts deeper. I'd rather bear the sharp edge of his anger than the heavy weight of his surrender.

However, I'm used to all of this now, know this song and dance. Used to this tone of voice from people right before they run, right after I let them down, right after they've used me up and decide what's left isn't worth it. This time, I'm going to get ahead of it. I turn, meeting the side of his face. "Then leave," I tell him. My voice wavers, but I pull myself together.

He whips his head towards me as best he can while barreling seventy miles an hour down a highway. "What?"

"Just drop me off at the train station in Richmond, and I'll get a train down the rest of the way." I'll figure out the rest —lodging, everything—on my own. As always.

Silence.

I clench my jaw to keep my voice from trembling, but I'm not successful. It shakes when I say, "We'll just tell May we drove down together, and we'll avoid each other during the wedding, and then we'll never have to see each other again."

More silence. I think I hear my insides churning.

"Then I don't have to listen to your inane—"

Nico suddenly jerks the wheel and veers off the highway onto a rest stop ramp.

My heart slams into my ribs. "Are you serious?" A knot the size of a fist lodges itself in the upper part of my esophagus.

He doesn't answer, just drives all the way into the parking area. He pulls up to one of the curbs.

"Get out of the car," he orders.

I will not cry. Don't you dare let him see you cry. "You won't even give me the courtesy of dropping me at the train? Literally any train station?" My voice cracks. Agony slices through my ribcage.

He steps out, rounds the car like an angry bear, and wrenches my door open. "Get out of the car," he repeats.

"Please," I whisper. "Just drive me to a train station." I fail. A tear gets out. Then another. I'm done.

He reaches into the car and bodily hauls me out.

And then, Nicholas "Nico" Giannuzzi, my childhood neighbor, high school nemesis, source of all teenage anxiety, and the kid who ruined my life...

...Wraps me in a hug.

Pulls me to his chest and wraps both his meaty arms around my shoulders.

At first, I'm stiff as a board. Confused. But then he squeezes even tighter, and then I... dissolve.

Something about this feeling—safe, squeezed, secure, supported? That's it. All I need. And then... I just let it all go. The regret and guilt of the past week, of the last year, maybe even eleven? I let it all go and sob into his shirt.

His hands smooth down my back, through my hair. His lips press, soft and warm, against my forehead. I cry harder, and he shifts his arms to curl around my head, mashing my face into his chest.

"I'm a mess," I sob.

"It's okay," he says, squeezing tighter.

"I'm fucking insane," I cry.

"Aren't we all?" he says, petting my head.

"I hate you," I sniff.

"I know," he says, pressing his mouth into my hair.

Nasty, selfish, problematic, miserable hurricane of serious issues. I take it all and soak his shirt with it.

This goes on and on and on until I run out of juice and I'm an empty husk of a human. It could be a few seconds or minutes or maybe an hour, I'm not sure, but Nico's arms don't relax in the slightest, remaining strong. Sure, dependable, unwavering.

When he feels my breath even out, Nico Giannuzzi puts my face in his big hands and uses his thumbs to swipe under my eyes. I can't look at his, afraid of what I'd find, so I focus on the giant wet spot I put on his shirt. Again.

"I'm still tough," I tell the spot.

"Tough as nails."

"And pretty."

He tilts my chin up, forcing me to meet his gaze. The brown eyes filled with warmth instead of judgement. "Fuckin' beautiful, honey."

I sniff, step away. Wipe my nose. "I'm still not your honey." *But please don't stop calling me that.*

Nico drops his hands to his sides. Chuckles. "You need a second," he tells me, and he's right. "I'm gonna go get you a soda in the meantime. The high fructose corn syrup will activate your dopamine receptors and make you feel better," he says, and then he walks away.

I sink down to the ground and watch him walk away. Inexplicably, the first and only thing I think is that he has a really nice butt. Then I rest my head in my hands and let myself disassociate.

His sneakers eventually enter my line of vision. I look up, and his hand is outstretched. I take it, and he hauls me up and shoves me back into the car. He walks around and gets in, hands me the soda, then wordlessly pulls back onto the highway.

———

We pull into an almost-mansion in Richmond in the evening. This one has a pool and a separate pool house.

We haven't said a word to one another since the rest stop, but my brain has been a whirlpool of anxiety and overthinking and thinking in circles and then thinking some more.

I recognize it now. Sister Annie reached the frayed edge of her rope, the knot slipping, the fibers splitting. I was triggered, unraveled, ashamed, lashed out. I wanted to go out and do all the things and was upset that I'd fuck something up while doing it. And then I made another ridiculously reckless choice.

But that's why Sister Annie took her vows. No indulgence, no temptation, no slipping into the arms of bad choices disguised as good nights. But something in me is starting to wonder—maybe this isn't discipline. Maybe this is just another way to disappear. I can't be a problem if I'm not there.

I think about the response I got from Chef right after we pulled out of the rest stop, the one that almost had me bursting into tears and then feeling horny all over again.

> From: chef@nakedreactions.com
>
> To: ali@hawkpublishing.com
>
> *I don't think you're mean. You've been nothing but kind. Why do you think you're mean? Maybe you're scared? Defending yourself against something? Or someone? Also, "impulsive" doesn't bother me. Impulsive is fun. Gets me [Redacted for Work Email], like I said. Miserable, I can work with. Maybe that means you're fighting for something better. But don't act like everyone's given up on you—I haven't and never will. I'm on your side.*
>
> *You're writing our book, after all.*

Could he be right?

It forces me to think about what Nico did at the rest stop. Because he saw right through the mean and the scared, saw me while I tried to disappear and yanked me clear out. But I hate Nico. I've always hated Nico. But maybe just not right now?

I take one look at the pool house and decide I'll be hiding in it until tomorrow morning. I'm not ready to learn to hang out and be cool tonight at the fancy restaurant with all the cool restaurant people and cocktails. Maybe I'll try in the next city. Maybe I'll relax tonight.

Maybe I'll watch some old Chef videos to *really* relax. *Don't even start with me right now, Sister Annie.*

Nico turns off the car, and the small space fills with the buzzing, relentless energy of silence as we both stare ahead.

"Thank you," I finally say.

He looks over at me, nods once.

"I'm..." I look towards the pool house. "I'm exhausted. I'm gonna hide in there until we leave in the morning. I'll just get some food delivered for dinner."

"Okay."

"Please don't help me with my luggage. I've got it."

"Sure?"

"Yeah. Have fun tonight." I get out of the car and take my luggage out of the back and start moving towards the front door of the pool house.

"Annie."

I stop and look back towards the car. At Nico, my worst enemy and award-winning hugger, with his arm hanging out his open window, handsome face shrouded in the warm, sepia and lavender toned shadow of the sunset.

"You good?"

"Trying," I answer truthfully.

NINE

Nico
______

I FIND MYSELF IN THE EGG AISLE THINKING OF
elementary school grammar lessons.

Particularly the one Mrs. Harrison gave about adjectives.
Adjectives are describing words. They describe nouns. Looks
like, feels like, sounds like.

Easy enough, I remember thinking. *Smooth desk.
Fluffy dog*.

Then, *loud Annie Li. Smart Annie Li. Tough Annie Li.
Scary Annie Li.*

Because Annie Li was taking that particular lesson to lay
the fuck into Steven Choi, who was sitting to our right,
because he had called May a nerd during recess. Annie Li
being Annie Li, however, was using adjectives at a level far
beyond any of our comprehension.

Ignorant Steven Choi, she hissed, her feet unknowingly
kicking the back of my chair in her agitation. *Nauseating,
revolting Steven Choi. Repulsive, disfigured, pathetic Steven
Choi.*

Then in my head I added, *sad Steven Choi*, after he started

87

crying, then *sorry Steven Choi*, after Annie made him apologize to May, who was sitting behind her.

In high school, there were two different sets of adjectives. Junior year? *Funny, intelligent, hardworking Annie Li.* Senior year? *Nasty as fuck Annie Li.*

Standing there in the egg aisle, buying supplies for the *NakedReactions* video I plan on filming tonight, my thirty-year-old self is able to think of more advanced adjectives to describe Annie.

Tenacious, unyielding, abrasive Annie Li. Guarded, wary.

When I woke up with her all but riding my dick? *Supple. Sexy. Lascivious. Soft and wet Annie Li.* A quiet miracle of soft curves, impossible considering her razor-sharp edges.

And after holding her sobbing body at the rest stop? *Fragile, delicate. Complex. Wounded.*

I grab a pack of eggs and a pack of bacon. Some bread and butter and cream. I've gotta take advantage of this pool house situation and the fact that Annie will be hiding there overnight. Something quick, something easy, like breakfast food.

I've gotta work on my fancy pants voice, the over-the-top professor type-shit, 'cause I've been Brooklyn Nico for the last two weeks, so I practice a few lines in the car on my drive over to the restaurant for a quick in and out before filming.

Once I get back to our place, it's late enough that all the lights are off in the pool house. I quietly gather all my camera equipment and make my way to the main house. On my way past, though, one more adjective pops into my head, unbidden. *Complicated Annie Li.* And that's the absolute last thing I need, with everything going on in my life right—

A sound cuts through the silence.

I freeze, and I listen.

Another.

I know, just *know* that I shouldn't—am absolutely positive, in fact—but I make my way towards where it's coming from, towards a window of the pool house with a faint light illuminating—

No.

Yes.

Hell yes.

Another sound—a *moan*.

The dim light of a laptop screen illuminates Annie. And hey, as far as lascivious peeping can go, it's ain't too bad, 'cause she's entirely under the covers, but there is no doubt as to what's going on, what she's doing, or what she's watching, even if I can't see the screen.

Fuck yes.

Fuck—

My ring light falls out of my hand and drops to the ground with muffled *thud*.

I throw myself on the ground right behind it, lay myself as flat as possible, the only thing still up in the air my, well. You know.

Lying here in the dirt, seconds away from being put on a national sexual offender list, some new adjectives pop into my lizard brain.

Creepy Nico Giannuzzi.

Fucked in the head Nico Giannuzzi.

Hard as fuck Nico Giannuzzi.

With that, I creep away like an ashamed fuckin' Labrador, tail and erection between my legs.

———

From: ali@hawkpublishing.com
To: chef@nakedreactions.com
Thank you, Chef. That helped me more than you'll ever

know. And if I ever get brave enough to say nice things out loud, I hope I say them half as well as you did.

I'd like to think that I'm fighting for something better, but right now, I'm just fighting to keep my head above water.

———

From: chef@nakedreactions.com
To: ali@hawkpublishing.com
Anytime. Don't be afraid. Open up and make everyone listen. Be brave and soft and loud and aggressively Ali.
People will want to hear your voice. I know I do.

———

Annie is leaning against the passenger-side door when I walk outside in the morning.

I approach slowly, not sure what Annie adjective I'm going to get this morning. I don't have the energy for *hissing and spitting* Annie, but will be able to make do with *grumpy*.

"Morning," she grunts.

Grumpy Annie I can work with, especially if I can't look her in the eye after last night. "Hey."

Suddenly, in the span of two blinks, she's in my space and thrusting two things into my hands. "Here," she mumbles, before scurrying away and into the passenger seat of the car.

I stand there a little confused, now holding a large book and a cup, its liquid sloshed over and onto my hand because of the force of Annie's assault. "What is this?"

She shrugs, busying herself with the books at her feet.

Oh boy. This is some good shit. "Annie," I press.

She ignores me.

I plant my feet, trying but failing to smother a grin. "Did you get me *gifts*?"

"No."

"Then what is this?"

She opens a book at random and begins flipping through it. "I was already in town getting coffee for myself, and I stopped in this adorable bookstore to look around after... so I just..." She waves a hand in a way that's probably meant to convey nonchalance. "Got some random shit," she finishes.

Fuck it. I'm grinning from ear-to-fuckin'-ear. "This random, gift-like shit? I'm gonna look this gift horse right in its damn mouth. You ready?" I taste the drink. "A tasty, probably overpriced latte and..." I look down at the book. My smile grows even wider. "A cookbook that focuses on the science of cooking."

"A total coincidence," she mumbles.

"A coincidental purchase of a book related to my entire life's work."

"It was being displayed on the counter next to the register. Saw it while I was paying."

"This book published ten years ago was being displayed on the counter next to the register?"

She finally looks at me. "You know this book?"

"Of course I know this book. This lady works in my field." I forgot it existed, though. Maybe I'll flip through it and send some ideas over to Ali.

"Oh." She looks a little dejected.

"I never got the book, though."

She looks up again.

I shrug. "Just read her academic papers. But now it'll be cool to look through it."

She makes a noncommittal noise and looks back at her book. The book may as well be upside down, the cursory way she's flippin' through it, but her posture is more relaxed.

"Thanks for the random shit, Annie," I say cheerfully,

before walking around the car and getting into the driver's seat.

Annie grunts.

I take another sip of the latte. "Still seems pretty gift-like, though."

Her hands clench into little fists. "I was trying to thank you, okay?!" she finally bursts out. "It's kind. A kind thing to do. To get you a latte and a book."

Oh boy. This is some real good shit. She's red as a freakin' tomato and I'm pretty sure I can hear her molars grinding together.

I grin. "I knew you'd try to kill me eventually, but never thought in a million years Annie Li would try to kill me with kindness."

"Believe me—when I kill you, it won't be with kindness."

I can't help myself. I bust out laughing.

Annie rolls her eyes.

I pull out of the driveway.

"Thank you," she says after a long moment, so soft I almost miss it.

"For giving you a hug?"

She doesn't answer until we pull onto the highway. "For not leaving me," she finally says to the window. "And you didn't just hug me. You held me together," she murmurs.

I blink. *Broken Annie Li?*

Forget Mount Olympus. Forget Jon Snow. I am The Whole Freakin' Wall. A jillion feet tall and a gazillion miles long, made of solid ice, constructed with magic and defending the Annie Realm against everything scary and dangerous and painful in the north. I have a sudden and distinct urge to throw a large rock and roar and pound my chest like a fuckin' gorilla and protect this new, *soft and vulnerable* Annie Li at all costs, baring my damn teeth at anyone who dares cross her. Complicated, be damned.

"Anytime," I finally respond.

———

We don't say another word to one another until an hour into our drive, when I look over and see that Annie is again crying and trying to hide it.

My heart sinks. "What's wrong?" I'll take him or her or them or it on in a heartbeat.

Annie glances over and sniffs. "No unsolicited 'honey's' or knee touches?"

"You just called them unsolicited for a reason, sweetheart."

She shakes her head, but I see a smile out of the corner of my eye. I ignore the way my chest puffs up.

"What are you crying about?" I try again.

She gestures at the book open in her lap. "It's beautiful."

"What's so beautiful it made you cry, Annie Li?"

"When you sat there and looked pretty for an hour straight while being my chauffeur."

"You think I'm pretty?"

"I told you, when your mouth is shut—yes."

I heave a sigh.

We're silent for a few minutes.

She starts so quietly I almost miss it with the wind flying through the open window. "There's this scene where this guy and a girl are walking through the countryside, and everything is written so delicately, like one wrong word could shatter the moment," she says. "She starts talking about her past, about how lonely she feels, and you can sense that she's slipping away from him even though they're right next to each other. And then she says, 'I want you always to remember me. Will you remember that I existed, and that I stood next to you here like this?' and... it *hurts*."

What the fuck? I look over at her. I don't think I've ever

heard Annie sound like this. I got a taste of it earlier, but... I don't have the words to describe this Annie. Not like Annie does. Heartbroken, almost. The bluster all gone. I glance over at the book cover. *Norwegian Wood*.

"The way the author writes it... I don't know. The landscape feels like it's grieving with them, like the wind and the trees understand something." She huffs a laugh. "It's not just sad." She pauses, thinking.

When she speaks again, I can barely hear her. "It's that quiet kind of sadness where love and loss exist at the same time, and there's nothing anyone can do to stop it." She shakes her head, looking out her side of the car. "His prose is just beautiful."

Beautiful Annie Li. Open. Introspective. Soft instead of jagged edges of steel meant to protect her more vulnerable insides. I want to tell her this, but she thinks I'm prettier with my mouth shut, so I don't. This earns me a glance and another small smile, and it's so beautiful it hurts. It's painful. It fucks me up. I keep my mouth shut about it, but something has unlocked. Those were the most words Annie has said to me in fourteen years.

Pretty soon we pass a sign. I get an idea.

"Wanna see some beautifully sad nature shit in real life?" I ask.

She nods, and I make the turn onto the Blue Ridge Parkway.

———

Now, I'd like to think I'm a pretty easy guy. Science and math. I like to describe complex concepts in simple ways. Think it's elegant that way.

I've driven through the Blue Ridge Mountains before, did while I was at Duke. Thought they were mad pretty.

Driving through them for the next few hours with beautiful, complex, intelligent, articulate Annie, though, is a whole new freakin' experience.

She describes what we're doing and seeing in that quiet, poetic voice of hers, forcing me to notice the elegance in the complexities of the world around us. Changes my whole worldview, shifts the narrative into something... beautiful.

The road winds through the mountains like a ribbon, rolling and dipping with the curves of the parkway. Sunlight filters through the trees, casting golden patches onto the pavement, the world stretching out in all sorts of layers of deep evergreen and soft, smoky blue. A different flavor of blue. This should be called Blue No. 1, not that artificial nonsense. The valleys below are hazy; the peaks above kissed by the last light of the afternoon.

She leans forward at one point, pointing at a hawk circling lazily overhead. I end up watching her more than the damn bird, though, the way her eyes light up, the way the wind through the open window makes the strands of her hair fly all over the place.

"I can see why you're a writer," I blurt out after we pass a break in the trees. It's like the world opens up—a sheer drop to our right, an endless horizon of mountains stacked against each other.

"Like waves frozen in time," Annie had said.

She looks at me now, then looks away. Doesn't comment.

"I wish I could write like you," I try again, but I really do. If I could write my cookbook in that voice of hers, making everything sound good—feel good? I'd be a millionaire twice over. "Would I be familiar with any of your work? Anything published?"

She drums her fingers on the handle of the door. "Maybe," she finally says. "There's some stuff out there, some of it big, but none of it under my name."

"Don't most writers have a pen—"

"I failed, Nico," she cuts in softly, as the road twists some more, pulling us deeper into the heart of the mountains. Wildflowers dot the roadside—yellow, purple, white—tiny bursts of color against the deep emerald grass.

"Huh?"

"I'm..." she begins. "I'm just... not."

"Not what?"

"Not anything."

The vulnerability in her voice makes me glance over. And at the look on her face? I find the next overlook and pull the car over and turn it off.

"Let's go be in the beautifully sad nature shit," I say. "It'll make us feel better." We both get out of the car.

The two of us sit right down in the grass, looking beyond at the vast expanse of mountains rolling endlessly into the horizon. Dusk is beginning to settle, painting the sky in soft pinks and oranges, the mountains shifting into the deep indigo of their name. The air's cooler now, tinged with the crisp scent of pine and the faint, distant smoke of a campfire somewhere.

Annie pulls her knees up, arms wrapped around them. Her voice is quiet, like she's talking to the wind. "I think I'm learning that I'm just a costume. One that doesn't come off easily. And when you wear one long enough, you forget what's underneath. If there is anything underneath. And now I'm not a voice. I'm someone else's voice. It's easy to be someone else when you're nothing at all."

I glance over. Her face, at first glance, seems neutral. No tears. No theatrics. But I'm getting better at reading her, and it reads *silent devastation*.

And it does something to me. Cracks something open. The look on her face and the fact that I knew what it was.

I lie back in the grass, hands behind my head, and stare up at the sky, letting the silence stretch for several minutes.

"I get it," I say finally.

Her eyes flick over to me. I'm not too sure but it seems like she inches closer.

"I'm hiding, too. I've done shit I'm not proud of," I continue. "Things I never thought I'd do. Things that make it really hard to look people in the eye sometimes. Especially the ones who think they know me."

She scoffs. "Look at you, Dr. Nico. There's no way you've done worse than I have."

"My mom is one of those people I can't look in the eye, Annie."

She pauses. "Well, you can't tell your mom anything."

"How do you know?"

"Because Mrs. Giannuzzi is a saint."

A smile cracks out of my face. "You remember my mom?"

She looks at the ground. "Of course I remember your mom. She was a chaperone on that field trip to Six Flags and stayed with me in the bathroom while I puked my brains out."

"You got sick?" I think I spent that trip on a bench reading about astronauts.

She shifts, staring at something in the distance. "I rode that huge roller coaster three times in a row."

"The one with all the loops and flips?"

"Obviously."

Obviously. "That's funny you remember that."

"It's because she called me brave," she says in a small voice. "Instead of getting pissed that I was puking because I rode the roller coaster so many times like an idiot, she told me that no one else in our class was brave enough to ride it except for me."

I grin at this. "She was right. I spent that trip parked on a bench reading about NASA scientists."

Another soft smile.

"Anyway, here's the thing," I say, sitting up again. "You're not a nobody, Annie."

She lets out a bitter scoff, but I shake my head.

"I mean it. You walk into a room and rearrange the air. Ever since we were kids. Like some sort of volatile reaction—change the temperature, shift the pressure, and suddenly nothing around you is the same. Something lights on fire. And yeah, maybe you fucked up. Maybe you lost yourself for a while. But that doesn't make you nothing."

I meet her gaze, steady now.

"You're definitely something. You're Annie Li."

A pause.

"Which is, frankly, my worst fuckin' nightmare. But impressive and terrifying as hell."

She laughs, choked and surprised.

Annie stands suddenly, like she can't help it, like she needs to move, like she's finally uncomfortable in this costume she's wearing. I stand with her. We both keep looking out, the wind the only sound besides the steady rhythm of our breathing and the quiet, unspoken understanding that something is happening here. Something bigger than the road, bigger than the mountains, bigger than our hatred for one another. Bigger than high school. Something is different. Something is complicated. Something has unlocked. It's right now—it's Annie Li, the beautiful, grouchy writer, and Nico Giannuzzi, the porn star chemist, a coupla smart, weirdo kids from Bensonhurst who only sort of hate each other.

She hugs herself against the breeze, and without thinking, I shrug off my hoodie and jam it over her head, my hands brushing over the soft silk of her ponytail. She looks up at me, surprised, and for a moment, neither of us says anything.

We stand side by side, the silence between us thick with that weird unspoken thing. The wind tugs at her hair, and I look down. I hear her breath catch. I search her eyes. She doesn't move. I don't either. The world seems to narrow, the vastness of the mountains disappearing into the space between us, the only sound being the rustling leaves and the distant chirp of crickets.

Then, she exhales—a soft, shaky breath—and looks away, breaking the spell. It's for the best, but it kills me to do it, and I step back just slightly, enough for the moment to slip away. She smiles, small and knowing, her shoulders loose and languid. The sky darkens, the first stars flickering to life, and without a word, we turn back toward the car.

Complex? Or complicated? Too much of either is not what I need right now, anyway. But I get it now, I do, after this drive. Something so beautifully complex that it makes me want to cry.

TEN

Nico

I PULL THE CAR RIGHT INTO THE LOT, WON'T TAKE no for an answer. Because for some insane reason I want to hang out with Annie "My Worst Fuckin' Nightmare But Also My Wettest Fuckin' Dream" Li.

She pulls herself out of her book-hole as I turn the car off. We haven't said much since turning off the Blue Ridge Parkway. I think both of us were afraid of popping that bubble of an unspoken truce.

"Where are we?"

I look over.

She's blinking a lot.

"Asheville. We gotta eat, so we're at the restaurant that wanted me to visit."

Her eyes dart around, reminding me of a terrified baby rabbit. There's a subtle shift in her demeanor, and I can't pin a new adjective to it. She suddenly shuts it away, and I can almost hear the clang of her walls smashing down as she seems to come to a decision. She looks at me. "Cool," she says, and that's all I get.

We both get out of the car and meet at the front of it.

She's still swimming in the ratty Duke hoodie I pulled over her head at the overlook, the tattoos on her hands and fingers peeking out of the frayed sleeves, the soft, heather gray a stark contrast to the dark tattoos all over her exposed legs. She pulls her hair out of its elastic, the silk curtain of it spilling into the hood.

The whole thing makes me stop dead in my tracks.

"You want it?" she asks.

I squint at her and attempt to decipher her meaning. The legs? Yes, I want it. Wrapped around my head. Or waist. Again. But maybe without clothes this time. Maybe. But I'm not picky. The hair, though? Twisted in my fist.

"The hoodie," she thankfully clarifies.

"Absolutely not," I tell her.

With this, Annie seems to burrow further into it, tucking her chin into the collar and shoving her hands in the front pocket. This makes me want to take her hand out and hold it, rub my thumb over the tattoos on her fingers, but I'm not going to disturb the new armor she's created for herself with *my* freakin' sweatshirt. I shove my hands into my own pockets. "Let's go."

"Sorry, our kitchen is closing in five minutes," the hostess tells us when we walk in.

"I'm Nico Giannuzzi from NYU," I tell her. "Claire's expecting me." Claire is the head chef of this fine establishment. I'm proud of her. We crossed paths a million years ago when she was a sous-chef at a restaurant in the city. Hooked up once. She and I had been chatting earlier this month while I was planning the trip, and our texting hinted at a... reunion when I came down here. But honestly, I hadn't thought of her once until right now, and that likely has to do with the woman standing right next to me.

This has been a grave miscalculation.

"Oh. In that case, you can go sit by the bar. I'll let her know you're here," the hostess tells us.

I let Annie walk ahead of me, and she slides onto a bar stool with practiced ease. I watch her put on a costume. It's a little scary. That soft Annie Li has transformed into something else. She's armed herself and is ready for battle.

The bartender walks over, a tall, good-looking guy covered in as many tattoos as Annie, maybe more. That feeling comes back, the urge to bare my teeth and pound on my chest like a gorilla.

Annie gives him a look, a sly and knowing smile meant just for him, but the weight of suggestion and the force of the pheromones are so strong it probably brings every straight man, gay woman, and pansexual person within a mile radius to their fuckin' knees.

He recovers quickly. "Can I help you?" he asks her and not me, because I no longer exist.

She licks her lips—unconscious or conscious movement I don't know—but he for sure catches it and I suddenly feel like throwing this barstool at the wall.

"I'll just have a sparkling water, but my friend here might want something stronger," she tells him, *immediately* fuckin' friend-zoning me, and I should be happy I've been elevated to the level of 'friend' instead of 'worst enemy,' but sure as hell am not. Forget the wall, the barstool might need to smash him right in the fuckin' teeth.

He doesn't even glance over. "I can make you a mocktail," he tells her, practically salivating at the need to serve her.

"Oh, yes. Please," Annie purrs, in that voice meant for dark, private spaces like under the blankets or bent over a table, and with that, he's in and I'm out.

I sigh.

Simple, I remind myself, and force myself to tune out of their conversation after he introduces himself to her as

"Mark." Would love a drink but it probably ain't happenin' unless I leap over the bar and get it myself. Mark wouldn't even notice because of the thrall she's captured him in.

A familiar voice cuts through the angry buzzing in my ears.

"Nico!"

I turn just in time to catch Claire barreling toward me, eyes bright, arms already wide. "I'm so happy to see you!"

I slide off the stool and pull her into a hug. "Hey, you."

She grins. "How's your drive going?"

I don't even know how to answer. "It's definitely... something."

Claire laughs, and I turn to Annie to introduce her, but something makes me pause. Something's changed in Annie's demeanor, a teeny tiny shift of that something I sensed in the car. "This is—"

Annie gracefully steps off the stool, extends her hand. "I'm Annie," she says. "My sister's marrying Nico's friend so I decided to catch a ride to their wedding," and with that I've been demoted even further, kicked out of the friend-zone and into the *just-my-ride* zone and I decide that I fuckin' hate it here.

They continue their introductions while I sit there like an idiot. When Annie sits back down, she puts an entire barstool between us, which somehow feels like an empty, yawning chasm.

"What do you think?" Claire asks.

"Well, your menu looks awesome. Actually, everything about this place is incredible," Annie shares, tone genuine. She looks around. "It feels warm, but elegant. Like you package comfort and serve it with good wine."

"Wow," Claire laughs at Annie, eyes alight. "That's exactly what I was going for."

"You did good, girl," Annie grins back.

I continue to sit there like a potted fern.

"You hungry?" Claire asks us. "I can whip something up real quick for you guys."

"Starving. That would be much appreciated. Really excited to try it," Annie replies with a smile.

"I'll send it out with one of the guys when I'm done." Claire turns back to me. "You wanna come back to the kitchen?" Claire asks me, her eyes sparkling.

"Uh..." It's the plant's turn to speak. I turn to Annie. "Do you—"

Annie glances at Claire, then looks at me. "I'm good," she says with finality. "You won't even remember I'm here."

I will never forget about you for as long as I live, Annie, a strange voice says in my noggin.

Mark takes that opportunity to swoop in like a fuckin' hawk, and Annie redirects the force of her smile at him.

Simple, I remind myself. "Let's go," I tell Claire.

This is one of my jobs and everything I love about this job, but for the life of me right now I can't get into telling Claire how she can improve her foams. I say all the right things, mention *lecithin* and *gelatin* and *agar* and *methylcellulose* and *xanthan gum*, use a whipping siphon with nitrous oxide gas, but I try to keep it short and sweet and simple, trying to wrap it up quickly, keep it copacetic. It doesn't feel fast enough, though, and by the time we're done, the kitchen's closed and cleaned and the kitchen staff has wandered out and it's just me and Claire.

This entire time I'm really feeling some type of way leaving Annie out there with fuckin' Mark.

Eventually, there's nothing left to talk about, and the

conversation switches gears into more catch-up, personal topics.

"I kinda want a drink," I tell Claire. I can't take it any longer. "Could we go back out there?"

"Oh," she says. "Sure! Mark will hook you up."

That's all Mark better be hooking up.

We step back onto the floor, and it's a pretty standard sight. Staff lounging around, holding beers, stepping out for a cigarette, vape pens being handed off. I finally find Annie, and she's still by the bar but now surrounded by a group of guys.

She looks fine. She looks at ease. I remember what my sister said about Annie. Annie knows how to party.

Claire and I wander over to the group, where they're talking about Annie's tattoos, of all things.

"Yeah, they're Pete Cheser's," she's saying.

"Sick," Fuckin' Mark says. "I've always wanted a piece by him. His waitlist was like a year long last I checked."

She chuckles. "Well, his waitlist is now probably ten years long, because that's the length of his incarceration."

The guys, including me, wince.

"How'd you get so many then?" someone else asks.

She shrugs, a picture of nonchalance, but I can tell now that it's forced. "We dated for a bit."

Everyone marvels at her.

Annie notices us now. She glances back and forth between me and Claire. "Hey," she says simply. "How'd it go?"

"Wonderful," Claire grins. "I love this guy," she says, bumping me with her shoulder.

"Wonderful," Annie answers with a smile, looking anywhere but at me.

Wonderful.

Mark finally gets me a drink. As parties do, it ebbs and flows—groups shifting, splintering, reforming; people trading puffs, bumps, and questionable decisions. I eventually claim a spot on a couch across the room, keeping an eye on Annie.

And there she is.

Holding court like she was born for it, even though she doesn't know a single soul here. She's got a circle of people hanging on her every word as she teaches them a drinking game that seems to involve lies, deceit, scheming, screaming, and the kind of rule changes that should be illegal. Within minutes, she's orchestrating chaos—calling out bluffs, assigning shots, dragging shy people into the fray, and turning the whole room into a rager. Laughter erupts around her in waves, the kind that makes coworkers cling to each other like lifelong friends.

Through the raucous roar of laughter and playful shoving, I find myself stunned.

Annie's not loud and jovial and bubbly. No freakin' way. She's loud but wry and sarcastic and witty. She has a dry-ass sense of humor. She doesn't bounce around from group to group. No, people gravitate to *her*.

Annie talks to everyone as if they're in on some long-running inside joke, like she's swapping secrets and talking shit with her closest friend. She sizes you up in an instant, delivering just the right dose of teasing—anywhere from a polite pass to a playful 'silly you' to an all-out, no-mercy roast if she thinks you can take it. And somehow, she always gets it right, making you feel like you've known her forever.

Thirteen years ago, she must've decided I could take the full-force massacre. But back then, the stakes were lower. We were just kids. I also "fucked her over," so maybe I had to get a very specific, hurt Annie Li, lashing out at me when she thought she was in danger.

Regardless, everyone loves her and tries to get caught in her web. Everyone wants to share an inside joke with her. Because it's all genuinely Annie, the way she's carrying herself and talking to people—none of this is a show. With a start, I realize this side of Annie isn't a performance. It's not a costume or armor—it's simply another layer of her. Still sharp, still real, just as true as the rest.

It's in this moment, as I watch her smile at Mark, that I suddenly understand what's happening to me. Fuck everyone else, because I'm winning the race. 'Cause as friendly as she's being, no one is allowed in. *In* in, to see the real Annie Li. Except for fuckin' *me*. She's shown it to *me*. Not all, but some, and some is more than all these losers. Grouchy Annie Li, permanently sucking on a lemon. Protective, loyal Annie Li. Sexy, horny Annie Li. Dry, funny, friendly Annie Li. Then soft, vulnerable, poetic Annie Li. Those parts she seemingly spends her entire existence protecting. Maybe a little bit broken. She let me see her cry. I held her together while she cried. She's using my hoodie as armor.

Fuck Mark—I'm the only one who's fuckin' earned it.

I get looped into a conversation with the kitchen staff about the restaurant scene in Asheville. How all these awesome breweries have popped up, how Asheville is now a solid beer destination. They go behind the bar and get me little sips of different beers, but I'm driving, so I don't get crazy.

Out of the corner of my eye, I notice it's just her and Fuckin' Mark at the bar. They're both sitting on stools facing one another, their knees maybe touching. While I'm busy convincing myself not to storm over there, Mark takes something out of his pocket. It's a baggie. He dumps a bunch of what's probably coke right onto the bar, takes a card out of his wallet, starts cutting lines.

Annie freezes. Gets stiff as a board. Her posture is all wrong.

She stares at the lines. She looks at Mark. Mark leans in, mistaking that look for interest. She looks at the lines again.

Looks at Mark again. He shifts his stool closer, so that she's practically between his knees.

Her eyes begin darting all around the restaurant, looking for something. I'm shocked to realize that she's looking for *me*.

Her eyes finally hook onto mine, and it seems like there's a line that pulls taut. Tense. Something isn't right. She has the same expression she had when I pulled her out of the car at that rest stop. She looks like she's going to cry.

And then Claire comes over and wedges herself right into my side. She rests a hand on my thigh. "Hey, big guy," she says. She's drunk. I can smell the liquor on her breath; she's that close.

I'm still looking at Annie. Her eyes dart to Claire, and the line gets cut. Snaps right in half.

By the time I get Claire's hand off me, Annie isn't looking at me anymore.

Am I supposed to do something? Am I supposed to go over there? She won't even let me open her car door for her, for fuck's sake. Will she lay into me if I go over there?

Claire strikes up an energetic conversation with the people around us. They start asking me questions about my work, and by the time I look up again to look for Annie, she's gone.

ELEVEN

Annie

Can you send me the rental info I'm gonna catch a cab

I SEND NICO THE TEXT AND SLUMP DOWN ONTO THE pavement, leaning my back against the building. I take shelter in Nico's sweatshirt, pulling it over my knees, pulling the hood over my head so that I likely resemble a soft boulder. I'm surrounded by fuzzy warmth and his smell, cozy and familiar after three days and hours and hours in a car, and it's this feeling of safety that lets me think.

I was doing great until I wasn't. Sister Annie held strong in the face of everything in the beginning—the people, the drinking. The flirting. But it was the one-two punch of the Mark and the coke that did me in.

Something I've learned about myself over the last ten years is that I give good party. I don't know if it's a scent I give off, like a bitch in heat, except a bitch in erratic, fun decisions or something, but it's always been this way. People take one look at me and say, *this girl can hang.*

It really used to work for me. Now, Sister Annie hates this about herself. She's been unable to find a balance.

> Where are you

What I'm one hundred percent sure of, though, is that I don't want to be an issue for Nico, because that would be the icing on the intricately frosted cake. Perfect Dr. Nico the Active Listener, swooping in to save the miserable fuckin' hurricane of serious issues who causes fuckin' problems for everyone around her. And he's the type of person, I'm learning, who will drop everything, including a fun party and a beautiful woman who is clearly into him, to make sure I'm okay. And that's not okay with me. So I'm not going to be a problem.

I ignore the odd thing chewing at my insides, but I suddenly find myself on the verge of crying again.

I need to get out of here.

> Don't worry about it just forward me the
> email

I text him from inside the soft cavern of the hoodie, the phone lighting up the small space. He texts back immediately.

> Are you outside?

I mean, obviously. I can't get anywhere else without the keys to the car or the information about the house. I'm in the middle of typing out another request for the house information when I hear the door to the restaurant swing open. Goddamnit.

"Hey, you," I hear, and it's not Nico. It's Mark.

I groan.

"Are you okay?" he asks.

I'm clearly thriving here, says the girl curled into an upright fetal position on the ground and hiding in a hoodie.

"Are you out here to smoke? Do you want a cigarette? You smoke Parliaments? That's all I got."

Mark has clearly done the blow he laid out for us on the table, because he hasn't stopped speaking and I'm still in my hoodie shell and haven't spoken one word and he hasn't noticed. I'm actually quite jealous of his emotional disconnect right now. "Mark—" I attempt.

"Ah, shit, I left them inside. I can go in and grab them? Or I can sit next to you? You okay? Wanna talk about it?"

I sigh. "No, Mark. Please go back inside."

"Are you sure? I mean, look at you. You clearly need someone to talk to."

I finally pop my head out an inch to eye him. He can't stop moving. "Probably, but that person isn't you." I retreat back into my shell.

"Why not? I'm a great listener, and I thought we were getting along in there, and I thought—"

I don't hear whatever profound realizations Mark's made because he's suddenly cut off by a rich voice with a Brooklyn accent that mostly comes out to play when he is feeling a strong emotion. "Hey, honey."

The wave of relief that rushes through me is overpowering. "Hi," I answer, and even that small word comes out strangled. I stay in my hoodie cave.

"Mark, go back inside," he says. Commands, actually.

"Whoa, sorry, bro. I didn't... I wasn't... are you two—"

"No," I say, at the same time Nico says, "Yes."

"Right, man, well, sorry, I didn't know. Claire seemed to think you two were, or you two seemed pretty, you know—"

I take deep, centering breaths.

"Inside, Mark," and then I don't hear his cocaine-fueled rambling anymore.

Suddenly, I feel the warmth of Nico's body as he takes a seat right next to me on the pavement. Settles himself right into my side without any concept of personal space.

"I would actually kill someone for a cigarette right now," I manage after a minute of warm, comfortable silence.

"Same," he says.

"Do you have any?" I ask him.

"I quit after you told me it was gross."

There's a burst of warmth in my chest. "You said I was so sexy, it was gross."

"Still true."

I'm glad I'm still in the hoodie. "I quit everything," I confess.

I feel his body stiffen. "Everything?"

"Everything. Just up until the wedding."

His big body expands with the breath he takes. "And I brought you here."

I shrug. "It's my problem, not yours."

"Still, Annie—" he starts with aggravation.

All coziness halts. I hate that tone in his voice, sick and tired of people getting aggravated with me, like I'm a permanent piece of gum stuck on their shoe. I'm really trying my best! Am I really that aggravating to be around? This is what I wanted to avoid in the first place! "Can you please tell me the info for the rental now?"

He scoffs. "Absolutely not. I'm taking you home."

I whip the hood back and look at him. "No."

"What do you mean, no?"

"I told you I was taking a cab."

"Don't be fuckin' ridiculous, Annie."

"How the hell am I being ridiculous—"

"I brought you here, so I'm fuckin' taking you home—"

"Just give me the info—"

"*No.*"

"Nico—"

"What the *hell* is your problem?"

Problem, problem, problem. "Hello? You said it—I'm a miserable—"

"Enough about that," he roars. "Do you need another fuckin' hug?"

I stand and rip his hoodie off. "I don't want *anything* from you," I snarl, throwing the bundle into his lap.

He looks down at the hoodie as if it were a spear I've just launched into his stomach. "Why won't you let me drive you home?"

"I don't want to make you leave," I finally shout, pacing back and forth across the pavement. "I don't want to be the crazy one you need to bring home. I don't want to 'cause fuckin' problems for everyone around me.' I want you to stay here and have a good time with your fucking friends and fucking Claire!"

Nico stands, too. "I think your brand of crazy is mine, honey, 'cause I'd rather solve all your fuckin' problems than spend any amount of time with anyone else, including fuckin' Claire." He catches up to where I'm standing on the pavement, jams his hoodie back over my head, and marches me towards the car.

I've lost the use of my arms, so I try to push back using only my feet. "Nico!"

"Get in the *fuckin' car*, Annie," he roars for the eighth or ninth time in three days.

"Hey!" Mark suddenly yells from the door of the restaurant. "Is everything okay?"

"Fuck off, Mark!" the two of us shout.

Nico presses me against the side of the car, his hand solid

at the center of my chest so he can use the other hand to unlock the car and wrench open the passenger door.

I push forward, but his hand holds me firm. A second later, his body follows, pressing me into place. I struggle, twisting against him—until I don't.

Until I freeze.

Suddenly, I'm aware of everything. The solid weight of him. His thigh wedged between mine. My breasts flush against his chest. My lips grazing the heat of his neck.

My fight dissolves. In fact, I think I melt.

He finally gets the door open, but neither of us moves. He looks down. At us.

His breathing, already ragged from our struggle, turns uneven. I watch the pulse in his neck hammer.

He tilts his head down. Instinctively, mine lifts.

Neither of us blinks.

His breath ghosts over my lips, warm and shallow. The soft, pretty pink of his mouth is right there, close enough to taste.

"Nico!"

My head whips towards the restaurant. I look over the car, on the other side, towards the door. It's Claire. I look back up at Nico. He hasn't moved an inch. Hasn't even shifted his eyes.

I use the weight of my body to shove him off me, and I get in the fuckin' car.

I hear a repetitive thud against the metal of the car. If I'm not mistaken, Nico is banging his head against it.

While I'm buckling up, Nico rounds the car towards Claire. He wraps her in one of his award-winning hugs, and I throw the hood over my head so I can't see anything else, closing myself off from the thoughts of the heavy press of his body against mine.

"I hope you told Claire she could come back to the house," I tell him, ten minutes into the silence of our drive.

He doesn't answer immediately. "Shut up, Annie," he finally murmurs.

I clench my teeth together.

Fuck Sister Annie.

———

The next morning, the sun fully illuminates the gorgeous details of my room, of this house. I check my phone and shoot Chef a quick reply.

From: ali@hawkpublishing.com
> *To: chef@nakedreactions.com*
> *Yes, Chef. I did what you asked. I opened up. Just a little bit, though. But mostly because I found someone who might've been willing to listen. Am I a good girl now?*
> *Now it's your turn. I'm writing your book, after all. Tell me all of your deepest, darkest secrets. Open up. I'm on your side, too.*

I stay in my room as long as possible so I don't have to run into Claire doing any sort of Walk of Pride. That's what Izzy and I have renamed the Walk of Shame, by the way. No one should ever be ashamed of their nocturnal choices. Well, maybe everyone except me, because of my dubious choice of partners, but whatever. Getting some is something to be proud of. And Claire is gorgeous. I'd bang her too. She would probably be Walk of Shaming away from me, though.

I stay as long as I can. I get myself off two (or three) more times to a combination of one (or three) of Chef's old videos. But then I start smelling bacon.

I wander over to the staircase, dip my head down and take

a peek into the kitchen. Nico's alone and frying something (likely bacon) at the stove. I dart my eyes around and only catch the one coffee mug next to him. I take this as a sign it's safe to walk downstairs... wearing Nico's Duke hoodie and some underwear and nothing else. Because, fuck Sister Annie.

"Hey," I call out.

Nico turns. He gives me a lengthy once-over. His eyes go lazy, and I let myself appreciate it for one second before I walk to the coffee machine.

When I finally turn, Nico's still looking at my legs. He finally mutters something, shaking his head and turning back towards his cooking.

"Claire still here?" I ask.

"You're really into Claire," he says, no longer looking at me.

"*You're* really into Claire," I remind him.

"I'm really into Claire," he mutters disbelievingly, shaking his head again. It's a wonder he doesn't have permanent neck damage from being around me for the last four days.

"Well?" I press, walking over to stand next to him at the stove and leaning against the counter.

Nico puts his spatula down. He steps over, takes his hoodie by the strings, wraps them around his fist once, and drags me towards him. He meets me halfway and glances down into the wide opening of the collar.

My body lights up. My mouth goes dry.

He licks his lips. "If you thought Claire was here, kinda nasty of you to come down here wearing nothing else but my sweatshirt."

I shiver. He's not wrong.

He drops the strings and moves back to the stove. "You know she never came here, honey."

"I'm not your honey," I say weakly, leaning heavily on the counter for support.

He smirks. "But you're dripping all over my kitchen."

I blink slowly, somehow scandalized by the Science Olympiad Captain of our class.

Nico navigates the kitchen with the same sort of confidence he just looked down my shirt with. "We have about a three-hour drive to Durham. There are some really nice... forests we'll pass on the drive that we can... take little walks in."

I frown. "You can just call it a hike, you know."

"For some weird reason, I get the impression that you equate hiking to getting a root canal."

He's not wrong. I don't tell him. "Fine. Let's go on the flattest little forest walk, then."

He grins. "Then we got an entire free afternoon in Durham. Wanna go check out my old stomping grounds? We can go see some more beautifully sad nature shit in Duke Forest."

I stifle a laugh at the "beautifully sad nature shit" comment, then realize it's the first time I haven't had the urge to massacre him for the Brooklyn in his voice.

It might (read: definitely) have everything to do with the beautifully sad nature shit he showed me on the Blue Ridge Parkway, when he mostly kept his mouth shut and drove me through the most wondrous of mountain views, blues and greens and purples and pinks pervasive through the car window. Nico, a sentry with his eyes roaming around the land-scape, flicking over towards me to gauge my reaction. Then, at the overlook, so unfortunately handsome in the fading sun and encroaching moonlight. So calm and solid and strong it made me feel like giving him a piece of myself. A realization that popped up just sitting there with him, like it felt safe enough to come out and show itself. All of this while surrounded by the smells of cool wind and smoke and damp and earth before being enveloped by the distinctly safe and warm smell of Nico's sweatshirt.

How strange it's felt, to be wrapped up in Nico, my worst enemy. Arms, clothes, body. I don't feel the need to disappear.

"There's a library I wanna show you that's also kinda tragically beautiful. Rubenstein," he goes on. "It's for rare books and all that shit, and in it there's the Gothic Reading Room."

"A room where goths can read?" I ask.

"Gothics, actually."

I hum.

"And Duke Forest has some more nice little walks in it. We can wander around for a while."

"More beautifully sad nature shit," I say with a smile at my coffee.

He stops what he's doing and takes in my face. His gets soft for a moment before shifting into a smirk. "You really are so beautiful when you smile, Annie."

I make a big production of scowling and rolling my eyes to distract from the warmth spreading through my arms and legs.

He tilts his head back and laughs. "Anyway, all that sound good?"

He slides a plate over to where I stand at the counter. Bacon and eggs could be considered boring, I suppose, but this bacon and these eggs look like nectar from the gods, like they belong on a table of decadent delights. Golden breads, jewel-bright fruits, overflowing cream, and Nico's bacon and eggs all in a row.

All of a sudden, Sister Annie makes herself known and shakes me by the shoulders. My heart sinks as she forces me to remember. "I don't want to put you out."

His eyebrows furrow.

Go on, Sister Annie presses. "And I'm sorry for last night. For making you leave. I know you wanted to hang and I feel bad for making you drive me home."

Nico tilts his head, looking at me in that way that says he's trying to figure me out. "It wasn't a problem until you made it one, Annie," he says slowly. "And even then, it wasn't a problem for me at all." He peruses the length of my body again, and just like that we're both remembering the press of our bodies against the car. In the bed, under the blankets at the murder motel.

I push that out of my head. "And I'm sorry for making you drag me around everywhere. Entertaining me. I can go off on my own—"

"I want to, Annie," he says simply.

"Why?" I whisper.

He shrugs. "I wanna hang out with my worst fuckin' nightmare. Turns out she's more of a fun dream."

It's there again, that feeling of warmth and existing, of being enveloped by Nico Giannuzzi.

"Consider this a gift," he continues, the tips of his mouth curled up.

"Oh."

"But not for you," he says. "Spending the day with you is a gift to me. Treat yo'self, and all that," he grins.

It turns out I have no idea how to deal with a flirtatious Nico, so I decide the best course of action is to grumble at my plate in self-defense instead.

"Eat," Nico demands, with a laugh in his voice.

I won't look a gift horse in its mouth, but these are the best bacon and eggs I've ever eaten in my entire life.

TWELVE

Annie

Back on the road, we settle into our appointed car roles. Nico drives and blasts music with the occasional podcast thrown in. I don't mind in the slightest—because my role is to read, and when I read, it's like stepping into a soundproof room and locking the door behind me.

As a kid, my parents never minded that I loved books. What drove them bananas was the way I disappeared into them. The *Annie has turned into an inanimate object* part. I'd sink so deep into a story that the real world ceased to exist—chores forgotten, homework abandoned. It would take several attempts to get my attention. I wouldn't come when called. I became a living gargoyle, curled in a ball in a corner somewhere, unblinking, unmoving, and utterly gone.

It seems that Nico doesn't mind, though, because when I finally hear my name and look up, his eyes are laughing and his hand is on my knee, and it's clear he's been trying to get my attention for a while now.

"We've arrived at the flat little forest walk," he says, squeezing my knee once.

This I feel like lightning shooting up my spine, and for a

reason entirely unknown to me I feel almost heartbroken when he removes it. My nipples go on strike and start a picket line. *Nico's hands are a basic human right!* their signs say.

I distract myself by looking around. We're in a small lot at the trailhead in the middle of a thick forest of evergreen. There are no other cars around.

"The location you've chosen for my murder is tragically beautiful," I announce. "Fitting for someone like myself."

He laughs as he gets out of the car. "As someone who deserves to be murdered or as someone who is tragically beautiful?"

"Yes." I climb out and take a deep inhale.

He gazes at me from the front of the car, eyes warm and alight. "Nice, right?"

I guzzle it all down, over and over again. "I don't leave the city very much, but I'm getting addicted to this smell," I tell him.

We start towards the trailhead.

"What smell?" he asks.

I take several more samples. "The smell of cool, dark, damp earth. Life," I say. "We're both city kids, so you get it. I've always defined 'life' by the hum of traffic, the crush of people, the constant movement of millions of lives intersecting." I glance around, feeling something shift. "But this... this is life in its rawest, most primitive form."

I glance over, and Nico is looking at me, one corner of his mouth tipped up in a way that makes me want to lick it.

"Pretty," he says.

Our flat little forest walk takes us deep into the trees, and I suddenly feel like a wolf with the way the scent deepens in here. My head is clear, my heart rate a little elevated (the forest floor is not entirely flat, mind you, not to mention a little spongy, meaning it takes a little more effort than walking on pavement). I get the urge to walk across a log like those Pacific

Northwest influencers on social media with the beanies and the long and loose hair that seem entirely inappropriate for aerobic activity.

I find a suitable log and walk across the length of it. When I reach the end, I suppress the urge to squeal and throw my hands in the air. The smile gets out anyway, and Nico's matches mine.

However, that was enough adventure for one day. Luckily, the trees take this moment to part like a secret unfolding, revealing a sun-drenched clearing with soft beds of moss and tiny purple wildflowers. I lean against a tree to take it all in. The air is thick with the scent of earth and pine, the quiet only broken by the distant trill of birds and the rustling of leaves in the breeze.

It turns out there is truth to the trite captions under those aforementioned Instagram posts. I think of an overused one, "nature is healing," right before blurting out some more truths to my worst enemy.

"I'm a hurricane of serious issues," I tell Nico, who's standing maybe twenty feet away in the middle of the clearing, drinking water and looking right at me, the brown of his eyes lighter in the sun.

He caps his bottle. "Annie—"

I interrupt him. "I went kind of wild after high school."

"Everyone does," he says, visibly frustrated. Why is he frustrated? He's the one who said it. "Letting a bunch of freakin' eighteen-year-olds out into the world on their own for the very first time will do that."

"But most people are safely contained doing keg stands on campus. I was out doing it *all* in the middle of the wildest city in the world." I shake my head. "And it didn't stop after college. It got worse, in fact."

He drags his fingers through his hair. "You looked comfortable last night. At least in the beginning."

I nod. "That was nothing. That was just like a regular Tuesday night in the East Village when I was twenty-one. But Nico, I did it *all*. Warehouses, raves, clubs, sex clubs, alcohol, drugs. People. *Dubious* people. *Groups* of people. *Groups* of *dubious* people."

He frowns at this. "Like Mark."

"There were a lot of Marks, but he was like a monk compared to—"

Nico holds up both hands. "All right, I get it."

I lean my head back on the tree. "It got to be a big issue," I say quietly.

His handsome face is the perfect picture of concern.

"Not in like, an addiction way, but more in like, a sad Peter Pan way. Or actually, maybe in an addiction way—addicted to doing whatever the hell I wanted to do, and fuck everyone else. It was my say. Blacking out and waking up in my sister's bed at two in the afternoon with a random person. Dating a coke dealer for free coke *and* free tattoos, while he used me to be the hot little thing on his arm at parties." I let Nico see this ugly side of me, like the forest wants me to come completely clean.

Understanding shines in his eyes. He's starting to get what happened last night. He doesn't say anything, but it's flowing out of me now.

"One night—or morning, I guess, I was at this stranger's apartment in Williamsburg, in their living room, and I looked around and realized the person that I had come there with was gone and I didn't know anyone there. But we were all so messed up it was like we were all the best of friends."

Even through the emotional blunting, I found it strange to be squished onto a strange couch between strangers as the sun started to peek up over the horizon. I was sitting on someone's lap, his arm wrapped tightly around my waist. We were debating the twin telepathy thing. The impersonality of this seemingly personal moment was jarring.

"I didn't have any real friends. Everyone I surrounded myself with was someone I could use for something. But the worst part was that anyone else I actually did care about—and let me tell you this included maybe three people, one being May—I was so, so cruel to."

May finding me in her bed, in the bathroom. Once, in the lobby of our apartment building in Chinatown. Not showing up for countless Sunday dinners at my parents' house. Not showing up for my grandmother's grave sweeping because I was out until six in the morning. Not showing up for my mother's birthday several years in a row.

I look at Nico, who would never miss his mom's birthday party. "I don't think you'd get it. You're like the Bensonhurst golden child. Valedictorian, Duke, PhD, postdoc, doing... whatever you're doing now. Clearly like rich and successful—"

"I told you I've made some pretty fuckin' dubious choices myself, Annie," he interrupts.

I sigh, unwilling to pop this magical forest bubble of uneasy truces. "Okay," I say simply. "Anyway, there it is. Some of Annie Li's serious issues." I confess this, and it's out there.

Why did I just tell him that? I think, and then, *I'm glad I just told him that.*

Like a weight lifted off my shoulders is another one of those trite phrases from influencer Instagram, but I feel it here in this grand forest with this terribly handsome man who is currently radiating *genuine care and concern*. Looking at me like I'm delicate, like I'm something to be treasured, tragically beautiful. Maybe not a serious fucking hurricane of issues or a giant pain in his ass. I smile despite the topic of conversation; let out a big breath.

"It felt good to tell you that," I admit.

Something shifts with that confession. The air grows thick

here in this sun-dappled clearing, surrounded by trees and wildflowers and the buzz of insects. The atmosphere hums with a low vibration, and time becomes suspended.

His answering smile is soft and careful, his eyes and body lazy. The entire effect is ruinous, and I find that I can't pry my eyes off him. When did Nico Giannuzzi get this hot? Did that just happen? Did he buy that shirt yesterday, pre-dampened with sweat, knowing it would drape over his chest like that? A chest that seems even broader than it was two days ago, when I was on it? Did it rise like proofing bread dough? I want to take a bite out of the meaty flesh over his heart. Really sink my teeth into it.

"What kept you doin' all that for so long?" he wants to know.

I shake myself out of an image of worshipping the veins in his forearm using only my tongue. "I don't actually know." I'm not willing to get into high school right now; that's a whole other emotional vomit, and I don't think that's what he's asking, anyway.

Nico takes a step towards me. "I mean, something about it had to feel good."

I trace the dips of his cupid's bow with my eyes. Something about it makes me breathless. It's hard to think. "It did feel good," I admit.

"What felt good?" He's a few inches closer.

"I guess... the adrenaline rush, maybe? The loss of control," I say, heart starting to flutter at his proximity, increasing exponentially in beats per minute.

"Yeah?" His eyes are searching for something on my face. His, I learn, has three tiny moles on the otherwise flawless olive expanse. One by his left eye, another on his right cheek, the last just underneath the right side of his bottom lip.

"The fact that it was something new or different—" He takes another step closer. "—or a really, really bad idea," I finish. I hear my heart pumping blood now, surging through my ears, up my temples.

We're inches apart. The back of my head presses against the tree as I look up at him, the edges of the bark a sharp punctuation to my sudden dizziness. His eyes that clear, solid brown. Warm, sure, dependable. Melted chocolate.

I want to fall in—
slip into that sweet,
greedy for wonder,
willing to drown.

"Impulsive," I tack on. I'm whispering now. Anything louder might break the fraught fragility of this moment. "I get off on being impulsive. On the adrenaline that comes with it." There's an internal pressure pushing against my chest and throat. My breasts, my shoulders, everything feels heavy. He's so close I can feel the heat of him through our clothes. One more thing leaves my mouth, unbidden. "Fun," I sigh. "It was just *fun*."

The corner of Nico's mouth tips up as he finds what he's looking for. He moves in.

It's not what I expect, though, because he diverts at the last second. Runs his nose up the line of my jaw, his exhales dragging hot along my neck.

"Fuck," I breathe out, my hands reaching behind me and gripping the tree for dear life.

"Oh, honey," he breathes into my ear, activating every single nerve ending on my neck. His own breathing is erratic. "I can see your pulse fluttering like a pretty little hummingbird. I haven't even touched you yet."

He shifts down. Hovers right over my pulse point, pulls gently at it, open-mouthed, then presses his tongue against it, feather light.

My knees buckle.

He moves again, his mouth millimeters from mine as we share several breaths for the span of several moments.

The first brush of our lips is whisper soft. A question.

The second is a definitive answer. Nico's never been so sure of anything in his life, the way he finally takes my mouth and lays claim.

The weight of his lips on mine is perfection. Soft yet firm, top lip then bottom. Insistent. I let out a sigh of relief. This spurs him on, and he uses his thumb to open my mouth so he can slide his tongue in, a delicious draw and suctioning pull, and I melt between his body and the tree.

A hand tangles in my hair, fists it by the root and tugs lightly in a way that sparks down my back. He angles my head in another direction, his tongue winding around and across mine, playing, toying, fucking. Learning the inside of my mouth and taking notes. His solid weight presses like a slow roll of electricity, just like last night against the car, just like a few days ago, except it's a freaking tree behind me this time. But it's so nice to be back.

I need to get my hands in his hair. I want to be the reason it's a mess, but I get distracted by the firmness of his arms, his stomach, his chest, and the way he sucks on my tongue and nips at my lips. Finally, I get there and it's soft, so soft, and I tug at it, my nails scratching at his scalp.

Nico likes that, letting out a groan from deep in his gut. One of his hands moves to my throat, the other down my thigh, and so slowly, he lifts my leg and wraps it around his hip, and now I know I was right. I get off on the adrenaline rush, because it spikes through my veins and directly into my clit.

He presses his length, impossibly hard, right where I need it, a place he knows and is familiar with.

I gasp into his mouth.

He grunts.

On the second thrust, we both open our eyes. His forehead leans against mine, and I stare into brown eyes that have gone unfocused and hazy.

We blink.

That's when the comedown happens.

Shit.

I bring my leg down.

"I didn't tell you about Sister Annie," I say into the space between our lips.

Nico Giannuzzi, with hair mussed and pretty mouth swollen from my nibbles, stares at me. His eyes clear up. He takes my hands and presses them against his heart but takes a tiny step back. I mourn the loss of his warmth.

"Because of all that, because of everything I just told you... I'm Sister Annie until the wedding." I can barely catch my breath. I feel like I've just done a dead sprint. "I'm not going to cause problems for anyone. I'm not letting myself do anything. Nothing fun, new, or different. No bad choices. No impulsive ones either. No drugs, no alcohol." I have to swallow before this next statement. "No sex," I grind out, even while peeking down at the tent currently occupying the front of his shorts. "I've messed up a few times, and..." And what, though?

Nico still grips my hands, enveloping them in his own. He clears his throat. "That what you want?" he asks, voice hoarse.

"It's what I need," I say weakly, with so little conviction it's a wonder he's even listening to me in the first place. "Especially with someone... well, someone like you," I admit.

He braces himself. I feel his hands tighten. "And who am I?"

My high school nemesis, source of all my teenage anxiety... my worst enemy? The labels cycle in my head, but they're starting to hold less and less merit. "Someone... who's a bad idea," I go with, but as soon as it leaves my mouth I regret it.

Something flashes across his eyes—understanding, resignation, hurt possibly—then disappears. He seems to come to a decision. He looks down at my hands, drags his thumbs across the tattoos on my fingers with something that looks like reverence and regret.

He finally drops them and steps back, and my ears pop with the immediate snap of the magical forest bubble.

"Yeah," he says, but he's searching my face for something else. "It's a bad fuckin' idea." He gives me a small, unbothered smile, then strides out of the clearing without looking back.

Fuck Sister Annie.

THIRTEEN

Nico

"Sister Annie seems like a religious fuckin' zealot," I tell Annie "Bad Idea Yet Excellent Kisser" Li in the car.

"That's the point," she says quietly.

Annie's right—me and her? It's a bad fuckin' idea. Annie is Complicated with a capital C and the opposite direction I need to be moving in if I need to start simplifying my life.

And on her end, Sister Annie maybe should not be having sex with a glorified porn star. That would be the definition of A Bad Fuckin' Idea.

She's right about all that.

But I'm thinkin' she's wrong about somethin' else.

"I get the renouncing sex and drugs and alcohol shit," I tell her, "but renouncing 'fun' is fuckin' ridiculous. Renouncing 'new' and 'different' seems like life is living you and not the other way around."

Annie won't look at me anymore, been looking out the window the last thirty minutes. "It's what I need to do until I'm absolutely certain I won't screw something up. I just haven't been able to find a balance yet."

"How are you gonna find a balance all holed up in a cave? Seems pretty unhealthy, too."

"You saw what happened back at the restaurant. That shit just finds me. It can't if I stay home," she grits out.

"So Sister Annie is actually a monk."

She shrugs, body tense.

"That's no way to live, Annie. And I think you're setting yourself up for failure."

"You just want to get your dick wet again," she mutters. Her walls are back up. She's back in her shell. But not the Nico shell, because my hoodie has been tossed in the backseat.

"I'm not gonna deny that I think you're hot as fuck. Been thinkin' of getting my mouth on that tattoo on your stomach ever since you first sat down in that slutty little excuse for a shirt."

A switch has been flipped, apparently. Like we got it all out of the way, and now I can talk freely about wanting to plow her. Maybe because I finally got to taste her but am secure in the knowledge that we won't be taking it any further.

Annie presses her fingers into her eyelids. "That isn't helping."

"Sorry." I'm not. "I just don't think disappearing is the answer."

"What's the answer then, big brain Dr. Nico?" she snaps.

I drum my fingers on the steering wheel, thinking. My big brain always brings me to chemistry. "You can control chemical reactions by changing the surrounding environment. Like cooking. You can adjust heat, ingredients, or time to change how food turns out. You can change different factors to speed up, slow down, or even stop a reaction."

"So I can stop the unwanted reactions from happening by controlling my environment. In other words, staying home."

"*Home* and *parties* aren't the only two freakin' environments out there, Annie." I shake my head. "Pick a different safe environment and adjust the heat."

She doesn't answer.

"What about your writing? Your own personal writing? Or your books?"

"What about it?"

"Seems safe to me. You're surrounded by the things that you love. And it's safe to lose yourself in book worlds or whatever you do when you don't answer after I call your name a hundred times."

Annie looks at me then. "I do volunteer at an actual book world. The library."

"There you go. What do you do there?"

"I read books to kids and their families, mostly."

I pause, attempting to picture Annie Li in the company of young children. "What, like the *Necronomicon*?"

"That," she says, "or *Dante's Inferno*. Sometimes *The Tibetan Book of the Dead* if the mood's right."

I bark a laugh, now willing to pay money to watch Annie interact with young children. "Did you make friends there?"

"Yeah."

"Okay, well, that's a safe environment. You needed a real community that wasn't built around fake relationships, so you built it with your library. That's amazing. What kind of things do you do with your new friends?"

She looks back out the window. "We... watch shows."

"What kind of shows?"

She pauses before answering, like she's weighing her words. "Cooking shows," she finally says, with a hint of embarrassment.

I glance over but refrain from telling her that there are some cooking shows that are not lame. *NakedReactions*, for one. But Sister Annie wouldn't let her subscribe, because porn definitely seems like something you'd renounce. "There are some cool cooking shows out there," I offer lamely instead.

Annie pins me with a long look. I can almost feel the weight against my side. I look over again. She's frowning at me. Again.

"What?" I ask.

She doesn't answer.

"Okay, well. The library sounds like a safe environment where you can have some fun. And watching TV with your new friends. I dunno, you could take up bachata lessons or something. Crochet. There's a cool pottery studio in Clinton Hill. Go for a flat little forest walk. Go outside and touch grass, Annie. Go to Prospect Park. Go to Green-Wood Cemetery. I think we just proved you can get a nice little adrenaline rush in the woods. I won't be fucking you against a tree, but you can walk across a log or something." I grin. I can't resist now. "You seemed to like that log just as much as you liked mine—"

"I get it, Nico," she mutters, rubbing her temples now.

"Honey." I take my right hand off the wheel and go for her. Fuck her knee, I go right for the soft skin on her inner thigh. Squeeze that tattoo of the skull and crossbones with a dagger jammed in the skull, right at the top of her thigh, the one I've been looking at for four fuckin' days. "Just sayin', you've got options. You keep yourself all locked up, don't get control of all the factors, you're gonna end up with a disastrous and unwanted reaction."

She grunts, but she doesn't tell me she's not my honey, and she doesn't move my hand. "Jesus," she says. "You're too much."

"What do you mean?"

"You're just so," she gestures towards my body. "Much. A lot. Big. You take up so much space in this car."

I glance over and wink. "I'd take up a lot of space in something else, too, sweetheart."

Annie bangs her head against the window.

"Fill her right up," I add, because now I can't help it. "And yes, *it's* a *she* now."

——————

I take her on a tour of Duke campus. I try to make it fun and pretty. We start at the Duke Chapel, its towering Gothic spires cutting into the sky like something out of a book. A fairy tale. Inside, the stained-glass windows cast colorful patterns onto the stone floors, and the hush of the space feels almost sacred. She tilts her head back, taking it all in, and I can't help but smile 'cause this place has that effect on everyone.

We walk through the bustling West Campus, past students hanging out on the quad and racing between classes. I lead her toward the Perkins and Bostock Libraries, pointing out the glass bridge that connects them. But it's the Rubenstein Library that I really want to show her. It has a certain smell—the smell of history itself—with its rare manuscripts and archives and shit. Centuries-old books. I watch her trace a tattooed finger over the spines of leather-bound volumes, her expression shifting from curiosity to something more reverent. I think of the way I traced those tattooed fingers with the exact same sort of reverence.

We wander towards the gardens for some more tragically beautiful nature shit, where the scent of fresh flowers lingers in the air. The winding paths lead us past koi ponds and cherry blossoms, and for a short moment when no one else is around, the world closes in, just like it did in that clearing in the forest, like it did at the overlook in the Blue Ridge Mountains.

Annie drops her walls again. "I think the quiet beauty of places like these makes everything feel softer and easier," she says into the air. "There's not so much noise. I feel like I can breathe."

God fuckin' damnit, where the heck does she come up with this shit? It makes me wanna kiss the hell outta her.

We eventually end up at the Science Center, home to Duke's chemistry department. The sleek, modern building stands in contrast to the older Gothic architecture on campus, its glass windows reflecting the late afternoon light.

"Wanna go in and see where the real magic happens?" I ask her with a grin.

She laughs. "Sure, Dr. Nico."

"This is actually where Dr. Nico's origin story began."

I lead her inside, past rows of bustling labs and whiteboard-covered walls filled with complex equations. She pauses at a display showcasing breakthrough research. She hovers two fingers, the ones with the spade and the heart, over a diagram of molecular structures.

I take those two fingers and rub my thumb over those tattoos again. "I like these two," I admit.

She stares at my hand holding hers. "Why? They're so small."

"I dunno. I can't stop looking at them. They stand out. A heart and a spade? Love and a little bit of chaos."

That gets another small smile.

"What does *PLUM* mean?" I ask, referring to the tattoos she has on the knuckles of her other hand.

"It's May's nickname."

"Why Plum?"

"It's an inside joke we had as kids. May thought she hated plums. Thought they tasted like garlic."

I frown. "Why?"

"Turns out someone always used the same knife used for cutting garlic for cutting the fruit for dessert afterwards," she says with a laugh. "What's the science behind that?"

I grin, because finally—something in my wheelhouse. "Garlic's loaded with sulfur compounds, things like allicin, that bind like Velcro to surfaces. Metal, plastic, knives, cutting boards, whatever. They're oil-soluble, so once they stick, they spread into whatever fatty or porous food comes next. Plums, peaches, chocolate cake. You name it, they all end up tasting like the ghost of garlic."

She wrinkles her nose. "A lot of things about my childhood are starting to make sense."

"Yeah. Once it's on the blade, it doesn't rinse off easily. Soap works, but you have to actually scrub because those sulfur molecules cling to surfaces. Some people swear the stainless steel trick helps, but the real solution is cleaning the knife well or switching to a fresh one for fruit or sweets."

"Huh. Cool," she says, then: "What's your bad tattoo that Tom was talking about on the beach?"

I shrug, feeling the back of my neck get hot. "Just a dumb joke." I walk away before she can ask me anything else. There's no way she subscribes to *Naked Reactions*, but I ain't riskin' it.

A bit later, I'm in the middle of explaining some of the classes and research I did here when I hear: "Is that Nicholas Giannuzzi I see?" *Fuck. Of all the fuckin' people...*

"This fuckin asshole," I mutter under my breath. I turn, body already tense. "Hey, Turney," I manage.

The man whose skin always reminded me of cottage cheese ambles over. "Nicholas, what are you doing in Durham? Aren't you supposed to be up in New York? Line cook for the Times Square Olive Garden, right?" He chuckles at his little fuckin' joke.

I let out a deep sigh, resigned to doing this. I look at Annie to start introductions but jolt with surprise to see she isn't paying him any mind. She's reading me instead, her little eyebrows furrowed. Concerned.

"Annie, this is Professor Damien Turney. He was my

advisor for a hot second." *Before I finally dropped his ass.* I look at Turney, who's predictably salivating over the insanely magnetic woman standing next to me. "Turney, this is Annie Li, my—"

When I analyze this moment later, I will realize that the next minute is a calculated power move by *scary* Annie Li. Because in the span of a few moments, Annie reads my body language and tone of voice, analyzes his sleazy look and the maybe twenty words he's said, figures out this guy is a piece of shit, decides I am in need of *protective* Annie, and chooses to do that by eviscerating him.

"Girlfriend," she finishes for me. She seems to vibrate with a low hum of terrifying energy. Turney looks disappointed. Even more so when Annie glances down at Turney's outstretched hand and doesn't take it. Instead, she looks down her nose at him even if she stands half a foot shorter. "You must be the 'has been' who's been trapped at Duke for the past forty years," she says with absolutely no fuckin' shame at all.

Both Turney's and my mouths drop open.

This might also be the moment that I fall a little bit in love with Annie "My Lord and Savior" Li.

He takes a second to recover. "I'm only forty years old," he sputters.

"Oh," she says, which roughly translates to *I know, but I wanted to emasculate you.*

I can't help it. I wrap my arm around her neck and pull her into my side. She takes my hand, the one hovering by her shoulder, links our fingers together and brings them to her mouth for a kiss that I feel all throughout my body.

Turney blinks. "So how is the Times Square Olive Garden? Heating up frozen breadsticks?"

My ears still get hot when this dude talks to me like this, but the woman under my arm has surrounded us in a force field made of knives and barbed wire. "Postdoc, actually," I tell him. "I work with some of the best restaurants in the world."

He chuckles. "Oh, wow, listen to you. You probably fit right in with the kitchen staff. *Fuhgeddaboudit!*"

I am ashamed to say this gets past the force field. I wince. I'd forgotten to use my academic voice, probably 'cause I've been spending the last several days with someone from home.

Don't matter though.

Annie moves forward.

Turney steps back.

For a moment I'm halfway convinced Annie might unhinge her jaws like a snake and swallow him whole. Instead, she bares her teeth before tearing him limb from limb.

"How does it feel to be churning out the same research for forty years that no one cites?" she hisses. "Advising undergrads who surpass you before they even graduate. Watching them go on to careers you've dreamed of while you're still stuck here, recycling the same lecture notes from the '90s." I love that she's chosen this decade to ruin him with. "Must be humbling. Or maybe you've convinced yourself that tenure is just another word for relevance."

Turney seems to shrink into nothing while Annie only grows sharper and more lethal.

"That must be the real research project—figuring out how to stay important when the world has already moved on. But hey, at least your name still shows up somewhere... even if it's just in the acknowledgments. Maybe one day they'll even name a garbage can on campus after you, though I'm sure it'll be the one in the basement of waste services."

Am I levitating? I look down at the ground to make sure I'm not. Then I take pity on this motherfucker (*sad Damien Turney, sorry Damien Turney*) and pull Annie back towards me. "Retract your claws, honey," I whisper in her ear, then kiss the top of her head. "We gotta go," I tell Turney, who looks as if he's just been disemboweled. "I hope you continue to have a mediocre life."

I pull Annie out of the building.

"Nico," Annie laughs.

"That was so hot," I say as I drag her around the corner. "That was the hottest fuckin' thing I've ever seen." I find a giant bush and pull her behind it before pressing her into the wall of the building and kissing her senseless.

She lets me in immediately, her hands flying into my hair, her hot little tongue in my mouth. Dragging against and dancing with mine with the same sort of skill and confidence and energy she just tore Turney apart with. I band an arm around her back, arching her into me and feeling her tits against my chest. It's frantic and aggressive and far too vulgar for broad daylight.

"*Shit*," I mutter, tearing myself away.

She looks up at me with swollen lips, her dark eyes heated and sparkling. Fists my shirt and pulls me back in.

I offer no resistance, take her mouth immediately and all but shove my tongue in.

This time when I try to step back, she pulls my bottom lip between her teeth. Traps it there while I move, the slight tug going directly to my dick. I rest my head against hers and try to catch my breath. I get Annie's whole addicted-to-adrenaline thing, because I'm gone for the way she has my heart rate up. "I could tear you up against this wall right now," I admit.

She laughs, shakes her head a little. "Bad idea," she whispers. But she takes me in her arms for a hug. I rest my head on her shoulder while she scratches my scalp through my hair. "Are you okay?"

These three words make me want to melt into a puddle or explode into a thousand little butterflies. "Fuckin' amazing."

<hr>

"Who the hell does that guy think he is?" She's still so angry on my behalf on the ride to the house, and I could not for the life of me explain how exhilarating it feels to be on this side of the wrath of Annie Li.

"I mean, honestly, you called it," I tell her. "Exactly what you said. He was my advisor for all of about two seconds before I realized what a dick he was. He was one of my professors and had a massive chip on his shoulder. I think Duke hired him as some sort of promising young professor, but his research never amounted to much of anything. I guess just enough for tenure, since he's still at Duke."

She huffs.

"How did you figure it out?" I demand to know. "How did you know he was such a shithead?"

"He looked like someone who wraps his entire mouth around a water fountain spigot."

The car swerves, the force of my laughter twisting the wheel.

"Why did he have it out for you so badly?" Annie is so grumpy I could tickle her.

"Because I was better than he was," I admit. "Smarter. Excellent grades. I was accepted into some of the best PhD programs in the country—Cornell, MIT, Stanford. But then he decided he could lord one over on me when he found out I was going for an unconventional concentration. Food chemistry is kinda frowned upon. Also when I decided to go to NYU. 'Cause NYU's good, but it's not the best." It also paid PhD students the least amount of stipend money, at least relative to the cost of living in New York City.

"Go Bobcats," Annie mutters, with an enthusiasm reserved for airport security lines. "Why'd you decide to go to NYU?"

"Ma got sick," I tell her. "Wanted to be close to home." It was so soon after Dad died that I freaked out. Would've dropped the PhD dream altogether and worked in a kitchen somewhere close to Bensonhurst if I hadn't gotten into a New York program.

"Oh." Annie reaches over and squeezes *my* knee. "I'm sorry. I didn't know. Is she okay now?"

"She's doing better. We finished paying off all her medical debt." Entirely thanks to *NakedReactions* and the advance for the cookbook from Hawk Publishing.

"Well, good for you," she says indignantly. "You should be damn proud of all the choices you've made."

We pull up to the rental. This one also has a separate pool house, which is definitely for the best considering I'm in the mood to show Annie my gratitude with hundreds of orgasms. Would eat her pussy for three to four hours—

"Like, come on," Annie says. She waves her hand at all of it. "Handsome, successful, rich Dr. Nico. Taking care of his mom's medical bills. This is amazing. Look where we are. Own every single one of your choices that brought you here, and fuck what everyone else has to say. You deserve to do what you love."

I stop the car and smile over at her. You know what? Maybe she wouldn't judge me for *NakedReactions* after all. After that whole shpiel? I should put her in touch with Ali.

On second thought, maybe they should never meet.

"Thanks," I tell her, "but can you take your own advice? Why don't you own all the choices you made? Look at you now. And you say you regret them, but how fucking cool are you? You've had all these crazy experiences and an amount of fun that most people only dream of having."

She looks out the window and doesn't answer.

I'm dropping her off before heading to the restaurant in town. She decided she didn't want to go, and I'm not arguing with her about it. Not arguing with her about anything after the stunt she just pulled for me.

Before she gets out of the car, though, she gets all quiet. "That comment he made about your accent."

I shrug. "I've had worse." *From you*, I don't say.

"He wasn't used to hearing you with an accent because you got rid of it. You wrestled it out. You changed your whole voice. Because of me. Because of the way I bullied you about it."

I shrug again. "Successful scientists definitely don't sound like Tony Soprano dollar slice dimwits. Probably would've dropped it even if you hadn't harassed me about it."

She turns and looks me directly in the eye. Hers are fierce. "I'm really sorry about that, Nico."

I'm kinda taken aback by the force of it. "It's okay, Annie. We're past it."

"I don't care. I want to apologize for being such a bitch. You're one of the smartest people I've ever met. I'm sorry."

I take her hand and kiss the finger with the heart on it. Her middle finger. "Apology accepted, honey."

She smiles and my world ends, because Annie Li is smiling at me and it's so debilitating it's apocalyptic. *I did that*, I think. I suddenly cannot breathe. It's warm instead of ice, it's directed at me, and it fries my brain with the force of a laser beam. I decide in that moment that I'm going to spend the entire rest of the trip working for more of them.

"Since we're doing big apologies, is now a good time to talk about the rest of high school?" It's mostly a joke, but I'm currently brainless.

Clang. Wrong move, buddy. Her steel reinforcements slam down. She sighs deeply and opens her door. "Let's end today on a positive note," she says, then shuts the door. She walks around to the trunk and gets her own luggage, starts rolling it up to the pool house. "Have fun tonight. Later."

I rub my neck to help alleviate some of the whiplash and bang my head on the steering wheel a few times. Get out of the car, load all my shit into the house, then get back in and start driving.

———

I'm almost to the restaurant when I realize I unpacked the Pacojet that was meant for them. Sometimes our lab gets random kitchen tools, and we promised this Durham restaurant this extra Pacojet we had lying around. The thing purees deep-frozen ingredients into super smooth textures without needing to thaw them, so the head chef wants to give it a try with sorbets.

Thirty minutes later, I'm aggravated as hell and pulling back into the driveway. I jump out of the car, don't even bother to close the door, run in the house, and grab the damn thing.

On my way back out, I glance over at the pool house, wondering what Annie's up to and if she's gonna be all set for dinner. Maybe I could ask the kitchen to whip her up a little something and I can take it back for her. I'm here already, so I may as well go ask her.

The pool house is angled away from me, so I gotta round the side to get to the front door.

I peek in through one of the windows as I walk by.

And then I die.

———

Once I'm resurrected, I sit on the ground. Sit right there on the ground, crisscross fuckin' applesauce, because my blood and soul and dignity have drained out of the top of my body at lightning speed and are promptly replaced by adrenaline and now I am dizzy and a little bit nauseous.

Am I fucked?

Because Annie "My Worst Fuckin' Nightmare" Li is sitting on the couch with her back to the window. And Annie Li's laptop is open on the coffee table in front of her.

And Annie Li is watching me cook bacon and eggs in the nude.

FOURTEEN

Nico

Fuuuuuck.

Does she know? Is she fucking with me? Has she known this whole time? Did she put two and two together that food chemistry is really freakin' niche? Is that where the "own your choices" shpiel came from?

There's no way, though. No fuckin' way! If I know anything about Annie from the four fuckin' days we've been trapped together, it's that there is no version of Annie—grouchy, gentle, friendly, crying, or otherwise—that would give up an opportunity to fuckin' shit all over me for having a paywalled dick.

I gotta know.

How do I find out?

Because I have a death wish, I crawl closer to the window.

I hear myself through the wall, hear my academic fancy-pants voice talking about the coagulation of egg proteins. *She doesn't recognize that voice.* She's never heard it before.

"There's just something about his dick that makes me want to put it in my mouth," Annie suddenly declares, and I lie down right there in the dirt under the window, fully fuckin' horizontal, and I perish.

"Glad to see he's all healed!" a voice says. Who?

I cover my face with both hands and take deep breaths.

"Someone needs to make a cast of this man's cock and put it in the Louvre," someone else says. Someone old. Someone who sounds like a grandma. Yuck. I mean, I'm flattered but... yuck.

"There's still a little blotch on his weird surprised duck tattoo," another voice says. I rub it. That splatter messed with the color a little bit 'cause it healed and scabbed all weird. Poor little mallard.

Someone shrieks dramatically. "I swear my blood pressure goes through the roof every time he turns around," someone else says. Also someone old.

What in the messed up, Golden Girls pornography watch party is this?

There is a lot fuckin' goin' on right now. Too fuckin' much. I'm currently feeling a hundred different feelings, lying in the dirt under Annie's window, listening to her and her elderly girl band salivate over my naked body and wax poetic about my dick.

"He's so hot. Good for him. Honestly, whoever this guy is, he's my hero," Annie is saying. "Making a little space for himself in this weird little section of the internet and raking it in."

"Little?!" one of the old ladies shouts. I wince. "Fuck your 'little'. He's gotta have carved out a full eight in—"

This is about as much as I can handle.

I crawl away. All the way back to the car. Slither like a snake in the grass. Grab the Pacojet from the middle of the driveway, where I apparently left it in my panic.

I close the car door as quietly as possible.

My ears buzz in the silence.

Annie Li doesn't know.

Annie Li thinks I'm hot.

And... I am Annie Li's hero?

Do I fuckin' believe that?

Yeah. Yeah, I do.

Not just because she said it when she didn't know I was listening—although that helps. That makes it feel really real. No performative teasing, no bravado, no games. Just Annie and her opinions and her absolutely unfiltered mouth, talking to a room full of old ladies about my dick like it's a national treasure.

But it's not just that. It's what she said to me at the lookout. In the forest, too.

She told me the truth. Her truth. She didn't have to. She could've shrugged it off or made a joke or steered the whole thing back to *My Cousin Vinny* or grisly murders or industrial techno, but she didn't. She let me in. Told me her mess and her history, the shit she went through after college and how it changed her. I saw it—the jagged parts under the veil. The realness underneath the mask.

And that's been her pattern, hasn't it? Every day, a little more. Not the whole story, not all at once. But enough. Enough to know she's choosing to trust me.

I... I kinda wanna give her the same thing.

I could keep this to myself. I could let her keep thirsting over the version of me behind the camera, the faceless cock on the internet.

But something about Annie makes me want to show her. Makes me want to own it.

Makes me want to say: yeah, that's me. All of it.

But I also wanna mess with her a little.

A laugh bubbles up in my throat, low and involuntary. It startles me. Feels like it came from somewhere deeper than humor.

I want to see her gorgeous fuckin' face when it clicks. When she connects the dots and realizes she's been talking about my dick like it's a museum artifact. I want to be there when her eyes go wide and she short-circuits. I want to see the carnage. I want to be the carnage.

Because Annie is mayhem—grumpy and stubborn and brilliant and unfiltered—but she's also honest. Loyal. Not nice, but kind in that bone-deep way that makes you feel like maybe the world isn't total trash.

And I want her to know me. Not just the guy she used to hate. Not just the one who flirts and bickers and cooks. Me.

The illiterate gorilla of a man she doesn't realize she's been drooling over in two different formats.

I lean back in the seat, grinning slow and wide, heat rising in my chest like it's got nowhere else to go.

She is so fucked.

———

I call Michelle, the head chef of the restaurant, tell her I'll swing by tomorrow. Ask her what she's making for family meal. I go right to the grocery store. I buy a steak.

I drive back to the house. Lock all the doors and pull all the blinds shut. Set up my camera equipment.

I start recording.

FIFTEEN

Annie

Nico is in a very good mood. Frankly, it's extremely unbecoming to conduct oneself in such a manner at this hour.

"Get dressed, honey," he said, after pounding on the front door at eight o'clock in the morning and all but knocking me over the second I opened it. "We're havin' some fuckin' fun today."

Now I'm sitting in the front seat of the car, all the windows rolled down, the cool, sweet Durham air blowing in, and some horrible classic rock blasting over the speakers. Nico periodically grins over at me.

It puts me on edge. I feel a little terrible. The fact he's *this* thrilled after someone stood up for him to some yogurt-faced nobody? That *I* used to be as shitty to him as that yogurt-faced nobody?

But he ruined my life. Sister Annie exists because of him, because of what he started twelve, thirteen years ago. But then, *tone down the nastiness*, Sister Annie says. *Also*, she continues, and I want to smack her, *you cannot renounce your vows for your hot enemy who hugged you while you cried, even if he'd fill*

153

you right up with that monstrosity you rubbed on. I shake my head. How many days is this bitch gonna be around? I count down. Four more days.

Four more days where you'll just have to make do with old *NakedReactions* videos.

I burrow deeper into his sweatshirt and pull the hood up.

"We're having ice cream for breakfast," he tells me as he parks the car in front of a modern-looking restaurant.

I look up at the sign. "Didn't you go here last night?"

"Nope," he says cheerfully. "Didn't make it."

He's out of the car before I can ask him about it further, opening my door in the next second. He takes my hand and draws me out of the car. I am elated but refrain from telling him so.

"The restaurant doesn't open until lunch," he tells me, squeezing my fingers once. "Sister Annie is safe here." He moves to the trunk and pulls out a medium-sized box. "Let's go."

I follow him in.

"Nico!" A beautiful, curvaceous Asian woman with a topknot walks towards us from the back. Goddamnit, the universe is *tempting* me today.

"Hey, baby!" Nico shouts at her. I ignore the pull in my stomach at the use of the nickname. I eye the two of them while he puts the box down and wraps her in his gorilla arms. Every gorgeous woman I see this Mathletes Captain embracing really has me reconsidering everything I know about the natural world and its laws.

"Honey, meet Michelle de la Cruz," Nico says, and I realize with a start he's referring to me. *That's right*, I think. *You might be his baby, but I'm his honey.* "Michelle and I went to Duke together. Had some science classes together. She's the owner of this fine establishment."

"Hey," I say with a smile instead. "I'm Annie." I shake her

hand. I wonder momentarily if her hand's ever been on Nico's dick.

Michelle rakes her eyes up and down the length of my body with interest. O-kay. Maybe she hasn't touched Nico's dick. I stand a little straighter. I wish I weren't wearing this massive, shapeless hoodie.

"Uh, uh, uh," Nico scolds Michelle. He wraps a thick arm around my neck. "Mine," he tells her.

Some internal being starts jumping and squealing and clapping its hands. *Who the* hell *are you?* I scold it. *Pipe down!*

But I don't move his arm.

She throws her head back and laughs. "Welcome in, you two. Have you eaten yet?"

Nico thrusts the box towards her. "Brought you the Paco-jet. Figured we could try some sorbet and mousse for breakfast."

"Awesome," she says. "Let's go have some breakfast."

———

"Fuck," I groan.

Nico and Michelle stare at my mouth.

"Definitely this one. Which one is it?" I look down at the ingredients piled on the counter. "Pandan and kaffir lime?"

"Whatever the fuck it was," Michelle mutters to Nico, "it's going on the menu tonight."

He nods brainlessly.

"Make her do it again," she whispers.

I crack up. "Stop."

They break into mischievous grins.

"Why that one?" Nico asks.

I think about it. "You get a whisper of vanilla and coconut from the pandan. It's like silk. But then the kaffir lime cuts through—bright, citrusy, electric." I take another bite and put my dramatic commercial voice on. "Then it all lingers, a dance of sweet and tangy, like sunlight filtering through emerald-green leaves."

Michelle nods, impressed. She pulls out her phone and starts typing. "I'ma write that onto the menu."

There are about ten bowls of different sorbets we made in the machine, loading in different ingredients and herbs and syrups and other things I wouldn't ever imagine putting into a dessert. I said something silly after the first one we made, mango and calamansi (golden silk, citrus kiss), and after that we made it into a fun little game. Dramatically and poetically describing each of the flavors like I've been doing with the cookbook.

The two of them are hilarious together. I can't remember the last time I laughed this hard. But maybe I'm all jacked up on the sugar.

"Hey, Téo!" Michelle suddenly says.

We look over, and a tall, lanky man walks into the kitchen.

"Guys, this is my sous, Téo Gutierrez. Té, some friends. Nico and Annie."

He nods his head down at the bowls. "Which one we serving tonight?"

"Annie says pandan and kaffir lime," Michelle tells him. "And what Annie says, goes."

I smile.

Nico, Michelle, and Téo start discussing something about the Pacojet, throwing around words and phrases I don't understand—*superfine emulsification*, 2,000 RPM, *breaking down fat globules and evenly dispersing water molecules*. I stop listening after *shear-thinning effect* and *micro-aeration* and try to finish all the gelato on the counter instead. I mean, if I'm having ice cream for breakfast, I'm going all out. God, I can't believe how delicious these are.

"I gotta go over some stuff with Téo, but feel free to hang

out," Michelle finally says. "I can whip up some real food in a sec." The two of them start walking towards an office in the corner. "But don't get in the way of all the guys. They're gonna start coming in soon."

We wave.

Nico smiles down at me. "Having fun?"

"Yeah," I have to admit. "Michelle's a blast."

He slaps a pout on his face. "Sister Annie better not be renouncing her vows for Michelle before me," he mopes with false jealousy.

I can't help but laugh. I feel light, airy, somehow, like I was just all whipped up in the Pacojet and filled with tiny air pockets.

Nico squeezes a hand on the curve of my waist. It lights me up. "I dunno, Annie. I think I like that one," Nico says, pointing to the furthest bowl on the counter. "Black sesame and coconut honey." He drawls the words, drips them off his tongue. "Try it again," he demands.

I take a bite. I make it slow.

"How would you describe that one?" he asks, voice a shade deeper.

I make a show of licking the spoon. Curl my tongue around it.

Nico's eyes turn feral as he lasers in on my mouth.

"The black sesame hits first—deep, toasty, and rich, like a whispered secret against your lips. Then the coconut follows, smooth and sweet, curling around it like warm breath at the nape of your neck, softening the bite into something—"

I don't get the last word out because Nico darts in. He takes my mouth, tongue licking in and tasting once, then twice, a wet, hot slide against the cool stickiness left from the sorbet.

He groans softly. "The honey," he murmurs down at me,

while I stand breathless, blood thrumming through my veins, "makes it fuckin' delicious."

———

Michelle comes back out and announces she and Téo are making steak and eggs for "family meal."

Nico is positively *thrilled* about this.

"Remember that reaction I told you about back in Philly?" Nico says.

We're leaning against the wall, drinking the black sesame lattes Michelle made for us while watching Téo put steaks on the grill.

"The one Gino used for his cheesesteaks?"

"Yeah," he says. "Pop quiz time. Tell me what you remember about it."

"Uh..." I try to think back to a few days ago, except most of what I remember is the feeling of being sliced open in the middle of the small restaurant. "Really hot grill. Browning. No steam. All that equals caramelization or something?"

He squeezes me with glee. I'm very confused.

"Close. Caramelization occurs when sugars are heated, but this reaction occurs when sugars *and* proteins are heated."

"Does beef contain sugar?"

"Sure does. Natural sugars. It also happens when you bake bread, 'cause flour contains carbs that have both sugar and proteins. Coffee beans, too."

"And you need heat."

He nods, and I'm reminded of a golden retriever puppy. "You're right about needing a really hot grill. The reaction happens when the food hits about 350 degrees. That's why boiled foods, which have an upper limit of 212, will never brown. But with high-temp searing or roasting or frying or whatever, browning goes crazy."

"And browning is good?" I want him to clarify.

"Browning is fuckin' delicious. Think of the last good steak you had. Think of its color. It wasn't gray, that's for sure."

I nod in understanding.

"Also, Annie, check out how I've spread the steaks out far apart," Téo adds.

Nico's smile is pure satisfaction. "Remember what I said about steam?"

"Steam is bad."

His eyes get dark and delighted. "Steam is bad for making steaks brown." He leans in, his breath hot against my ear. "But steam is very, very good when it refers to spanking something pink."

I'm surprised I don't collapse right there on the kitchen floor.

"There's a whole bunch of shit I could tell you about what type of fat to use, too. Interested?" he goes on, as if he doesn't owe me a new pair of panties with the way he's just ruined mine.

"Not interested," I let out weakly, because I'm currently using all my mental capacity to process the size of the handprint Nico would leave on my ass.

"'Kay. Well, wanna know what it's called, at least?"

"What is *what* called?" I breathe. I've lost the plot.

"The reaction."

"Sure."

"It's called the Maillard reaction," he tells me, eyes sparkling.

"What's that?"

"Maillard." He spells it.

"Like mallard?"

The massive grin that splits across his face comes out of nowhere. "With an 'i,'" he says.

Something about this inexplicably tugs at my brain.

Nico searches my face, and his grin grows even wider. Jesus, it's like staring directly into the sun.

"Anyway," he says, "It's pronounced *my-ard*. It's French. Named after a French dude, a chemist. Louis Camille Maillard." He pronounces his name with an awful approximation of a French accent.

Téo eventually finishes up and throws everything onto platters. The kitchen and front of house staff descend upon it. We let everyone take their share first before loading up our plates.

We take it out to the front and dig in.

"Holy shit," I find myself saying again. "It's honestly shocking how something so easy and boring can be so incredible."

"And that," Nico declares around a mouthful of eggs, "is what I think you big-brain writer people call a *metaphor*."

———

"Nuh uh," I tell him.

He turns the car off. "Uh huh."

"Nope."

"What's wrong?" He's grinning.

"It starts with 'this is a lame cliché' and ends with 'I don't want to do this,'" I tell him, but he's already out of the car and on my side, opening my door.

He holds his hand out. "C'mon."

"No."

"Get out of the car, Annie."

"I refuse."

"*Get out of the fuckin' car, Annie.*"

"N—"

He reaches in, unbuckles my seatbelt, scoops me up, and throws me over his shoulder like a sack of flour.

I'm in the middle of screeching when I feel his teeth sink into the side of my hip. "Shush," he says.

"Did you just bite me?" *Do it again.*

"What, Sister Annie isn't allowed to eat?"

"Sister Annie isn't eating anything!"

"Can I eat Sister Annie?"

"Nico," I groan.

"She wouldn't have to do anything," he adds on conversationally, while carrying me like a bag of potatoes into a building labeled *Bachata Soul Durham* alongside dozens and dozens of other couples. "It'll get messy, but I'd take care of all the prep work and clean up."

"Oh my god."

"With my tongue," he adds.

I sigh.

"That's a metaphor for *I want to eat your pussy*," he clarifies, and I explode into giggles.

———

I almost turn and run back to the car once Nico puts me down, but he puts me down in front of the most adorable elderly couple and immediately says, "Hi! I'm Nico, and this is Annie, my—"

I blow out a breath. "Worst enemy," I finish for him.

Nico is nonplussed. "She means that in a good way now."

"Hi, Nico and Annie," the woman says. She has to be at least seventy-five years old, but you never know. We don't raisin, and all that. "I'm Jing, and this is my husband Elton."

He inclines his head.

"We own the place, and we're going to be leading the class."

She turns to me. She asks me something in Mandarin.

"*I don't understand Mandarin*," I say in very badly mangled Mandarin. "*Do you speak Cantonese?*"

She switches with ease. "*Have you fucked him yet?*"

My mouth drops open.

"*Because if you haven't, you sure will after this class.*"

Her husband chuckles.

I blink.

She switches back to English. "Good to have you two in," she says with a wink. They move on to greet another couple.

"What'd she say?" Nico asks.

I'm still standing there gaping after them. I shake myself out of it. "She said, 'Nico is an asshole for making you do this, and you should probably leave before you embarrass yourself.'"

He drapes an arm around my shoulders. "That's funny. To me, it sounded like 'something something *unresolved sexual tension* something something.'"

I elbow him in the side and look around. The studio is packed with couples, some people nervously shifting their weight, while others look like they were born to do this. I wonder which Nico is.

"Have you done this before?" I ask, as one of the people nervously shifting their weight.

"Few times," he answers, looking like he was born to do this.

Jing claps her hands to grab everyone's attention. She has everyone gather around, and then she and her husband begin giving a short introduction of what to do and what to expect, which all roughly translates to "grind your pelvis into Nico's dick for an hour." I can't believe this. My palms, my neck, my face, everything is sweaty. My nipples are hard.

Nico is looking like the cat that ate the canary.

Jing claps her hands again. "Let's get started. Ladies,

follow me. Gentlemen, you're going to lead. Don't be shy," she says to my dismay, "feel the music!"

I feel like I'm about to vomit, but also? Honestly? There's something about Nico's presence that reassures me. Like I'm not totally alone in this. I would never tell him this, though.

The two of them demonstrate the basic steps, stepping forward and back, making the movement look so effortless that I almost believe it's easy. The two of them glide with a sensual fluidity that makes them look forty years younger, while I all but tear my hair out at how close they are.

"Now, ladies, you're going to mirror your partner," Jing announces. "Gentlemen, lead them through the steps."

Nico looks down at me, his lips curving into a small, amused smile. "Don't worry. I've got you, honey," he tells me, low and coddling. "I can lead."

Adrenaline suddenly spikes through my body. I feel like a rabid dog, salivating and snapping at my leash, demanding to get Nico's hands all over me. I nod and step closer.

He takes my hand in his, his grip warm, strong, and steady, thumbs brushing over the tops of my fingers as he gently pulls me toward him. There's something comforting about the way his hand wraps around mine, like I'm not just learning to dance—I'm learning something else, something big, and somehow, that feels even harder than getting the steps right.

Nico steps back first, pulling me along with him. His movements are smooth, graceful, confident—and I feel like I'm stumbling in slow motion. My feet don't quite match his, and I step on his toes more than once.

"Sorry," I mumble, wincing.

"It's okay," Nico purrs, gaze lazy and molten. "You're doing so good. Just relax, baby."

I stumble again with the force of the sudden deluge between my legs.

We go through the basic steps again, this time a little

smoother, but still—his movements are so fluid, while mine are still stiff and awkward. I can feel my face flush with embarrassment, but Nico just gives me that encouraging yet horny look that somehow makes it all feel okay.

"Okay, now let's add some hip movement," Elton says, clapping to the rhythm. "Let your hips follow the beat—don't be shy!"

"For fuck's sake," I groan at the ceiling.

The corners of Nico's lips are twitching. "It's all in the hips, honey," he growls playfully. "Don't be shy." He guides me through it, his hands steady as he moves us in time with the music. His own hips sway effortlessly, and as he glances down at me, there's a teasing glint in his eyes. "Relax, really. Stay with me. Trust me. Just follow my lead."

I feel a little ridiculous, my hips moving awkwardly, but Nico doesn't stop. His hand slides from my lower back to my hip, pulling me closer as he sets the rhythm. My body follows his, albeit not with the same grace, but I try to match him.

I start to get the hang of it, and after several marginally successful steps, his fingers press gently into my side. My breath hitches. He increases the pressure, and there's something about the way he touches me—nothing overt, just the press of his hand that sends a spark straight down to my toes. He's guiding me through the dance, but with every step, every slight shift of his hand, something between us builds, slow and deliberate.

Suddenly, Nico pulls me closer. Too close. I can feel the heat radiating off him, and I'm so close I could sink my teeth in like I've been dying to. His strong arms steady me as I teeter on my own two feet. I glance up, and his eyes are dark, focused on me, as if the dance has become secondary to something much more intimate.

"Annie," he murmurs, his voice low and husky.

I swallow hard, suddenly acutely aware of how close we

are. My heartbeat is thudding in my ears, and I feel his breath on my skin as he leans down just a fraction closer.

We move together, our bodies in perfect sync now. Nico's hands glide with precision over my back, guiding me through the steps, but there's something more, something electric in the way our bodies align. I can't help but notice how strong he feels beneath my touch, how steady and controlled his movements are.

"Now, lean into me," he says softly, his voice barely above a whisper, guiding me into a dip. His hand slides lower on my back, the pressure firm, possessive, but gentle.

I lean into him, my chest pressing against his, and for a split second, I forget about the rest of the class, the music, everything around us. All I can focus on is him—his hands, his lips that are just a breath away, his body that's holding me steady. The entire room has faded away, and there's only him, his body against mine, the heat between us building.

When he pulls me back up, his hand doesn't leave my waist, keeping me close. I'm breathless, my body buzzing with the closeness, the magnetic intensity. His eyes flicker to mine, the air thick with unspoken words.

"See?" Nico says, his grin back, but it's different now. "Told you I could lead."

I laugh, breathless, but there's something undeniable in the air, palpable, something you could stick your tongue out and taste. "Yeah, well," I say, "I think you might be leading Sister Annie down the wrong path."

His smile softens, and for a moment, the world is still. He pulls me even closer, his breath hot against my ear. "Maybe. But I think *Annie* is more than willing to follow me wherever I go."

The lights go dim. The music gets louder.

His lips graze my neck, sending a shiver down my spine. The music swells, and I can feel the heat of his body with mine, the friction between us as we move, slow and steady, as if we're the only two people in the room. Our bodies are slick with sweat, the temperature rising, the rhythm of our movements mirroring the pulse building between us. He's half-hard, I feel it now, and I can't help but press against it, thrilled and panting over the low groan in his throat and the slight thrust he gives back.

Our breaths are shallow and erratic. His Adam's apple bobs in his throat. A drop of sweat drips down his neck. It's so close; it's right there, and I have the uncontrollable urge to taste it. Something takes over me, and I do. I lick it. It's delicious. Warm and salty, a little sweet, like the lingering taste of summer heat and something distinctly him. There's a hint of whatever soap he uses mixed with the intoxicating scent of sweat and desire. Addictive—earthy, masculine, utterly consuming. My tongue barely flicks over the spot, but the taste floods my senses, leaving me desperate for more.

He leans down, presses an open-mouthed kiss right under my ear, doing his own tasting. He's all but holding me up now; I'm trembling in his arms. "So," he murmurs, his hand sliding lower on my back as he pulls me into the hard length of him again. "Am I fuckin' you in the car, or back at the house?"

SIXTEEN

Annie

I'M WHITE-KNUCKLING THE BAR ABOVE MY SEAT.

What I'm not doing, however, is riding the fuck out of Nico Giannuzzi in the back seat.

He grips the steering wheel, ten and two.

"I. Fuckin'. Hate. Sister. Annie," he grits out between clenched teeth as he drives us home. After I told him it's not happening. "Look at you," he says, but it sounds slurred, like "*lookatchu*," because his accent is back in his voice in full, full force, like he's lost all control. "Look how bad you want this," he says to my crossed thighs that are currently trying to strangle an orgasm out of my clit. "Just from having my hands all over you. You're dyin' for it but won't take it. And for what? For *what*, Annie? Depriving yourself of something you're convinced is bad for you. You know what'll be good for you? Having me on my knees. My mouth all over that tiger on your stomach. Everything in my mouth. Anything on my tongue. Your perfect fucking tits, that hot, wet, tight little pussy, your—"

"Oh god," I breathe out, starting to rock, my head pushed back onto the headrest.

He cuts his gaze over to me again. "Fuck, baby, look at you. I can make you come right now without even touching you. You're so close. Can you imagine how it'd feel once I fill you up? When I—"

I can't. Can't do it. "*Stop*, Nico. No means no," I tell him, but I don't mean one ounce of it.

Nico, though, Mr. Manners, Mr. Good Fuckin' Person and Consent King, immediately takes it the other way. He stops, and I could kill him. He takes a deep, shuddering breath, shaking his head like a dog. I'm half convinced he's going to crack the steering wheel into three separate pieces. "God. Fuck. You're right. I'm sorry. Shit. I'm sorry."

I TAKE IT BACK, I'm about to shriek at the top of my lungs. *I TAKE IT ALL BACK; TAKE ME NOW*.

I don't say any of this.

We're both panting at this point, like we've run a half-mile. The energy, the tension in this car is thick, viscous, dripping all over us, down my neck, in between my breasts, in between my thighs. I try to swallow and can't, the inside of my mouth like sandpaper.

Nico wordlessly rolls all the windows of the car down, tension rippling out in waves from his body. The cool air on my skin isn't helping; it's making it exponentially worse.

When he finally turns the car off in the driveway, it takes thirty years of self-control not to leap over and straddle him.

He glances over at me, and my heart jumps for a second at the possibility that Nico is not actually a gentleman and will instead pull me over his lap for that really steamy spanking he mentioned earlier. He does not do this. I hear an audible swallow before he says, "I'm sorry," he rasps, in a voice that sounds more or less under control. "For pushing you. I'll stop."

I feel like bursting into tears. Instead, I clear my throat.

"It's not only you, Nico. It's not your fault. I'm not exactly sending clear signals," I say to the windshield.

"*No* is a clear signal, Annie."

There are a million things I want to say to this, but nothing comes out. I nod instead, then get out of the car and walk on shaky legs into my house.

It takes an embarrassingly short amount of time to get myself off.

———

Afterward, I lie in bed, staring at the ceiling, drowning in post-nut clarity. But this time, the regret feels... different.

For what, Annie? Depriving yourself of something you're convinced is bad for you. Before the filth (Christ, the filth... where the hell did that come from?), Nico had a point. A very good point after that, too, but that's neither here nor there.

Almost a year of Sister Annie, and I can barely remember why the hell she exists. Or at least, what I was trying to accomplish with her. No sex, no drugs, no alcohol—for what? Because those things led to reckless choices, choices that *hurt* people. That hurt *me*. And the logic was simple: I can't make bad choices if I remove the things that tempt me.

But sitting here now, skin still buzzing, heart still racing, I wonder—am I giving up bad habits, or am I just giving up living?

I get the renouncing sex and drugs and alcohol shit, but renouncing 'fun' is fuckin' ridiculous. Renouncing 'new' and 'different' seems like life is living you and not the other way around. Because cutting out sex and drugs and alcohol? Sure. Makes sense. I can follow that train of thought. But cutting out fun? Cutting out new and different just because they might lead somewhere uncertain? That's not self-control—

that's hiding. Letting life live me instead of the other way around.

How are you gonna find a balance all holed up in a cave?

That's no way to live, Annie. And I think you're setting yourself up for failure.

And finally, my own words echo back to me, mocking me. *It's honestly shocking how something so easy and boring can be so incredible.*

So now I have to ask myself—Is Nico bad for me? Is Nico easy? And if he is, can he be incredible?

Relax, really. Stay with me. Trust me. Just follow my lead.

Handsome, successful, *kind, safe* Dr. Nico. The one who knows what he's doing with his life, who has it all figured out, with the graduate degrees and the mansions and the Tom Ford sunglasses, moving back home to take care of his mom. The one who shredded up my titanium shields as if they were made of tissue paper and replaced them with his hoodie and his hugs. The one who was bad for me fourteen years ago, who fucked me over, but now is trying to convince me to live it in an easy, boring, incredible way?

Do I let him in?

————

I don't get much sleep, and whatever light dozing I manage is shattered by the sun shining through the window. I peel my eyes open, grab my laptop, and attempt to be a responsible, easy, boring, tax-paying adult by answering some work emails.

The *NakedReactions* page is still up in my browser. Before I go to close the tab, though, I notice that he's posted a new video.

You know what? It's way too early to keep being Responsible Annie, anyway. So, priorities. I hop out of bed and make a sweep of the house, shutting every single blind.

I run back to bed and throw myself and the laptop under the covers before pressing play.

This kitchen is different from his usual one. The one from his last video was different, too. The only thing that's sure and dependable is his absolutely scrumptious body taking up space.

I close my eyes, listening to that smooth, languid scholarly voice that would win awards narrating smutty audiobooks. He never really says anything overtly sexual in his videos, but I could imagine thousands and thousands of people getting off to him saying things like "You're doing so good," "You know what'll be good for you?" "Having me on my knees," or my personal favorite from last night, "Fuck, baby, look at you."

Instead, this guy starts talking about "—the Maillard reaction."

I open my eyes.

He has a steak out on the counter, his thick hands gesturing towards it. "—named after Louis Camille Maillard, a French chemist—"

I blink.

"—complex series of chemical reactions that cause food to brown. It's often confused with caramelization, but caramelization only involves sugars. Onions, carrots, actual sugar—those things are caramelized. But the Maillard reaction refers to the heating of both sugars *and* protein. The browning of things like meats, bread, and coffee beans."

I sit up. Turn the volume up.

"Remember, we want brown. Browning is good. Browning is delicious. Think of the last good steak you had, the crust on it. It wasn't gray, that's for sure."

A dull roar floods my ears, causing me to miss a bunch of what he says next.

"—high heat. I have a gas burner here, so I'm going to turn it all the way up. We want the reaction to happen very quickly. Now, the Maillard reaction happens above three hundred and fifty degrees. This is why boiled foods don't brown, because water has an upper temperature limit of—"

"Two hundred and twelve Fahrenheit," I say at the same time as him.

I look down at this man's hands. At his forearms. At his chest, his shoulders, his torso. He turns around to get something from the other side of the kitchen. I run my eyes down the wide expanse of his back, the curve of his ass. A sudden thrum of energy pulses through my veins.

"We don't want any steam," he's saying, and *oh god*. "Steam will stop the reaction and the browning from happening. In this case, steam is bad."

He pauses.

No. *Nooooo*.

"But steam can be very, very good for making things pink."

I slam my laptop shut.

A rush of adrenaline sends my pulse into overdrive.

What?

No.

What?!

A laugh escapes my mouth.

Chef?! *Nico*?! There's no way. Is this for real? Did he do this on purpose? Is this why he was so happy yesterday? Does that mean he trusts me with this information? I don't even know where to begin with that. Is this some sort of twisted "as per your last email" response?! *Does he know I'm Ali?!*

But what if I'm wrong? What if this is some fucked-up coincidence? I don't recognize his voice. But maybe this is what it sounds like when he gets rid of his accent.

There's only one thing I need to see—physically see—to confirm. And when or if I do, then what?

From: ali@hawkpublishing.com
To: chef@nakedreactions.com
Haven't heard from you in a while. Been keeping busy?
I'm still waiting to hear your deepest, darkest secrets.

SEVENTEEN

Nico

LIKE I SAID, I'M A SIMPLE GUY. THERE IS NOTHIN' complicated about the fifty-four different Annie Li-related fantasies I've concocted for myself in the last twelve or so hours.

Annie in the backseat of the car.

Annie against a tree.

Annie bent over the kitchen counter.

Annie on top of the kitchen counter.

All right, all right, I let my imagination run a little wild with the Annie-in-the-pool scenario 'cause it required a blatant disregard for the laws of chemistry. Water, after all, strips away natural lubrication by dissolving mucus and lipids, making things drier and more abrasive. Plus, unlike oils or silicone-based lubricants, it lacks the viscosity to reduce friction, turning smooth strokes into a struggle. So maybe in this fantasy we weren't in a pool of water—we were in a pool of lube.

I have a new one right now, knowing that Annie is probably wearing nothing under my sweatshirt. And won't stop looking at me, all over my body.

She looks brighter today somehow. Her eyes are animated and her body's tense but excited, like she's holding something in that's ready to explode all over the place. Much, much different from the way she left the car yesterday, frustration with a touch of regret. Holding a different sort of explosion in. But maybe that was just me projecting.

Regardless if it's good or bad or whatever, I just want to see her *let go*. To trust herself, not hide behind Sister Annie like some twisted security blanket of abstinence. To trust *me*. 'Cause I've fuckin' got her.

And I ain't touchin' her again until she gives it to me.

She's given me little peeks at it. On Duke campus. At the restaurant yesterday. Dancing with her last night. *Fuck yes*, last night. But she showed me letting go. And it was fuckin' beautiful.

So today I've decided to open myself up even more. Make myself vulnerable, trust her with something big. I'm gonna give her the last thing that's mine. Enough fuckin' with her. And she might shit all over me, but that's fine. Somehow in the last few days, her merciless roasting has gone from semi-malicious to... fun. Cajoling and silly. I like it, like the way it makes me feel. Like we share an inside joke. She's got me too.

So, in case she hasn't seen the latest *NakedReactions* video, or missed all those hints I dropped yesterday about my side-gig?

"Where are we going today?" she asks me in the kitchen of the main house, barefoot and likely naked under my hoodie.

"We're going swimming."

The same extra-wide grin crosses our faces.

———

Ma calls on our drive over. I glance at Annie. "You mind if I take this?" I ask her.

She shrugs. "Of course not."

I put her on the Bluetooth speakers. "Hey, Ma."

"Hey, Nico. How's it goin'? Just wanted to check in."

"Great. The drive down's been pretty painless." I wink over at Annie, who rolls her eyes at me. "I'm actually drivin' down with Annie Li. Remember her?" I hope to god Ma doesn't mention anything about her being the crazy one.

"Hey, Mrs. Giannuzzi," Annie says warmly.

"Hey, beautiful girl!" Ma shouts. "You the one who stood up for my Valentina when youse was all kids?"

I glance over; Annie looks confused.

"Yeah, that's her," I chime in. "You kicked Bobby Pinto in the nuts after he pushed my little sister when we were all playin' Manhunt," I remind Annie.

She smirks. "Oh yeah. Fuck Bobby Pinto."

Ma cackles over the car speakers. "Where you guys at now?"

"In Durham now. Been hittin' up all the old spots."

"That's good, honey. Get to all your restaurants?"

"Most of 'em." I grin over at Annie again.

"How 'bout the quarry?" Ma asks in a softer voice.

I drum my fingers on the wheel. "Headed there now," I finally answer. This is something I decide I'll give to Annie, too.

Annie turns her head at my tone.

"It's a real beautiful place, Annie," Ma says. "You been?"

She shakes her head, even if Ma can't see her. "No, I haven't been."

"It's gorgeous," Ma says. My throat tightens at the pain in her voice. "The last weekend we all had with Joe. Nico's father. Spent the whole day swimmin' there before flyin' back to New York." I grip the steering wheel tighter.

"Oh," Annie says, voice delicate. "I had no idea."

"Yeah," Ma goes on. "We were down there visiting Duke

your junior year. Joe was so proud of Nico for his grades. Wouldn't stop talkin' about it in those woods. *Nico's gonna be valedictorian. My boy, the Stuyvesant valedictorian. Nothing's gonna stop him. No thing, no one.* He was so excited for Nico to apply to Duke. He passed away the day after we got back."

Annie stares at me.

"I'm so sorry," Annie finally says, voice thin and reedy and not like anything I've ever heard before. "I really had no idea."

"It's okay," Ma replies more fondly. "Joe'd be so proud of Nico today."

The twinge between my ribcage grows. "He wouldn't," I mutter.

Annie surprises me by reaching over and taking my hand. Twists her little fingers through mine. I glance down, seeing the heart on her finger peeking through my fist. "He would," she says quietly, for my ears only.

I shake my head. That I make a living off of people paying money to see my naked dick? Hundreds of thousands of people? Nah. He wouldn't.

"Nico?"

"Yeah, Ma?"

"Say hi to him for me when you're there, yeah?"

My eyes sting. "Yeah, Ma."

Ma clears her throat of emotion. "All right, you two," Ma tells us. "Be safe. No lifeguards there. Text me when you get to Miami, Nico, okay? Love ya."

"Bye, Ma. Love you."

"Bye, Mrs. Giannuzzi."

I pull the car into the small lot shortly after. This place normally gets crowded on weekends, but since it's early on a Wednesday morning, there's no one here. I take a deep breath and look over at Annie.

She's staring at me with that look that means she's about to cry.

"It's okay, honey," I say. "It was a long time ago. I still miss him, but it was a long time ago. I'm okay now. We're okay now."

Annie gnaws on her lower lip. "When did he pass?"

"Huh?"

"What month?" she whispers.

"Oh." I scratch my head. "May of our junior year."

Her face collapses. Her body folds in on itself.

"What? What's wrong?"

Annie gets out of the car, slams the door shut, and strides into the forest.

EIGHTEEN

Annie

HE DIDN'T DO IT ON PURPOSE.

"Annie."

He didn't ruin your life.

"Annie!"

You ruined your own.

I turn around and walk towards him, towards his warmth and security and care, eyes full of concern. But I change my mind, because, fuck. I... *fuck*. I turn back and blindly find a trail marker and start walking towards it.

"Annie!" His voice cuts through the trees, his footfalls crunching through the dead leaves and the underbrush of the trail.

He grabs my hand and swings me around. "Sweetheart."

I wrench my hand away and realize I'm crying.

"Talk to me," he orders.

"No."

"Fuckin' talk to me, Annie."

"*No.*"

He takes a deep breath, his giant chest expanding, contracting. When he speaks, it's evident he's really trying to keep his shit together. "I'd appreciate it if you didn't take this new information you've gathered about my dad dyin' and turn it into something about you without telling me what's wrong."

With that, something caves. "I'm sorry, Nico." I swipe at my face. "Shit, I'm sorry. I'm sorry."

He opens his arms.

I don't hesitate.

He wraps me up, but this time I squeeze back. We stand like that, tangled in each other, surrounded by bad, tainted, incorrect memories. But also there's his scent—clean soap, warm skin—and the quiet hush of the forest morning, and the rhythmic thud of his heart under my cheek.

Eventually, I pull back. "I'm so sorry about your dad, Nico."

Nico cradles my face in his big hands, wipes tears from under my eyes for the second time. Soulful brown eyes searching my face with concern, as if he can find the source of my hurt there and make it all better, when I should be doing it for him. "Come," he tells me, dropping his hands only to twine his fingers with mine, tugging me further down the trail.

He doesn't let go. "What just happened?" he asks me eventually, probably knowing I needed a minute. Again.

I exhale slowly. Step over a tree root. "I had no idea."

"What, that Dad died?" He peers down at me. "Why would you know that? I didn't share it with anyone. Well, except for my teachers and the principal. Just left school for the rest of the year. It was actually during that Chem project we—" He stops short.

Nico's face shifts. Realization dawns.

I look around. We've stopped at the edge of what feels like the end of the world. Below us yawns a vast, glittering basin— an old quarry, its waters deep and still. It's carved out of solid stone and cradled by a halo of green, trees crowding the rim like they're guarding a sacred secret. The silence hums, thick and alive.

"During the AP Chem project *and* the AP Physics project we were partners on," I finish flatly. "The classes I needed the college credits for. The projects I ended up doing alone. The ones I bombed, tanking my entire junior year GPA. And when I asked our teachers what happened to you—they said you wouldn't be working with me anymore. That you'd already finished them. On your own. And had gotten A's."

I let out a dry laugh, no bite to it—just regret and resentment. Not at him. Not at the kid who ruined my life. At me. At the girl who ruined her own.

"Fuck," he breathes, low and hoarse.

"You didn't answer my texts or calls," I continue. "I even stopped by your house once." I shake my head, remembering. "Your sister answered the door. I asked her if you were going to come back to school, or if you were around to help me finish the projects. She looked at me like I was out of my mind."

I pause. My throat tightens.

"She said you weren't available. She said—" I swallow. "She said, 'What fuckin' projects? Nico doesn't need that shit. Nico's—'

I look at him. He already knows.

"'Nico's gonna be valedictorian. Nothing's gonna stop him. No thing. No one.'" *Especially you,* she had said, along with some other harsh expletives and vague threats that led seventeen-year-old me to believe he was sabotaging me, but I don't tell him this, because I realize now that the face his sister had on? The twist in her face, the curl of her lip? She wasn't taking her brother's side in some new competition. The face wasn't one of malice. It was one of grief.

"You know the rest," I mutter.

Senior year, after I was sabotaged, used, disposed of,

bested? I took it all out on the person who had done it to me. The perfect valedictorian with the perfect family and loving parents. And after high school? It was all downhill from there.

"I don't know the rest," he says gently. "Tell me the rest, Annie. Let me in."

Open up. I drag my fingers through my hair, fist it at the crown, tug like I can root the shame right out. I pace to the edge of the cliff, where sunlight crashes off the water—blinding, brutal, and bright enough to carve me open.

It makes everything inside me rise to the surface.

But I don't think that's what's giving me the urge to tell him. It's not because the pain is unbearable or the silence is too loud or whatever trite bullshit.

It's because he's still here.

Because he's seen the worst of me, *nasty, problematic Annie,* and was okay with it. Liked it, maybe. And didn't flinch. Gave me a hug instead. Told me I was something. I was Annie Li.

And he maybe wanted some of it for himself.

Somewhere between Brooklyn, New York and Durham, North Carolina, in a Mustang convertible and a Honda Civic, my worst enemy carved out an Annie-shaped space inside of himself.

So I can't hold the rest back from him—not now.

Because Nicholas "Nico" Giannuzzi, my oldest nemesis, is somehow the only one I want to give it to.

"In high school, I pushed myself so hard I forgot what breathing felt like," I start.

I feel Nico come up next to me, a steady, silent sentry. We stand next to each other, staring out at the water.

"Straight A's weren't enough. Honors weren't enough. I had to be valedictorian, as you know. Student council, volunteer of the year, write award-winning essays for shit I didn't even care about—because if I didn't, my parents would eviscerate me."

He turns to look at me. "Define eviscerate."

I shake my head.

"Like, physically?"

"Among other things," I admit. "Mostly verbal. And I wouldn't get my ass totally beat, but... Little things. Maybe it's a cultural thing," I add weakly, not sure why I'm feeling the need to defend them, but the truth is a lot of us grew up this way.

He blows out a breath. "Annie. Baby. I'm so sorry." He squeezes my hand. "Just in high school?"

"Since childhood, it had been like that."

"What the fuck, Annie? And how about May? Why?"

I inhale some of that beautifully sad nature shit for strength. "Only me. Not towards May. Not if I could help it, at least. Because since childhood, I took it all, so she didn't have to. I shielded her from it. By being louder, *smarter*. By being *the best*. I didn't *want* to be the best. I *had* to be the best. I took it all on—all of their attention and their wrath, just so they would leave May alone. I got straight A's so that I would be the one berated for a B+. I was loud and talked back so that they wouldn't look twice at May—she was the good one. The silent, deferential, perfect one. I played piano and violin really, really well, so that May could sit happily as a second chair clarinet player."

"So I was never allowed to be average. I wasn't allowed to rest. So that May could be happily average—so that *she* could rest. So I hustled." A bitter laugh escapes me. "And for what? So I could get into Harvard and be their shiny little trophy?" I shake my head. "Didn't get in. I blamed it on my GPA. I blamed it on *you*. Got into NYU instead, and the second I got out from under them, moved into the dorms, I fell apart. No rules, no parents, no pressure? I went feral."

My voice drops.

"I exploded. No curfews, no parents breathing down my neck, no one watching. I partied in the best city in the world for partying. Slept too little, drank too much, hooked up with people I didn't even like because they could get me something." I shake my head. "Even if that something was just a funny story in the morning."

Shame washes over me, hot and tight, but Nico's hand brushes against mine. Gentle. Intentional.

"Every relationship I had was a transaction. Attention for validation. Sex for connection. Proximity for status. We used each other as social currency. And I told myself I deserved it—after everything, I was owed some pandemonium. I was allowed to be selfish."

"After we graduated high school, I was a huge fucking embarrassment to my parents, obviously. But then it was May's time to shine. She thrived. And I was so proud of her—I am so fucking proud of her—but... But then I kept swinging, swinging, swinging, and my poor decisions started impacting her. Like... we used to live together in Chinatown. She'd come home from her MBA program to find me in her bed with some rando. Or she'd come home and I wouldn't be there at all. For days. Without answering my phone. Or she wouldn't be able to work because I'd have people over. That sort of shit."

"She made me move back home, even if it was hell, because that was the kind of overbearing structure I needed again. She made me go to therapy. She made me get my shit together. It was her turn to watch over me. And then..." I blow out a breath.

"The engagement party," Nico finishes for me.

"The engagement party," I confirm. "And then..."

"This."

"And then this."

Nico wraps me up in his arms. In *this*.

"Thanks for telling me the rest," he murmurs.

I shake my head.

"That's not—I don't think I'm done."

His arms tighten.

I cling to him, now taking a hit of that Beautifully Sad Worst Enemy Shit directly into my lungs, my bloodstream.

"I'm either nothing, Nico," I say, "or I'm just a bad fucking person."

I'm surprised at how saying it out loud makes it feel smaller, as if it's not pressing quite so hard on my ribs anymore.

Nico holds me tighter, and I can feel it in the way his whole body wraps around mine like armor that he wants to fight that thought for me. But he doesn't say anything yet.

"I was jealous of you—I recognize that now. And none if it was your fucking fault. What a shitty fucking thing." I tear at my hair while Nico tries to swat my hands down. "Also? Even when I got out of my mess? After the engagement party? I didn't fix anything. I didn't become a better person. Or at least... I just started hiding better. I keep Old Annie on a leash and hope she doesn't maul anyone. I don't... *do* anything, see anyone." I'm rambling now. "I don't have my name on anything and—shit, Nico. I don't exist."

Something about the way he has me, though, makes me doubt that, a little. One hand smoothing over my hair. The other tracing circles on my back. Slow, steady.

"You're not a bad person," he says once he feels me settle, quiet but resolute. "You were just a kid under too much pressure—too many unstable variables, not enough control. So you did what you had to do. You protected the person you loved. And when she was finally safe, you tried to rebalance the equation. You just over-corrected. You're not empty, Annie. You're still trying to find equilibrium."

Jesus. I let out a laugh-sob hybrid. "Big-brain Dr. Nico."

But something, I realize, has shifted in those few words.

Not an explosion, or a full epiphany, or some miraculous transformation. Just... something. A softening and a slight easing in my chest.

So I breathe. A real, full breath. And when I exhale, it's like I'm letting go of something I've been clutching too tight for too long. I let it drain out of me, slow and quiet.

And what's left isn't nothing.

What's left is warmth. Faint, but something. A flicker of light where the weight used to be.

"I'm sorry," I exhale, with this renewed invigoration. I peer up at him, at the kindness in his eyes, and become even stronger. "I'm so sorry, Nico, for the way I treated you. You didn't deserve that. *I* didn't deserve that. I'm so, so fucking sorry."

He holds me at arm's length now, staring at me like he's seeing me anew. He nods once, accepting my apology without words, but his eyes say it all. He forgives me. I may not deserve it, because I'm still a raging, fucking bit—

He pulls me close again, softer this time.

"You are *good*," he says, voice barely above a murmur. "You are *fun*. You are strong. Appreciate that, at the very least. And you exist. You do."

I snort. "To who?"

"To May."

"Well, obviously—she's my twin—"

"—to me," he interrupts, low and slow.

I look up at him. He's so intensely serious about this that his jaw is clenched. His brows are pulled tight. But his eyes— those warm, brown, soul-deep eyes—don't waver. They hold me steady, safe, secure. Maybe that's what I should name those three moles dotting the smooth expanse of his disgustingly handsome face.

"You don't know me," I say, trying to deflect that thought, shoo it away.

"I think I do," he replies. "Because if we're talkin' ghosts—Annie, I've been one, too. Just a different kind."

I breathe and wait.

"You gave me the rest," he says with a faint smile. "Now you can have mine."

Before I can speak, Nico kicks off his shoes, the sound of them hitting the dirt absurdly loud in the stillness. He peels off his socks with exaggerated care, like he's putting on a show. He starts walking backwards, slow, theatrical steps, retreating toward the edge of the cliff.

"What are you—?"

He just winks.

And, with ridiculous, arrogant confidence, he reaches over his shoulder, grabs the back of his T-shirt, and pulls it off in one smooth motion.

My breath catches so hard I actually stagger.

It's *that* chest.

With that *fucking* tattoo.

But the grin on his face—wild, unrepentant, teasing—says it all. It's the grin of a man who's just shattered a wall.

My face cracks open, like I can't hold emotion in anymore. Like joy is pouring out of me from every seam. There's a sound—a real, sharp, dizzying thing that comes from somewhere low in my gut. A noise of pure, undiluted delight rips free from my throat, half-scream, half-laughter.

With that, he backflips off the edge of the cliff.

NINETEEN

Annie

______

Nico's head breaks through the surface of the lake, whips back and forth as he clears the water from his face. His smile is as blinding as the sun's reflection on the water surrounding him. He leans back and assumes a casual float, that duck on his pec bobbing through the water, while I stare and stare and stare.

"Well, what are you waiting for?" he finally calls up. "Get in here and wash away those sins, honey."

Another hysterical giggle breaks free. "Wow," I say.

"Wow," he agrees.

I sit at the edge of the cliff and dangle my legs. "Are you the Jesus in this baptismal scenario?"

He starts kicking, swimming in small, leisurely circles. "If that's what Sister Annie wants to call me when she's screamin' later, sure. But I prefer Nico."

I shake my head again. "Wow."

He grins.

"How about Chef?"

Nico tilts his head, his smile turning quizzical. "I'm not

technically a chef, so maybe not. But whatever floats your boat."

One sec. Does he... not know?

"Nico."

"Hmm?"

I stand.

"Nico."

"What, babe?"

"You are making a *NakedReactions* cookbook." I kick off my shoes and my socks.

A line appears between Nico's thick eyebrows.

"You asked Hawk Publishing House to get someone to ghostwrite it for you." His hoodie, my shirt, my shorts come off.

The smile starts growing on his face as he comes to understand.

"That ghostwriter is not me."

I close my eyes and leap.

————

Turns out washing your sins away in a quarry lake is a frigid experience. My lungs seize as soon as I'm under, but the shock of it all is pretty cleansing, I guess.

When I surface, Nico is laughing so hard I'm afraid he might drown.

"Annie," he huffs, "and I mean this lovingly—shut the fuck up."

"Yep."

"No way."

"Yes way."

"Wow."

"Wow."

Nico throws his head back and laughs again, my own

giggles (do I *giggle* now?) joining, the echoes of us bouncing on and across the water, against the rock cliffs surrounding us.

We swim towards each other without discussing it, both deliriously giddy with the truth.

"Hey, Chef," I say, when we're inches away, our knees and toes knocking together under the water.

He smiles, and it's devastating. "Hi, Ali."

"A. Li," I grin.

His laughter wraps around me, warmth blooming through the cool hush of the water. "I'm such a fuckin' fool."

"Same."

"You've been on my side this whole time," he says more softly.

"Same," I repeat, throat clogging with something.

"I know you."

I clear my throat. "Same."

The water droplets on the tips of his eyelashes sparkle while the ones on the pink of his pretty lips scream, *lick me*. When I look up, he's looking at my mouth like he's hungry for it, too.

He meets my eyes. His Adam's apple bobs as he swallows.

"You're so beautiful it hurts to look at you," he starts. "I'm dying to put my hands all over you."

Is it possible to melt in cold water?

"And... I'm waiting for you to find equilibrium and say 'fuck Sister Annie' and make the first move..." he trails off, trying to make it a lie, "...with the *utmost* patience. The most freakin' patience anyone has ever had in the history of the universe."

"Fuck Sister Annie," I respond immediately. I move in and lick the water droplets off his lips. "First move."

His eyes darken, his smirk turning sharp, before looking up and around. "Unfortunately, despite how easy it may look in the movies, I can't make out with you while treading water. I'm not that strong a swimmer."

Laughing, I start making my way towards the cliffs, towards a vertical path of rocks where it looks like you can climb back up to the top, but Nico cuts me off. "This way," he says, swimming to somewhere on the other side.

He stops at the base of the cliff, at a small series of rocks sticking out of the water, the top just flat and wide enough for him to pull himself out and sit on. That's it, though. No more room for me or anything else.

"So, I, too, only have a few minutes of treading water in me—" I start, but I am interrupted when he hooks his hands under my armpits, bodily lifts me out of the water, maneuvers my knees to either side of his hips, and settles me into his lap.

Like this, we're eye-level, his radiant under the sun.

"Hey, Nico," I say, already breathless.

"Hi, Annie," he answers, then drags me to him by the back of my neck.

There's no preamble this time, just Nico using a thumb to wrench my jaw down so he can fuck his tongue right in, immediately fisting my hair and using it to control our angle, velocity, depth, not that it matters, because our teeth still clash together with the force of our mutual assault.

Who in the world taught this *Dungeons and Dragons, Magic the Gathering* motherfucker to kiss? I owe them my life. His tongue is obscene in the way it tangles with mine, hard, demanding, hot, and rough, lewd when he uses it to drag a long stripe up my neck.

He traps my bottom lip between his teeth and tugs as he pulls away, his hand caressing my jaw, then my throat. A finger moves lower. We both watch as it traces the tattoos on my chest with reverence and care.

"It's been a year, Sister Annie. How would you like me to

break your vows?" he murmurs with an upward thrust of his hips.

Whoa. Jesus.

"I told you—I prefer Nico," he says, and I guess I said that out loud.

"I've wanted to put your dick in my mouth for months now," I breathe, "so maybe there?"

He groans, pulsing up once more. *Jesus motherfucking Christ.* "I heard you say that to your perverted geriatric girl gang. I haven't been able to stop thinking about it since."

"Thinking about what?" I breathe. I have no idea what he's talking about anymore.

Nico pauses the winding, searching path of his hands for a moment to lean in and suck on the skin on my chest, drawing it between his teeth, breaking the blood vessels and shooting a bolt of electricity directly to where it counts. He smiles at the artwork he's left behind, right between two tattoos. "I've imagined doing that for days now. So pretty." He circles the rapidly reddening mark with his fingers.

I grind down on the behemoth currently between my legs. I think I'm whining, but Nico doesn't seem to care. He gently angles me back. His fingers wander, dance up the string of my bikini, following the line of it down, down, down, until he reaches the triangle and traces over the seam hugging my breast.

He swipes a finger in, pulls the cup out, and hooks the entire thing under.

And then it's his turn to stare. And stare. And stare.

I grin.

Nico is shellshocked. "Wh—This entire time..." He tugs on the cup of the other side and does the same thing, both my tits now bracketed by my bikini and lifted and presented to him in offering. He wets his lips. "Don't fuckin' tell me these pretty little nipples were pierced the whole time? Three feet away from me? The entire time?"

"Are you going to salivate over them or salivate on them?" I demand to know, hips still circling, needing *something*, anything but his eyes to touch them *now*.

Evil glints in his eyes as he rakes a hand over his open mouth. "Both," he finally says, spitting on the right one before wrapping his lips around it.

I would have fallen back into the water if he didn't have an arm around my back. I grip onto his hair and hold on for dear life.

He uses a thick hand in tandem with his tongue and mouth, lifting the heavy weight of my breast towards his face while licking, sucking, tugging, tonguing the bar back and forth. For minutes, *hours*, slurping and squeezing and moaning as if he hasn't eaten in years.

I am not proud of the sounds leaving my own mouth, the heat of it all shooting through to my fingertips, down, down to where it aches so badly that I'd come if Nico so much as looked at it.

"How could you hide these from me, honey?" he croons on his way to lavish the other side, rolling the abandoned one between his fingers.

"How *dare* you?" Nico says, minutes, *hours* later. And with no warning at all, he lifts me slightly to land a sharp slap directly on my clit.

Wh— I scream, the shocking force of my first non-self-induced orgasm in a year bending me backwards, light and color swirling, and Nico, dear Nico, gives me the flat of his palm to ride out every single wave.

"Wow, baby, look at you," he's muttering into my ear. "You're so pretty when you smile, but you're even prettier when you come. Was that your first since Sister Annie? How did that feel?" he murmurs in between deep draws of my tits as he tugs the bottom of my bathing suit to the side.

"Who the fuck are—" I gasp, but I am rudely interrupted by one (*two?!*) finger(s) sliding right up into my trembling pussy with no fucking warning and forcing past any resistance.

He hisses. "Does this tight pussy need to be stretched after an empty two years?"

"Dildos are a thi—" I try to retort, but I am again rudely interrupted when I quickly realize that my collection of dildos has nothing, actually, on Nico's (*three?*) fingers. He rubs my front walls with the tips, my clit with his palm, gripping my entire fucking cunt in his big hand and working it. Back and forth, while I pant and moan above him.

"Give me another," he whispers with a rough jiggle, and *oh fuck*.

"*Nico!*" I sob, this orgasm even bigger, stronger, more painful than the last, my vision whiting out at the corners. My spine might be broken with the force of it, and then I no longer exist.

When I finally float down, Nico pulls his hand out, the entire thing embarrassingly shiny with my wet. "Salty," he says, as he licks a tear sliding down my cheek; "Sweet," as he licks his own hand from palm to fingertip.

My heart slams out of my ribcage. I rest my head on Nico's shoulder, now red and inflamed from my nails. He wraps his arms around me in a tight hug while I try to lower my heart rate.

"Who are you, and what happened to the kid who cried during fourth grade dodgeball?" I ask after catching my breath.

I feel him smile against my hair. "He grew up to be a meticulous scientist with a deep-seated obsession with empirical observation and rigorous data collection." He pauses. "And to have a big dick."

Laughing, glowing, radiant, I pull my head back. "Speaking of which," I say, grinding down on it, "give me a taste."

"I want to eat first," he says, his tongue licking into my mouth again, taking languid, leisurely sips. "But maybe if you're good, I'll feed it to you later."

I need a second, so I draw my legs down and lower into the water. My feet find purchase on some rock, and I tug on the sides of his swim shorts. "I'm hungry now," I say, and he lifts his hips so I can pull it down the rest of the way.

I stare, and stare, and stare.

Nico leans his head back, exposing the arrogant slope of his jaw and his neck. "Don't look so surprised. You've seen it before, honey."

"But—" I blink. "But not like this," I sputter, gesticulating wildly. "I'd ask you if you've considered porn, but..."

He laughs, brown eyes sparkling in the sun. "Good one, Annie Li. Now shut up and suck that dick."

And finally, after months of waiting, I do.

I lick it like it's the last fucking ice cream cone I'll ever eat. Trace my tongue up his length, wiggle it under the sensitive underside, swirl and suction around the broad head, before taking him as deep as I can. Salty heat and sweet musk. He's delicious.

"Stop," he grunts suddenly. Nico fists my hair to keep me down and thrusts up into my throat once, letting out a moan from deep in his belly. He uses his other hand to wipe the tears leaking from my eyes, then traces my lips stretched around his girth. "Yeah. Good," he says, and, "I knew it. You're even prettier when you're gagging on me."

Another burst of warmth in my chest, luminous under his words. I want more. I want it all, so I go to motherfucking town.

"Yeah," he groans, "just like that," "take a little more,"

"perfect," "pretty girl, your mouth is heaven on fucking earth," he's saying in between my explicit slurps. "You're gonna make me come, beautiful," he breathes, impossibly large in my mouth, thighs trembling, and then...

Laughter.

Laughter, from far away.

From... up the cliff and down the trail.

I go to pull away, but Nico now holds my head in both his hands. "Nuh uh," he scolds. "Hold on tight, Annie."

I dig my nails into his thighs, our moans a low chorus as he fucks my face. One, two, three, four... before he pulls out. I take a deep inhale of air while he strangles his own cock, jerking the swollen tip aggressively.

"Let me paint those tits, honey," he grits out, impossibly handsome, impossibly imposing above me, the cords in his thick neck straining. I give them to him, and he aims his dick right at the mark he's sucked and comes in spurts with a muted, drawn-out groan.

Chest heaving, he opens his eyes and admires his artwork, rubbing some of his release into the hickey and swiping what's gotten on my nipple piercings onto his fingers.

"Open up, Annie," he whispers. "Tongue out."

I do as I'm told, moaning softly as he drags the come on his fingers onto my outstretched tongue.

"You taste so good," I tell him, after swallowing it down.

The resulting look he gives me can only be described as tenderness. Maybe devotion.

There's a splash in the lake behind us.

Nico fixes my bathing suit and slides us into the water. "Shame," he whispers. "I wanted to appreciate your new artwork a little longer." He kisses my head and takes my hand to swim us over to the other side.

TWENTY

Nico

Candid, intricate, fractured, adrift Annie Li.

Hot, tight, wet, *pierced* Annie Li.

Languid, post-coital, content Annie Li.

My Annie Li.

"Ouch," she says, and I realize that I squeezed her hand a little too hard with that last one.

We're "lizarding," as Annie had called it moments ago, sunning ourselves on a large, flat rock wide enough for the two of us to lay side by side, a few meters away from the jump-off point of the quarry.

I want to cuddle my soft, lost Annie Li, but she is not, to anyone's surprise, Annie "Big Cuddler" Li, but she seems happy with the way we're playing with each other's fingers, dancing and twirling them together above our faces.

"Sorry, honey," I tell My Annie Li, Annie "Who is Now Mine" Li, and *what the hell is wrong with me?* What the hell happened to simple? But at this point it's kinda hard to not to think about it considering I just marked her like a mother-fucking animal at the first opportunity I was given.

"How did you know?" she asks.

"Know what?"

"Or rather, when did you figure out that I watched *NakedReactions*?"

I turn on my side to face her. "I saw and heard you watching an episode in the pool house. You were watching it with what sounded like a perverted Golden Girls crew."

She laughs, her entire face transforming into sunlight. The silk of her long hair a stark contrast to the rough rock. Unfettered, joyful Annie Li. "Those are my friends from the library. Fernanda and Betty like to objectify the aggressively male chefs on cooking shows, so I shared your channel with them. They're obsessed. We try to have a watch party for every episode."

I trace the purpling hickey I left on her chest with puffed up satisfaction. "Do they know you're ghostwriting my book?"

Her face shutters a little at this. "No. No one does. I'm contractually not allowed to tell anyone."

"Why the long face?"

She chooses her words carefully, but gone is that wariness that came before telling me anything at all. I internally roar and beat my chest with pride. "Remember how I said I didn't exist? That I didn't have a voice? I'm someone else's voice? I meant that literally. The term ghostwriter couldn't be more true. I am a ghost. I don't exist. My name is on nothing. Not the work that's famous, the shit that people quote. Nothing."

I pinch a nipple through her bikini. "This is something." Now that I'm looking closely, I can see both barbells poking through the fabric. How the fuck did I miss that?

She sighs—a deep, satisfied sound. "That is something."

"If you could do anything, what would it be?"

"You mean what did I want to be when I grew up?"

"Sure."

"A writer. But not this fucked up, Sad Invisible Peter Pan version."

I want to growl when she talks about herself like this. I twist her nipple as punishment.

"Ouch! Nico!" she says, shoving my hand away.

"Stop talking about yourself like that," I warn.

"It's true!"

I pinch the other one.

She sits up and tries to run away, but I grab her arm and tug her back down. I notice her shoulders are getting pink, so I dig into my pocket.

"Here," I say, handing her the sunscreen bottle. "You're pinking, and not in the good way. That's comin' later, though."

Annie stares at the bottle as if it has suddenly sprouted wings and a tail. She looks at me. "Did you bring that for me?"

I shrug. "Yeah. On the beach you said the best form of tattoo aftercare is sunscreen."

Her face becomes unreadable.

But now I'm the lucky motherfucker who's learned how to read her.

"Come here," I order, sitting up.

She doesn't move.

"Sit in my lap and let me fuckin' take care of you, Annie."

Annie grumbles (So adorably! Like a disgruntled kitten!) and shuffles into my lap.

"Good," I whisper in her ear and wait for... yep. The goosebumps down her neck, the stiff of her nipples poking through the fabric of her bikini. My Annie Li likes a bit of praise. And how lucky was I that I figured it out with my dick in her mouth?

Makes sense though. After spending the entirety of her youth trying to impress people, convince them that she was the best or whatever?

I squeeze some sunscreen onto my hands and start rubbing it into her shoulders and arms. On my way down her left arm, though, my thumb brushes against something under her skin. Something maybe two inches long and the width of a glow stick.

I am suddenly lightheaded with the way the blood leaves my head and flows directly into my dick. "Uh oh," I rasp out. "You're in big trouble, Annie."

Annie realizes what I'm rubbing and shivers. "If you want, later," she starts. I hear her swallow. "You can—" but she cannot finish because I've got my fist in her hair and my tongue down her throat.

She pulls away once she feels my hand sneaking down the front of her bathing suit. "Nico," she sighs.

"What?"

"Think of the children," she laughs.

My mind becomes static as I try to parse all the information now zooming in loop-de-loops through my brain. *No children; that's the point of the implant. I'm going to come in Annie Who is Now Mine Li. I can mark you from the inside. Fill you up, drive it in, let it drip. Do you want kids? Will you bear my children? Should I rip the implant out with my teeth? What the hell is happening to me?* And then, *Do I have a breeding kink?!* And last and most alarming, *No, just a "pumping Annie Li full of my come" kink. So... yes?*

She clears her throat.

My eyes refocus.

Annie is looking at me with concern. "There are kids swimming over there," she says slowly.

"Yes," I solemnly nod. I shake my head to get rid of the insanity and resume my task.

"You brought me sunscreen because I mentioned it several weeks ago," Annie mumbles after a while.

"Yep." I move onto her chest. "You might not be used to

people taking care of you, honey, but that's just 'cause you hadn't met me yet."

"Nico, we grew up together."

"I amend. You hadn't decided that you liked me yet."

"I hate you."

I land a sharp slap to her clit again, loving the whimper that leaves her throat. "Lie."

I don't see it but I know she's smiling, especially when she relaxes in my arms and lets me fuckin' take care of her.

I suddenly cannot breathe. The oxygen up all the way up here on Mount Olympus is pretty thin.

"Do you write anything else?" I ask after getting all her visible skin covered.

"Hmm?"

I plant a kiss on the side of her neck. "Do you write for fun?"

"Yeah," she rumbles. "Poetry."

"Any of that published?"

"No."

"Can I read some of it?"

"No."

"No matter," I reply, unbothered. "I'll make you read it to me while I go down on you later."

We watch the sun glittering on the lake, still playing with each other's hands.

"So... ghostwriting." I ask. "Why'd you start?"

Annie doesn't answer immediately. She shifts her weight on my lap.

"It wasn't some noble calling," she says finally. "I didn't sit up one night and think, 'I want to devote my life to writing memoirs for wellness influencers who think drinking chlorophyll cured their depression.'"

I smirk. "You sure? Sounds poetic."

She laughs, dry and soft. "It just fell into my lap. A friend of mine from a writing group got offered a ghostwriting contract she didn't want. She passed it to me. Said, 'You're good at sounding like other people.' I needed money, and it wasn't self-publishing poetry that no one read."

She says the last part like it's a joke, but her voice goes a little hollow at the end.

I angle my neck to better look at her face. "But you kept doing it."

She shrugs, eyes still fixed on the horizon. "It pays the bills. And it got easier to sell other people's truths than keep digging around for my own. There's a weird kind of relief in that. Like... if the words flop, it's not really your failure. And if they fly, you just pretend you weren't even there."

I let the silence sit.

After a while, she says, "It was easier to hide behind other people's voices than admit mine wasn't loud enough to matter."

I shift closer. "Well, too bad. I've heard it now, it's fuckin' beautiful, honey."

Annie giggles, and I want to bottle the sound up to pour over pancakes at a later time. She turns sideways and snuggles deeper into my lap. I'm not sure she realizes she's doing it, but she's rubbing her cheek against the hair on my chest with her eyes closed. Maybe she ain't used to cuddling because she hadn't met me yet, either. "Nico," she says suddenly.

"What, baby?"

"I'm dying to know about the surprised duck," she says, poking it with her finger.

I smile. "Mallard."

Annie's body grows tense in frustration. "There's a connection that's been on the tip of my tongue for days now but I can't fucking get it."

"It's a mallard, Annie. A mallard having a reaction."

She looks up at me with gorgeous eyes. "Maillard reaction."

"Yup."

A pause, then, "That's the corniest fucking thing I've ever heard in my life."

I bust out laughing. "It's amazing. It's hilarious. You love it."

"I hate it."

I spank the side of her ass. "Lie."

"It's okay," she grumbles, eventually.

———

We ended up hitting the road way later than I'd planned 'cause Annie fell asleep on my arm while lizarding, and despite the jagged bits of rock digging into my ass and skull I was not gonna move her. We've gotta haul ass now, 'cause we've got a big six hour push to Savannah.

Annie's got her laptop on her lap and has been barraging me with questions for the last few hours.

"Okay," she says, fingers still clacking, "explain the difference again between caramelization and the Maillard reaction. But this time, say it in the Nico voice."

"I don't know what you mean," I mutter. "My voice is my voice."

She huffs out a laugh. "I want your actual voice in this thing. I want it to sound funny and sexy."

I glance at her. "You think I'm funny and sexy?"

She ignores me. "This book needs to feel like you. Not a version of you dressed up for a publishing meeting. I want people to read this and hear how you talk about pan-searing like it's foreplay and emulsification like it's an enemies-to-lovers relationship."

"I do not talk about emulsification like it's an enemies-to-lovers relationship."

"You literally said, 'Mayo is a miracle of cooperation and stubbornness. Like any good relationship.'"

I pause. "Okay, yeah, I did say that."

She grins.

I rub my neck, suddenly weirdly shy. "I just want it to feel... honest. You know? Like it's about more than just technique. The best food I've ever made wasn't about the exact grams or temps. It was because someone I cared about was gonna eat it. That's the part I don't wanna lose."

Annie's hands still on the keyboard. "Then don't."

I glance over. Her expression's open, serious in a way that pulls at my insides.

"You know," she says, "I've read a lot of cookbooks as research after getting this project. And I've never once read one that made me feel like I understood the person writing it. But this one? This is gonna be a book about love. About food. And how they're the same thing. With a little porn sprinkled in."

"There is definitely porn sprinkled in," I say, shaking my head. "It's an offshoot of my porn channel, Annie."

"I know," she says. "But it's also about chemistry. Literal and figurative. You and food. You and people. You and—" she stops herself and clears her throat. "Anyway. I just want to get it right."

"You will," I say, because I know this to be true. "I mean it. All the poetic shit you been sayin' this whole trip, that's what I want our cookbook to be."

She hums. Then finally, "Yours."

"What?"

"It's your cookbook."

I furiously shake my head. "Hell nah. It's ours. Our cookbook. And your name's gonna be on it and everything. Annie 'The Best Writer Ever' Li."

"That's not how contracts work, Nico."

"Contracts are meant to be broken."

"Again, not how contracts work, Nico."

Fuck that. I start messing around with the digital screen on the dashboard, scrolling through contacts, while Annie mutters, "The two of us have got to be Hawk's worst fucking nightmare." I find who I'm looking for and press *Call*.

"Hey, big guy." My agent Kate's voice echoes through the speakers of the car.

Annie's little body tenses next to me. "Big guy," she murmurs.

I slant a look at her and radiate joy. My Annie Li is jealous, and it sends driving pulses of pleasure through my veins. It makes me feel... wanted.

"It's not like that," I whisper, and she settles immediately.

"Kate, is it in the contract with Hawk Publishing that the ghostwriter of the cookbook's gotta stay anonymous?"

A pause. "What?"

"Can I add the ghostwriter's real name as the author of the book?"

Another pause. "Why?"

"Because I want her to be." I glance over at Annie, who is uncharacteristically quiet. "Because she deserves to be." I squeeze her knee.

"I don't know, Nico. I'd have to look through the contract."

"Could you do that for me, honey?"

Annie's body tenses again, but Kate's mumbling something that sounds suspiciously like "the confidence of cis-het white men," and Annie smothers a grin.

"I'll look, Nico. Is that it?"

"Yeah. Let me know, Kate. Later."

"Later."

———

Turns out Annie is even more beautiful surrounded by shellfish carcasses. Like some sort of devastatingly beautiful Disney villain of sea crustaceans. It's a marvel to watch her deftly navigate the peeling of crawfish, even more so when she sucks the juice out of their heads like it's a sacred maritime ritual passed down from Poseidon himself.

"What?" she frowns, a single rogue antenna caught on her wrist.

"You're so hot," I tell her.

She rolls her eyes but the tips of her lips twitch. She plucks a potato from the tray, blows on it, then pops it in her mouth with a satisfied hum. "Tell me about the science of a low country boil," she says, licking Old Bay from her thumb.

My brain short circuits remembering the feeling of her mouth wrapped around my dick. Hot, warm, silky heaven. I wonder what her pussy will feel like. Probably—

"—Nico."

I blink. "Yes."

She squints. "You have no idea what I just asked."

"*Yes* to anything and everything you ever ask of me for the rest of our lives," I blurt out, and did I just fuckin' go there? What in the actual fuck is happening to me? Jesus fuckin' Christ.

Annie has that scared baby rabbit look in her eyes again.

Oh god, you fuckin' ridiculous asshole.

"Sorry," I half-shout, waving my hands around like a lunatic. *Dial it down you fuckin' weirdo.* "That was weird. I didn't mean—"

"Obviously not," she says, eyes still huge, shaking her head up and down, then side to side in a daze.

"Right, obviously not," I echo. "I meant like, for the cookbook. The duration of the cookbook. Professionally."

She nods harder. "Of course."

"Of course." Not of course. For the rest of our lives. I meant it. I'd let her name our kids after shellfish if she asked. *What?!* I clear my throat. I do it again. "What did you ask me?"

Annie blinks at me. "I..." she trails off. "I don't remember."

"Science of low country boil!" I declare.

Vigorous head nodding from both of us.

"Okay, okay," I recover, scooting closer and grabbing a crawfish for her like it's a peace offering. "First off, low country boil is with shrimp, so this technically isn't low country boil. This is just a crawfish boil."

She shakes herself out of it, eyes still locked on mine, but now I can see the gears in her adorable noggin turning. "Okay."

"First rule of a good boil? The water should be seasoned. Like, aggressively seasoned. Salt, cayenne, paprika, garlic, bay, Old Bay, lemon—you want that pot to punch you in the face with flavor before you even drop anything in it."

"Punch me in the face," she deadpans, "got it."

"The water isn't just cooking things—it's infusing them. The food doesn't have long in there, so you need that seasoning to go hard from the jump. The starches and proteins will absorb flavor as they go, like little sponges of spicy, steamy goodness."

"Okay."

"Now—potatoes first. Because they take the longest to cook and absorb flavor."

She pops a potato in her mouth like she's testing my claims. She nods slowly.

"Next: corn. But here's the thing—" I lean in slightly.

"You don't want to just boil the hell out of it. Corn gets water-logged fast. You want to steam it more than drown it. So you put it in close to the top, let the steam from everything below hit it gently. Otherwise, it's sad corn. Nobody wants sad corn."

Annie smirks. "Steam is good, here."

I wink. "Steam will be good later, too." I could be wrong but I think she shivers.

She smirks. "Go on."

"Sausage next," I croon.

She glances down at my lap. That's right, baby—

Annie is snapping her fingers in my face. "Focus, Nico," she says, but her eyes have gone lazy.

I make an attempt. "Ideally Andouille," I continue. "High fat content, firm casing. You drop it in just long enough for the fat to start rendering—adds richness to the broth, layers of smokiness and spice. But don't overdo it or it goes rubbery."

"You're really selling me on this sausage technique," she murmurs, a glint in her eye, licking her thumb again.

I raise an eyebrow. "You really wanna play this game, honey?"

"I do," she sighs dreamily. "But preferably somewhere near a bed."

I stand so violently the table rattles. A few shells drop onto the ground. "Let's get the hell out of here."

"No, Nico!" she laughs. "Sit. Finish telling me about the crawfish."

"Fuck the crawfish."

"And don't you want dessert?"

"Depends," I say. "Can I eat it off your asshole?"

Annie gapes at me, leaning over the side a bit.

"Is that a yes?"

"Who are you?"

"The dude who isn't gonna let you disappear. The dude who wants you to have some fun. The dude who's got you.

The dude who wants to bang your motherfucking brains out." I think there's a lot more that I can add but I need to unpack it at a later point in time. Preferably after I bang her motherfucking brains out.

"That was a rhetorical question, Nico," she breathes, that dazed look back in her face.

I slap a hundred down on the table and round it to take her hand and draw her out of her chair. I suck the Old Bay off every single fingertip while she melts in my arms on the way to the door.

"Let's go have some fun, Annie. I got you. And I'm gonna bang your motherfucking brains out."

TWENTY-ONE

Annie

NICO QUITE RUDELY AND UNCEREMONIOUSLY throws me over his shoulder and sprints through Savannah to get back to our house.

Just kidding.

I wish.

Instead, after dragging me out of the clatter of dinner and stepping into the thick, honey-slow air of Savannah at night, Nico takes one look around, gently takes my hand, and begins a romantic stroll.

I hate it.

Lie.

"This is nice," he says.

"This is awful."

He swats my ass.

More, I want to say.

"This is some beautifully mundane shit, Annie. Enjoy it with me before I break your back."

Despite the persistent flood in my panties, Nico is right, unfortunately. It's quiet now, the kind of hush that blankets the city when it's too dark for tourists and too early for ghosts.

We wander past wrought-iron fences and crooked cobblestone paths, under the draping canopies of ancient live oaks. The streets shine faintly under the glow of old gas lamps, amber pools of light flickering across cobblestones slick with humidity.

"I love the Spanish moss," I offer, nodding towards where it drapes over most visible tree branches, swinging like whispers in the slight breeze. "Soft, secretive, sacred."

Nico stops us under a huge clump of it on the branch of a massive oak and swings me around to face him. He's wearing a lazy smile, his eyes shining with something that looks like affection. He starts tracing the lines of my face with his fingers—god, those fingers—across each eyebrow, down the length of my nose, across my mouth. It's all too much.

"You are disgustingly handsome," I blurt out, and I almost regret it, expecting that arrogant smirk, but instead I get a grin that seems like it's just for me. Soft, secretive, sacred. Enchanted.

Somehow, in the span of almost seven days, my worst enemy has made nasty, problematic, selfish Annie Li feel *enchanting*.

"Dance with me under the moonlight, Annie Li," he says, and *girl, you are so fucked*.

I step into my rightful place, the place he's made for me, a place that's strong yet pliant, that can accommodate my force field of spikes and knives and swords and other manners of sharp things—not that they've come out around him, lately. Wrapped up tight, his arms squeezing my entire torso, my forehead tucked against his chin—my place, I realize, is in Nico Giannuzzi's arms.

I experience another moment of sheer panic at this, the fortieth in two hours. The first being earlier, at Nico's allusion to "the rest of our lives." At how, in the span of five days, I'd gone from "I'm going to kill this asshole" to "I want to spin in slow circles while hugging him under the moonlight." At two thick fingers breaking Sister Annie's two-year-long vow of celibacy, two days short of the goal. At being a miserable hurricane of serious issues—

Nico presses his lips to mine, and all panic is entirely replaced by gooey warmth and a sense of belonging. This kiss is different from the others. This is a worship of my mouth, a tender caress, a slow drag and dance of our tongues, my jaw reverently cradled in a big hand. It's one that says, *I've got you, Annie Li*. I see you, and I want you.

I'm wholly unfamiliar with this feeling. Of safety and security and something else. I am unmoored.

I take his bottom lip between my teeth and tug, trying to ramp it up and move it along. Get to the good stuff. Detour around this other stuff I don't want to, *cannot* get into.

But he knows. He knows what I'm trying to do and is unbothered. He takes my hand and drops a kiss on the pointer and middle fingers, directly on top of the spade and the heart, before looping his fingers through mine and continuing our leisurely moonlit stroll.

"Can we pick up the pace?" I attempt.

"Crawfish," he answers merrily. "I didn't tell you about the crawfish. That's the fun part, but it's where people really fuck up."

"Tell me more about fucking and upping."

"Be good, Annie," he chastises gently. "I'll give it to you if you're good," and then my brain shuts down and enters Overachiever Autopilot so that I can not only be good, but will also be the best.

"Okay."

He cuts a glance down towards me in contemplation. Then he leans down.

"Look at you, beautiful girl. Much, much better," he breathes into my ear, and I trip over a crack in the sidewalk.

Nico catches me and moves me into the dark, presses me against one of those wrought iron fences so it cuts into my back with just the right amount of pain. "Data collection," he explains, before sliding his hand down the front of my shorts and into my underwear and gliding his fingers between my lips. He chuckles, dragging back and forth in a sopping wet slide while all but holding me up with his other arm. "Noted," he muses while pressing the hard length of himself against my hip.

I grip onto his arm with my nails like an actual cat in heat when he tries to pull away. "No, please, Nico," I whine, and great. I'm now a whiner and a beggar along with being a giggler.

However, this does something for Nico. I feel it in the way he gets even harder against my hip and thrusts.

"Say it again, Annie," he grunts.

I'm all but climbing him now, grinding myself along his fingers and using my hand around his neck for leverage. "Please, Nico, please. I need you." I don't recognize this voice. "I need you now. I need you to fill me up. It hurts."

"Fuck," he hisses. "You're even prettier when you beg." He gives me a finger in reward, slides it in and up and out and in, and I swallow a shout. "Even more when you're dripping all over my hand."

Yelling, then laughter, from the other side of the fence.

Nico looks up and around, collecting some more data while knuckle deep inside me. "Shit," he reports. He pulls his hand out and licks his finger. "Fuck the romance. Fuck the crawfish." He starts dragging me down the path. "Time to break your back, honey."

———

We barely make it through the front door. We do not make it past the foyer.

Between the hot thrusts of tongues and groping, searching hands, Nico drags us down to our knees immediately after slamming the front door shut. He whips a hand under my thighs, manhandling my body to lay me on my back so he can rip my shorts and my panties down in one particularly aggressive drag.

"Shirt off," he says, reaching back to pull off his own. "Shirt and bra off, Annie, then use those two favorite fingers of mine to spread those lips and show me where it hurts."

I do as I'm told because I'm being so good, laying back and planting my feet and making a 'v' of my pointer and finger to spread myself where I'm aching.

"God, Annie, fuck," he groans. "There she is," he says, his eyes dragging the length of my body in reverence. "You are the most beautiful fuckin' thing I've ever seen." As if he can't help it, he tugs the waistband of his boxers and those fucking athletic shorts that have been haunting my nightmares for days and hooks them right under his balls. I lose my mind at the image of him like this, of him looming above me on his knees and impossibly large in a leisurely, stroking hand.

Girl, you are so fucked. "Nico," I wheeze out, grinding on emptiness. "Please."

He plants a hand on the floor and leans down, licking the tops of my fingers on either side of my pussy, right on top of the spade, then the heart, his tongue just grazing where I need it most. He groans again. "I'll give you anything you want if you beg for it like that."

He spits on my clit, right at the apex of my fingers, and I shouldn't like this as much as I do, even more so when he mutters, "mine," before going to fucking town.

The first drag of his tongue is animalistic, a blistering slide that splits my flesh down the middle. An inhuman sound leaves my throat, at this first oral contact in two years, somewhere between a screech and a gasp, and my hand flies to cover my mouth before Nico swats it away.

"Nuh uh," he chastises. "Loud, Annie. I wanna hear how I'm making it better."

Fine, then.

I receive a satisfied rumbling from deep in his chest. Both my hands immediately fly into his hair as he tosses both my legs over his shoulders. "Yes, baby," he grits out in between wet laves and circles and sucks, "Grind that sweet pussy all over my face," and I realize that my hips are moving on their own accord as I try to chase my third non-self induced orgasm in over two years.

"Fingers, please, Nico," I gasp, needing that stretch, and he obliges with two that move right to the spot he's already located with a scientist's precision and rubs. Hard. "Oh, fuck," I breathe, as the wave starts to build from the base of my spine. "Oh god. Nico. Here it—" I am interrupted by a brutal suck to my clit, then the wave swells and then crashes, exploding into a million pinpricks of confetti and white noise.

When I open my eyes, Nico is again looking down at me with that look in his face. The one of reverence, or awe, or maybe devotion.

And again, a sound tears out of me. It bubbles up from deep in my gut and bursts into the air, something between a laugh and a cry, too full of joy to be just one or the other.

He grins, kissing up my body, following a line of tattoos up—the tiger on my belly, the butterfly on my sternum, the hickey from earlier, then lays the side of his head against my chest, his ear against my heart, lays the full weight of his body on mine while I wrap my arms around his head and try to catch my breath.

"Thank you," I whisper.

"Thank me later," he says, then, "I'm just getting started."

He hauls me up onto my feet, spears his hands through my hair and his tongue into my mouth, walking me backwards with slow steps towards what I assume is the kitchen. "Now," he says in between kisses, "is a good time to tell me what you want for your first dicking down in two years."

I have had two entire years to think about what I've been missing and one week to think about what I've been needing. I've also had five days and maybe nine months to learn to be completely honest with Nico. "I want it mean and fast and rough. I want you to spank me. Hard. Like, *leave a big, red, Nico-sized handprint* hard," I ramble, shivering. "Sex for me has always been about conquering. But now I want to be conquered. I don't want to think. I don't want to make any decisions. I want to give up control. And I have the implant. I want you to come inside m—ah!"

Nico twists both my nipples at the same time with a hiss. "Oh god, baby," he moans against my neck. "That's so fuckin' hot. I want that, too," he's nodding. "Need it. Need it. Fuck," he breathes. "You're so good. You're perfect. Made for me."

My heart does the explode-y thing again. "And I think I just discovered that I like being praised," I whisper.

"Got that," he croons. My butt finally hits the edge of a table. "My turn. I like a bit of teeth. I want those gorgeous fangs of yours," he says, with a nip to my collarbone. "I want you to fuck up my back with your nails, Annie. I wanna toss you around." He moves over to the hickey on my chest and kisses it. "And I think I just discovered that I like hearing you beg and I like marking you up. Inside and out. And I say that I just discovered that because I've never wanted that with anyone else in my life."

Warm, glazed eyes meet my panicked ones. "We'll unpack that later," he whispers gently. "Yours too. 'Cause it's the same thing, I think. But is everything else okay?"

I blink. "Yes."

A predatory smile, a lopsided grin. He turns me around. "I know what you need, honey. You want me to tell you exactly what to do," he murmurs as he bends me over the table, "and then you want to do it well."

I nod against the hard, solid surface now pressed against my face, whimpering and relaxing with relief at the same time. That he gets it. Because he obviously gets it.

"And then you want me to tell you how well you're doing. How well you're taking me. How perfect you are," he says, thrusting his hard length between my thighs once, inhaling sharply when the head brushes against the wet of me.

I nod again, closing my eyes, letting go.

He pulls away, leaving me cold, but warming me back up with a hand slowly tracing down my back and over the curve of my ass. I feel it stop to smooth over a tattoo on my back. "I'm gonna do that for you, honey. I've got you," he says, fingers dragging back up through my pussy and up my back again and into my hair, petting and caressing my entire body into a semi-catatonic state.

Suddenly, his voice is right next to my ear.

"But I'm gonna make you beg for it, too."

Crack.

A blast of sharp, white-hot fire spikes through my skin, my flesh, through my bloodstream, while the air around me shifts into every color of the rainbow. I soundlessly scream into the table, my mouth pressed open against the woodgrain while I melt into warm, syrupy honey.

"I'm so fucked, Annie," he sighs, soothing the burn away with a tender hand. *You?!* "I like the look of this a little too much, I think." He traces the shape of a hand into my skin. "You're so gorgeous, Annie, *this* is so gorgeous because it's mine. This is from my hand, and you did such a good job of letting me put it there."

I suddenly feel like bursting into tears.

The caresses increase in horniness, his fingers brushing against my entrance at every pass. I start squirming. "Another," I breathe. "Other side."

"What was that?" he murmurs, dipping a finger into my pussy. I'm embarrassingly wet, his finger meeting little to no friction. He rubs circles on my asshole as a reminder, in a promise.

I make a choked sound into the table. "Another. More. Please, Nico. *Please*."

"That's right, babe."

Crack, on the other cheek.

"*Fuck yes*," wheezes out of me as I claw at the tabletop with my fingernails.

"I can't wait for you to see what this looks like," he tells me. "It's unreal."

There is a rustle of fabric hitting the floor.

"I should probably ask if you want me to stretch you out with my fingers first," he says in a conversational tone, as if he were commenting on doing the laundry. "But you don't wanna think." I feel the blunt, broad head of him splitting the flesh of my cunt. Oh *shit*. "You just want to feel. And I think you're going to take me like a good g—*fuck*," he chokes.

During his filthy monologuing, Nico had attempted to push in. However, Nico had met resistance after only a few inches. There is simply no more room. My feet currently scramble for purchase on the floor, every vein in my body ending in a live wire. "Oh shit, oh shit, oh shit," I cry. "It's so good, I'll be so good, give me more, Nico."

"Fuck," he grits out, "let me in, Annie," pulling out slightly and gaining another slow inch when he presses back in with an agonized moan.

"No, please," I sob, trying and failing in my pleasure and torment to explain that I need the burn of him punching the fuck through. "Just do it, I want it all, *GIVE IT TO ME*—"

He tears through the rest with one long, sure, brutal shove, a shocking invasion, making room for his own damn self, and I scream and I come and I black out in a dazzling explosion of gunpowder and glitter all at once.

When I come to, Nico is fucking me in mean little strokes that are simply hitting the spot because of his size—because his size hits all the spots. "You did so well, Annie," he's panting, tilting my hips exactly how he wants them before sneaking a hand around to pinch my clit. "You gorgeous, perfect girl, you."

I come again, a horrible, delightful, slobbering mess. The table is wet with either my drool or my tears.

"Do you know how many times I've imagined fucking you over a kitchen table?"

"How many?" I pant.

"I lost count." He lifts me up by the neck and thrusts up twice, my feet no longer on the floor, held up by a strong arm around my stomach. "Bedroom, now," he says, lifting me off his dick and somehow turning me around to face him, all in one go. My legs wrap around his hips, and I'm so, so pleased to have access to his pretty, filthy mouth again, his wild hair, the salty skin on his neck damp with sweat.

He carries me—moving and making out and stopping short and turning in circles.

"Why aren't we in the bedroom yet?" I sigh in between deep, drugging kisses.

"I've never fuckin' been here before, Annie—" another spin, "—I have no fuckin' idea where the fuckin' bedroom is," Nico grits out with frustration.

I giggle (*what the hell is happening to me?!*) and give him what he needs, a bite right in the meaty part of his neck.

Nico gives up and gracefully deposits me on my hands and knees on what appears to be the fluffy area rug of the living room.

I look over at the kitchen. "We didn't get very far."

He rewards me with a sharp slap to the underside of my ass. He lies on his back next to me, his cock a hard, angry-looking leviathan. "Hop on, Annie. Ride it."

I have to stop for a moment.

"What?"

"I'm calculating an improbable physics problem," I say to his erect dick, "or maybe math."

He laughs, tucking a hand behind his head with supreme arrogance. "It fits. Scientifically proven just a moment ago, in fact. Over there." He points towards the kitchen.

"Displacement, volume, dimensions. Is this what they mean by abstract math?" I ramble. "There's also something about gases or maybe liquids taking the shape of a container, or maybe filling the available space?" *Is my pussy made of liquid? Feels like it.*

The sound of Nico's rich, booming laughter filling the available space of this room somehow feels better than the countless number of orgasms he's given me. (Five—it's five, not counting the ones I gave myself. Because I've lost count of those.)

I swing a leg over while he grips his shaft and angles it towards where I need it. I do not let myself adjust, just sink down as I watch Nico's beautiful eyes fall shut and pretty mouth fall open to exhale a slow, extended, "Fuuuck."

I get it, I really do, a whimper leaving my mouth at the sharp sting of the stretch. I plant my hands on his broad chest, leaning down and biting his mallard, that fleshy part of his pec.

His eyes fly open, blown with lust. "Fuck, baby. Does that fill you up nice and tight?" he slurs, bouncing me up and down with his hips like I'm a rag-doll riding a mechanical bull. He grasps my hips and wrenches me back and forth while arching his hips up, and I lean back, a hand on his thigh, a foot on the floor next to his torso so he can hit it right...

Six is a slow rippling, like a pebble falling into water, concentric circles of tingles out my arms and legs.

"Shit," Nico says, all arrogance gone, a wild look now in his eyes, his jaw clenched and fingers digging into my hips so hard I know they'll leave marks. I want them to leave marks. I want them all over my body, scattered throughout my tattoos. A twisted collection. Gotta catch 'em all.

His chest is crisscrossed with raised red lines from my nails. The smug satisfaction that bursts through my body is entirely unexpected.

"My turn," Nico is saying, and somehow I'm spinning or falling or turning and I'm on my back. "Spread those legs and let me finish rough," he grinds out in between deep, merciless, dirty drives that make the rug burn my back and leave me gasping for air. He moves my legs open, knees up, leg over, a container, a vessel, for him to fill and use and take the shape of. Grunts and moans and wet, lewd slapping now fill the space around us, a chorus of lust and sexual tension getting fucking resolved.

I've never had it this good.

"Beg me," Nico orders, handsome face in a snarl, "beg for it, Annie," and I'm being good for him, so I do.

I rake my nails across his shoulders. "Fill me up, Nico. Please."

His hips piston, then stutter, and with a needy, filthy groan, he does.

Something flashes in his eyes when he watches himself leak out of me like a pervert, but he silently closes my legs and carries me to a bedroom, which turns out to be up a flight of stairs.

He doesn't let me clean up, muttering something about unsound UTI research and wanting me full of him all night. He lays me down under the covers with tenderness before climbing in himself.

"Nico," I mumble, already half gone.

"Yes, honey."

I yawn. "That was the best sex of my life. I don't hate you anymore. And I think I hate cuddling you."

He smiles, turning me and tucking my back against his chest, winding his legs through mine.

Through the blanket of sleep already weighing me down, I hear, "That was the best sex of my life. I love cuddling you. And I hate you, Annie Li."

TWENTY-TWO

Nico

In the morning light, My Annie Li sleeps like a rock, as if she'd spent her night slaying her enemies and drinking their blood.

Or at the very least, fucking one three or four times.

It's wild, the way that she or I pulled towards one another throughout the night, drawn together like magnets, mouths and hands searching and learning, slow, languorous, dreamlike fucking with whispered laughs and gasps under the covers, under the blanket of night. Falling asleep right after, only to wake up a few hours later to do it again.

When I wake up, she's in my arms, her head buried in my chest, arm and thigh thrown around my waist like an adorable little koala. Everything below our waist is sticky. Normally I'd be horrified, but I feel nothing but proud and really fuckin' pleased. I should probably digest this myself before we digest it all together. Because now we're running out of time.

It's Wednesday, and there's one more stretch 'til we arrive in Miami tonight. Tomorrow is the welcome party. When real life will burst through this little bubble of daggers that Annie's only just let me into.

Which side of the bubble will I be on tomorrow? Which side do I *want* to be on? Is My Annie Li only Road Trip Annie Li? Will she be different when she's around her sister, parents, family, friends? Will I?

As if she can hear me thinking, she snuggles deeper into my torso with a contented sigh. From here I can see the freshest mark I've left on her body, on the side of her neck from just a few hours ago.

I'm so fucked.

I clear my throat. "Babe."

Nothing.

I peel myself away the slightest bit. "Sweetheart."

"No."

"Honey."

"I'm not your honey."

Lie, but I'll take it easy on her this morning. I chuckle and lift some hair out of her face. "We've gotta hit the road soon."

One eye opens. "How soon?"

I lean back and check my phone. "Two hours."

Silence, then, "Are you fucking kidding me, Nico?" She wrenches herself around, buries her head under a pillow, and throws the covers over for good measure. "Wake me up ten minutes before we have to leave," a muffled grumble says.

I am so very tickled. I leap out of bed and round it to her side. I bunch everything in my hands—covers, sheets, pillow— wrench it all off onto the floor, and smack her ass.

Annie screams.

I admire the pink of my handprint in the morning light, relishing, yet again, in the shock of power that explodes through my body, before scooping up her thrashing body and hauling her over my shoulder. "We gotta get in the shower. I need to wash myself off of you," *regrettably,* "and I need to get some food in you. And I gotta do this laundry 'cause no one should have to touch it."

I deposit her in the en-suite walk-in shower and turn it on. It happens to be one of those dual showerhead systems, so she's blasted on both sides. As Annie glares at me through the wet hair in her face, like she wants to gut me from stomach to neck, she resembles a bedraggled, angry kitten who's just slipped into the bathtub.

I'm gonna marry this girl one day.

I step into the shower and get down on one knee in a twisted foreshadowing, dazed by the promise I've just made myself. "Let me make it up to you," I tell her, and I have my breakfast.

———

"Get naked and do the voice," a much more chipper Annie tells me over the sound of bacon sizzling.

I'm unable to respond because I'm currently speechless at the image of Annie kicking her bare feet while perched on the counter next to the stove, wearing nothing else but my hoodie, reinforcing all these ridiculous notions I'm having of "forever" and "permanence" and "mine."

How did this happen? In six days? Or maybe it's been months in the making, considering the Ali/Chef correspondence. Regardless, this can't be real, can it? But it certainly seems real, especially when I suddenly feel Annie's arms wrap around me from behind, when her face snuggles into my back between my shoulder blades. "Nico." I realize I've been wordlessly staring at the bacon as if it held all the answers. It usually does, but not right now.

"Yes, honey."

"Take your pants off and do the sexy professor voice and talk to me about the science of eggs."

"Hmm..." Something about this makes me feel wary.

"What?"

"I'm not sure."

"Are you embarrassed?"

I think about it and try to answer that in a way that won't put that panicked look back in her face, and *we'll never be embarrassed in front of one another because I'm going to watch you shit on a table while birthing our children and you will be picking me up from my colonoscopies* won't cut it. "No, I don't think that I would be embarrassed to do anything in front of you."

"Wait," she says suddenly, taking the spatula from my hand and placing it on the counter. She turns me around, and the ease and the familiarity of it is almost painful. "Let's make a video!"

"Right now?" I consider my whole rig. "We don't have time. We gotta be out of here in an hour, and I can't get all my camera stuff unpacked and repacked by then."

"Can I use my phone?" Annie is adamant and earnest and enthusiastic about this in a way that I haven't seen before.

"Maybe?"

"What's wrong?" She squints at me before her gorgeous eyes light up like a damn pinball machine. I think this is Impulsive Annie Li. "Can I do it with you?" she asks excitedly.

There is a sudden roaring in my ears. "No."

She frowns. "What do you mean, no?"

No—from this moment forward, I am the only one who is ever allowed to see your naked body. "I don't want you to," I tell her instead.

It's in this moment that I learn that saying *no* to My Annie Li is the equivalent of telling her to *do it, and do it more and harder.*

"Well," she announces to the kitchen, "now I'm doing it. More, and harder."

"I just said 'no.'"

"You promised me 'yes' to everything for the rest of our lives!" she fires back.

There is a new roaring in my ears, and it's the sound of shocked silence as we stare at one another, digesting this thing that has permeated the air around us since I released it last night.

The smile that spreads across my face is slow and measured. "You ready to talk about it?"

She throws the hood of my hoodie on. "Never mind. We don't have to make a video." She tries to move around me to leave the kitchen, but I don't let her.

"We don't have to talk about it right now. But what should the video be about?" I ask her gently, reaching down to the hem of my hoodie and peeling the whole thing off her body, grateful when she lets me. "I just did one on breakfast foods, and this stuff is done already." I rub the various love bites I've left on her body, and the nonsensical animal in me is soothed knowing that anyone who sees her naked body will know she is mine.

Annie melts in my arms. "It has to be fast, right? Easy?" She scans the kitchen. "Coffee? Tea?" Her eyes light up again. "Caffeine Chemistry."

I ponder this, running through factoids in my brain. "There are a bunch of specifics with brewing coffee and tea that I don't remember off the top of my head. Things like water temperature and steep times for different grinds or types of tea. I'd have to look those things up, so I don't think I can just do those things off the cuff." I keep scanning the kitchen. "How about add-ins?"

Annie's already moving through the kitchen, gathering things like a sous-chef hurricane. "Milk," she says, opening the fridge. "Wow. They have whole, skim, half-and-half, oat, and almond."

"That's perfect. Those all do different things that I can talk about."

She moves to various cabinets. "Sugar. Spices?"

"Cinnamon," I say, after a moment. "And cardamom is used in Turkish coffee."

"Oh," she exclaims. She takes one last thing out of the cabinet and slams it on the counter.

"A supersaturated solution." I grin. "Good girl."

Nico

"—HOW DIFFERENT MILKS MAKE COFFEE TASTE better," I say towards the phone that's propped up on the counter.

Annie sits cross-legged on the floor, munching a piece of bacon. She blinks.

I gesture to the containers of milk. "Beginning with dairy: cow's milk contains both lipids and casein proteins. These molecules act as binding agents with bitter compounds—specifically chlorogenic acid lactones and phenylindanes—found in medium to dark roasted coffees. This binding action counteracts the bitterness. Whole milk provides superior mouthfeel and flavor longevity because of its higher fat content. Skim milk provides minimal effect."

"So does this video," I think I hear Annie mutter.

I move on to the oat milk. "Now, with plant-based alternatives, oat milk has the most favorable emulsification characteristics because of its beta-glucan content. The viscosity creates a mouth-coating texture that simulates dairy while adding a toasted, carby sweetness."

Annie is now lying on the floor and staring at the ceiling.

"Soy milk contains a higher percentage of protein relative to other non-dairy options, theoretically enabling similar binding reactions. However, its interaction with acidity at high temperatures results in a higher likelihood of precipitation, which is curdling."

"Are you being punished? Blink twice if this is a hostage situation," she whispers.

"I'm sorry," I can't help but cut in. "Is something wrong, dear sous-chef of mine?"

"This isn't working for me the way I thought it would," she mutters.

"Hundreds of thousands of my fuckin' followers might disagree with you," I shoot back.

"Well, it sucks," she declares.

"Not according to the paycheck."

She stands up suddenly.

Strolls over to me, swaying her hips. Strokes the skin under my belly button on her way past.

I cough.

I don't know what the hell I was expecting, but I am not prepared for this: the sight of her standing naked in my kitchen, light slanting through the blinds and catching on her tattooed skin like she's been shellacked in gold.

She dips those two fingers into the jar on the counter. Love and a little bit of chaos. Brings them to her mouth and licks.

My neurons fire. All of them. At once. I can practically feel the synaptic overload—dopamine, norepinephrine, complete hormonal cascade. It's not fair.

"Tell me more about this," she says, licking a second slow spiral off her finger, like she doesn't already know she's short-circuiting my prefrontal cortex.

"Honey?" I croak.

"You said it's super-something?"

Right. Supersaturated. Focus, Nico.

"Supersaturated solution," I manage, voice automatically slipping into my practiced academic cadence. Safe ground. "Primarily glucose and fructose. Hygroscopic. Antimicrobial. It doesn't spoil because it—"

She sighs, loud and dramatic. Leans against the counter and casual as anything, drags a slow, gleaming smear of honey across her collarbone.

I freeze.

My mouth opens, but nothing comes out. I have a fuckin' doctorate in this shit—these words are supposed to be my thing. But right now? Nothing in my brain works except the primal throb of want. I blink. Swallow. Try to remember the bullet points I had queued up in my head—viscosity, hygroscopicity, aromatic stability—but they all dissolve in the heat of watching the sticky shimmer spread on her skin.

She raises an eyebrow, challenging. Playful and powerful.

And just like that, something clicks.

Annie reads it, too, 'cause that's what she's fuckin' good at. So she presses on, dipping her fingers in the jar again, this time rubbing a stripe of honey over one pierced nipple—slow, deliberate, 'cause she knows I'm already two seconds from losing it. Then the other.

My jaw clenches so hard it aches. So does my dick.

She leans back just a little as she drizzles the last of it lower. Between her legs. Just a hint of amber sheen disappearing into the heat between her thighs.

My control snaps like brittle sugar glass.

I step toward her, slow and deliberate, until her back hits the edge of the counter. Her breath catches, barely, but I feel it. Her body knows before her brain does—she's mine.

"I was gonna talk about how honey retains volatile aromatics," I say, voice low, words dragging like molasses.

"How its glucose-to-fructose ratio affects mouthfeel. How it coats everything it touches."

I skim a finger across the line she's drawn on her collarbone and lift it to my lips. Suck it clean, eyes never leaving hers.

"But now?" I murmur, dropping my mouth to her throat, my breath hot and humid against her pulse. "Now I'm thinking about how I'm going to taste it off your perfect skin, inch by inch."

She exhales, shaky. Sweet fuckin' music.

"Messy girl," I say, dragging my tongue along the curve of her collarbone, chasing the trail she left. "I can't wait to clean you up."

I shove the jar aside, grip her hips, and hoist her up onto the counter in one movement. Her legs fall open like an invitation.

I lean in and lick across one sticky nipple, slow and firm, tasting sugar and salt and her skin beneath. She arches into me, lets out this gasping whimper that shoots straight to my cock.

"You know honey is antibacterial?" I murmur against her gorgeous tits before sucking one into my mouth. I make sure to tongue every last drop from her piercing. "It preserves everything it touches. Lucky me."

She tries to pull me in, greedy now, but I don't let her. Hell no. I want her begging.

"Wanna learn something else?" I say, grinning against her sternum as I trail kisses lower. I press her thighs wider, hooking one over my shoulder. My breath ghosts over her slick skin. Beautiful. Mine.

She stares down at me, a glorious, sweet angel of wrath. "Yes, Chef."

That does something to me. A shock of power that would have brought me to my knees if I weren't already on them.

"Honey is hygroscopic," I growl. "Means it draws moisture to it. Makes everything wet as fuck."

"Nico, *plea*—"

I dive in, tongue first, chasing every trace of honey she's left on her body—every inch she's tried to turn into a challenge. She moans, high and ragged, clutching my hair as I lick into her with meticulous precision.

"So sweet, baby," I mutter, relishing in her taste, dragging my mouth up her inner thigh.

"Jesus fucking Christ," she breathes.

"Was he the one who called this the land of milk and honey?" I taste her again, deeper this time, getting all the way in there, sucking and lashing and letting her grind against my face like I was made for it. Because I was. I fuckin' was.

When she finally shatters, when her whole body jerks and writhes and she moans my name like it's the only word she knows, it's then that I yank her to the edge of the counter and plunge myself in hard and deep, start fucking her in the rough, brutal rutting she likes, licking honied Annie from my lips like the feral fuck I've become, the one she's made me.

Annie screams again. It's my new favorite sound after "Nico" and "please."

"And on the sixth day, they made a sex tape," Annie says in the car hours later, fiddling with my phone. "What do you think is the best way to get this from your phone to mine?"

We were a little late leaving the house. Lots of cleanup.

Now we're hauling ass to Miami. This is our last stretch in the small space of this car, this car that we've filled with truth and lies and more truth, hugs and words and more hugs. And sex tapes.

"Dunno, sweetheart. Try the drop thing."

She fiddles some more. "Done."

"Just make sure no one sees it," I remind her. After very little consideration, I decided not to post the video to *Naked-Reactions*.

Annie's silent.

I look over, and she's vibrating with tension. Her eyes brighten again. Hello, Impulsive Annie Li.

"What if we posted it?" she exclaims.

"Huh?"

"We could post it to your page and make people pay more for special access!"

I frown at her. "I don't want that."

"Why not?" she demands to know.

"Why do *you* want it?" I push. "This seems like something Sister Annie would douse with holy water."

She flinches. But then she breathes in, slow and steady, like she's trying something on.

"Sister Annie is tired," she says quietly. "She's been tired for a long time. And she's not wrong, she just... never lets me want anything."

I stay quiet. Let her speak.

"She thinks she's protecting me," Annie goes on, staring out the windshield. "Every bad decision I've ever made, she shows up after like the fucking angel of regret. No sex, no shame, no ridiculous ideas allowed. She doesn't trust me. She doesn't think I know what I'm doing with my own life. She thinks I should be ashamed of everything I've done. And maybe for a while, and maybe for some things, she was right. I didn't. But..."

Her voice falters. Then steadies.

"I don't think this is a mistake. It's fun."

I swallow hard.

Annie glances over, eyes sharp but vulnerable. "You know what's different? I don't want to post a sex tape to blow my life up or get someone back or prove I'm hot. I just... You make me feel—"

There's a beat of silence. The kind that hums in your spine.

"Maybe Sister Annie needs to die," she finally says, not finishing the rest of that damn sentence, even if I'm dying to hear it. "Because real Annie wants to live a little."

I grin, deciding to let it go for now. "You want to make a sex tape *and* a point."

She flashes a smile, crooked and reckless and soft. "Exactly."

I let out a low whistle. "You're wild."

"I'm getting better," she says, too quickly. "And maybe it's not a bad thing."

I reach across the console, hook my pinky through hers. "Yeah," I murmur. "I'm trying to, too."

She grins down at our hands. "So... we post it?"

I laugh, loud and startled, because of course she circles right back to insanity. "Annie. I'm not ready."

"Fine," she says. "I'll wait." She drums on the door with her fingers. "Why don't you show your face or tell anyone who you are or use your real voice?"

"Isn't it obvious?"

Annie shakes her head.

"Well... a bunch of reasons," I admit. "Didn't want to lose my PhD or postdoc spot, although that's over in a month. Didn't want my mom knowing that I paid her bills by showing my dick for money. And I guess... It's just embarrassing. I mean, I'm embarrassed." I shrug. "Plenty of adult entertainers own it. I don't."

"So no one knows?" Annie is incredulous.

"Except for you."

"Except for me," she breathes. "Not your sister, best friends, exes? No one?"

"No one, Annie. That's why I've had such short-lived relationships. I could never be completely honest with any of my partners about what I do. I would keep waiting and waiting for the day they would somehow stumble across a video and be like—I know that body, that tattoo, that kitchen. It was just constant deception and anxiety on my end, so I would end it. It wasn't fair to them." I wasn't being fair to myself, in a way, either.

I can tell that she has the beginning of that look in her eyes, so I choose my next words carefully. "You're the only one in the entire world who knows, Annie, because you're the only one I've ever felt comfortable telling." I give her this.

I didn't choose carefully enough, because Annie's little body locks up.

"Nuh uh," I tell her, reaching over and grabbing the strings of my hoodie and tugging. "Don't you dare kick me out. I just got here. Just take that at face value, Annie. Don't overthink it. But we're gonna have to talk about it. 'Cause something is happening here, and you fuckin' know it."

She tries to pull away, and I think the only way to keep her is to give her more of myself.

"I just can't help but think of my dad," I give her, and the tension leaves her body.

She peers over at me with new concern in her eyes. "He'd be proud of you," she says firmly, and this right here is why I'm doomed.

I shake my head. "I loved the fuck out of him. He was never shy with his support. Constantly telling me how proud he was of me and my sister, of how smart we were, how successful we would be. Valentina didn't always do too hot in school, but she still got the same sort of praise any time she improved her grades. He was such a good guy, and I really did love making him proud. But he was... a pretty traditional guy."

"In what way?"

"In like a... go to Mass every Sunday way. Pretty socially conservative. FDNY." I shrug. "And the worst part is, if he ever did find out I had a porn channel, he would never reprimand me about it. He'd just be quietly disappointed." Which would be worse.

Annie drums her fingers on the door again, digesting this. When she speaks, it's with conviction. "I don't think I ever met your dad, but if he's anything like your mom, or what I remember of your mom twenty years ago, then he'd be proud as hell. Your mom got sick, you didn't follow your dreams to go to Cornell or whatever, you settled for somewhere at home because your mom needed you. What dad wouldn't be proud of that? And then you paid for her medical bills, Nico. What was that, like tens of thousands of dollars?"

My mouth is a flat line.

"Wow, okay. More. But it doesn't matter. What if you hadn't done that? What would your mom be doing now?"

"We'd figure it out another way."

"Yeah, and she'd be stressed as hell and maybe that would lead to another medical issue."

I mull this over. "Yeah. Maybe."

"I've already told you this, but I think what you're doing is cool as fuck. And I think you should own it. When do you finish with your postdoc?"

"In a month."

"Would you consider putting your name on the cookbook then?"

"Nope."

Annie glares at me. I feel it in the side of my skull. "You can't tell me you want my name on the book without yours. It's our book, Nico."

I search for her hand and bring it to my face, kiss her knuckles. "I'll think about it." But definitely not.

"You're not gonna think about it," she pouts.

"How do you know?"

"Because I know you."

I nod. "You do. You do know me. More than anyone else. And vice versa. And that's what we're gonna have to talk about at some point between here and Miami."

She doesn't answer.

"You have me, Annie. All of me."

TWENTY-FOUR

Annie

———

"GET THOSE FUCKIN' SHORTS OFF," NICO GRUNTS AS he pulls onto a dirt patch in the middle of some trees in the middle of nowhere. I do as I'm told seconds before he puts the car in park and hauls me over the center console to straddle him.

It's just too easy to distract him from things that are hard. Just make him hard.

I find and meet his mouth immediately, groaning when our teeth collide when his tongue licks in and searches the inside of my mouth to meet mine. We fly back as Nico pulls the lever under his seat, moving us as far back as it goes, tearing his mouth away only to rip off my hoodie. He's hard—so hard already, and I'm already panting for it, grinding down and feeling the heat of him through his shorts and my panties while his hands squeeze my ass in delightful points of pain.

"I need it," I exhale the second we come up for air. "Faster. Please, please—"

He shoves me back against the steering wheel, balancing me on his knees while he manages to get his shorts and boxers down.

Then, "Nico?" echoes through the car speakers.

We freeze.

"Hello?" Tom's stupid fucking voice reverberates against all the windows.

Fuck. *Fuck*. I reach behind me blindly to start pressing random buttons on the steering wheel to hang up the call, when Nico traps both my hands behind my back.

He grins at me, pupils dilated and sparkling with evil delight. "Hey, man," Nico answers.

Oh, *hell* no. I try to rip my hands out of his grasp, but his fingers hold tighter.

"Hey! Just wanted to see how your trip was going. You driving now?"

Nico reaches over himself with his free hand. He pulls his seatbelt out as far as it will go until it locks with a *snap*. He brings it behind my back.

Be good, he mouths, and I halt all movement.

"Nah, not driving right now," he says.

I feel him wrap the belt around my wrists, fidgeting with it, his eyes locked on mine in question.

I nod.

When he lets go, all the slack gets pulled back with a series of *clickclickclicks*, and I am trapped. My wrists are entirely immobilized.

"Ah. Good. Where are you right now?"

Nico tugs up my shirt, baring my tits. "Not sure," he says. "Bumblefuck, Florida, I think." He licks at a nipple with the flat of his tongue, jiggling and bouncing it before pulling it into the heat of his mouth.

I try to be good, but a whimper leaves my throat.

He pinches the other one in punishment.

I try harder to swallow it down this time, and I'm rewarded. He draws me over him with two large hands at my ass.

"How's traveling with the spawn of Satan for a week been?"

I frown but keep my mouth shut.

"I dunno, man," Nico begins with a pleased smile, his hand drifting down between us to pull my underwear to the side, sliding his fingers back and forth and across my slit, spreading my wetness all over me before slathering some on himself. He draws me down.

"I think she's being—" I feel the thick head of him pushing against my entrance,

"—really," he pulls me down onto his cock, sheathing himself with my pussy slowly, so fucking slowly, watching my face the entire time,

"—really," there's still a burn, a stretch he's learned I love, and he forces past until he's seated to the hilt,

"—good."

He must read something on my face because he reaches behind me and jabs at a button on the steering wheel a half second before I come. Very, very loudly.

I get a sharp spank on the side of my ass, and that combined with the cut of the seatbelt into my wrists only adds hot, tingling fire to the warmth of the orgasm spreading through my core.

"Fuck," I sob. "Yes, it's so good. I'm so sorry, I'll be good, I'll be good."

"It's okay, Annie," his soothing words a sharp contrast to the way he now manhandles me back and forth, ogling my bouncing tits. "It's okay. This dick is just too nice. You tried your best, honey," he murmurs.

"I did," I breathe, relishing in the wet sounds filling the space of the car, the overwhelming feeling of full and stretched and *used*, "I tried."

"Lean back," he orders suddenly. "Use the seatbelt as leverage and grind it. Roll that tight little body—*yes*," he hisses, when I do. "Make it all better for me, Annie. Good girl —just like that."

He watches where I move on him, where he's filling me, for the span of several minutes, all before shoving his thumb in my mouth and getting it wet. He brings it down to my clit and starts rubbing circles in tandem with my movements.

"Yeah, girl. Give it to me. Make me come. Fuck me up, Annie," he groans into my ear, angling his hips just *right* and using my body with both his big hands clenched tight on my ass. "Chase it—yes—fuck yes, I feel it. You're gonna make me come, *fu—*"

I lose all bodily control on the second one, leaning down and latching onto his shoulder with my teeth, just for something to hold on to, legs twitching like mad, mindless writhing, cold then hot, while he shouts with his own release, pulsing endlessly inside me.

Nico wraps me in his arms while I pant against his neck and consider incorporating some cardiovascular exercise into my weekly routine. I feel a hand leave my back, and then:

"Hey. Sorry, man," Nico says. "Must have gotten disconnected. Service is spotty here."

I sink my teeth into his neck. He shakes with silent laughter.

"No worries. Anyway, you were saying? How's the week with the crazy twin?"

"I was actually saying it's been really good," Nico replies, voice calm but firm. He turns to me, his hand cupping my chin with surprising gentleness, and tilts my face to his. "Amazing, actually," he says, eyes locked on mine. "She's fucking incredible."

"Wait a second," Tom says. "Have you guys fucked this week?"

I freeze.

And furiously shake my head.

"We—" Nico begins.

"If you did, I don't hold it against you, bro. And I wouldn't be surprised you fucked her. It's hot as hell to stick your dick in crazy once in a while," Tom drawls.

Nico's still inside me. Currently twitching inside 'crazy.'

The shame hits me like a cold slap of reality, of real life. I move to climb off, humiliated, nauseated, furious at myself. Because I'd forgotten, in this car, on this trip. Of course. I'm the experiment. The story. The one you brag about, not the "for the rest of our lives" one.

But Nico tightens his grip, doesn't let me go. His voice, when it comes, is low and sharp.

"Careful, Tom."

The words hit like a warning shot.

"We're all fuckin' crazy, man. Every last one of us. And turns out, Annie is *my* brand of crazy. She's the fuckin' brilliant kind of crazy. And what you just said? That is not a joke. That is not funny. That's you showing your whole ass."

Tom starts to retort, but Nico cuts him off, eyes never leaving mine.

"You meant something else. So I'm gonna say this once— don't ever talk about her like that again."

He says it to me.

He says it for me.

And he smashes the button on the steering wheel.

"Hey," he says, brown eyes full of concern.

I want to believe him. I do. But even now, even with his hands gentle and his voice fierce, my stomach twists into knots. I'm the fun. The joke. The problem. The one-night story that doesn't fit anywhere in the morning. People like me don't get this kind of defense. Don't get people who say she's mine like it's a promise and not a mistake.

And even if Nico thinks he means it, he doesn't know the full inventory of my chaos. The way I sabotage things, break them.

Maybe he will. Maybe it's only a matter of time.

But then—

He's still looking at me like he sees all of that. And he's not blinking.

"I meant it," he says again, thumb brushing under my jaw. "All of it. In real life, in real time, outside of this damn car and this road trip."

My throat is so tight I can barely swallow. "Why?"

Nico gives the softest huff of breath. It's not a laugh exactly—it's more like a knowing sound. His forehead presses against mine.

"I see all of it," he murmurs. "All of you. And I'm dying, wishing, hoping, praying—that I'm gonna be the lucky motherfucker who gets all of it for himself."

My eyes sting.

And for a split second—just one—I believe him.

Before my phone starts ringing on my seat.

And it's my sister.

———

"Annie. What's happening?" she asks the second I pick up.

I blow out a breath, pace *way* away from the car. Try really hard to keep my shit together and not burst into tears.

Because of course she's calling me about this. The day before her wedding weekend, and I've become A Problem Again. She should be finalizing flower arrangements or getting her nails done, not checking to see if her maid of honor is fucking something up. And I am. I did. God, what the hell is wrong with me?

"May," I begin slowly. "I'm really, really sorry—"

"What for?!"

I don't know—everything?! For being me. For trying to have some fun, find some equilibrium and messing it up, anyway? I flounder for the right words. There aren't any, so I go with the truth.

"For fucking Nico," I blurt, ripping it out of my throat like it'll hurt less that way. "But it's not—May, it's not just that, I swear. It's not just fucking around. I—." *Too much.* "I'm not being reckless for fun this time. It's not a game."

I'm rambling now, desperate to make her hear it, believe it. "I swear to you, on everything, on my life, I would never let this affect your wedding. I will disappear into the wallpaper if I have to, I will make myself invisible, I will not cause drama, I—"

"Annie—" she interrupts.

"I'm sorry, May—"

"Annie, *stop.*"

I stop pacing, scrub a hand down my face, and brace myself. Here it comes—I've upset her, I messed it all up again, I—

"I wasn't calling to yell at you," May says. Her voice softens, threading in through the cracks of my shame, like she's reaching through the phone and touching the side of my face. "I was calling to make sure you were okay."

I blink. "What?"

"Annie," it comes out as a sigh. "Tom just told me you had sex with Nico, and that you *hate* him. I want to make sure you're *okay.*"

I short-circuit.

"I'm so, *so* sorry. I really had no idea you hated him when I asked you to travel with him. I thought you had a crush on him in high school. I really thought I was helping—"

"You were," I cut in. "You didn't do anything wrong—"

"Let me finish," she says firmly.

I clamp my mouth shut.

"That's a huge lift to ask of you, Annie, what the heck? To sit in a car for seven days with someone who hurt you? And I'm freaking out right that you're dealing with it in an unhealthy way because you didn't have a choice, and that is entirely *my* fault."

Her voice breaks on the word "fault," and I feel it crack right down my chest. Tears spring to my eyes, fast and hot and completely unwelcome.

"Annie," she says, and this time it's my name wrapped in so much love it nearly levels me. "I almost feel like you did this because you didn't want me to be upset. That's not right. Now, I repeat my question. Are you okay, or do you want me to get you a train ticket from wherever you are to Miami?"

I glance at Nico over in the car, through the windshield. He's sitting in the passenger seat, fiddling with his phone. He doesn't even look over, but I know he's aware of me, attuned to me in a way that makes everything... too much.

"I'm... okay."

"Annie," May warns.

I drag in a shaky breath. "Plum." I swallow. "I didn't mean to fuck this up. I swear. I didn't come here planning to—" *To what?! Fall in love with my worst enemy?!*

"You didn't fuck anything up," she says quickly. "Fuck what up? My wedding?"

I glance over again. Now Nico's looking at me—really looking. His eyes meet mine through the windshield, and they're soft and unwavering and devastatingly kind. His brow creases, like he knows I'm in a moment. Or, like he's just waiting for me to come back to him.

I swallow and decide to go for a subject change. "Your wedding is going to be perfect. I'm going to make sure of it."

"Annie," she enunciates. "Are you sure you're okay?"

Am I?

"I'm fine," I say with force. "Don't worry about anything other than yourself and your wedding."

"You're not fine." She sighs. "But I'll see you tomorrow, and we are having a long chat. Got it?"

"Got it. I am at your command, dear bride."

I can hear her rolling her eyes over the phone. "I love you."

"Love you."

——————

Am I okay?

When I get back to the car, I don't say anything. I just open Nico's door, climb into his lap, and curl myself up, knees to chest. He doesn't flinch, doesn't question—just wraps his arms around me like it's the most natural thing in the world.

Sitting there for half a second, after six days in this car, I come to a realization.

I'm not afraid here. Not of him, and not of myself.

His chest rises steadily under my cheek. I press my ear to it and try to match his rhythm, absorb this feeling, the feeling of Nico, a cool flow of water down an eternally parched throat.

I could stay like this. I could stay right here. I could be this version of myself—the one who doesn't always break the things she touches, who can finally appreciate her younger self for giving her so many wild, joyful memories... and the grace to walk through the world more gently now.

I'm not just okay.

I'm anchored.

I'm *safe*.

We sit there like that for several moments, my ear against the heart beating solidly under his ribs, my head tucked under his chin.

"I love my sister," I tell the car.

He nods, arms tightening just slightly.

"I hate Tom."

He snorts.

"I hate you," I whisper.

Nico turns my chin, tilts my face up to meet his. He presses a kiss, soft and gentle and knowing, against my lips. "Lie."

TWENTY-FIVE

Annie

THE AIR IN MIAMI IS THICK WITH HEAT AND SALT and the promise of trouble. I step out of the car and take a deep breath, the warm wind curling through my hair like a dare. I adjust my sunglasses and throw Nico a look over my shoulder that says, *What now?* He just smiles, slow and knowing, as he rounds the car to meet me on the sidewalk.

We don't have a plan. That's the point.

I used to live without plans. That was my whole thing—chasing the thrill, making wild decisions, doing whatever the hell I wanted, never thinking past the next hour. And it got me into some serious shit. But it also gave me some of the best stories of my life, and today I find myself feeling... proud of them. And now, here, with Nico's hand warm and steady at the small of my back, it doesn't feel reckless. It doesn't feel like I'm bracing for fallout. It feels like balance, or like maybe spontaneity isn't dangerous when it's built on trust.

And it's not that my brain has gone quiet. It still zings and sparks with all the old ridiculousness. But with him beside me, grinning like mad, I can finally hear the part of me that says, *You're okay. This is good. You're not screwing it up.*

He takes me shopping. Not like a weird sugar daddy—or, you know what, maybe just like that. I think he likes paying for me or taking care of me. But he says, "Let's go get some clothes for dinner."

The boutique we stumble upon is sleek and intimidating in that minimalist, art-gallery way, but Nico makes it easy by giving each mannequin ridiculous names and fake backstories in his fake academic voice. I try on dresses I'd never normally pick. Soft, muted colors. Conservative necklines. But also something gauzy and gold that moves like water when I walk.

He waits outside the dressing room like a carved statue, impossibly gorgeous and annoyingly relaxed, his eyes locked on me with something that makes my stomach dip and my heart ache. When I step out in the gold dress, he doesn't say a word. He just stands, takes my hand, and twirls me slowly in front of the mirror.

And for a second—I see it. What he sees. Not "nothing" or a mess or a problem or a mistake waiting to happen. But someone beautiful. There is someone there in the mirror.

That dress goes into the bag.

I buy him a shirt, too. Crisp white, fitted just right across his shoulders. He grumbles, but he lets me, and there's something so warm in his smile I want to wrap myself in it.

Dinner is at some candlelit spot with oysters on ice and soft jazz playing somewhere just out of sight. We sit outside under tall, lazy palm trees, my bare leg brushing his beneath the table. I order something just because I like the name. He watches me lick aioli off my finger and doesn't bother pretending it's not doing things to him.

We don't talk about anything heavy. Not tonight. I laugh too loudly. My heels pinch, but I don't care. I feel buoyant, like I could float all the way down the block.

We find the club by accident. Music bleeds out into the street, low and hot and magnetic. Inside, it's all hips and rhythm, lights flickering like heartbeat. I hover at the edge of the dance floor, hesitating—until Nico takes my hand.

He doesn't ask. Just pulls me in.

I still don't fucking know bachata. I barely know how to sway with rhythm. But I know the way his hand fits against the small of my back, the way his thigh presses between mine, the way his breath curls against my cheek as we move.

And I let go.

I let myself be led. Let myself be seen. Let myself be the girl who gets spun and dipped and kissed in the middle of a dance floor. I let myself be the kind of girl who dances too close in a hot club in a city she doesn't know, wearing a dress that shimmers and clings and makes her feel golden. And yes, I've done that before, countless times, but never with a man so good. So safe.

There are moments—tiny stabs—where the self-doubt claws back in. *You're too much. He's not going to stay. You're making another impulsive mistake, and you'll regret it, just like always.* But then Nico's lips brush the curve of my shoulder, and that noise quiets down.

I'm not disappearing this time. I'm not shrinking to fit someone else's version of lovable. I'm expanding. Becoming.

I'm having fun.

I trust myself to hold this joy without breaking it.

We dance until our clothes are damp and my feet ache and our mouths are pressed so close together that words aren't necessary.

And when we step back out into the night, the Miami air clinging to our skin, I think:

This.

This is what equilibrium feels like.

The hotel where we're staying, where May is getting married, is absurd. All sleek marble, soaring ceilings, and enough velvet to make a burlesque dancer blush. The suite Nico booked has a balcony with a view of the ocean and a bed that looks like it belongs in a music video. I don't even want to know what this cost.

Nico doesn't brag, though. He just opens a chilled bottle of champagne and pours two flutes like this is something we do all the time.

We're still dressed from the club. I kick off my heels and sink my toes into the plush carpet with a groan. He sits on the edge of the bed, hair a perfect mess, his shirt half unbuttoned, pants unbuttoned and unzipped, skin golden from the dance floor heat.

He pats his lap.

"Come here, sweetheart."

I sit on his lap and notice the giant mirror that spans the opposite wall.

He moves each of my legs on either side of his thighs, my dress riding up as he settles his hands on my hips.

"Look at that," he murmurs, voice thick. "Look how fuckin' good we look together."

I see it. My gold dress glinting in the dim light. His strong hands sliding up my sides. My flushed skin, his blown eyes.

He pulls the straps of my dress down, exposes my breasts. He dips a finger into his glass of champagne and drips it down my neck. The cold shocks me, and then his tongue is there, lapping it up.

"Could live off this," he groans. "Sweet, fizzy, and fuckin' mine."

I can feel the hard steel of him beneath me.

"Watch," he says, indicating to the mirror with his chin. He peels my panties to the side and takes himself out of his pants, cock angrily hard. "Watch," he repeats, and he slides in, and I watch as every inch of him disappears inside me. He doesn't give me time to adjust. Just rocks us both in front of the mirror, gripping my hips, fucking me slow but deep, in and out, each thrust purposeful in the mirror and bouncing my tits like he wants it burned into memory.

"Look," he says again, voice rough now. "This is us. You see that? Look how perfectly we fit together."

I do. Every inch of him, coated in my arousal.

He makes sure I come first and watches my face in the mirror before finishing in me with a growl, pulling me tight to his chest. But he doesn't stop. He slides down and lays me back on the bed, peeling my dress off, throwing it somewhere behind us.

Then he reaches for something.

I don't even see it coming until I hear the soft glug-glug-glug of liquid being poured. Cold champagne streams over my belly, down my thighs, pooling in the softest, most sensitive parts of me. I yelp at the shock.

He disappears between my thighs like a man starved.

Lapping, groaning, drinking our combined release in like it's all nectar and indulgence. Like we're something decadent, meant to be consumed.

His voice is hoarse when he finally lifts his head, lips slick with the both of us.

"We taste good together, too."

I break apart in his mouth.

———

When he tucks me into his arms in a bed sticky with champagne and come, I realize I'm wrong. I am afraid.

This is what fear feels like.

Real fear.

Because this is love.

TWENTY-SIX

Nico

Annie "Whom I Love" Li is gone in the morning.
I check my phone, though, and she's left me a text.

> I've gotta be with May all day today. But
> we'll talk.

> Thank you.

I scrub my face and throw the phone on the pillow next to me, right where her head used to be.

The sheets still smell like her warm and faintly citrusy, sweetened with skin and sweat and the ghost of champagne and sex. The whole room is haunted by her. Her gold dress is draped over the back of a chair. A single heel lies on its side next to the balcony door, like it made a break for it.

God, I love her.

There. I said it! Mentally, at least. Quietly, in the echo chamber of my skull, because it's something I don't know what to do with yet. But it's true.

Annie Li, the girl with impossible compassion and loyalty,

who will defend me to the death. Not just to others—but to myself.

I hadn't realized how small I'd gotten, how much I'd been hiding. From the world, from my family, from the version of myself I didn't want to explain. But she makes me want to be seen again. Not just tolerated—claimed and fuckin' proud.

And not a nameless, faceless, fuckin' porn star, some ghost floating through fuckin' postdoc purgatory. Just a man. A man with his hands on a woman who is somehow too much and not enough and exactly right, all at the same time.

I sink back into the mattress and stare at the ceiling. It's white and perfect and impersonal. It cost me a lot of fuckin' money a night to feel this detached.

And still. There's this tiny, minuscule part of me that's waiting for the other shoe to drop.

Because Annie is... complicated.

Not just emotionally. Though, yes. That too. Her feelings arrive in full technicolor, with their own weather system. But she's also restless in a way that makes my bones ache because I'm afraid I wouldn't be able to keep up if I tried to follow her forever. And what if she doesn't want to be followed? What if she just wants to burn hot and bright and then vanish?

What if I'm just the guy she kissed in a car on a borrowed week?

I sit up and stare at my phone again, like it might cough up some answers.

Seven days.

It's only been seven days.

That's not enough time to know the full story. Not really. Right? There are chapters I haven't read yet. Pages she hasn't let me see. Maybe whole volumes she's burned before anyone could get to them.

And don't I know better than anyone that people are full

of secret selves? Hell, I have one. A whole identity I've kept hidden for years.

I told her everything, though. Not all at once. Not perfectly. But she knows. And she didn't flinch. In fact, she called it hot as fuck.

But what if she's still hiding something from me? What if the next version of Annie is one I don't know how to hold?

But it hasn't only been seven days. It's been nine months, hasn't it? Nine months of Chef and Ali.

I press my palms against my eyes and blow out a breath.

This is what happens when someone cracks you open. When they sneak in through the cracks in your logic and nest there, quietly rearranging the furniture.

Now I'm sitting here, fuckin' alone, wondering if I've fallen for someone who might bolt the second she thinks she's become a burden. Who might sabotage us just to prove she doesn't deserve to be loved.

But damn it—I want her. All of her. I don't just want the easy parts. But wanting it doesn't make it easy.

I'm going to have to work for it. That's the real truth. She's not the kind of woman you win once and coast with forever. She'll test me and push and run as fast as she can. Which probably isn't very fast, but still. I'll have to hold my ground and chase her. I'll have to make it safe for her to come back, every single time.

And some part of me—a tired, cynical part, the part of me alone in this bed right now—wants to ask: Is that what you want, Nico? Are you ready to exhaust yourself for someone who might not stay? Someone who might always think you're just another one of her bad ideas?

But then I remember her face in the mirror. The way she looked with my hoodie as armor, covering the marks I made on her skin underneath. The way she gave herself to me, and the way she is mine.

What's the truth I want to live with?

––––––

The next time I see Annie "Who I'm 99.9% Sure I Love," she is a beautiful, bossy whirlwind of activity.

She flits across the vast, yawning space of the trendy restaurant that is currently holding the welcome party. She's fixing flowers, checking in with her parents, getting them water, getting May drinks, getting Tom drinks (begrudgingly, but still doing it). Asking waiters and waitresses if they need help. Grilling the wedding planner, but in a firm, supportive, *I've got you* way. Stopping to socialize with every single person in this room, putting the "Welcome" in Welcome Party. Drawing everyone in as she does, muttering inside jokes under her breath, making them laugh and stare in awe of this gorgeous, spectacular woman and feel lucky as hell to be granted her genuine attention.

I can't help but smile, because I fuckin' get it.

I spend the first ten minutes here just standing by the bar and watching her. On high alert.

It turns out to be worth it, because there's suddenly a moment, a split second in time, when panic crosses her face while she's talking to May. Something is wrong. And I wait for it... and her eyes fly around the party. Looking for something.

She's looking for me.

I all but shove through the crowd, plowing whoever the fuck over to get to her. And when she sees me, the relief that crosses her face almost brings me to my knees.

I open my arms, and she comes home.

"Nico," she breathes, all the tension immediately leaving her body once it's wrapped up in mine.

I love you, I don't say. "What's wrong, honey?"

She sighs. "Nothing, anymore."

It's on the tip of my tongue to say it.

"May just told me there was a massive miscommunication with some of our cousins." She peers up at me, resting her chin on my chest. "They're all bringing their kids, Nico, and this is supposed to be a child-free wedding. But it's fine. I can handle it."

"You need my help with anything?"

"No," she says firmly. "This is on me. There's a bookstore down the block. I'm gonna go get some books, and we're having story time. They'll probably have crayons and coloring books and arts and crafts, too."

"I'm gonna go get it, Annie," I tell her, with a kiss to her forehead. "Let me."

She shakes her head. "You should be enjoying yourself—"

"Stop. I'm gonna go for you."

"For May. And Tom, you mean."

"Sure," I say. "But mostly for you."

She suddenly has that (previously to me) unreadable look in her eyes. And then, shocking the hell out of me, she says, "I missed you this morning." But the way she says it is almost like a dare.

"Annie. Baby." I'm so relieved that I squeeze her so hard her ribs flex. "This was the worst morning I've had all week."

Her face gets gentle and dreamy. She gets on her tiptoes and presses a soft kiss to my lips. "We'll talk, Nico."

I can't help it. I grab her whole face and make out with her in the middle of this Welcome Party. 'Cause her mouth is throwing a Welcome Party for my tongue.

She finally peels herself away, laughing softly. "Go," and I do.

———

Later, I find myself wandering over to the corner of the room, where Annie is reading to a whole bunch of kids. Because I want to watch Annie interact with kids. For no reason at all.

I am waylaid by Tom.

"Thanks for this, big guy," he tells me, with a slap to the back that sort of misses the mark.

"Welcome," I say, but I don't feel welcome. 'Cause after what he said about Annie in the car?

"So you're fucking Annie," he grins. Leers, almost. His eyes are drooping and unfocused. Jeez. Has this guy always been like this?

"Careful," I warn him, that murder and danger tone coming back into my voice.

"I want *you* to be careful," he slurs. "Outside of getting your dick wet—it's a bad fuckin' idea, Nico," he tells me, leaning over to one side, repeating my own words from just... a few days ago. "She is batshit insane. She is selfish and narcissistic. Main character energy, chaos monster—"

I see red, then black. Rage. I grab his arm. "Listen to me, Tom. If this weren't your fuckin' wedding right now, I would beat the shit out of you." I probably wouldn't, but maybe I would ask Annie to help me set his car on fire. "Never, and I mean *never*, *ever* say shit about her to me or her or your fuckin' fiancé and her fuckin' twin ever again. Do you hear me? Because if you don't, I'm gonna make you fuckin' hear me," I whisper in his ear with an arm wrapped around him and a fake-ass smile pasted on my face. "Because we're not gonna have any problems here. For Annie's sake. For May's sake. Got it?"

Tom frowns at me, a sort of vacant look in his face. He doesn't look like he hears me. He shrugs and walks away.

I blow out a breath and refuse to think about it.

I move towards Annie.

And this is an Annie page I have never read.

She's sitting cross-legged on the floor regardless of her fancy-ass dress, a book open across her knees, six kids practically draped over her, all wide-eyed and slack-jawed. And Annie? Annie's not the sharp, sarcastic woman, or that bold, impulsive, terrible-at-dancing, grouchy force.

She's soft here. Unarmored. Animated.

Her eyes are wide and bright, her hands flying with each sentence like she's physically painting the story into the air for them. Her voice lifts into silly accents and singsong rhythms, and she laughs loud and open and delighted. The kids are rapt. And so am I.

She glows. Not in that sexy, slow-burn, feel-my-wrath way I've gotten used to. This is something easier, more sunshine. Warm. Effortless. Kind.

It hits me all at once how much of herself she's still hiding from the world. From me. How many versions of Annie exist, raw and unexpected and real. How many I haven't even earned yet.

I am so fucked.

"Hey, Nico," May's voice says from next to me.

I snap out of it and go in for a hug. "Hey, you." It's wild how similar she feels to Annie, but also completely different. I could tell them apart with my eyes closed, just by how they felt in my arms. "Congratulations."

She smiles. "Thank you."

We watch her sister as she quacks like a duck and barks like a dog. The tiniest kid is laughing so hard he's barrel rolling across the restaurant floor. Annie looks unbothered, majestic.

"I wanted to apologize to you for making you bring Annie on your work trip, but I'm not so sure I should apologize anymore."

"Yeah?" I mumble, only half paying attention because Annie is currently using the *skin on her arm* to wipe another kid's nose. I am not well. My body is trying to reach towards her on a cellular level, my sperm shouting for her eggs.

May's laugh brings me back from my daydreams regarding the color of our daughter's hair.

I blink. "What?"

"You've been staring at her this whole time like she's just arrived on a bed of sunshine and rainbows."

I finally meet May's eyes. "If you mean clouds of hellfire and darkness and other equally impressive, terrifying things—then, yeah."

May's grin changes into something knowing. "You get it."

"I get it," I say, dead serious.

Her face shifts again, and suddenly... it's Annie's. Not literally, but enough to make me tense. Same tilt of the jaw, same flash in the eyes. She leans in. "Then it's time for me to tell you this," she says, voice low. And murder-y. "Annie is the best person I know. Don't you ever hurt her."

"I won't," I vow, but now I'm a little scared. Jesus. The Li sisters are like a fuckin' Category 5 hurricane. Of knives. "But honestly, I'm worried about the other way around," I admit.

Her face doesn't change. "She will *never* hurt you. Not purposefully. If she does, then it's an accident. But even if she *thinks* she's hurt you, she'll retreat." May seems to grow ten times her size. Did her teeth just get sharper? "And that's when you fight for her, Nico. You fight for her because she deserves it. Because she's worth it."

I rub my arms. Did it drop thirty fuckin' degrees in here? "Okay!" I half-yell. "I will! I promise!"

"Good," she says brightly. "Have fun. Enjoy the ride. I hope to see you at Christmas." She strides away with perfect, delicate posture.

Annie catches my eye and raises an eyebrow in question.

I love you and I will fight for you, I try to say with my eyes. She smiles.

———

Towards the end of the party, I decide to treat myself to a scotch. Something peaty and sharp, methinks. I'm halfway through mentally sorting the shelf by distillation method when I spot him.

It's that big, handsome, goofy fucker who I owe my millions to—Charlie Fischer.

He's leaned against the bar, half-slouched, dress shirt rumpled, sleeves pushed up. Drunk. Like, capital-D Drunk. His eyes are aimed at something directly across the room.

"Charlie," I say, clapping a hand on his shoulder. "How's it hangin'? And I don't mean literally," I add, tipping my head toward his crotch.

Because Charlie Fischer is a porn star. A real one. A real-life sex worker, who has sex on camera for money. And he's one of those people who own it. So much so that he recommended it to me a few years after I had just moved home to be with my mom, had started my PhD program, and was severely strapped for cash. We were out at a bar with May, I think, maybe a year after he and May had broken up, once they were in the 'comfortable friend-zone.' He'd always been a chaotic sort with a hundred different jobs, an artist and philosopher and wanderer and model and bartender, and he had just stumbled into the porn industry (filming for *Harlot*) and was raking it in. He took one look at me and told me I could do well on their new subscription-based creator content platform.

Never got to thank him for it, though, 'cause I ain't telling anyone. Except Annie.

He blinks over at me, slow and glassy. "Nico. My man." His grin is loose and toothy. "He's been hangin' in private. I've been out the game for a bit now."

Huh. "Nice. Why'd you get out?"

He shrugs and takes a healthy swig of his drink.

"Whatcha drinkin'?"

"What aren't I drinking?"

"Touché. Nice of May to throw us a classy-ass, top-shelf party."

He hums. "May did good," he replies. It's quiet and the opposite of what I'm used to from him. Neutral, and maybe resigned, and I've never known Charlie to be neutral about anything.

I nod, even though he's not really talking to me. I follow his gaze—May is dancing now, in a cute white dress, smiling as her wasted fiancé tries to spin her in a circle. Elegant. Collected.

Some things click into place in my head. "She looks happy," I offer.

Charlie mutters something that sounds suspiciously like, "Does she?" under his breath. He lifts his glass in a lazy, saluting motion, like maybe he's toasting her or maybe he's warding off a punch to his stomach. "She was always gonna end up like this. Stable and centered." He doesn't clarify; instead, he takes another big gulp of whatever brown substance is in his glass.

"I saw you with Annie earlier," he says, changing the subject with the subtle grace of a wrecking ball. He smiles, and this one is genuine. "Pretty different from the last party we were all at."

I laugh. "Yeah, we didn't set anything on fire this time, so I'd call that progress. We spent the last week together road-tripping here."

A ghost of a smile now. "Annie's got that thing," he says. "She's like me."

I look at him.

"She's fucking anarchy. She's fire," he adds. "Annie. You don't date a woman like that to settle down. You date her to burn through a phase of your life."

Why is everyone testing me tonight? "You don't know her," I warn.

He doesn't push. Just shrugs. "Neither did you, a week ago, seems like."

Fair. But unfair, too.

"Sorry," he murmurs.

I nod.

A long pause stretches between us.

He drains his glass and sets it down on the bar. Then turns and studies me. "You think you can build something real with someone so messy?" He seems genuinely interested in knowing the answer.

I shrug. "I think everything's complicated. It's just a matter of whether it's worth dealing with."

He nods slowly. "Huh."

I watch Annie gathering flower arrangements and throwing them in boxes while complimenting the wedding planner on tonight's success. And I come to a conclusion.

"Maybe," I say, more to myself than to him, "stability isn't peace and quiet. It's staying. It's choosing someone. Again and again, even when it's messy. *Especially* when it's messy."

Charlie looks away. "That's a nice idea."

"It's not an idea," I say more firmly. "It's a plan." *A tentative one, but still.*

He blinks slowly. "You're serious, then."

"And you're full of shit."

He laughs, and it's a real one. Tired and a little grateful. He raises his glass, eyes a little clearer now. "To anarchy, then," he says.

I clink my glass against his. "And to the people who make it feel like home."

Home. A place where I'm safe and protected and unafraid. I take a deep breath, and from this new place, the one Annie helped me find, the anarchic fortress she let me into, I decide that maybe... I should give something a shot.

"Hey," I say, shifting awkwardly on my stool. "I never said thanks."

He raises an eyebrow. "For what?"

"For the *Harlot* suggestion," I admit, scratching the back of my neck. "You said I'd do well. You were right."

His brow lifts a little higher. "You actually did it?"

I nod once. "Yeah. PhD wasn't paying, Mom got really sick, bills started stacking up, rent was high—I needed to. But it turned out... I was good at it. Made real money. Kept it quiet. Still do."

Charlie whistles, low and impressed. "Well shit. Must have left before you got big. Good for you, man. Proud of you."

I huff out a laugh, surprised by the rush of relief I feel. I'm not even sure what I was expecting. Judgment? Mockery? But of course not. It's Charlie. He's a very, very famous porn star.

"You ever regret it?" I ask.

Charlie doesn't react right away. He just rolls the empty glass between his palms, eyes back on May across the room. "Yeah," he finally says. "But not for the reason you think." He shakes his head. "Does Annie know?"

"Annie's the only person I've told," I say after a beat. "She didn't flinch. Said I shouldn't be ashamed of any of my choices. Should be proud of them, even."

Charlie nods slowly. "That's a good woman, man."

My chest swells. Not just with love, but with something sharper and quieter beneath it. Permission. Not to change, but to stay and to grow around the things I used to hide.

"Yeah," I agree. "She is."

He looks at me again, more sober now. "So what's the issue?"

That one takes me a minute.

"Because being proud of something means I have to admit

it matters," I finally say. "And if it matters, then it's not just something I did. It's... part of me."

Charlie lets that settle. Then he claps me on the back, harder than necessary.

"Congrats," he says. "You're officially in the emotional nudity stage. Way scarier than the full-frontal kind."

I bark out a laugh. "No shit."

"You gonna tell more people?"

"Maybe."

He grins. "Start small. Like your mom."

I grimace. "Jesus."

"She loves you. She'll be fine."

"Would you be?"

"Hell no," he says cheerfully. "But I'm not a mom. I'm just the porn star who accidentally talked a PhD student into becoming one, too."

———

I catch her in the hallway leading to the bathroom and press her against the wall. "Hey."

"Hi."

"Wanna come back to my room?" I say into her mouth.

Her entire body shivers. "I do, but I told May I'd stay with her tonight. She's sleeping in my room because Tom's a wreck."

I groan so loudly I ruffle the hair on the top of her head. "Fine."

She looks up at me, almost shy. "I also think it would be good for us to spend a night apart. Really think things through."

"I've thought it through, Annie."

She plays with the buttons on my shirt. I notice she's

covered up my hickeys with makeup, which makes me unreasonably upset.

"But what if you're wrong?" she asks quietly. Fragile Annie Li.

I blow out a breath. "Here it is, honey. I l—like you. Really like you," I decide this is a normal thing to say to a Currently Scared Annie Li, With Whom You Fell in Love With in the Span of a Week. "And I think you like me too, but you don't know what to do with those confusing things called... fuzzy feelings. But we're always gonna figure it out. And I'm going to prove to you, over and over again, that I am not wrong."

Some infinitesimal part of her relaxes, but her face doesn't change. "It's only been a week, Nico," and I know what she means.

No matter.

I'm gonna fight for it, and it begins today.

"It's been months, Ali," I remind her gently. "And even so, it's only a tiny fraction of the rest of our lives."

Annie blinks at me like an owl.

"Annie."

We look back over my shoulder. It's her dad. He says something in Cantonese.

When I look back at Annie, she has already retreated behind her force field of barbed wire. It's actually fuckin' terrifying how quickly that happened.

"I gotta go bring my parents home," she mutters to me. "After the wedding, okay? We'll talk."

"Annie, honey."

She lifts up and gives me a peck on the lips. "Later." She walks away.

Leaving me, forcing me... to really think it through.

TWENTY-SEVEN

Annie

May and I lay under the covers in my giant bed, eating Pocky and watching a reality television show where everyone shouts at each other.

"Ready to talk about it?" she asks, as we watch a piece of bread fly towards another cast member.

I groan.

She opens her arm. I curl into her side without hesitation, like I've done since we were little. Same dynamic, same comfort, just with more adult problems and better snacks.

"I don't know how to do this," I mumble into her shoulder.

"Do what?"

"Not fuck it up," I admit.

She doesn't push. Just rubs my arm in those long, even strokes she's perfected since childhood. She used to do this when I'd lose my mind after getting in trouble—when I'd scream at our mom for being cruel, when I'd take the fall for May's broken vase or missing homework because I could absorb the punishment better than she could.

"I don't know how to be in something that isn't already

halfway to disaster," I whisper. "I only know how to crash into things. Not keep them."

May stays quiet, which is how I know she's really listening.

"I like him," I say, then exhale. "I really, really, really like him."

May raises an eyebrow.

I ignore her because she knows exactly what I mean.

"And it's been—what, a week?" I continue. I don't mention the months of Ali and Chef. "That's ridiculous. It's ridiculous even for me. And that's saying something."

May makes a soft sound in her throat. But she stays calm. Always calm.

I keep going because if I stop, I'll lose my nerve.

"Something in me is screaming that he's just another one of my flaky, self-destructive choices. That I'm just doing what I always do—jumping into something dramatic because I'm bored or sad or lonely. That I picked the hot guy with a weird job and good dick because I thought it would be a good story or because I liked the chaos."

"You think Nico is chaos?"

"No," I say instantly. "That's the thing. He's not. He's... good. He's stable and safe. Kind. And I don't know what to do with someone like that." I pause, fingers fiddling with the Pocky wrapper. "He's the kind of person who makes careful decisions. Who thinks about other people." I look at the television, where something else goes flying across a table and towards a head. "I think he's the first person I've ever liked for who he is. Not for what he can do for me."

I stare up at the ceiling, overwhelmed by the weight of everything I feel.

"What if I ruin it?" I whisper. "What if I scare him off? What if he figures out I'm not actually funny or hot or interesting—I'm just crazy and exhausting and high maintenance and dramatic? Or that I'm too loud or cranky or cry too much. Or just *too much*? What if he realizes I'm not a partner, I'm a liability?"

May finally pulls back enough to look at me. She's got that look on her face, the one that says I am your sister and also your fiercest advocate, so shut the fuck up with that nonsense.

"Annie," she says, steady and certain. "You've always been a lot. You know that."

"Thanks."

"I mean it in the best way. You've always been full-volume, full-color. Big feelings, big loyalty, big everything. You've always been big enough to take up space for both of us."

My throat tightens. "That sounds suspiciously like *exhausting, high maintenance, dramatic, loud—*"

"It means you're fierce. You feel everything, and instead of shrinking from it, you use it. You turn it into fun and love and protection and wildly inappropriate reactions."

I let out a watery laugh.

And I feel a piece of me heal.

May's voice softens. "Nico isn't scared of you. He watched you today like he wants all of it. Like he was so lucky, like you're the best thing that's ever happened to him. He's a great guy—he deserves someone who loves and protects like you do. And *you* deserve that kind of love more than anyone in the word."

I nod. Because maybe... I do.

We fall silent again for a moment. The TV blares in the background—someone screaming about betrayal and hair extensions—but there is a kind of quiet that isn't silence so much as a shift in temperature.

"I know that you love me. And... I know what you've done. But..." she swallows. "I want you to stop."

I rear back. "What?"

"You made yourself big so I could be small."

I blink at her.

"You were the lightning rod, so I didn't have to be," she says. "You took up all the air so I could breathe without being noticed. I didn't get yelled at because you were already screaming. I didn't get questioned because you were already in trouble. You made it easy to be the good one, because you took all the heat."

I feel my throat tighten. "I wanted to."

"Did you, Annie? Did you really? At the expense of your own happiness? Sacrificing yourself over and over again—"

"I could take it, and I *wanted* to, May—"

"You were protecting me. You always have. But also sometimes... protecting me meant making all my choices for me. Even when I didn't know it."

I flinch a little.

May notices, but she doesn't stop. "I let it happen. I liked that I didn't have to be messy. I liked knowing you'd always stand in front of me if something went wrong. I liked being good."

There's something bitter at the edge of her voice. Not about me—but about the cost of all that goodness.

"But I've lived my whole life by the rules because I was afraid of what would happen if I didn't. Afraid of being like you. Afraid of what would happen if I weren't good. If I didn't make the 'right' choice."

There's a long pause. "He's the right choice for me," she says eventually.

Tom. She doesn't have to say it. I read the name on her face.

"He's... safe."

There's that word again, but it carries a vastly different weight than the way I just used it to describe Nico. Because "safe" got wasted the night before his wedding and is god knows where right now.

She stares at the television, her expression glassy. "He's predictable. Respectable."

And suddenly, I see it. The shape of her life. The rigid outlines she's drawn around herself so nothing unexpected can slip in. The lines that have kept her calm, composed, reliable.

She picked a path. And now she's walking it with her eyes closed.

I reach out and hook my pinky around hers. "You know I'd murder him and make it look like an accident if you asked me to, right?"

A smile ghosts across her lips. "I know. But please don't. I'd like tomorrow to be drama-free, please."

We fall silent again. The TV's still loud, someone's still screaming about betrayal and extensions, but it all feels very far away.

I stare at the ceiling.

I'm thinking about Nico. About how good it felt to be safe with someone and still fully myself.

And I'm thinking about May. About how maybe I've spent so long protecting her that I never gave her the space to learn what she really wants. Maybe she thinks love is what happens when no one yells. Maybe she thinks respectability is the same thing as happiness.

She deserves more than that. We both do.

But it's not my place anymore. I don't need to protect her. She can make her own choices. Even if they're ones I wouldn't make.

Even if they break her heart.

Even if they break mine.

———

We wake up to room service knocking on the door. Yes, I ordered us room service in advance, because I am the most honorific of all maid of honors ever. I hop out of bed before May even opens her eyes and let the woman in.

She rolls in a cart full of all of May's favorite breakfast foods.

May sits up in the bed, only for me to tackle her right back into it. "It's your big day, you big, beautiful bride, you. Congratulations."

There is a minor scuffle while she attempts to shove me off of her, but I latch onto her waist, pull open her robe, and blow a raspberry right on her belly.

She screams. "Get off me," she shrieks, but she's smiling.

The day is gorgeous outside our window. The sun is shining bright, and the sky is blue with a smattering of clouds. It's really not a bad day for a wedding. I start popping lids off of the platters and uncover a tiny jar of honey that makes my insides feel like gooey warmth. Or honey, I guess.

"Tom's okay," May announces from the bed, looking at her phone. "He and the other groomsmen will come down to the big suite after they're done getting ready."

"What constitutes getting ready?" I ask, unable to resist dipping a finger in the honey pot and taking a lick. "Drinking from matching flasks? Smoking illegal cigars?"

She shrugs. "I don't really want to think about it."

"Then don't think about it," I tell her. "It's your perfect day, Plum."

———

Getting Ready is *fun*. Even if it's hours of hair and makeup and *giggling*, I'm having fun. Even if my mom is here, wearing her fake maternal smile that tricks everyone into thinking she's an adorable little old Asian woman. Even if May's bitchy friend Elodie keeps making snide remarks about every tiny little detail. But Izzy's here, and the rest of the bridal party are great, so loving, and a hilarious bunch to be around. I'm so happy for May, to have found her people. Her girls.

There's an energy, a camaraderie that exists in the air. A little bit of nerves, a lotta bit of love and excitement. It only increases after five hours of Getting Ready. I could be into this. I take some notes. For no reason, and for no person at all.

But I do text that person to come up to the suite with Tom and the groomsmen and the rest of our family for pictures.

"Annie, sit down for a second," May calls from across the room, while I'm checking her hanging *qi pao* for wrinkles and texting with the wedding planner for the eighteenth time to make sure everything's okay and *is she sure she doesn't need any help* and *you're sure the string quartet has arrived to the hotel?* "Relax," she laughs, consummately calm.

I take deep, centering breaths and force myself to look at my sister.

Immediately, I begin to bawl my eyes out—huge, dramatic crocodile tears. "You look so beautiful," I sob. "I can't believe it. You're so perfect and amazing. Look at you." She's so radiantly gorgeous I can barely breathe. Her hair in soft waves framing her face just right, makeup impeccable. Her dress makes her look like the Goddess of all the Sparkly Princesses.

May just grins at me.

"Annie," my mom says in Cantonese, "stop making a scene." She says this in a bright tone, with a smile, so no one else realizes she's shitting on me.

May and I ignore her. "Watch your makeup," May tells me.

"This shit isn't going anywhere," I assure her, dabbing at my face. "It's like permanent marker has been shellacked onto my face, but it still manages to look naturally effortless. This bitch right here is a queen. *Kuh-ween*." I point to one of the makeup artists, Vanessa, who smirks.

I squint at her. "Do you do weddings in New York City? Or maybe Durham? North Carolina? Never mind."

May shrieks with laughter, and I think it's my favorite sound in the universe.

"Shush," I tell her anyway, feeling my cheeks get hot.

Izzy is suddenly standing next to me. "No," she says.

"Yes," May tells her.

"No," I say firmly. "Stop looking at me like that, Iz," then, "Get away from me, Iz," when her wide eyes are inches from my face.

She punches me in the arm.

"*Ow.*"

"Shut up," Izzy laughs. "Really?" she asks May.

"Really," May replies.

"No," Izzy repeats.

"Yep," says May.

"No," I insist.

"This one just couldn't get anything right," Elodie the horrible one says out of nowhere, indicating to Rosalia, the other makeup artist. "I had to do it myself."

I don't even blink. "Yeah, well, maybe the problem's not the artist. Maybe your face just rejects beauty."

May coughs hard to cover a laugh.

Izzy doesn't bother and cackles like a witch. "Rosalia could make a potato look luminous. But she's not a magician," she adds on for good measure.

Rosalia tries to hide her grin.

"Excuse you?" Elodie says to us.

"You're excused." I smile. "You're free to take a walk. I hear nature is healing. Maybe some fresh air will fix your face."

Elodie mutters something under her breath that sounds

like "fucking bitches," but she grabs her bag and strides out of the room.

Izzy waves.

I whirl towards May. "What the hell?"

May sighs. "I know. She's Tom's best friend. I had to include her. She's not usually this bad."

"Want me to slice up her dress?" I ask.

"Nope."

"Break one of her heels?" Izzy offers.

"Nuh uh."

"Cut off a piece of her hair?" I try.

"I'm good."

"Because we will," I assure her.

"I know you will—that's why I'm good." May smirks. "No problems, remember?"

"But *she's* the prob—"

"Annie."

"Fine."

"Your tea ceremony is in an hour," Michelle, one of the bridesmaids, announces. "Is everyone ready?"

I glance around the room. "No! We are *not* ready." I start moving around the room and start tidying, cleaning, hiding things, putting things away. "The photographer is coming to take pictures of all of us before that. We've gotta make it look nice."

May stands.

"No," Izzy reprimands. "We'll clean. You sit and look beautiful."

May sits, and the rest of us get to work.

Half an hour later, there's a knock on the door. We all squeal. Apparently, I squeal now.

The boys walk in, and I immediately look for—

Wow.

Wow.

Is the world tilting on its axis?

Why is my mouth so dry?

Are those angels singing?

I'm still gaping like a fish when Izzy brushes past, throwing a smirk back at me.

"Hey, Nico," she purrs. "You clean up real ni—*ouch*."

Izzy inexplicably flies sideways several feet.

"Was that an actual hiss?" She is cracking the fuck up with her hands on her knees, but I do not know what is so funny. "Did you just hiss at me?"

"Mine," I hiss at her, before walking towards My Worst Fuckin' Nightmare but Wettest Fuckin' Dream Wearing the *Fuck* Out of a Tux. And the smile that he's shining down on me is filled with adoration, devotion, a little bit of shock, and a whole lotta... love.

"Hey, Ali," he grins.

"Hi, Chef," I say, and I pull him down to my mouth by the lapels of his hot-as-fuck tux.

We are getting very reacquainted with each other's tongues when I hear my dad's voice call my name in a sharp rebuke.

We ignore him, but we pull away a fraction, our noses and foreheads still touching.

"It's not fair," I tell Nico, stomping my foot a little. "It's uneven. You can't just *look* like this. I don't look as good as you do in formalwear."

The tux is cut perfectly, accentuating the width of his shoulders and the strength in his arms and his thighs. His face is freshly shaved, revealing the line of his jaw, and his hair is styled to perfection. Is that *pomade*?

"Nah," he says. "You look better. Fuckin' beautiful, honey." He traces a thumb along my cheek, runs a hand through my hair. Twirls me around by the hand once to check out my ass, presumably. There he goes, making me feel things like *precious* and *enchanting* again. He leans in close to my ear. "But I much prefer you wearing nothing but me."

Are my legs broken? Do I need to change my underwear?

"Where's Tom?" May calls from somewhere behind us.

Nico's smile is tight when he looks back at May. "He said he'd meet us here. Had to check something on the roof for the ceremony."

I whip my head back to her face just in time to see a crack in her perfect, unflappable expression.

She bites her lip.

"I'll go get him," I declare.

"I'm going with her," Nico loftily proclaims.

"*No.*" I put a hand up in the *halt* position. "I have to go to my room to get my clutch, too—"

Nico raises his eyebrows.

"*Definitely* no. Then we will all be very late for photos."

"That sounds like a challenge," he whispers.

"It's not. It's a fact."

"I should inform you," he says, deadly serious now, "that I am extremely competitive. Mathletes, remember? Science Olympiad? Speed, time—"

I bolt. "Stay away from me, nerd!"

His laughter echoes behind me.

I start on the roof patio where the ceremony's being held, but I don't find him. What I do find is... well, magic.

The whole rooftop has been transformed into a kind of floral dreamscape. The arch is massive, built entirely of blush and cream flowers, vines twisting together. There are tiny white flowers woven into the backs of the chairs. Gauzy drapes float in the breeze, soft and translucent and impossibly elegant. Everything is delicate and romantic and expensive in a subtle, effortless way. I definitely don't take notes.

a rooftop in bloom—
so soft it nearly shatters.
love tucked
into every petal,
every ribbon of wind.
an altar at the edge of sky.
forever
doesn't feel so far.

Nice, Annie, I compliment myself.

I clock the string quartet tuning near the glass railing, their instruments gleaming like jewels in the sun. The wedding planner is crouched next to them.

"Looks perfect," I call out, flashing her a thumbs-up. "Did you see Tom?"

She shakes her head, distracted.

Of course not. Probably snuck off to the bar for some overpriced scotch to center his soul. Whatever. I spin around and hop into the elevator, punching the button for my floor.

As the doors open, I'm greeted by the rhythmic *bang, bang, bang* of something heavy slamming against drywall. I freeze. It's the door across the hall, vibrating like it's about to shake off its hinges. Then, a high, breathy moan echoes through the corridor.

My brows lift. Damn. Get it, girl.

The hallway stretches ahead like a runway, and it takes forever to reach my room at the far end. I kick through the war zone of clothes, shoes, and makeup scattered across the floor because my suitcases have obviously exploded. Somewhere beneath it all is the tiny clutch.

I finally find it buried under some underwear, and then I fire off a quick text to Nico.

Did he come back yet?

The walk back to the elevator feels even longer. I glance at the noisy door again—it's quiet now. I wish the best for them and hope they finished strong. Today is a celebration of love, after all.

I press the elevator button. The doors glide open.

Behind me, I hear the soft creak of another door swinging wide.

I turn.

And my smirk suddenly dies a sudden death.

TWENTY-EIGHT

Nico

———————

THE SUITE SMELLS OF HAIRSPRAY, DEODORANT, perfume, and mild panic.

I'm sitting in the corner of the room in a tux that cost more than my monthly rent, holding a flute of champagne I don't particularly want, listening to the groomsmen argue over whether the groom should wear a pocket square or not. It's mostly irrelevant, considering Tom has been missing for an amount of time I'm trying not to think too hard about.

May looks good, though. Or at least she's doing a damn good job pretending. She's in the center of the room, sipping water from a straw and accepting gentle preening from her makeup artist. She's glowing. Literally. I think they put something sparkly on her clavicles.

"Hey Nico," one of the more annoying groomsmen, Kyle, says, nudging me. "You're the science guy, right?"

I nod warily. I can feel a terrible question brewing.

"What's like... the pH of champagne?"

There it is.

"Low," I reply. "Maybe two or three."

"Shit," he says, like that means something to him.

"Champagne is acidic," I clarify, because he's looking at me like I said something life-altering.

"Ohhh," he says, like that explains something.

There's a weird comfort in being surrounded by bedlam that isn't mine. At least not right now.

I take another sip of champagne and look out over the crowd of pastel bridesmaids adjusting straps and bobby pins. Everyone's buzzing. I'm the only one who seems still, and that's because I'm not really here.

I'm thinking about Annie.

Annie in her silk bridesmaid dress and heels, hair swept up, lips pink and eyes smoky. Annie looking like a perfect, polished woman. Everything about it was immediately overwhelming. She looked incredible. So fuckin' beautiful I lost my words when I saw her.

But... I don't know. She also didn't look like Annie. Not really. That is, until she screeched like an alley cat and shoved Izzy Flores a full nine feet away from me, which was arguably the most romantic thing anyone has ever done for me.

I love her with no makeup and messy hair. I love her in tank tops and cutoffs and my ratty twelve-year-old hoodie that comes down to her thighs. When she's barefoot in my kitchen.

That perfect imperfection, though, makes me think of a whole lot. I'm still kinda reeling from how she left me last night.

I'm mulling it over when the door slams open.

Annie barrels into the room. I immediately move towards her, drawn to her, when I see the look on her face. That expression—she looks like she's going to cry. Her eyes are darting all around the room, looking for something. And I realize with a start that she's *not* looking for me.

"May," she breathes.

TWENTY-NINE

Annie

THE ELEVATOR DOORS SLIDE SHUT, AND I JAB THE button for the bridal suite. I'm clutching my stupid little beaded bag, sweating through my dress, and willing myself not to cry or scream or both at the same time. I need to get to May, and then I need to tear this motherfucker to shreds.

But just as the elevator jerks, a manicured hand catches the doors.

"Wait up," Elodie chirps, smug as shit, stepping inside with fake fucking innocence. Tom follows, adjusting his cufflinks like he's walking into a boardroom, not the goddamn reckoning.

You can kick his ass after you tell May, I tell myself. *Don't let anything stop you from getting to May.*

"What a coincidence," the bitch says. "All of us heading up at the same time. Isn't that fun?"

I don't answer and focus on taking deep, centering breaths, but I'm shaking like a leaf.

Tom does, though, answer. "So what's your plan, Annie?" His voice is cool. "You gonna go cry to May? Cause a huge fucking scene?"

My jaw locks.

"She's not going to believe you," he says, stepping a little closer, crowding my space with his stupid fucking face and smugness and cologne. Filling the elevator with fear. That Tom is right, and May isn't going to believe me.

I can see it—her face turning tight, her voice going small. Getting hurt and saying I've misread it and it can't be true, he would never.

But even as the fear tightens in my chest, I know the truth: It doesn't matter.

It's not my job to decide what May does. It never should've been. Not when we were kids. Not in high school. Not even now. It doesn't matter if she's going to be upset.

I'm not here to save her. I'm here to tell her the truth. And this time, she gets to decide what to do with it.

I snap my head toward him. "Fuck you, Tom."

The elevator dings.

I step out into a perfectly carpeted hallway that smells like roses and furniture polish. My heels are too loud, even through the carpet, my heart punching in my ears, a muffled click-click and a pounding of impending doom. My stomach is a twisted knot, my mouth bone-dry. I barely hear the elevator ding shut behind me.

Tom and Elodie are two steps behind me.

"You don't have to do this," Tom says, low and threatening, the kind of whisper that wants to slap. "You're going to ruin her wedding. Make it the Annie show, like always."

I whirl around. "Fuck you, Tom. There is no wedding."

He scoffs, all teeth and superiority. "You think she's going to believe you? You think anyone will?"

I don't answer him and turn away before I commit a felony.

Inside the suite, I'm vaguely aware of other things happening—all white chiffon and blush florals, hairspray and champagne, flower girls twirling in sparkly shoes, someone fixing May's veil, Vanessa touching up lipstick, groomsmen and half empty fruit platters—but it's all happening outside of the tunnel, and the tunnel is leading me directly to May.

I call out to her, but she turns before I speak.

Her eyes find mine, and something in her face shifts instantly. Alarm and fear. A sister's radar. She sets down her bouquet and takes one step forward. "Annie?"

I shake my head, motioning her over, adrenaline carrying me across the room. "Come here. Please."

She meets me quickly, her heels quiet on the rug. I tug her to the far corner near the balcony doors, away from the others.

"I need to tell you something," I whisper, my throat closing around the words. "I just—I just saw Tom and Elodie."

She freezes.

"What?" Her voice is thin.

"Together. Walking out of a room. I heard them fucking against the door, May."

Her lips part. No sound comes out.

The door to the room slams open. "What the fuck is going on?" Tom says loudly as he enters behind us. "May, baby, don't listen to her—"

I see red and lose my fucking mind. "Don't you 'baby' her, you motherfucking piece of shit."

"What are you even talking about?" he sneers. "You're making shit up because you're a miserable little attention whore."

Gasps around the room. Izzy comes to stand by our side. Elodie tries to hang back near the door, face red. People are standing now. Someone whispers to a groomsman. Someone else knocks over a glass of champagne. A tiny flower girl starts crying. Nico moves towards Tom like he's going to wring his neck. Good.

May steps between them, pushing Nico away, voice shaking but loud. "Tom, were you with her?"

"No! Jesus, baby, she's making this up—"

"Annie wouldn't lie to me," May cuts in.

Tom steps forward, the light catching on his tie clip like it's a dagger. "I wasn't, May."

"Then where were you?" May demands to know.

"I was—"

"I watched you walk out of a room with Elodie, and I heard you fucking her against the door," I answer for him.

"She's insane, May—"

"Then what were you doing?"

"I was up on the roof, checking—"

"I went up there to look for you. The wedding planner said she hadn't seen him. You can ask her," I retort.

Tom steps towards May. "Are you seriously going to let her hijack this day?" His voice is a weapon—measured and sharp. "This is classic Annie. Stirring up chaos, screaming in the middle of someone else's moment because she can't stand not being the center of attention."

"Enough, asshole," Nico spits, trying to get to Tom, but May stands her ground and doesn't let anyone past her.

Tom sneers at him. "Shut the fuck up, dick."

His eyes land back on me. His smile is cruel. "She lies and plays victim and leaves a mess for everyone else to clean up. That's what she does. That's who she is."

"This is not about me. You are not doing this right now," I manage to spit, low and guttural, but he barrels over it.

"She can't help it," he says with a bitter chuckle, looking at May now, like he's trying to reason with her. "It's pathological. She gets off on ruining things for other people. She needs to be the loudest. And you—" He gestures at May. "You always let her. You bend your spine backwards trying to make her feel like she belongs here, like she's not a walking disaster."

Nico is suddenly by my side and wraps me in his arms, his knuckles white. Safe, steady, secure. The room is heating up. A bridesmaid stifles a sob. Izzy is ready to throw the fuck down the second May says the word.

"She can't stand that you have a real relationship," Tom spits. "That someone like me—stable, smart, with a future—chose you. Because she's never had anything like that."

"Shut up," I growl, but I'm shaking while Nico squeezes me tighter, like he can protect me from the slaughter. Safe, steady, secure. But my voice still breaks in the middle, and he smiles like that was what he wanted.

"You're just going to take her word for it?" Tom shrugs. "She's jealous. That's all this is. Jealous and lonely and attention-starved."

"I'm gonna fuckin' kill you, Tom." Nico says it like a promise.

Tom turns to him with a smirk. "Oh yeah? And you're what—her latest fuck toy?" He looks to May now, loud and smug and sharp as a whip. "And you're going to believe the one who's fucking the porn star?"

Every single muscle in Nico's body goes tight behind me.

Time stops. For one heartbeat, the room doesn't breathe.

"What did you just say?" May asks.

Someone whispers, "What porn star?"

Tom doesn't blink. "He's a porn star. He gets paid to be naked on camera. Again, May," he drawls, "You're gonna believe *her*, when she's fucking *him*?"

My blood runs cold.

I turn.

Everyone turns. I can feel it—the shift of the entire room swiveling, eyes clicking into place like dominos falling. On him.

Nico looks at me. And his face... it crumples.

"I didn't tell him," I whisper quickly. "Nico. I swear."

But now his face is scarily blank, devoid of any and all emotion. He takes a step back, a step away from me, and the sudden loss of warmth is paralyzing.

Something in me collapses, crumbles.

The noise hits all at once as everything begins to unravel.

Voices rising. Groomsmen trying to reason with May. May's hand trembling as she stares at Tom. Izzy getting in Tom's face. My mother: "What are you doing, Annie?" My father's voice like a whip: "You've humiliated all of us, again." A bridesmaid whispering, "Oh my God," to someone else. The flower girl crying.

Nico, now several feet away from me, standing motionless, except for a slight shift in his eyes. The flicker of something breaking.

And then—finally—Elodie steps forward.

"It's true," she says. Her voice is loud, the shrill tone of her voice isolated from all the noise. "He and I... it's true. For a while now."

May flinches. Her face drains of all color.

"I'm sorry," Elodie adds weakly, as if that helps.

May bolts.

I try to follow, but my feet don't move. My lungs don't work. I'm stuck. Watching Nico. Watching May fly out the door. Watching the whole room devolve into chaos.

Then Izzy punches Tom in the face.

I snap.

"You fucking piece of shit," I scream at Tom, who's holding his bleeding nose. I shove myself between him and Iz, my voice shaking with rage. "You emotionally abusive, manipulative little coward. You don't deserve her. You never did."

Years and years of pent-up thoughts and aggression uncork. *Pop*. The dam breaks, and I flood the room with anger and vitriol. "*How dare you?!* You used May like a mother-fucking sponsor for your sad little country club cosplay. The boat shoes, the brunches with your awful finance bro friends who all talk about women like they're interchangeable LinkedIn endorsements. You treat her like a lifestyle accessory. Something to show off, not someone to love."

My voice rises, disgust dripping from every word. "She paid for your future. She gave you stability, status, image, and you paid her back by lying, gaslighting, and cheating. On her wedding day. In a hotel room she paid for."

I step closer. "You don't love her. You love the version of yourself you get to pretend to be when she's around. And the second she stops sacrificing herself to keep that illusion going, you find someone else to validate you. You're not just a bad partner. You're fucking evil."

People are staring. Someone's phone falls. No one breathes.

"And don't you dare come for Nico," I spit, tears hot in my eyes. "You think you're better than him? Because he shows his dick on camera? At least when he uses his dick, he uses it for good. He's not sneaking around, lying, manipulating. He's kind. He's brilliant. He's better than you in every measurable way."

Tom scoffs, but I walk over to him and kick him right in the fucking nuts because I'm on a fucking roller coaster without brakes. Three times in a row, bitch.

"And he prefers the term 'adult content creator,' dick. And you know what's amazing about adult content creators?" I shout over his groans. "People choose to watch him. Every single time. He's not just fucking people in secret, hiding behind NFTs and crypto and chinos and his fiancé's money. He gets paid to be seen. You? You couldn't pay me to look at your dick. I hope it's broken now."

"And you," I hiss at Elodie, who has since run over to help Tom off the ground. "Not fucking cool. Haven't you ever heard of girl code?"

There's a beat of stunned silence.

Then my mother shrieks, "Annie!"

I turn to her and fire back in Cantonese. "You should be yelling at him! Your perfect little son-in-law was getting his dick sucked by the maid of honor fifteen minutes ago, and all you can say is my name?"

My dad tries to speak. I talk right over him.

"For once in your lives," I say, trembling, "you could thank me. Or check on May. Or ask if she's okay. Or maybe—just maybe—you could drag Tom out by his hair and ask him what the fuck he thinks he's doing cheating on her minutes before the ceremony!"

I gesture around us, to the stunned wedding guests, the shattered silence, the pieces of a lie they all helped build. "You want to be mad at someone? Be mad at him. Not me. I didn't destroy this. I just refused to let her walk into it blind."

My voice keeps rising, sharp and fast, powered by years of held-back rage. "You've called me selfish since I was twelve, when I told you May didn't want to be a doctor. You said I was poisoning her, corrupting her, dragging her down. But you didn't want to hear what she wanted—only what you wanted."

"I got grounded every time I told you the truth. You told me I was difficult. Dramatic. Disobedient. But I was just trying to protect her—when neither of you ever did."

I step forward now, my hands shaking. "I cleaned up her messes. I took the fall. I stood between her and every cruel thing you said when she didn't meet your expectations. I made myself the bad one so she could be your good one. And guess what? I'd do it again. I will always protect her."

My mother's face is white. My father is stone. But neither of them moves.

"Just once," I say, breathless now, "I wanted you to see me. Not as the problem child. But as the person who's been holding this family together by the seams, even when you were too proud to admit it was always broken."

The silence is brutal. No apology. No thank-you. Not even a blink.

"You can all go to hell," I finally announce to the room in English. "I'm gonna go get my sister."

I search for Nico on my way out of the room. But when I do finally find him, I stumble over my feet, as if it's now dark, because someone has blown out the final candle lighting the space.

He's looking at me like I am someone he doesn't know. As if the mask has cracked, and what's underneath is something ugly.

And when I finally leave the suite, heart splintering in my chest, I feel something deeper underneath the panic and fear for my sister. I feel grief for both of us. For love lost, right there in that room.

———

I can't find May, and she finally picks up the phone after I run all around the hotel for fifteen straight minutes.

"Plum," I breathe, voice cracking. "Where are you?"

"I'm gone," she sobs. "I left."

"*What*? Where are you? Can I come get you?"

"No, I—" There is a rustle of fabric, and... a deep voice murmuring to her in the background. "It's okay, Annie."

"*Plum*. What the *fuck*?! *Where are you? Who is that*?!" I shriek.

"Annie, I'm okay. I'm going to be okay," she cries. "I swear I'm okay and I'm safe. I swear. I have to go. I can't be around —" she heaves a shaky breath. "I love you. Thank... Thank you for telling me. None of this is your fault. Thank you. I love you. I'll see you back home." She hangs up the phone.

I stare at my phone, feeling adrift and totally lost, standing on the carpeted floor of a random hallway.

And then I get a visit from a friend.

Old Annie taps me on the shoulder. The miserable little attention whore that Tom was talking about, the one whose parents have scolded and blamed and harassed her whole life. The Annie who dated a coke dealer/tattoo artist/criminal for free coke and tattoos. Nasty, selfish, problematic Annie. The Annie that Nico finally got to see. *I'm here*, she whispers in my ear. *Let's go*.

I nod. *Okay*.

I text the wedding planner and tell her the wedding is off. I tell her I'll pay her whatever she needs to do to take care of it.

I walk with purpose back to my room. I throw all the important, expensive shit into one of my suitcases. I leave everything else.

I take the elevator down to the bar.

I order a martini.

I cry.

I fix my makeup.

I find a man sitting alone.

"Hey," I smirk.

He looks me up and down. His hair and his eyes, really, his *everything*, are all wrong, but he will do. "Hey," he says with a smile.

THIRTY

Nico

I'LL ADMIT THAT IT TAKES ME A SEC TO GO AFTER Annie.

I do leave that damn room almost immediately after her, but it's to get away from my worst fuckin' nightmare—stares and whispers and a barrage of questions and glances at my crotch. I go to my own room to wage my own war in my own damn head. The arguments on both sides are equally loud.

This is exactly what you were fuckin' worried about, and it's only been eight days. Complicated, guarded, cryptic, mysterious Annie Li, who you thought you could trust.

There is no fuckin' way Annie told anyone about you. Annie, who gave you all of herself. Who you gave all of your own damn self because you knew she'd guard it with her life. Fierce, loyal, protective Annie Li. Ali. My Annie Li. Annie "Whom I Love" Li.

I glance around my room. Housekeeping has been here twice, and the previous hurricane of this room, gold dress and heels and my new shirt and everything, is now perfect. Too perfect. The dress and shirt are side by side in the closet, shoes neatly arranged just underneath.

I hate it.

A flurry of images flashes through my mind. Annie with the gold dress banded around her waist, hair cascading across the sheets, open, smiling, glowing, vulnerable and covered in *me*. Annie with some kid's snot on her arm. Annie verbally bodying Tom. Annie physically bodying Tom. Annie protecting her sister, eyes flashing, hair everywhere. Annie defending... me.

Annie against the world. Annie, with no one on her team.

Except for maybe three people.

May.

Izzy Flores.

And me.

We're the only ones who fuckin' earned it.

Fuck.

Fuck.

I've gotta go chase Annie. I've gotta fight for her. I promised.

Maybe we'll figure it out.

I pull out my phone and call her. It goes straight to voicemail. "Annie, honey. Where are you? Please call me," I say. I send her a text with the same thing, stare at my phone, then hear the blood rush into my ears.

Undeliverable.

Fuck.

I jump off my bed and run to the elevator, and when the doors open... lo-and-behold. I step on anyway because I'm still feelin' like I gotta murder this motherfucker.

"Nico," says Tom.

"Don't say my fuckin' name," I warn him.

He huffs a laugh. "It's like that, then?"

I whirl around and face him with a newfound understanding of a "crime of passion." I've got him on size, and I use it to get in his face. "Fuck you very, very much, man. I hope to never see you again."

He lifts a snide fuckin' eyebrow. "So you believe the crazy bitch, too."

An *oof*, as Tom inexplicably finds himself strong-armed against the wall of the elevator. "Stop with the 'crazy' adjective use, asshole, because she was always right about you."

He shakes his head. "I'd say I can't wait for her to destroy your life, too, but I know you're just her flavor of the week. She's probably gone and left your ass already, anyway," he sneers.

In saying this, he's voiced my greatest fear. The elevator doors open to Annie's floor, and I find myself being pulled to leave and find her and forget about this asshole for the rest of my life. So I step off.

"Lose my number," I tell him, with barely suppressed rage. "And while you're at it, lose May's and Annie's."

He laughs, sharp and cutting, like what I said was fuckin' hilarious. "I don't have Annie's number, anyway. Like she would ever, ever talk to me in any capacity about anything."

Something about this makes me pause. Did Charlie tell him? No, from what I saw last night, Charlie would never speak to this asshole either.

I slap a hand on the door to keep it from closing. "How did you know about the porn thing, Tom?"

He laughs again, and it takes everything in me not to wipe the smug look off his face. "I didn't mean it in a bad way. I think it's pretty cool. You're clearly making bank."

"How did you know, Tom?"

"I'm on that porn site a lot," he shrugs, like it's a totally normal thing for someone with a fiancée to say. "You're pretty popular. I see your content pop up all the time, and I recognize that weird duck tattoo you have."

Everything inside me goes still while the ground shifts beneath me. Panic prickles at the edge of my vision.

I turn and stride away without another word.

She was telling the truth.

After forever, I bang on her door. "Annie."

Nothing.

"Annie," I yell, banging even harder.

I'm such a fuckin' asshole.

I press my ear to the door. It's silent.

"*FUCK*," I scream at the ceiling.

I stride back to the elevator.

You stupid, stupid motherfuckin' asshole. Of course she was tellin' the fuckin' truth.

I take the elevator to the roof, where I find the wedding planner.

"Where is Annie?" I all but yell at her.

"Whoa, dude, back up," she says, frowning at me.

I take several deep breaths in a row. "I fuckin' apologize. Have you seen Annie? May's twin?"

She shakes her head. "She texted me a while ago and said the wedding was off. She asked me to take care of closing it down. But I haven't seen her."

I turn on my heel and go back to the elevator, adrenaline punching through my veins.

Of course she fuckin' took care of things for May. OF COURSE SHE DIDN'T TELL TOM ABOUT YOU, YOU MOTHERFUCKIN' ASSHOLE.

I get to the bridal suite, the scene of my worst fuckin' nightmare, but I could give two shits about who sees me right now. I bang on the door. "Hello? Hello? Is anyone in there? *HEL*—"

Izzy Flores opens the door with an equally panicked look in her eyes.

"Where's Annie?" we both shout in tandem.

I peer behind her. The room is empty. "I don't know," I pant. "She's not with me. My calls and texts aren't going through to her."

She gives me an inscrutable look. "I just got a text from her a minute ago that says, 'I'm okay.' I want to make sure she's really okay."

Something heavy settles behind my ribs. I'm out. I'm on the other side of the force field. "Where else have you checked?" I grit out.

"Her room and this room."

"I checked the roof. She's not there."

We lock eyes, some sort of understanding passing between us. "Bar," we say in tandem.

We move back towards the elevator. May's fine, Izzy tells me. Well, not fine, but fine considering. She's safe. It makes me worry about Annie even more.

"So," she says, with an eyebrow raised. "Sex work, huh?"

I blow out a breath. Shrug.

"Where do you have your content?"

"*Harlot*."

"Nice. What kind of stuff do you post?"

The tips of my ears burn up. "Uh…"

"Nico," she says.

Her tone makes me look over.

"I'm sort of an escort. I get paid a disgusting amount of money to work for and occasionally have sex with people. I am not the person to be embarrassed in front of," she tells me, matter-of-factly.

I blink.

What the *fuck*? I give Isabel Flores—fellow Mathletes champion, chess team co-president, and the third-ranked student of our high school class, right behind me and Annie— the full force of my attention.

She gives me a totally unbothered smile. Owning it.

My mouth hangs open and only briefly closes to form the word, "Wow."

"Yep."

"I..." Well, I guess there really is no reason to be embarrassed. "I cook," I admit. "I cook naked, and I explain the food science behind everything I make."

The grin that spreads across her face is slow and understanding. "No way." She looks me up and down. "You're the *NakedReactions* guy."

I blink again. "Yes."

She laughs and laughs. "I watch your videos with Annie and some friends."

I blink again. "Are you part of that geriatric girl gang?"

"Yes!" She chuckles. "Betty and Fernanda. No way. That's so awesome. Annie never told me."

My chest hollows out. Of course, Annie didn't even tell her best friend, who knows both *NakedReactions* and Nico Giannuzzi, that they were the same person. I bang my head against the wall of the elevator. "Fuck," I mutter.

"Oh boy," she says cheerfully, unaware of my internal struggle. "You definitely have nothing to be embarrassed about."

When we get downstairs, I scan the room, not seeing her. My pulse climbs. I approach the bartender with all the grace of an angry rhinoceros. "Was there a gorgeous Asian woman here? All tatted up? Arms and chest and legs and shit?" *Alongside some of my hickeys.*

He eyes me. "Yeah."

Every muscle in my body pulls tight, including my tongue. Izzy takes over and slams her hands on the bar. "What did she do? What happened? Did she look okay? Where did she go?"

The bartender shrugs. "She got a martini. I always remember orders." He tilts his head and looks up towards the ceiling. "She was crying. Pretty hysterically actually."

My pulse falters, skipping several beats.

"She was crying so hard that I was gonna go talk to her, but..."

"But what?!" I roar.

"Whoa, dude, chill—"

"If one more fuckin' person tells me to chill, I'm gonna fuckin' break something. What happened?"

He frowns. "I was gonna go over to her, but she got herself together pretty quickly."

"And then?" Izzy shrieks.

The bartender looks at me with something that looks like fear. "She..."

"Dude," I warn, the murder very evident in my voice.

"She went to talk to some guy. And then... they left together," he finally says warily, like an apology.

It hits like a vacuum imploding. The air gets sucked out of the room, and everything collapses inward. Then I float— weightless, gutted, a single molecule drifting without a charge.

I don't remember sitting, but suddenly I'm on a barstool.

"Annie," Izzy yells. I look up. She's on her phone, pacing. I lunge, but Izzy blocks me with her arm. She's surprisingly strong. "Annie, I'm with Nico. We're so worried about you. Where are you? Are you okay?"

Do not attack the small woman for her phone, I'm chanting in my head.

Izzy's eyes flick to me before she turns away. "Okay," she says. "Okay."

I can no longer stand it. "Okay, what? Annie," I yell towards the phone. "Baby. Honey—"

Izzy paces across the room with the phone. "Yeah," she says. "Did you—okay. Okay."

I stalk after her, listening to her muttering into the phone. I follow her all around the bar and catch bits and pieces. "Annie, no." "Stop." "No." "That's not—"

She suddenly stops and whirls around. I swear she grows seven feet tall and sprouts demon wings. I take a step back with the force of her rage. Her eyes narrow to slits, and when she speaks, it's in the tone of someone who's about to exorcise me with her bare hands. "Back. The fuck. Up. Stop fucking following me, Nico. Go stand over there." She points towards the far side of the bar.

I go, obviously. I don't have a choice, lest I be smote. I sit on a stool like I've been put in time-out and watch Izzy as she shrinks back to human size, getting soft, gesticulating wildly on the phone.

Finally, seemingly hours later, she hangs up the phone, looking satisfied.

But then her head swivels slowly towards me.

Oh shit.

Izzy stomps over, a corridor of ominous clouds and wrath opening in her wake. She stops just short of me, eyes sharp enough to draw blood. "You didn't believe her?" she hisses.

"I—" The word crumbles in my mouth.

"She told you she didn't tell anyone about you. And she stood up in front of everyone and said something no one else had the courage to say, and you—you didn't believe her?" Izzy's voice breaks. "She *stood up for you*. She *defended* you. And you stood there and *didn't believe her*?" she shrieks.

I step toward her. "I panicked. I didn't—I thought—I didn't know what to think. It all hit at once, and I was scared—"

"No," she snaps. "No. You don't get to play scared. You're the one who was supposed to make her feel *safe*."

This is what destroys me. I stumble back a step, winded. 'Cause, fuck. *Fuck*. I was so busy being a selfish coward, thinking Annie was the strong one, that I forgot I was doing the same damn thing. Me and my fuckin' hoodie that she used as fuckin' armor—we were supposed to protect her, too.

And I let her down.

"She picked *you*. She let herself believe that you were different, and the moment she needed you most, you made her feel like she was alone."

She let me in. I forgot I was letting her in, too.

"She told me not to talk to you," Izzy says, crossing her arms, still breathless with fury. "She didn't want to make you feel bad. Can you believe that?"

I try to speak, but nothing comes out.

"Annie's on a train back to the city. Alone. She was crying so hard initially I could barely understand her. Saying she should've known better than to expect someone to stay. That it was stupid to think you'd still be there once things got real."

My throat closes. "She's wrong."

Her lip curls. "Looks like she was right."

Fuck, fuck, fuck.

She crosses her arms. Her voice changes, quieter now, dead cold. "She says to thank you for the ride."

Every single one of those words slices me open.

"She said she'll send you your manuscript through your agent."

Have I been stabbed? "Was she—is she okay?"

Izzy doesn't answer right away. Her jaw works. She looks away.

"Izzy," I whisper.

"She will be," Izzy says, jaw tight. "Because Annie always finds a way to survive. You think this is the first time she's had to pick herself up after someone let her down?"

I flinch.

"You know, if there's any good in this, it's that she's not spiraling because she thinks she's not good enough for you," Izzy says. "She's spiraling because *you* weren't good enough to stand beside *her*. She asked for something honest and real. She asked for someone who wouldn't leave the second things got messy. And you proved her right—about everyone."

I drop onto the stool behind me like gravity suddenly doubled.

"She told me not to tell you this," she repeats, "But she loves you, Nico," she says, and it's not gentle. It's a punch directly into my gut. "She loves you, and you broke her heart. She was finally starting to believe she didn't have to go through life being the one who takes the hits. She thought maybe this time, someone would stand in front of her."

A fresh wave of pain crashes through me. My face is suddenly wet. *You stupid motherfucking fool.*

"She'll bury it," Izzy says after a moment. "Just like she always does. She'll make it into a joke. Turn it into a story. You'll be a funny footnote in a monologue she tells at brunch."

I shake my head, furious with myself. How could I do this? "I don't want to be a fuckin' footnote."

Izzy studies me for a long, heavy beat. Then, softer: "Then do something about it."

Behind us, someone calls her name—familiar, from another life. We both glance up. The tall, handsome man version of Izzy, who I haven't seen since high school, walks toward us, holding a baby on his hip, a woman beside him.

Izzy waves them off for a second and turns back to me. Her voice is lower now, but no less intense.

"You want her?" she asks.

I nod. "I need her."

"Then fight like hell. Chase her. Apologize so hard she runs out of ways to argue with you. Remind her that she's not alone. That she doesn't always have to be the one taking on the world."

I'm already on my feet.

"She'll try to push you away," she warns. "She's scared

now. Scared in the way only people who've had to carry everything by themselves can be."

"I won't let her push me out."

Izzy looks at me for a long time before her face softens.

"She thinks she doesn't need anyone," she says. "But she needs you."

I nod again. "Her home is with me."

Izzy holds my gaze. Her eyes glisten for a second before she blinks it away and says, "Then go bring her home."

THIRTY-ONE

Annie

By the time I hang up the phone with Izzy, entire wars have been waged, empires have fallen, someone has been stabbed twenty-three times, and I have risen from the ashes and the carnage.

Old Annie? She made a brief appearance—sat at the bar, scoped out someone with decent bone structure and a black credit card, planned to fuck around just enough to get blackout and a free ride home. But she was vanquished somewhere between the lobby and the Amtrak kiosk.

By Sister Annie.

Now, Sister Annie tried to reclaim control, starting slowly, forcing me to lose the dude from the bar, buy my own damn train ticket and sit my ass on the train without getting up except to use the bathroom. She wanted me to slither back into my hole and be devastatingly crushed that I couldn't even make it the full year of her that I promised myself. Short by a few days and a big dick. She wanted me to go back to Rock Bottom, in my parents' basement, where I could safely remain leashed and caged.

But after sitting on that train, watching Miami slide backwards and behind me?

Only one bitch made it out alive.

Just me.

Annie Li, Chaos Bringer. Screaming and triumphant and feral. I rose from the motherfucking ashes.

Because I was *fucking* right.

I did the right fucking thing. I trusted myself. I did it all *myself*—the sum of all my experiences led to that moment right there.

I saved my sister's ass. This time, though, the self-sacrifice was right. I was my sister's keeper in an appropriate way.

I kicked Tom in the nuts.

I finally put my parents in their place.

I enjoy a brief, deeply satisfying fantasy of wearing my heaviest boots and stomping on some heads. Old Annie, Sister Annie. Tom. Elodie. My parents.

And one more.

Because I did one thing wrong.

I thought I could just give away my trust and my security to anyone else. Like maybe it was okay to depend on someone else, for once.

Like maybe Nicholas "Nico" Giannuzzi was different.

And I was so very, very wrong.

So it's back to basics. Me against the world. I polish my claws. Reinforce the steel plating. Harden the fuck up.

I text Izzy. *When I get back to the city, I'm moving into your place until I find an apartment*, I tell her.

Duh, she replies back.

I left some stuff in my hotel room in my dramatic exit. Will you bring it back to the city for me? I'll call the front desk.
Duh.

I pull up my contacts. *Block.*

I pull out my laptop. I email my boss. *The manuscript will be ready in a week.*

I pull up a contact. *Chef@nakedreactions.com.* I hover my cursor above the button next to it.

Block.

THIRTY-TWO

Annie

MY FORCE FIELDS ARE NOT FEELING PARTICULARLY intact two days later.

Maybe I didn't reinforce them enough.

All it took were flashes of memory, the waving of a tree branch in the wind, the reflection of the sun on a puddle. A bar of chocolate and a jar of honey in Izzy's cabinets and the disgusting bacon and eggs I tried to make us for breakfast. Each one pokes a massive, gorilla-sized hole in my shields.

Izzy's at work, and I'm simultaneously browsing for apartments in her kitchen and patching a hole I made in my armor after I squeezed my own damn knee, when her buzzer rings.

"Who is it?" I say into her intercom.

"Hey, honey."

For a brief, embarrassing moment, I fold. Just for a second. My vision blurs, like someone smeared tears across my eyeballs before I could stop them. That voice. That fuckin' voice. Warm and safe.

No.

No, no, no.

I remember who I am now. What I've rebuilt in the smoldering crater. I remind myself of my new and improved shield and my newly sharpened fangs.

I don't let him upstairs. Instead, I climb the steps down to ground level, checking my walls for weak spots. I pull my face into a sunny mask and walk down Izzy's stairs like I'm not holding the door shut on a screaming, sobbing version of myself inside.

When I open the door, I break all over again.

God, he looks wrecked. A big, beautiful wreck. Like he hasn't slept, like he's been walking around with a missing piece. He looks like me underneath this unhinged mask I'm wearing. His eyes land on my face, and they light up and fall apart at the same time. Hope and sorrow tangle in the lines of his face.

And I want. I want. I want.

I want to run into his arms.

I want to scream until my throat shreds.

I want to give in.

Instead, I chirp, "Hey!" My voice sounds like a cartoon chipmunk trying to sell perfume.

Nico's whole face collapses. "Oh, Annie."

I grin wider. Bigger. Stretch it across my face like Saran wrap. "What's up?" I say, like we're neighbors running into each other in the hallway.

He steps toward me, and I instinctively sidestep.

"I know you blocked me," he says, hands raised slightly, trying to show he's unarmed. "I just needed to see if you were okay."

"Oh, I'm great," I chirp. "I'm fine. May, on the other hand, is not okay. I mean, she's okay, like physically, but she's not in a good place. I mean, well, obviously. Her fiancé who she loved for who knows what reason was cheating on her on her fucking wedding day, that fucking asshole, and probably was for eons, and then she lost out on what, tens of thousands of dollars on all the wedding shit, and then—"

"Annie."

That word again. My name in his voice. It cuts through my rambling like a whip. I clamp my mouth shut.

"I'm not asking about May. I'm asking about you."

"Yup. Still fine."

He takes another step towards me, and I take another away in a twisted choreography, even if we're standing what has to be a good ten feet apart.

"You still owe me a talk," he says gently. "Let's talk."

"Iz told me she talked to you," I say, waving it off. "Thanks for the ride. No hard feelings, dude." Maybe if I avoid his name, this will hurt less.

He flinches. "Dude?" he repeats.

"It was fun. Really fun. You're great. Seriously. You're great and wonderful and like the coolest person I know—"

"Jesus, Annie." He laughs once, sharp and hurt. "These superlatives aren't makin' either of us feel any better."

"I told you, I'm fine." My teeth are clenched so tight my jaw will be sore tomorrow.

"Annie, honey—"

"Stop calling me that," I snap through my mask. "I told you a million times. I'm not your honey."

"Lie."

I blink.

He steps forward. "Let me in."

"Izzy's here," I lie again.

"She's not—she's the one who told me to come." *Traitorous bitch*. "Besides, that's not what I fuckin' mean, and you know it."

My throat is closing up. "Dude—"

"You haven't said my name once," he says quietly. "You're trying to erase me."

Because if I say your name, I'll remember how it felt in the dark. How it tasted against my tongue. How it sounded when I whispered it into your skin.

"I'm not okay," he says. "And I know you're not either."

My smile freezes. "You don't know me at all," I blurt out.

"Lie," he repeats, stepping forward. "I know that you are amazing and brilliant and also the coolest fuckin' person I know."

I step away.

"I know that you need a hug."

My eyes flick down to his arms, scan the width of his chest and the length of his hoodie, the one I wore for days. I want to crawl inside it and never come out.

"I know you deserve everything that is good in the world," he says with a step forward.

I don't move.

"And I know," he says, voice shaking, "that you belong with me," he says with finality.

Something tears across my ribcage. "Lie," I murmur, voice cracking. "I deserve someone better."

"Baby—" he tries, scrambling now, "Annie, I am so fuckin' sorry. I know I hurt you. I know I broke something. I froze, and I didn't believe you. I didn't go after you, I didn't defend you. The biggest mistakes I've ever made, I made within a ten-minute span." His voice rises in volume and frustration. "But that's a reflection of *me*, not you. On my own damn insecurities. But I should've fuckin' believed you, because you're the only person in the entire world I trust with my entire fuckin' life!" he explodes.

I freeze, and all of my organs collapse into a black hole that's appeared in my belly.

"I love you," he says. "I'm sorry, and I love you, and I'm here because I love you, and I love you so fuckin' much I can't fuckin' breathe. I know you," he continues, voice rough with feeling. "I know you're hurting. I know that letting people in has always been dangerous for you. But Annie, honey…" He tears his hands through his hair. "Please. Let me back in. Loving someone is not a weakness."

His words are a knife against my ribs. I don't let them draw blood. "It's the only one I have," I inform him, and it's the truth.

His gut caves in like I've kicked him. But he doesn't stop.

"Loving you is the strongest thing I've ever done," he says. "And I'm not gonna stop just because you're scared."

"Well, maybe you should," I say, smiling like the Cheshire fucking Cat now. "I'm not scared. I'm busy. I have a manuscript due. I'm apartment hunting—"

"Annie—"

"I mean it," I tell him. "You're a good guy. I wish you the best."

"Fuck!" He scrubs his face, and all I want to do is to give him a hug. He rips off his hoodie and holds it out. "Then take this. For now."

I stare at it as if it's laced with explosives. I feel it, I feel the tears welling in the corners of my eyes and making my weakness a show.

He doesn't move. Just stands there, holding it. Waiting. Hoping.

Something hot and dangerous rises in my throat. I clench my hands into tight fists. "I don't need anything from you," I finally whisper, voice shaking. "Not anymore."

My knees buckle at the broken look in his eyes, the warm, sure, melted chocolate of them, the sun shining into them and making this whole situation seem like a silly, merry joke. It almost gets me to cave. Those eyes that held me safe, supported, secure. Until they didn't.

He sets the hoodie down on the step like a peace offering. "Okay," he says. "Then I'll fight."

"For what?"

"To get back in the force field."

It takes a moment to answer, because I'm trying not to cry. *I will not cry. Don't you dare let him see you cry.* I take one last look at him—the messy hair, the three moles on his handsome face, his broad chest. The devastation and sorrow in his eyes. "It's not about that," I manage. "It's that maybe *yours* isn't strong enough for *me*."

As I turn around, I catch his big body slumping, and I feel a part of me break. So, I walk inside and shut the door. Quietly and carefully, away from him, and back to my cave where it's definitely safe. And I don't look back.

Not even once.

———

Lie.

Ten minutes later, when I'm sure he's left, I open the door and pick up the hoodie.

And I put it on.

THIRTY-THREE

Nico

THE HONEY CRYSTALLIZES IN THE JAR. I RUN MY thumb over the lid. It's the same kind she stole off the hotel breakfast buffet, pretending to be discreet as she shoved two into her purse. I teased her about it. She told me to live a little and made me taste-test a dozen honeys on her belly that night and rank them. This was the winner—dark, smoky, with a strange tang of wildflowers.

I mail it to her first.

No note. Just the honey.

It's ridiculous. I know it's fuckin' ridiculous. Izzy tells me it's ridiculous. "This is not *Amélie*," she says. "This is not *Love Actually*. She is not going to get the honey and realize you are soulmates."

"Soulmates in hell," I correct.

I can hear her rolling her eyes at me over the phone.

I rub a hand over my face. "I just want her to know I'm still thinking about her."

"She knows."

"Then I want her to know that I'm not done trying."

Izzy laughs. "Then maybe stop mailing her groceries and try giving her the truth."

———

I don't sleep much anymore.

There's a spreadsheet open on my laptop—six tabs, twelve columns, tracked expenses. After paying off Ma's bills and her entire mortgage, I have so much money I don't know what the hell to do with it. And for the first time in my adult life, I'm not surviving. I'm secure.

Annie was right about that, too. About everything, really. She made me want things that felt impossible—honesty, intimacy, a future with someone who doesn't look at me like I'm a fuckin' embarrassment.

She looked at me like I was inevitable.

And I broke that.

———

The second thing I send her is sorbet. Or at least, the recipe.

It's scrawled in her handwriting on a page she left in my notebook. She'd titled it "Sorbet for Illiterate Gorillas" like a little joke she knew I'd find, eventually. It lists three ingredients: black sesame, coconut, and honey. It's the one we made in Michelle's kitchen.

I recreate the whole thing from memory. I tweak the proportions a bit, adding my notes in the margins. I circle the part where she wrote, *Don't you dare add rosewater, you pretentious fuck.* I underline it twice and scribble back,

Noted, Ali. Miss you.

P.S. The honey makes it fucking delicious.

Izzy doesn't know about this one.

I mail it with trembling hands and a stupid, stubborn hope.

———

I ship the gold dress and the shoes to Izzy's apartment.

———

The truth.

Then maybe stop mailing her groceries and try giving her the truth.

After an hour of watching the sun creep onto my bedroom wall, I finally call Ma.

I've been avoiding it for months—years, really. But Annie was right. Ma deserves to know.

The phone rings twice. She picks up with her usual, "Hey, Nico. You good?"

"Hi, Ma."

"Is that a yes or a no?"

"It's a..."

"It's a no," she finishes for me.

I sit on the edge of my mattress, the sunlight dragging its way across the floor like it's too tired to shine. "Ma, I need to talk to you about something."

"I figured. You only call this early if someone's dead, in jail, or pregnant."

"I've literally never called you for any of those things."

"Well, it's the sentiment that matters." There's a pause. "Are you okay?"

"Yeah. I mean—no."

"Talk to me."

So I do.

I tell her everything. *Everything.* Not just about *Harlot* and *NakedReactions*—although I do avoid the more salacious DMs I get. I tell her about my PhD program, my choices, why I moved back home. I tell her about Annie. About the girl who made me brave. Brave enough to admit it to my mom. About the week that changed everything. About the night I didn't believe her, not fast enough, not loud enough. About how I lost her.

I wait for her disappointment. Or judgement.

"Huh," she says. "I wondered."

I brace myself. "What?"

"I wondered how a grad student could suddenly pay off my medical bills and start sending me care packages from Eleven Madison Park."

"You... you knew?"

"I didn't know, Nico. Didn't I just say I *wondered*? But I'm your mother. I knew something. I thought you were a drug dealer, to be honest."

"*What?!*"

"Oh, please! Is being a drug dealer better or worse than being a porn star, huh? Listen, times are hard for the ninety-nine percent, in *this* economy, everyone's gotta make sacrif—"

"But *me*? *Drugs?!* The guy who invented and experimented with lembas bread recipes until he found the 'accurate' one?!"

"You always have those pocket gummies!" Before I can remind her that they are now legal in the state of New York, there is a loud crashing sound, and I know Ma has thrown her hands up in exasperation and her phone has gone flying.

"But truly?" she says over the rustling of the retrieval of her phone from the ground. Her voice warms. "I'm proud of you."

My throat tightens. "Even with how I did it?"

"You betcha bottom dollar," she snorts. "You think I care if you showed your ass online to keep us afloat? Half the women on this block would pay to see you shirtless. I brag about you at bingo."

"Ma."

"You took care of your family. That's what a man does."

"But I wasn't honest."

"Well, now you are."

I clear my throat to try to rid it of the sudden onset of thorns. I attempt the question that's been keeping me up for years. "Do you think Dad would've been okay with this?" my voice cracks out.

She's silent for a long moment. "Baby," she finally says, her voice trembling with emotion. "Honey, Daddy died proud of you, so I think at this point we can consider it a permanent sentiment."

"But—"

"And I know, I fuckin' *know*," she continues, voice still wavering, "that if there is such a thing as heaven, he's throwin' a fuckin' party and dancin' bachata with Jesus and all his buddies up there, drinkin' Nebbiolo and havin' it catered by whatever shitty Italian restaurant they may have, celebrating everything you've done to take care of us."

The tears are flowing freely now. "Okay," I say after a swallow.

Something in me settles, a weighted blanket of peace.

Her voice softens. "But that girl—Annie. If she's the one who helped you believe in more than just surviving... then you better fix it."

I wipe my face and exhale. "I don't know if I can."

She pauses. "Nico, your whole life, you've been taking care of me. Putting yourself last. I had no freakin' idea you didn't go to the best program in the country so you could be home with me. That must've been hard as hell. This is the first time I've ever heard you talk like you wanted something for yourself. Don't throw that away just because it's hard."

I swallow.

"She still loves you," she says, certain.

"How do you know?"

"Because you still love her," she says. "And no one, not one fuckin' person on this planet, loves my son halfway."

———

"She hasn't said anything."

"She doesn't owe you that yet," Izzy tells me.

I nod. "I know."

"She hasn't taken your sweatshirt off, though. It smells kind of rank."

A spark, from deep inside my gut.

"Try something big."

———

I open the document on my laptop. No more hiding. No more shame.

The truth.

THIRTY-FOUR

Annie

From: pmaldonado@hawkpublishing.com
To: ali@hawkpublishing.com
Chef wants last min change to the introduction and now it
looks crazy can you pls fix it

"Annie," Fernanda calls over from a box in the corner. "Do your vibrators go in your closet or bedside table?"

"Bedside table, obviously," May answers. She pauses. "You put yours in your closet?"

Fernanda shrugs. "The special ones go in the closet."

I take a spoonful of wildflower honey straight from the jar. "Wouldn't the special ones go in the bedside table?" I want to know.

"Special means rarely used, in my case. My old reliables go in the bedside table."

Izzy frowns. "You have so many vibrators that they don't all fit in your bedside table?"

I tug on a string of Nico's hoodie, and surrounded by boxes, my sister, and my best friends in my old, shitty, beautiful-because-it's-mine studio apartment, I open the attachment in the email.

The new title page smacks me in the face and leaves a mark.

NAKED REACTIONS
Experiments in Taste, Touch, and Truth
Anne Li
Nicholas Giannuzzi

He did it. He's doing it. He's letting the world know who he is.

"*What?!*" May shrieks from behind me, and I nearly fall out of my chair.

"What the fuck, May—"

"Are you. Telling me. *That NICO FUCKING GIAN-NUZZI HAS BEEN THE NAKEDREACTIONS GUY THIS ENTIRE TIME?!*" she screams.

May has gotten a little spicier and a touch unhinged since returning from her honeymoon. The one she *took her ex-boyfriend on*. She curses now.

"You know the *NakedReactions* guy?!" Betty bellows from across the room.

"He told me not to tell anyone," I mutter.

May is losing her damn mind. "So you were ghostwriting this porn star's book. You had a crush on him. Then you went on a road trip with Nico, who you hated in high school," she rages, pacing back and forth across the room. "Then somehow, somewhere between Brooklyn and Miami, you fell in love with him, and then they turned out to be the same fucking person?!"

"*WHAT?!*" Betty and Fernanda shriek simultaneously.

I scrub my face. "I know."

"So... the porn star thing... and now... and this... and then..." I watch as the room malfunctions.

Izzy appears behind me, looking at the screen. "This must be the big thing," she muses.

"You knew?!" May fires at her.

She shrugs. "He told me."

"Everyone shut the fuck up and let's read this thing," May snaps.

Filled with something that feels suspiciously like pride, maybe elation, I keep scrolling.

If you're looking for a normal cookbook, I should warn you: this isn't it.

Yes, there are recipes. Some are precise. Others are more of a suggestion. A few were born during late nights in industrial kitchens, all burned fingers and bad lighting. Others came to life in the quiet—slow mornings, long afternoons, the only sound someone breathing across the counter. But none of them exists just for the food.

Because this book isn't just about food.

It's about the burn of wanting. The sweetness of trying. The strange alchemy of care.

It's about chemistry—the molecular kind, and the human kind. The kind that simmers low and slow, or sparks hot and irreversible. The kind that lingers on your tongue long after it's gone. The kind that sneaks up on you in a kitchen, when you're just trying to make something decent, and suddenly you realize you're making something that means something.

Cooking is chemistry, yeah. I can tell you the exact temperature beef fat begins to render. I can explain the molecular structure of an emulsion, the bonds in caramel, the slow miracle of a reduction. Science demands respect. Timing. Attention. The Maillard reaction doesn't give a shit about your feelings. It needs the heat high, the surface dry, and the contact exact.

But even the most scientific recipes can't account for grief. Or joy. Or memory.

They won't tell you how laughter gets caught in the shell of a crawfish. How bacon and eggs the morning after can feel like a truce. Or how ice cream for breakfast can feel like equilibrium.

How honey, slow and sticky on your fingers, can feel like love.

There was a time I thought I had to keep every part of myself separated—my past, my work, my body, my family, my future. Like I could compartmentalize myself into being palatable. But real flavor needs contrast. Sweet and acid. Soft and sharp. Something to burn, and something to cool it down.

This book came out of a season of undoing. Of unlearning shame. Of finding ways to say what I couldn't say out loud. It's full of recipes, yeah—but also full of risk. Of things I made when I didn't think I was allowed to want anything. Of moments that demanded truth when I wanted to hide. Of the ways I've tried to be brave.

Of mistakes I didn't think I could come back from.

Because sometimes, one wrong move can ruin everything. One missed cue, and you scorch the pan. Overbeat the eggs. Oversalt the broth. You lose the thing you didn't even know you'd been building toward.

But if you're lucky—and if you care enough—you try again. You taste as you go. You make adjustments. You get better. Not perfect, just braver.

Because cooking isn't about perfection. It's about attention. About presence. It's about watching something change under heat and not walking away. Letting it get messy. Giving it time. Giving it care. Trusting it to bloom.

You improvise. You ruin things. You start again. You remember how someone takes their coffee, and you try to get it right next time. You feed people the way you want to be fed.

That's what this book is about.

It's about split-second timing and slow forgiveness. About chemistry, memory, and the miracle of what softens when it's seen, what melts when you look at it long enough. About the truth that heat, when applied with care, can turn almost anything tender.

I've never been the one with the right words. That's her superpower. But I know what it means to try. To keep trying. To beg. To make something with both hands and hope it lands as love.

This book? It's messy. It's meticulous. It's full of heat, hunger, and a hell of a lot of heart.

It's: Here. I made this.

It's: I thought of you the whole time.

It's: You're allowed to want more. Please come back for seconds.

Let's begin.

—N.G.

I touch my face. It's wet.

There is a loud sniffing noise behind me. No, four.

"Wow, that's pretty bad," Betty squeaks out.

"Leaned on the metaphors a little too hard," Fernanda sobs.

Izzy swipes at her face. "It's better than the groceries."

"It's better than the handwritten recipe for sorbet that I can never make because I one, don't have a Pacojet, and two, have no idea how or where to get essence of black sesame."

"And the dress that he was *returning to you*," Izzy sniffs.

"For a valedictorian of Stuy, he's not very smart," May says.

"He's an illiterate gorilla," I agree.

"An illiterate gorilla who you love," Izzy says gently.

"And who loves you," Betty adds on.

Four pairs of arms, ages thirty to seventy-five, wrap me in a hug.

"I miss him," I admit.

It's the truth. As soon as I signed the lease for this place, the first person I wanted to tell was him. When I signed up for a pottery class, a bachata class, when I went for a walk through Green-Wood Cemetery—he was the only person I wanted to tell. When I put the gold dress on, I wanted to send a selfie.

After combing through my notebooks and napkins and scraps of paper and the files on my computer, typing, formatting into some semblance of order and organization, after sending a query letter off to some connections I've made through Hawk Publishing, for an anthology of poems?

He's the first person I wanted to read it. *The Naked Truth: Self-Erosion and Shame, Grief and Girlhood.* By Anne Li.

"Why won't you let him back in?" Betty asks softly.

I tell the truth. "I'm afraid."

"That what, he's been cheating on you for years?" May snarls. I kind of love it, but wow.

I don't answer.

May attempts to backtrack. "Nico made a mistake, Annie. It was a lapse in judgement, one that lasted minutes, not years. He's not perfect. Who are you, *Mom*?"

"Christ, May, what have you done with my sister?"

But she's right.

"He loves every version of you, even the pieces that are too big and too much. Can't you do the same?"

"I…" Fuck.

"You have proven to everyone that you are the strongest, bravest, most badass woman who's ever come from hell," Fernanda tells me. "But why are you still trying to prove it to yourself? By kicking him out, no less?"

"Loving someone is an act of strength," May murmurs sadly, knowingly, now. "Of bravery."

I squeeze my eyes shut and press my face into Fernanda's shoulder. The air smells like tears and old lady perfume and half-dried takeout. And comfort and love and strength and bravery.

I'm afraid. I'm afraid that loving someone means giving them a whole bunch of weapons and hoping they wouldn't use it on me. I thought I had to stay sharp, stay armored, stay alone to stay safe.

But Nico didn't break me. He made me softer without making me small. And in the aftermath, after the fallout and the fuckups and the fear, I'm still standing. I, Annie Li, Chaos Bringer. Still me. Maybe even more me.

And now?

"I think he just proved he will keep you safe," Izzy says softly.

The vulnerable spots in his armor, the mistake that he made, the one that failed to protect me? It was based on his own insecurities and anxieties. Fear.

And those cracks have been filled with a big, impenetrable "Fuck you, bitches."

I breathe. A real, full breath. And when I exhale, it's like I'm letting go of something I've been clutching too tight for too long. I let it drain out of me, slow and quiet.

And what's left isn't nothing.

There's a new fear.

Not of being hurt again—no, not that.

What if I miss out on something extraordinary because I was too scared to reach for it?

I've survived everything else. I'll survive love too.

———

From: pmaldonado@hawkpublishing.com
To: ali@hawkpublishing.com
I have an idea for a launch party. Call me.

THIRTY-FIVE

Nico

I'M ABOUT TO SHIT MY PANTS.

But at least I'm wearing them.

"Hey, everyone," I tell the crowd of approximately one fuckin' hundred, my voice only trembling a little. "Welcome in. My name's Nico, and this is *Naked Reactions*."

Hawk Publishing had this fuckin' idea for a launch party for the cookbook, that I do a live, fully clothed cooking demonstration for one of the recipes in the book, with a live Q and A session afterwards. So here we are, at this independent bookstore in Brooklyn, and I hope to freakin' god I don't shit my pants.

"Today, I'm gonna make you all brown butter grilled cheeses with hot honey drizzle," I say, gesturing to my rig, the portable induction burners, the cast iron skillets, saucepan, my mise en place—all things I'm staring at 'cause I can't for the life of me look anyone in this crowd in the eye, "and hope it's good enough to convince you to buy the cookbook."

That gets a laugh, which spurs me on.

"First on deck is the butter," I tell my saucepan, like it's my emotional support animal. "Regular and unsalted. Always unsalted, anytime you use butter. You want control over the salt levels."

It softens, then melts, then begins to foam.

"Now, browning isn't just melting. We're cooking the milk solids. They sink to the bottom and toast. That's what creates all those nutty, toffee-like aromas—Maillard compounds, lactones, all the good stuff. You'll know it's ready by the smell. Just follow your nose."

I swirl the pot as the butter hisses, then sings.

"If it smells like something you'd pour on your naked body, it's ready."

Laughter detonates across the room. A few gasps. I look up and grin.

"Hawk Publishing said *fully clothed* demo. They didn't specify the rating." Someone fans themselves with a promo postcard.

If Annie were here, she'd be rolling her eyes. *That's the corniest fucking thing I ever heard, Nico.*

Phones start to come up. I hear someone, someone old, whisper, "Wow, he's hot *and* smart *and* funny," and my soul leaves my body.

"Next, we gotta heat the pan." I indicate to the knob on the induction burner. "Cast iron, always. Why? One, heat retention. Once it's hot, it stays hot. Two, even heat distribution. No cold spots or patchy browning. You want a sear so even it looks airbrushed? Cast iron's your guy."

A camera shutter clicks. Someone goes, "Preach."

"Now," I continue, "brown butter tastes incredible, but it burns fast." I lower the induction setting. "So we keep the heat medium-low to low when it hits the skillet. Those toasted milk solids? They're flavor, but they're fragile. Too hot, and they turn bitter faster."

I swirl the browned butter in, slowly, carefully. The scent

blooms, nutty, caramelized, intoxicating. Someone in the crowd mouths "Oh my god" like it's a prayer.

"We're not drowning the pan," I go on. "Just giving it enough fat to crisp and conduct. Fat is basically an edible blanket. It insulates, browns, and carries flavor. Without it, you're just burning carbs and your dignity."

That gets another round of laughter. A girl near the front claps once, unironically.

I pick up the slices of sourdough.

"Sourdough's got chew. Tang. Structural integrity. If you're using soft white bread, that's fine, if you also enjoy disappointment."

One guy points and nods like I've confirmed a personal belief system.

I butter both sides, lay them in the skillet, and press down with my spatula. A sharp sizzle ripples out into the crowd.

"Now this right here is the Maillard reaction—amino acids meeting reducing sugars under heat. It's responsible for every delicious browned thing on Earth. Including toast that doesn't taste like the plain, joyless stuff you choke down when you're sick."

A woman in the second row gasps dramatically, clutching her friend's arm. Now I'm actively sweating.

"No flipping yet. This isn't pancakes. Give the reaction time to develop flavor." I peek underneath one slice. "You want the crust nutty, golden, and even."

I layer cheddar and mozzarella on the crisp side of one slice.

"Cheddar for boldness, mozzarella for melt. One's been aged, the other's a stretch queen. Together? Slutty in the best way."

The room howls. The indie bookstore owner in the corner gives me two very enthusiastic thumbs up.

I place the second slice on top and press again.

"One confident flip. You commit. This is not a situationship."

I flip and pray. It lands. The room gasps. Phones flash.

"This is why we browned the butter first," I say, smug now. "Richer Maillard flavor. More nuttiness. More depth. More pleasure. You're welcome."

As the second side cooks, I turn to the honey warming in the saucepan.

"This is hot honey. Red pepper flakes, apple cider vinegar. The vinegar adds acidity. Your contrast. Capsaicin activates heat receptors, which open up your taste buds. Basically, spicy makes everything sexier."

Someone drops their phone. I ignore it.

I lift the sandwich, slice it diagonally (because I have standards) and plate it. Then, I drizzle the hot honey in a slow, thick ribbon. "This last part is optional," I say. "Unless you have a soul." I hold up a half for the room. "Grilled cheese, brown butter, hot honey. It's Maillard, emulsification, fat transfer, capsaicin, and personal growth. Also, it's fucking delicious."

Pause.

Someone near the back calls, "Eat it!"

"Slowly!" someone else adds on.

I do not.

"I've got a bunch here on the warming plate for you to try," I tell them instead. Bookstore employees pick them up and start handing them out. "And if you like it, the recipe's on page seventy-six. Buy the book and make your situationship eat it slowly," I say with a grin.

The bookstore smells like bliss: butter, heat, toasted sourdough, and just a little vinegar-sharp sweetness. The applause is still going when the owner of the place—a guy in Warby Parkers and a vintage Death Cab for Cutie tee—steps up beside me.

"Can we get another round for our very delicious, very scientific, very fully-clothed chef?" he says, beaming.

The crowd laughs and claps harder. Someone, some old woman yells, "Take it off anyway!"

I grin. "You first."

More laughter. The owner pats my shoulder. "Seriously, Nico, thank you. This was incredible... and you will be making me that sandwich before you leave."

I nod, trying not to visibly sag with relief. "You got it."

He turns to the crowd. "We're gonna roll right into a little Q&A with our multi-talented culinary-chemist-slash-butter-thirst-trap. He'll be answering your questions for a bit, and then we'll open the signing line."

A chair appears out of nowhere, pushed behind me by someone with kind eyes and a lot of tattoos. Annie's are better. I wipe my hands on a towel, take a sip of water, and sit. The skillet behind me is still spitting faintly, the butter singing its dying notes.

I glance up and finally let myself get a real look at the crowd.

It's packed. Wall-to-wall Brooklyn chaos. Couples leaning on each other. Lots of women. Lots. Solo food nerds with phones still up. A few older folks scattered around, nodding like they'd seen it all, until I said "situationship," and they nearly fell out of their seats. There's even a baby in the back, chewing on a copy of the book. Honestly, same.

I take a deep breath before giving the mic a little tap. "Alright. Hit me."

A hand shoots up immediately, a wiry dude in the second row with tortoiseshell glasses and a pen tucked behind one ear.

"Okay, so, if you were doing this with rye instead of sourdough, would you adjust the butter or pan temp?"

"Great question," I say, enormously grateful the question is not about my dick. "Yes. Rye bread's denser and has less sugar, so it browns more slowly. I'd bump the heat just a touch and let it sit longer. But you also want more fat. Slather both sides."

He nods solemnly, as if I just blessed his sandwich marriage.

The next question comes from the back, a woman with a giant iced coffee. "What kind of cheese would you like, pair with like, fig jam, instead of hot honey?" The ice in her drink rattles as her hand flicks with each of her "like"s.

"I'd go brie or a goat blend. Something creamy with some funk. You want that smooth and weird counterpoint to the sweet." I gesture with my water. "That's the chemistry—fat, acid, sugar, salt. You play the levels."

Some murmurs of approval. Another phone click. This is going well. Too well.

The next question is annoying as hell, but I expected it, honestly. "So is this book real science, or just the sexy kind you use to get clicks?"

"Well," I say, scratching the back of my head. "I have a PhD in food science. And I just finished my postdoc. I also have hundreds of thousands of subscribers on *Naked Reactions*. So both, I guess."

Thank Jesus that gets laughs.

"How does your mom feel about your content being on a porn site?" the woman with the baby chewing my book asks.

"She feels fuckin' proud as hell!" I hear my mom yell from somewhere towards the back.

The crowd cracks up.

"Thanks, Ma," I grin.

The next hand is up before I can even find where she's sitting. A guy in a blazer, no shirt underneath, with his phone half-raised to record. Oh god. Here it comes.

"On that episode where you made that peach cobbler, was

it just the fruit you were plumping, or was there some, uh, extra juicing involved?"

There's a sharp inhale across the room. Half the crowd glances at me. The other half glance at their neighbors. I don't know where to look. My hands? The floor? Inwards, to ask myself, *How the fuck did you get here?* or *What the fuck are you doing?*

I'm still trying to form a reply when a voice slices through the air like a Katana.

"Are you really asking if he fucked a pie?"

Heads snap. Necks swivel. I think the baby gasps.

Every single atom in my body freezes, and the sweat on my body turns into ice.

Am I having a stroke? Am I dead? Did I just astral project into hell?

I look.

There, maybe six rows back. Standing with her chin tilted up and murder in her kohl-rimmed eyes, is My Annie Li. Annie "Whom I Love" Li.

Wearing my hoodie.

I suddenly cannot breathe.

I look to her right and see my mother and sister sitting next to her, grinning like this is exactly what they came for.

To her left: Izzy, two older women, Charlie, and May, all in some kind of seated Avengers-style formation. Izzy's already cracking her knuckles.

"Let me repeat the question," Annie says, stepping out into the aisle and towards the dude, hair loose and flowing behind her. Under my hoodie? She's wearing the gold dress, a majestic punctuation of fire and splendor. With combat boots. A glorious and resplendent angel of wrath, stepped out from a myth and ready for battle. "Did you just come to an event hosted by an independent bookstore, where an author is promoting a deeply personal cookbook, to ask if he was sexually intimate with a pie?"

The guy starts to sputter, backpedaling with his phone half-raised. "No—I mean, I was just joking—"

"Oh, thank god you were only joking," the old lady next to Charlie calls out sweetly, "because there's a cast iron pan over there and I was about to show you what one feels like."

"I call the butter knife," May announces.

"Let's caramelize him," my sister declares, and I refrain from getting into the specifics of human flesh technically qualifying for the Maillard reaction.

The crowd loses it.

The guy mumbles something and quickly exits, chased out by raucous applause and my mom yelling, "That's *our* chef, you crusty little meatball!"

I'm still in my chair, gaping like a fish, when Annie turns toward the crowd, serene and steady and strong.

"Hi, everyone. I'm Annie Li. I'm the one who wrote this illiterate gorilla's cookbook." she says. "Because he can't write for shit."

A beat. The bookstore falls silent again.

She turns to me. Our eyes lock. "But we can't all be perfect," she shrugs. "Otherwise, this illiterate gorilla is the bravest, most intelligent, beautiful por—adult content creator I've ever met."

I look around and make sure this bookstore isn't actually heaven. "Annie isn't perfect either," I manage to get out. "She thinks a cobbler is the same thing as a pie. Otherwise, she's fuckin' perfect."

"I'm proud of this book," she tells the crowd, but she says it directly to me. "And I'm proud of him."

I don't realize I've stood until I'm already walking toward her.

"She's not just the writer," I say, voice scratchy. "She's the reason I had anything worth freakin' saying."

I think the bookstore owner is saying something into the mic, looking like he's going to cry, but I'm not sure, because My Annie Li is where she belongs. Home. In my arms.

"Thank Jeebus," I say into her hair.

"I know," she says into my chest. "Let's finish this together."

Applause. Camera flashes. Someone yells, "KISS!" but we ignore it. For now.

She leans back and smiles at me, small and private, and I take her hand, brushing my thumb against the tattoos on her knuckles, love and a little bit of chaos, guiding her back and into the chair that's appeared next to mine.

"We're taking a few more questions," I say, and this time, I'm not nervous at all.

———

The bookstore's back room smells like cardboard and old paperbacks and hope. A crooked folding chair slouches in the corner beside a plastic storage bin overflowing with buttons and bookmarks labeled *Local Author Swag*. On the wall, a faded poster of a very famous fantasy author dons a Sharpie mustache.

I'm pacing like a lunatic.

The second the door clicks shut, I stop.

I don't turn around right away, but I feel her behind me. Her heat. Her breath. The hush of something fragile and alive between us. I rest my hands on the back of a folding chair and close my eyes, just for a second.

"I, uh... thanks," I say, throat dry. "For what you said. Out there."

"You lost a lot of color pretty fast. You were turning the

same shade as the bread," she replies, and I can hear the grin in her voice.

I turn.

There she fuckin' is.

Same gold dress, same mouth I can spot in a crowd of a hundred, same hands that rewrote my story and made it something I could stand behind. The tattoos on her fingers peek out from under the sleeves of my sweatshirt, her gorgeous face soft and gentle and radiant. The softest wrecking ball I've ever loved.

We crash into each other without even discussing it. She wraps around me like a little fuckin' koala, and I bury my face in her hair and exhale for the first time in days.

"God, I missed you," I say.

"So much," she agrees, her little body trembling.

I cradle her head in both my hands, winding my fingers through the silk of her hair, tilting her face up to look at me. "I'm so sorry," I say, with a soft kiss to her lips.

"I know," she agrees quietly.

"I fucked up."

"You did."

"God, there's so much I want to say to you," I go on. "That day, I made one bad call. A small one. I didn't say anything when I should've. I didn't shut it down."

She blinks, slow and careful. "And you think that's small?"

"No," I admit. "I just mean—it was a small moment. Barely a quarter of an hour. But the pain it caused you—us— was... massive. And that was terrifying. How one lapse, one second of fear, could break something like that."

When she exhales, it sounds like it's been sitting in her chest for weeks. "You didn't break it."

"Felt like I did," I say. "And I deserved that feeling. I didn't have your back when it counted."

Annie nuzzles into my chest.

"But the second I thought I'd ruined it? It gutted me. Because loving you has made me feel more like myself than I ever have before. And losing you didn't just hurt—it made everything else meaningless," I tell her.

There's a pause.

She says quietly, "You made me feel foolish. For believing you could be the one who didn't let me down."

"I know," I say, and I really do, "and I hate that. Because you've always been the brave one. You let yourself believe in something. In me. And I failed you."

"You didn't fail me." She shakes her head, almost amused. "You hesitated. You got scared. And yeah, that hurt—but I've had time to think. And... I think I've figured out the difference between someone who gives up and someone who fights to fix it."

I look at her. "And which am I?"

"The second one," she says. "God, Nico, you illiterate gorilla."

We're quiet for a beat. I let her look at me.

"You make me brave," I say. "You make me want to be better—not just for you, but for myself. I didn't know I could love someone like this and still feel like me."

She's quiet for a second. Then, "You make me gentler."

That's a surprise.

"You make me less reactive," she continues. "Not softer— just more deliberate. Being around you makes me..." She clears her throat. "Makes me want to slow down enough to care about things I usually bulldoze through. You make me want things. Real things. Not just goals or grudges or proving everyone wrong. And you make me feel like it's *okay* for me to want things. "

I swallow, hard.

"You're the first person I've ever trusted to give all of me. Even the parts Sister Annie tries to keep in a locked box labeled

'Too Much.' And somehow, you look at all of it and say, more, please."

"I mean it," I say, taking her hand, rubbing my thumb across the tattoos on her knuckles. Kissing every single one of them. "Every time."

She nods. "I forgave you the second I saw your name on the title page."

That hits me like a freight train of relief. "I realized that was the only thing holding me back from being able to be your safe place. I had to make it so I was impenetrable."

Her expression softens. "And you told your mom."

"She was proud of me."

She smirks. "Told you."

I give her a giant squeeze, feeling her ribs flex under my arms. "You're always right."

"So what are we saying here? We're both complicated, kind of dramatic, definitely chaotic, but we still choose each other?"

"I'm saying you make me stronger. And smarter. And honestly, probably way more tolerable to be around."

"That's debatable," she grins.

I pause. "I want to be the man you saw in me before I even saw him myself."

Her brow raises, and I trace the perfect arch of it with my thumb. "Good," she says. "Because I love him. A lot."

My ribcage expands, then explodes into confetti. I can't stand it anymore. I grip her chin and pull.

It's not some perfect movie-screen kiss. It's messy and desperate. Lips and tongue and tangling, pulling, loving. My nose bumps hers, and her hand knocks into my hip awkwardly before curling in my shirt. But her mouth moves like it remembers me, and I groan into it, cupping the back of her head like I could keep us here forever. It's soft. Then it's sharp. It's just us, our own messy little symphony of hunger and home. I love everything about it—the whimper that leaves her throat and the moan of relief that leaves mine.

When we finally break apart, she rests her forehead against mine.

"You make me more myself," she murmurs. "Not better or shinier or different. Just more."

"Same," I whisper. "You make me want things, too. And how to be proud of that wanting."

Another pause.

"Safe," we both murmur at the same time, and I stare down at the love glowing in her eyes and reflecting my own.

She wipes her mouth with the sleeve of my sweatshirt. "So. You gonna kiss me again, or was that just an amuse-bouche?"

I laugh, loud and surprised. "You're still a pain in my ass."

"A gorgeous pain in your ass," she corrects, wiggling her eyebrows. "And that's not a no."

So I kiss her again. Because of course I do. This time longer. Deeper. No more fear, just fire.

And when we finally pull apart, she tips her head, eyes bright and steady. Steady, safe, secure.

"You ready?" I ask.

"For what?"

"For seconds."

My Perfect Annie Li grins. "I'm fuckin' starving, honey."

Epilogue

Seven Years Later

"THIS MOTHERTRUCKER'S ABOUT TO EAT GRASS," Annie mutters to me.

"Honey—" I attempt.

"Gonna take his truckin' face and use it as an excavator," she continues with a glance down at our three-year-old.

"Digger!" Stella vehemently agrees.

"Honeys—"

"Ref!" Annie finally bursts out, her hands flying into the air, identical to and in tandem with our five-year-old daughter currently on the soccer field.

The beleaguered grandpa currently volunteering as a coach sighs down at my tiny angel of wrath.

"Excuse me, sir," Cleo seethes through the deep breathing exercises we've attempted to teach her. Her little chest doubles then halves in size as the exercise mimics hyperventilation instead of cleansing calm. "Lucas pushed me with two hands three times in a row," she fumes, really trying to keep her shit together. "Did you see? Are your eyes broke? That's a red card! That's three red cards!"

"Honey—" he begins.

"I'm not your honey," she sneers.

"You tell 'em, Cleo!" my wife shouts, aggressively rubbing circles on her swollen belly.

"Dig his face!" Stella yells, starting her march onto the field to defend her older sister to the death.

I grab her and plop her writhing body onto my shoulders, losing one of her sneakers in the process. "For truck's sake—all three of you, *stand down*," I roar.

"My shoe," Stella wails with a point to the fallen soldier.

"Cleo," the coach tries again. "This isn't a real game. This is just practice—"

"*Tell Lucas that*," Annie and Cleo yell simultaneously.

The coach scrubs his face. "Lucas," he tells his grandson, "can you please apologize?"

Lucas shrugs. "Sorry," he mutters, with little to no apology in his voice.

"Gotta try harder than that, kid," I inform him, at the same time Stella screams, "Sorry for what?" while tearing at my hair in her agitation.

Lucas kicks at some grass before looking at Cleo. "Sorry for pushing you three times with two hands."

"Apology accepted," Cleo sniffs after a moment. She stares at him, and then her gorgeous eyes light up in a familiar way. "I'm bored. Wanna get some ice cream?"

Lucas grins. He looks at his grandpa, who blows out a breath and looks at his watch.

"We still have ten minutes left," he says.

Annie cups her hands in front of her face. "Who wants ice cream? We're buying!"

Fifteen miniscule bodies display an athleticism not previously demonstrated in their thirty minutes of practice as they sprint towards the Mister Softee truck parked at the corner of the park. Stella flies off my body, lands on the ground like Spiderman, and runs after them.

"Stell, your shoe—" I try, waving it in the air half-heartedly for half a second before tucking it into my pocket.

The coach joins Annie and me as we follow behind them. "Any chance you guys want to take over coaching for the rest of the season?" he asks us.

"No thanks," I answer cheerfully. "We don't know anything about sports. We're just here for Cleo."

"And we're about to be really busy for a while," Annie adds on, rubbing her stomach.

"You're doing great, though," I assure him.

We haven't stopped being busy, truthfully. Our lives have been a series of chaotic, impulsive, beautiful decisions since leaving that bookstore.

Annie moved in with me mere months after our cookbook came out. Thank god she was paying month to month. I proposed to her in our kitchen a few months after that.

Well, I *half*-proposed. The second I got down on one knee, Annie tackled me to the kitchen floor, screamed, "*Yes, Chef*," and I barely managed to slip the ring onto her finger before her tongue was in my mouth—effectively cutting off my grand speech.

It's okay, though. She let me finish the speech later, in bed, while she sobbed over the new diamond resting over the diamond tattoo on her ring finger.

Our book went viral. Television networks and social media influencers had the two of us on their shows—I'd do the cooking and the science and Annie would provide the hilarious commentary. We had great chemistry, everyone had said.

I only made one more *NakedReactions* video. Annie wasn't involved. The end of *NakedReactions* was our only regrettable decision, but it was because we were sad about the additional income we'd be losing. It didn't last very long, though, 'cause not long after that, I started my own food consulting business. The two of us got to travel to restaurants all around the world—Tokyo, Paris, London, Bangkok, Mexico City, Singapore, Rome, Lima, Lyon, Marrakech— helping chefs improve their menus of kitchens big and small.

We danced in all those cities.

Annie wrote poetry. She's still publishing, and she's raking it the fuck in. Turns out her style of poetry has a solid market in millennial women who scream-cried My Chemical Romance into their iPod Shuffles.

We were married in a small ceremony overlooking the Blue Ridge Mountains, surrounded by the people who love us. Even her parents were there—Annie and May's compromise of staying no-contact except for big events and holidays. A boundary that protects their peace while still honoring the cultural respect that shaped them.

Cleo was born nine months after that.

Think of the children, I remind myself, before replaying the night Cleo was conceived. But hot damn.

We finally get to the overwhelmed ice cream man, where our youngest is leading a rhythmic "swirl with sprinkles" war chant. Annie moves to her side and uses her charm to begin negotiations for a deal on twenty ice cream cones. I step to her back and dig my thumbs into the base of her spine, right where I know she's sore, and she melts in my arms.

In three months, our Fort Greene brownstone we bought a year ago will be filled with four girls. My girls. Four majestic, terrifying, wondrous angels of wrath.

Life is stretched-out hair elastics, floor bananas (entirely peeled with only one bite taken out), big feelings, and little to no sleep.

We've never been happier.

"Daddy," Cleo asks me, as we step to the side. "How do they make ice cream in the truck? Is there a freezer in there?"

"Yep, there's a freezer in there, but the real trick isn't just keeping it cold—it's how you freeze it." I bend to sneak a bite of her cone. "You gotta keep it movin'. They mix cream, sugar, and flavors, then spin it while chilling it so that it freezes smooth instead of turning into one big ice cube. That's how you get soft, creamy ice cream instead of a block of frozen milk."

"It's like we did at home, Cleo, remember?" Annie looks at me when she says this, though, eyes sparkling, licking her cone slowly, in a way that's reminiscent of last night. In our bed, after the girls went down. While I straddled her face.

Think of the children, I mouth at her, pinching her ass.

"Oh yeah," Stella chimes in, now somehow missing the other shoe. And sock. "Daddy shook the plastic bag when we made ice cream."

"Our ice cream tasted better," Cleo says.

"That's 'cause it was made with love," I let her know immediately.

Three pairs of eyes roll in simultaneous choreography. Well, two pairs. Stella still hasn't figured out how to do it, so she just looks up at the sky instead.

"Hey!" I feign offense, but really, this is a reaction I'm used to. "I just love you all so much. Food tastes better when we make it together."

Annie, who has had my back for the last seven or eight years, depending on whether you count the Chef year or not, takes her place once more. "Daddy's right," she tells our daughters. "Think of the chicken parm we all made last night. It was the best chicken parm I ever had."

I think of the disaster of flour and egg caked into the crevices of our kitchen drawers and all of our hair, our identical grins. "Mommy's always right."

"Neither mommy nor daddy is always right," Annie reminds them. "But it's okay to be wrong sometimes."

Stella scrambles back up to my shoulders while holding her cone, soaking my shorts, shirt, and neck in chocolate-vanilla swirl. "Can we make more ice cream in bags when we get home?" she asks. "Mine is all gone."

I wipe a glop of it off my arm. "Sure."

There is suddenly a moment of buzzing silence, tense with energy.

Annie and Cleo look at one another, a shared under-standing passing between them. I watch as their bodies start to fill with a familiar freneticism.

Oh, fuck.

Annie nods at our daughter with a grin, and I brace myself for— "After-party at our house," she announces to the team. "We live just around the corner."

"We're makin' the best ice cream of your truckin' life," shouts Cleo.

Now it's Stella's and my turn. We stare at one another, wide-eyed.

"You thinkin' what I'm thinkin'?" I ask her.

"Yep," she replies with a frantic nod.

"Bags," I start to fire off, counting off on my fingers, as Stella keeps nodding. "Ice. We should stop at the bodega for ice. Heavy cream, sugar—although I think we have enough sugar. Paper towels for mess. Maybe some snacks, maybe get some juice. Cups. Do we have enough cups? We should get some more. Well, it's almost noon. We should just do a whole lunch, right? I'll call Russo's and see if they can whip up a bunch of heroes. What else? What were you gonna say?" I look down at her.

"Oh," she says. "I was gonna say I lost my shoe."

"Shoes," I confirm. "We need shoes." I pick her up and plop her back on my shoulders. Wait, when'd she get back down to the ground? "I got you for now. We gotta go. Babe? Honey?" I call backwards as I walk towards the other end of the park. "We're gonna run ahead. Meet you back at the house."

"Yes, chef!" Annie has to yell back, because she's currently swarmed by fifteen cheering five-year-olds and their hungover parents (Sunday morning practice can be a struggle). "I got you. Thanks, honeys. Love you."

"Can you find my shoes?" Stella wails.

"Already have them," Annie shouts back.

"I have your sock, Stell!" Cleo adds.

As I leave the park, Stella entirely barefoot and scream-singing a song about excavators on my shoulders, some adjectives pop unbidden into my head.

Pleased Nico Giannuzzi. *Content, satisfied* Nico Giannuzzi. So, so fucking happy. *Loved*.

All About Ana

Ana Kirk Shaw wrote her first romance at eight years old. It was a shifter romance starring Scar from *The Lion King* and Amelia Bedelia. It was weird.

She is now a teacher by day and romance author by night (plus weekends and summer break). She lives in Brooklyn, New York with her husband, kids, and cats.

Not ready to say goodbye to Annie and Nico? Want one more spicy scene? Want to be the first to receive updates, snippets from drafts, cover reveals, bonus scenes, and more? Check out Ana's website!

anakirkshaw.com